THE SHADOW OF THE RED BARN

What can the secret be, lurking in a sleepy Suffolk village, which shocks a hard-bitten pair of London cardsharpers like "Corinthian Tom" and his mistress, Lydia? What is it that sets these two, nothing if not experienced, dreaming of love like a couple of adolescents? And why should a cross-eyed youth—a mere "Johnny Raw" from the country—have the power to embroil them in the darkest, most sinister drama of their lives? In working out these unexpected themes Philip Lindsay gives us some of his cleverest characterization and some of his most vivid and vigorous descriptions. Readers who like their blood curdled will be delighted with this robust tale of low life, and will enjoy meeting again, in all its old horror, the most perennial of nineteenth-century melodramas, here blended skilfully with other themes. In this book, a subtle compound of fact and fiction, the author makes the fullest use of his extraordinary sense of period, painting a fascinating and unsparingly realistic picture of the underworld of London in the nineteenth century and falling himself readily into the boisterous colourful jargon of the period.

BY THE SAME AUTHOR:

Novels
The Merry Mistress
Queen Honeypot
Beauty or the Beast
All That Glitters
There Is No Escape
The Loves of My Lord Admiral
Heart of a King
The Queen's Confession
Whither Shall I Wander?
Sir Rusty Sword
He Rides in Triumph
Jack Laughs at Locksmiths
The Devil and King John
The Gentle Knight
The Fall of the Axe
Pudding Lane
The Nutbrown Maid
Bride for a Buccaneer
The Bells of Rye
Gentleman Harry Retires
The Duke is Served
The Little Wench
London Bridge is Falling
Here Comes the King
One Dagger for Two
Panama is Burning

History and Biography
The Loves of Florizel
The Queenmaker
Don Bradman
The Great Buccaneer
The Peasants' Revolt (*with Reg Groves*)
For King or Parliament
Hampton Court
I'd Live the Same Life Over
A Mirror for Ruffians
Kings of Merry England
King Henry the Fifth
King Richard the Third

For Boys
The Knights at Bay

The Shadow of
the Red Barn

A Novel by

PHILIP LINDSAY

HUTCHINSON
Stratford Place
London

Hutchinson & Co. (Publishers) Ltd.
London, New York, Melbourne, Sydney, Cape Town

First published 1952

Printed in Great Britain
by The Anchor Press, Ltd.,
Tiptree, Essex

DEDICATION

FOR

GERALD REITLINGER

My dear Gerald,

I know you have little interest in most fiction, but this is a tale set in the early nineteenth century, a period of which you are fond, and, if for no other reason, I hope it might amuse you for a few hours. "Amuse", perhaps, is scarcely the word to describe a tale centring on the notorious murder of Maria Marten in Polstead's Red Barn; yet I have tried to make this grisly subject amusing and, I hope, exciting. After all, Corder is not my central character, and the wretched Maria is scarcely more than a ghost, the interest being focused on imaginary figures who find themselves, almost by chance, involved with the tragedy.

Much has been written about Corder and the old melodrama is still acted, boisterously by Tod Slaughter and company, and by other actors— alas, too rarely—as serious drama. In particular, I recall a production at the Kilburn Empire in the early years of the recent war when Mr. T. C. Leybourne brought to his part a truly sinister, frightening quality and showed, what I had previously doubted, that this play—apart from its depressing comic characters—has moments near to tragedy.

The explanation I give of the famous dream is no invention. This is a theory still firmly held at Polstead, as can be seen in "The True Story of Maria Marten", by Dorothy Gibbs and Herbert Maltby ("East Anglian Magazine"), 1949, a small book which I strongly recommend to those interested in the crime, not only for its assembling of the facts but because of its many illustrations. The great work, however, remains J. Curtis's, with its interminable title beginning "An Authentic and Faithful History of the Mysterious Murder of Maria Marten", published in 1828 by Thomas Kelly of Paternoster Row. Although it was a rush job, its inaccuracies are surprisingly few, and the numerous other works on the subject fail to maintain Curtis's impartiality and their pages are sickly with sentiment, showing Maria as an artless village maiden and Corder her villainous seducer. Not only books, but ballads were written on the subject—the one I quote in

Chapter Twenty-two being contemporary—and a monument was built to Maria's memory in Polstead churchyard; today it rises a mere couple of inches off the ground, so greedy have been souvenir-hunters—the murderer's skull-less skeleton is still used for the teaching of anatomy in the West Suffolk General Hospital—many tales are told of what happened to the skull and of how it haunted one house until decently buried as a Christian—and in Moyse's Hall Museum, Bury St. Edmunds, you can see his death-mask—untrustworthy like most death-masks, for not only does death relax the muscles and the plaster tend to stretch the skin, but a violent death contorts the face, and in this mask Corder bares his teeth in a monkeyish expression—the pair of pistols with which he killed Maria and his sword that still shows the stain of blood, a portion of his scalp and a copy of Curtis's book bound in the dead man's skin—after it had been tanned, pieces of his skin were handed round in Bury, some people with scientific curiosity actually tasting it to see if it was different from leather. And, my dear Gerald, you must recall that day amongst the Willett Collection in Brighton's Art Gallery when we examined those charming potteries, one showing a top-hatted Corder holding Maria's hand, his other arm around her shoulder, dangerously near her throat; and the second portraying an accurate model—if we may judge by contemporary prints—of the Red Barn, Corder and Maria standing at its door, with a placid cow in one corner and some hens in the other.

Well, I must stand aside now for you to turn the page, and I only hope you will not be disappointed. That would, indeed, be a poor exchange for the happy and interesting hours I have spent with you amongst your precious Oriental porcelain and other treasures; and even should you weary of the tale, I hope you will forgive its faults, knowing with what affection it is offered.

PHILIP LINDSAY.

Sussex.

CONTENTS

Chapter I	SHARP OR FLAT?	*Page*	9
II	THREE'S COMPANY		20
III	WASPS IN COVENT GARDEN		32
IV	A LOVER'S TALE		43
V	POST-OFFICE CUPID		56
VI	CUPID IS NOT ONLY BLIND		69
VII	THE PRICE OF LOVE		87
VIII	A CALL FOR HELP		102
IX	IN THE FIRELIGHT		115
X	A BROKEN DREAM		128
XI	POLSTEAD		136
XII	OVER THE TEACUPS		151
XIII	THE HEART OF EVIL		162
XIV	THE SECRET OF THE BARN		176
XV	THE FETTERED MAN		191
XVI	THE TRUTH OF A LIE?		207
XVII	SURPRISE FOR LYDIA		218
XVIII	SHADOW OF THE PAST		233
XIX	LYDIA GROWS AFRAID		247
XX	LOVE MAKES THE DEAF TO HEAR		260
XXI	THE FIGHT FOR A LIFE		275
XXII	BEHIND WHICH DOOR?		293
XXIII	THE QUICK AND THE DEAD		308

SHARP OR FLAT?

GLANCING amongst the noisy crowd with her deceptively casual air, it was Lydia who saw him first. There was no need for her to speak or even to nudge her companion, the tall Corinthian, Tom Barsett. So many years had they lived and worked together that they were able almost to read each other's thoughts. A flicker of eyelashes, a lifting of eyebrows, a pursing of lips, a shrug, and the message was passed. With an assumption of boredom, the Corinthian gazed carelessly around the room in search of the prey she had sighted. At first on finding the fellow, he believed himself mistaken, so insignificant to him appeared this flat whom Lydia had chosen to be plucked. Eyebrows raised, he glanced again towards her and dully she stared back at him, giving merely a faint yet decisive nod. Yes, that was the flat she had indicated, and to the fastidious Corinthian he seemed a featherless pigeon, without that exhalation of wealth which, to the skilled sharp, cannot be concealed by drab garments or a dirty face. A johnny raw, and a conceited johnny raw at that; a small squire's son, perhaps, in London on a spree, and unlikely to carry much blunt. Amidst that glittering crowd of Greeks and Cyprians in the Piccadilly Royal Saloon as they drank and cuddled in the alcoves or strolled behind the iron trellis of the gallery above, he stood apart, watching the noisy throng with a supercilious grin on his thick yet shapely lips. A type of lout whom the Corinthian disliked. A flat who believed himself a sharp, a hobbledehoy fresh from the dung-cart who thought himself superior to London swells. Such men were not easily cozened. They wasted one's time for inadequate results. Yet Lydia had chosen him for plucking, and the Corinthian had never met anyone more skilful than she at snouting out flats.

The fellow was dressed in a black coat, black waistcoat, and grey trousers: the clothes were new yet ill-fitting. His hands gripping the broad lapels, he seemed to tug himself forward, poised on his toes,

and with out-thrust head he peered on all sides, pale e
up at the corners, a heavy shadow cleaving the wrinkled
though he were short-sighted and watching had become a s
nor was he drunk. Vanity perhaps had suggested his leaving
spectacles at home, and that, decided the Corinthian, proved h
stupid. One needed clear vision if one were to leave such place
as this with one's pockets unpicked. Many of London's most
experienced thieves mingled with this dandified crowd, and there
was scarcely a woman present who was not a professional ladybird,
ready to bargain at a wink and, whenever possible, to steal her
price beforehand without her victim feeling her caressing fingers
glide for his pocket-book to be slipped to a confederate. The
Corinthian knew them all, having in his novitiate years, when
exploring darkest London, learned disastrously the tricks of every
night-trade.

Under the dazzle of the glass chandelier, the drunkards, whores
and gamblers strolled, some of the women in gowns cut so low that
they might well have been nude to the waist, wriggling shoulders
and posteriors to demonstrate their charms, while some young
sparks lounged at the bottom of the staircase leading to the gallery
that they might watch the ascending women lift their skirts to show
their legs when they walked up. The stranger appeared indifferent to
the women, some of whom were beautiful and almost all of whom
knew how to give the promise of passion with a rolling eye and
gait. They minced past, some rubbing catlike against his sleeve and
breathing up into his face. He did not stir. Clutching his lapels—
perhaps to protect the reader holding his money in an inside-pocket
—he stood, blandly smiling at them, thick eyebrows raised, the
brown hair brushed up in an effort to make it curl. The chin was
heavy and faintly cleft, the nose broad, up-tilted, with curled
nostrils showing pink skin and the ends of hair, and his skin was
heavily freckled.

"He's no go. Thinks he's fly: just grins at you . . ."

The Corinthian turned to find his friend, Bertram Marley,
pressed against him by the pushing crowd. A big dark fellow with
soft brown hair and heavy mouth that rarely lost its derisory grin,
Bertram was as skilful a sharp as any in London, and where he
failed few could hope to succeed. Now, with ruffled cravat puffing
between the lapels of his bright blue coat, he stood, broad shoulders

back to withstand the shoving of late arrivals, a horde of young gentleman-drunkards tally-hoing as though at a hunt while squeezing their giggling ladybirds to make them prance like horses.

The Corinthian shrugged. "So I thought," he said. "It's Lydia's idea. And she's not often on a wrong scent."

Bertram smiled at Lydia, and bowed; coldly, Lydia inclined her dark head, the lids low over her sulky blue eyes.

"No, rum go," he muttered. "Not like her to make mistakes." And he watched her with calculating, desirous eyes, while, indifferently, she stared back at him, pretending to listen to the compliments of a fat bejewelled stranger quizzing into her bosom. "I'm thirsty," said Bertram suddenly, clearing his dry throat on a note of anger. "There's an empty table over there."

The Corinthian nodded to Lydia who nodded agreement and turned her back, with no farewell-word, on her admirer. Lifting her golden gauze skirt to show her ankles in white stockings, her feet in white shoes, she followed the two men elbowing a way towards the cubicles against the wall. Turning sideways the more easily to sidle through the promenaders, the Corinthian watched her from the corners of his eyes, and he noted how she wriggled in the direction of the short-sighted stranger. Had she been any other woman he might have suspected a sudden infatuation, but Lydia, as he knew too well, although passionate enough when the mood shook her, was at heart as cold as the jewels and cash which alone she really loved. In her lived no sentiment, no pity, little beyond greed and envy of women more prosperous or better-bred than herself. Indeed, she had often proved herself more merciless than he who would often have let a pigeon escape with a few coins for breakfast. Lydia would never let a farthing slide from her fingers. She would have stripped the most pathetic flat to his skin and then have had him thrown out of doors. Yet, unquestionably, something had attracted her towards this arrogant bumpkin with weak eyes whom both he and Bertram had dismissed as unworthy prey.

He saw her rub against the fellow, then turn to scorn him as though he had been to blame because her bosom squeezed his arm; and the fellow impudently grinned down at her, plainly unmoved by that caress and seeming with his squinting eyes to ask what might be her price. Eyes drowsily half-closed, she turned away with a gesture that might have indicated either indifference or invitation, so slightly did she nod her dark head towards the table at which Bertram was already seated and shouting for a waiter. Few were so skilled as she at the subtleties of seduction, appearing to promise whilst denying, baffling, maddening, conquering men to have them bemused for slaughter at cards or dice. On this bumpkin, however, the Corinthian felt that even she must fail; and the thought delighted his malice.

"I think she's hooked her flat," he grinned, sliding on to the chair opposite Bertram and leaning his elbows on the green cloth while he studied his shirt-cuffs to see whether they were ruffled.

Bertram shrugged. "She's wasting her time on that thing," he growled. "How have you made out tonight?"

"Nothing," murmured the Corinthian, frowning at a stain on his brown sleeve. "Went to Drury Lane. Nobody there. The usual Cyprians in the saloon with their flats, and the coves of cases keeping a sharp eye on 'em to see they weren't idle or didn't bilk 'em with a customer on the sly. Not a flat worth hooking. That's why we came here. . . ." He looked up, then drew aside as Lydia reached the table and pushed by him with rustling skirts to reach her chair. "No luck, my love?" he asked with an insolent smile. "Is your rustic blind to your opulent charms? I told you the fellow was a fool."

She did not answer. White-gloved hands in her golden lap, she sat and stared at the noisy perfumed crowd, and she did not even appear to breathe. These sudden silences always exasperated the Corinthian. Against them he possessed no weapons, as Lydia was well aware, and whenever she found herself caught in the wrong or defeated by argument, she turned thus into a statue. And the impression of becoming marble was made stronger by the whiteness of her skin which she rouged but faintly over her cheekbones, and the darkness of her blue eyes under the lowered lashes. Her black hair, parted in the centre and drawn back to tumble into curls, shone with bluish lights, the ostrich-feather rising from those curls nid-nodding in the heat and the gusts of talk and laughter. A tall woman, amply built, her firm yet well-fleshed shoulders gleamed as though polished, the plump arms, nude save for the short puffed sleeves, shimmering like mother-of-pearl until they ended at the kid of her gloves. And it seemed to the Corinthian, as often it had seemed to him before, that for all her soft, inviting woman's body, Lydia was not truly human. Cold she was, cold, cold to the bone. Cold the white face, despite the promise in the full lips and over-bright eyes; cold that Venus-body for all its voluptuous shape. That at times she could show herself passionate only intensified this inhumanity, the alteration in her moods being so sudden and so great. No longer did he love her, he told himself, although he still desired her. Passion had long since left them both; and they lived together like a couple married many years, their partnership having become more a business one. Yet tonight after her ogling of the cross-eyed stranger he was as jealous as any young lover might have been; and this jealousy perplexed him. Therefore he also fell silent and, after ordering three gins and water, Bertram was the only one to speak.

"I, too," he growled, "have had an empty night. London's not what it was. Damn' books like *Tom and Jerry* and poor bloody Thurtell's trial told too much, and the flats are frightened. They think they know everything, the fools, and they only know sufficient to sit on their readers and keep their pockets buttoned. I wish to God I'd been born a woman. That's a trade that never suffers, no matter what's written about it. Why, the more the bitches are abused, the more damn' fools of men race to be plucked. That flat's still got his cross-eye on you, Lydia. By jove! I think he's coming over!"

Lydia did not move, only the heavy lids lifted a little when her haughty stare rested on the stranger pushing towards them through the noisy crowd of coves with their covesses. He was making straight towards their table, and all three watched him slowly approach, the men faintly smiling, Lydia blankly.

"Hot in here," panted the stranger, lifting his tall hat and using it to fan his freckled face. "Mind if I sit down? I'm tired of standing in this heat."

No one answered, only Lydia inclined her head a trifle, and the stranger took the empty chair between the Corinthian and Bertram. Their indifference did not daunt him. Unruffled, smiling with his pale myopic eyes, he grinned at them. The squint was barely noticeable until one drew close; then one saw that the right pupil shifted towards the corner away from the nose, giving him a sly look. Now, slyly, he glanced from the Corinthian to Lydia and from Lydia to Bertram, grinning with shut mouth, the heavy chin, faintly cleft, pressing between the points of the high collar.

"This is a tame spot," he sneered, his voice soft and lazy, slurring consonants. "After all I'd heard about it, I didn't expect a place like this. Women showing off more than they've got, and young fools thinking themselves fine fellows because they've enough gelt to have the mollishers pretend to love 'em. There's more sport in a Suffolk barn-dance and hotter tits who'll not ask for payment more than a promise. If you want sport, gentlemen, take my tip and get into the country."

"Suffolk?" said Lydia in a low voice that was barely more than a whisper. "I thought I recognized the accent. I was born in Suffolk."

"You never told me that!" cried the Corinthian.

"You never asked," she said, not looking at him.

"What part of Suffolk?" demanded the stranger, staring hard into her eyes. "It's a large place, you know: largest county in England, next to Yorkshire."

"Lavenham," whispered Lydia, still looking at no one but staring mistily at the uproarious drunkards and their women swaying and staggering about the large room.

"Lavenham!" cried the stranger, smacking his thigh. "Now who'd have thought it! Hell's thunder, ma'am, but I don't come from far away. Do you know Polstead? The name's Corder, William Corder, at your service. You've heard of the Corders, haven't you?"

"No," said Lydia.

"Not heard of the Corders!" He raised his thick brows and pursed his lips in a soundless whistle. "Big farmers, we are; landlords, too. Everybody roundabouts knows the Corders, although my father's dead now and I'm the master. Both my brothers dead, too. But I've still got a sister, lecturing miss she is, like all her sex, and my mama's alive, God bless her noble heart, for I'm the stars in her eye, I am, and can do no wrong. That's why I've come to London. Got weary of hobbledehoys and having girls under hedges. They think I'm God Almighty up there and I can have 'em by the dozens for less than an apple. Growing tired of it, I thought I'd give London a go."

"Very good of you," jeered the Corinthian. "And what do you think of London, sir?"

Corder wrinkled up his curling nostrils. "Not what I thought it'd be," he said. "Not like what *Tom and Jerry* made it. Your name's Tom, ain't it? Must be, else they'd not call you the Corinthian, would they? But you don't look like Mr. Egan's hero. Not the way Mr. Cruikshank drew him, anyhow."

To his own annoyance, the Corinthian found that his legs were trembling and he pressed both feet firmly on the floor to keep them steady. If he had to listen much longer to this rustic, he feared he would thrash him. That he had been nicknamed the Corinthian after Pierce Egan's hero, his name also happening to be Tom, had always secretly delighted him, and he had attempted to look as like Mr. Cruikshank's engravings as possible until he had begun to believe himself that light-hearted daredevil's twin. And now for this hobbledehoy to question the resemblance . . .! He bit his lip, lowering his eyelids in his rage when he saw that Lydia was smiling.

"Our friend's name, Mr. Corder," she said, "is Thomas Barsett. Our other friend is Mr. Bertram Marley. And I am Miss Lydia Atherton."

"Delighted to meet you," chuckled Corder. "Liked you the moment I saw you, forgive my saying it, ma'am. Moment I set eyes on you, I said to myself: Here's a lady, Bill Corder, so mind your step. Here's something for your money, I says. I am very pleased to know you, ma'am."

"Thank you," she murmured, a smile twitching the corners of her tight lips.

"Never thank anyone for telling the truth, ma'am," he laughed, bobbing his dark head and ogling her with his squint-eyes. "I *am* pleased to know you, and I don't mind saying it. When first I came to London, I says to myself: Here's sport, I says; by glory, says I, here's the spot for a man to live if he likes living. Then I began to change my mind. The place's tame. Not like *Tom and Jerry*, by God. First I thought I'd go quiet, just look around a bit, then I'd visit the houses Mr. Egan wrote about, Almack's—East sounded better than the West to me—and down amongst those cheating beggars in St. Giles's. All the places he wrote about."

"You'll need a cicerone," said the Corinthian, "if you don't want your throat cut."

"I can look after myself, I don't need none of your what-you-call-'ems, these cicerones, thanking you all the same, Mr. Corinthian," smirked Corder. "Don't think I'd go anywhere dangerous with gelt in my pocket, do you? Not me. Just a few shillings is all I ever carry. Not that you could call me a mean man. Ladies could tell you different, and I've run through my hundreds —what am I saying!—thousands—before this; but I'm no fool neither. They might talk about Silly Suffolk! Let 'em say it, they'll soon learn better."

"Will you join us in a drink, Mr. Corder?" asked Lydia.

He shook his head, grinning shrewdly. "Thanking you—no, ma'am," he chuckled. "I'm no drinker. I always know when I've had enough. Had four tonight already, and that's sufficient."

"Four!" cried the Corinthian, aping surprise. "And you're not drunk! What a head you must have, my good fellow!"

"Ay," said Corder, "I can take my share when I have to, and you'll never see me stagger going home. But I think drinking's a waste of time and money. Prefer to keep my powers for daintier sport." He leered at Lydia, and the Corinthian doubled his fists. "A drunkard's no good to any lady, is he, ma'am?" he asked. "An insult to the ladies, that's what I call booze, wasting your potency on a bottle. Not that a drop now and then ain't useful. Always carried a flask with me when I went to a dance at home, most of the girls not being used to anything but beer, and a power of good it did me, too, after they'd swilled a bit. Worth the money, I always said. Why! I could tell you tales . . ." He cackled lewdly, stroking his chin, and his myopic gaze wandered over Lydia, lingering on her bosom cleft with deep violet shadow. "Not that they're like you, ma'am," he said. "You never know what you're handling till you get 'em alone, for most of 'em hide more than you can feel. I like fancy gowns, like yours now."

That none of the three spoke did not appear to trouble him. As though he chatted with old friends, he rattled on, and now and then he turned to quiz the women with a condescending stare, boldly appraising those nearest, but always he turned again to Lydia who sat with lowered eyelids, hands in her lap, save when she drank—which was often—and, to the Corinthian's astonishment, she did not seem to resent the bumpkin's ogling.

"It's time we went," he said, half rising from his chair.

"I want another gin," said Lydia, not moving.

"Waiter!" shouted Corder, "waiter, here! bring the lady a gin."

When four gins were brought to the table, one of which he accepted and diluted heavily with water, he made no attempt to pay for them. Smiling and nodding at Lydia, he ignored the waiter's tray, and the Corinthian, ever fearful of being considered mean, pulled his purse from his pocket and tossed down the money.

"Lucky I met you," said Corder. "When I saw you smiling at me, ma'am—well, not exactly smiling, but looking as though you knew me—I thought: Hey, boy! here's the lass for you if only she were by herself. . . . You don't mind my saying these things, do you, sir "

"I don't care a damn what you say," growled the Corinthian.

"Thankee," said Corder. "I always believe in saying what I think. Lying gets you nowhere in this world, 'cept into trouble. I learned that early. Always tell the truth, no matter what brawl it gets you into. It pays in the end. Honest Corder's what they call me at home. In Suffolk, my word's good for a thousand quid any day. Ay, that it is. Do you appreciate the country, ma'am?"

Lydia raised, then drooped, her heavy shoulders, as though she were too weary to answer, and the glass rim tinkled against her bright teeth.

"No, it's not the place for you," he said, after intently watching her long throat move as the gin trickled down within. "Not for you," he repeated. "Too delicate, you are. Too refined. Too lady-like. You'd want a feather-bed and not stubble to lie on. Aw, there! I talk too much! Shouldn't say such things to a lady like you, and I know it. But you don't know how lonely I've been. . . ."

"You are alone in London?" she asked, putting down her glass.

"Temporarily, yes," he smirked. "But I never expect to be lonely for long. Not William Corder of Suffolk, ma'am. And I find it restful, sleeping by myself for a while. You know, there's nothing like a change. Devil damn me! if only I'd met you earlier I'd never have had to advertise!"

"Advertise?" she repeated.

"Ay," he muttered, "advertise." Then gloomily he shut his lips. "But it's all for the best, I suppose," he said, "for I'm a great believer in fate. What is to be must be. Where, may I ask, do you live, ma'am?"

"In Bond Street," she said, watching the light twinkle in her glass. "Over Mr. Lowther's, the tailor's. I and my husband live there."

"Your husband?"

17   S.O.T.R.B.—B

"Yes. Although I usually prefer to be known by my maiden-name of Atherton, I am really Mrs. Barsett," and casually she nodded towards the Corinthian who sat, lips twitching, glaring at the tablecloth.

"So that's it!" cried Corder. "I was wondering . . . explains a lot, that does! . . . And, Mrs. Barsett, may I still call?"

"Of course," she said. "I will be at home tomorrow evening."

"That's a pleasure to think of!" he chirruped. Then with a crafty look, he added: "I don't play cards, you know: nor dice, neither."

"That is as you wish." Slowly, after letting the last dribble of gin sink between her lips, she rustled to her feet. "Doubtless," she murmured, "you'll find other amusements. My husband will make an excellent cicerone if you wish to visit any of the haunts mentioned by Mr. Egan: he knows all the lowest sluiceries in London. . . . Farewell, Mr. Corder."

He caught her gloved hand and kissed the kid over her knuckles, gazing up at her amorously. Then he pushed back his chair that she might pass.

Eyes glittering, lips tight-set, the Corinthian ignored his out-stretched hand as he followed Lydia into the press; but Bertram paused to tap him on the shoulder.

"Little man, little man," he said, "I'd forget that invitation if I were you. The Corinthian can use his fists as well as a pistol."

Corder laughed uneasily. "So can I," he mumbled.

"You're not in Suffolk now," said Bertram. "London streets are dark and many a man wakes in hospital and never knows what hit him. . . . Yes, yes, I know you're not frightened, but all the same I'd be careful if I were you; and I'd wish you luck, if I liked you."

Corder giggled. "Don't worry about me," he said, "and I don't need your luck. I've plenty of my own, more than most men, or I'd have been dead long since."

Before such complacency, Bertram knew that argument would be useless. He turned to follow his friends, puzzled that Lydia should have troubled to snare such an ill-bred, suspicious fellow, and then, on discovering his crudity, to have given him her address. He had always admired and desired her as the most dangerous of women. But then, he shrugged, after all, she was a woman, and therefore at times her actions were unpredictable.

Grinning, rubbing his fingers over his heavy chin, Corder sat back in the chair and twisted round, trying to squint at his reflection in one of the enormous mirrors that hung on the walls. But the crowd was too great for him to see himself, while the candelabra's lights were so strong that they seemed to explode in silver against the glass. Denied the satisfaction of self-approval, he took up his unfinished gin and, with a grimace, swallowed what remained. He did not really like the stuff, but someone else having paid good money for it, he could not bear to think that it might be wasted or licked up by a waiter.

Then he lounged back like a gentleman taking his ease in a harem, crossing his legs, and quizzed the many painted women, sniffing deeply of their perfumes which, in that enclosed and airless room, were sufficient to have suffocated anyone who did not relish femininity as Corder relished it. Country lasses or painted trollops, he did not care, knowing that with his fascinations he must always prove their conqueror, for he was male and they were merely female and therefore his destined prey.

Chapter Two

THREE'S COMPANY

EVER since, towards midday, he had woken up, the Corinthian had been trying to quarrel with Lydia. Unwashed, unshaven, he roamed about their Bond Street apartment, and, after being violently ill, sought to calm his stomach with brandy and soda-water. And he who prided himself on his dignified taciturnity rarely stopped talking, save to vomit. As ill as he, Lydia crouched before the fire, alternately shivering and sweating, her uncombed, un-pinned black hair straggling about her shoulders, and her loose satin *peignoir* so insecurely tied that she might as well have been undressed for all the covering it gave her when she moved. This *déshabillé* outraged the Corinthian because he considered it an insult. Had she been a coy girl with apparent innocence letting her gown fly open to excite him, or had she behaved like a purring mistress proud to display her beauty before her master, he would have been delighted; but he knew that Lydia's disregard for de-corum resulted from her contempt for him. So insignificant, so harmless had he become to her that she could act before him as though he were a little boy or merely another woman. Until this day, he had never considered this point of view. Indeed, he had relished her unselfconsciousness as proof of their emancipation and superi-ority over human sheep, but with his stomach wambling and his head aching as though a slab of lead pressed against the bone, he could not like Lydia, draped or undraped; and particularly, he felt, he disliked her half-undraped, as she was now. Everything she did exasperated him; her slightest gesture, every time she sighed or coughed, or when she ran from the room that she might retch in solitude, disgusted him until he had to turn away with clenched fists, fearful lest he try to beat her; and if he tried to beat her he would lose her, he knew, such being her pride.

Tugging at the tassel of his nightcap, he bared his hairy legs to the fire, as, sucking his thumb, he contemplated the thought of

20

living without a woman. It would offer both advantages and disadvantages. Although Lydia had never condescended to interfere with his occasional amours, he had always had the uncomfortable feeling that she might return home unexpectedly and catch him, helpless without his braces, with one of her best friends, for the Corinthian was terrified of being made to feel ridiculous. But escape from such possible situations would, after all, prove a small advantage when weighed against what he would lose if he left her—the most fascinating decoy in the game; and also, to be honest, the most satisfactory lover any man could desire when the fancy took her. No, he must not lose Lydia, however she might on occasions annoy him. And he wondered, and caught his breath with surprise at the thought, whether this morning's anger against her interest in this wretched Corder sprang from fear of losing her.

Never before had she shown other than a predatory interest in men. From her cupidity had come about their coupling, she mistaking him for a gull and he believing her to be a wealthy lady on a frolic whom, with threats of exposure, he could later milk of gold. At that time she had not been long on the town; and now that he came to think of it, he had never learned her history. Not that he had been interested. That she was beautiful, intelligent and a quick pupil in the art of flat-catching had been sufficient for him; and until now their partnership had proved profitable and, on the whole, amiable, although their quarrels these days had become frequent. And by God, the Corinthian told himself, he'd have truly loved her had she permitted it.

That was one of his deepest grudges against Lydia. Never had she said she loved him, even in a lie. He who was used to women's adoration therefore considered himself cheated of his masculine rights, and he had even felt—he had an uncle who was a parson —that there was something sinful in a woman who surrendered to a man for her pleasure and not his. Experience had long since taught him that all women were not saints, by any means, and in his heart he despised them for their carnality, his childhood faith insisting that only bad women and servant-girls could find pleasure in what was a man's privilege exacted against a woman's nobler instincts. Yet here was Lydia Atherton, who, if not exactly a lady, had been educated and genteelly reared, who shamelessly could act love's partner. And this the Corinthian's masculinity resented, for it made him, in some fashion, feel inferior, as though he were the woman rather than the man of that union. Nevertheless, for business reasons—besides, against his wish, he could not help now and then desiring her—he had never told her his thoughts and how he had begun to weary, dreaming of a tame, obedient mistress, allowing his resentments to show only obliquely in occasional sneers. The maddening part was that Lydia did not seem to care. She did not seem to care for anything or anybody other than money, money, money . . .

Certainly, the Corinthian cared for money, cared for it passionately because of the comforts it could bring; but, he told himself, he had not Lydia's greed. Besides, he needed money, while she, save for buying herself an occasional gown and paying half the rent of their apartment and the servant's wages, had no expenses. Wherever they went, always he had to pay for her as well as for himself: all food, drinks, theatres, masquerades and such came out of his pocket, although they halved whatever they might earn. When he had once attempted to remonstrate with her on the unfairness of this partnership, she had retorted that her task was the more odious as she had to submit to the handling—and in difficult cases, to more humiliating acts—with their clients before they could be lured to the card-table. On his continuing to argue, telling her how much each evening cost him, she had taken up her bonnet and carefully put it on. That had silenced him. He dared not lose her; and, damn it, she knew it.

Yet on the whole their partnership had been a friendly one. Until lately, they had rarely seriously annoyed one another and were able to live in tolerable amity, which was important. Other cozening couples quarrelled and fought and were continually changing partners. For roughly five years, the Corinthian and Lydia had worked remuneratively together and never once had they separated, each being aware of the other's value. Without her to tempt them, his victims would often have shown themselves more suspicious at being cheated, while she who had no inclination to act the harlot, save as a last desperate resource, would often have found herself literally naked before some flat's frenzy had not the powerful Corinthian been on call to arrive, the outraged husband, to be appeased, at her signal, only by gold.

For the first time now he felt that this lucrative sport stood in danger when Lydia should indulge an extraordinary whim for an ugly and, from the business point of view, worthless young man. That Lydia now and then should be taken by a whim, as he was himself when a fresh young face smiled in his dark world, and might choose a lover, if only for a brief diversion, he grudgingly accepted; but her liking for this cross-eyed William Corder remained to him inexplicable and therefore disturbing. The fellow was not even good-looking; he was either mean or poor; he was a simpleton bubbling over with his own importance; and doubtless he was a rogue and a liar. Yet deliberately had Lydia made his acquaintance. Why? They had been born in the same county, she had haughtily explained, but so had thousands of other men and women.

"What the devil you can see in that bumpkin," he roared for about the fiftieth time, "I can't make out."

Lying on the sofa, head back, limbs loose, wearily Lydia closed her hot eyes. "Then why bother about it?" she whispered.

"Because I don't like it," he growled, delighted at having at last evoked a response from this corpse-like creature. "It's not like you. You're sharp, you don't waste time on flats unless there's cash in it. And he's got no cash. Or if he has, he's too fly to let you get your hooks on it. We know this game, my dear, and you should remember that there's no flat more troublesome than a fool who thinks he's clever. If he won't play, how are we going to squeeze him?"

"I do believe," she said with a slow smile, "that you're jealous, my pet."

"Jealous!" howled the Corinthian, springing out of his chair to stare down at her, "jealous of that cross-eyed hobbledehoy! No, no, no, pretty, you'll not make me angry." Forcing a smile, he carefully sat down again. "I am merely curious," he said: "that's all. Yes, curious. Inquisitive, if you prefer the word. And puzzled. I've known you many happy years and if there's one thing about you of which I'm tolerably certain it is that you possess nothing resembling a heart. Not even a dried pea for a heart. That is one of the reasons why I love you madly. Because I also have no heart. We can't afford to own such vulnerable things suitable only to children who know no better. Our world's a dangerous one and we must walk carefully; and to have a heart is to open us to betrayal. Yet to my astonishment I find you deliberately picking up

23

an unprepossessing young fellow who has plainly no money to give us. Are you surprised that I am curious?"

"Nothing surprises me," she said in a dying voice. "I am a woman and I have my moods. Let that satisfy you."

"It far from satisfies me," he grumbled, trying to speak amiably. "You are decidedly a woman, and I am grateful for it, but I have never before found in you your sex's usual idiocies. O, you've liked many a pretty boy before, no doubt. I've not been blind although I've shut one eye. And that's never worried me, for, as you say, you are a woman and have your moods. But this little wretch is far from being a pretty boy, and I consider it an insult, yes, definitely an insult that you should favour him when you can't expect to squeeze a penny out of his reader. For the love of God, Lydia, what do you see in the dog?"

She sighed and did not answer. How could she answer, being as puzzled as he? All she knew was that in that noisy gathering last night, sickening at the smell of sweat and perfume, longing for fresh air and moonlight, she had suddenly heard the stranger speak and the gentle Suffolk voice had dizzied her with memories of her youth. So vividly that it had brought tears to her eyes, she had remembered her parents and the pink plaster of their thatched home in Lavenham. Lads speaking with accents like Corder's had wooed her in girlhood, and last night she had felt that she must speak to the man if only to listen to his voice. The Corinthian, she realized, was right to object to such a foolish whim. This Corder was an unpleasantly conceited young man, the kind of oafish youth she had always previously disliked, and she half-regretted the invitation she had given; and she would never have given that invitation had the Corinthian not behaved so boorishly. More to annoy him than to see Corder again had she asked the man to call. And now the Corinthian's nagging only strengthened her determination to be gracious when he arrived.

"O, please," she moaned at last, "be quiet. My head throbs, and you'll make me sick again."

"I merely want to know what you see in the rat."

"You've asked me about five hundred times, and if you ask me another five hundred times I'll not answer you. Did I question you after I'd found you'd locked me out that day and I could hear Sophie's voice?"

24

He flushed. "Do you want to be locked in with this Corder?" he asked.

"I've suggested nothing of the kind," she cried: "he's only a boy and I felt sorry for him. He comes from my county. That's all."

"And you want to talk to him about the flowers in the spring, showing that you're still a milkmaid under your dairies? Who'd ever have thought it! Piccadilly Lydia dapples her bottom in the dew! I'll take you to Hyde Park and buy you a pail of hot milk to drink with Mr. bloody squizz-eyed Corder. O, of course, you're only a child at heart, a maiden fancy-free until the traps nab you for having found too many bastards in your gooseberry-bed. Here's a new rôle for Lady Lydia!"

"Be quiet," she snapped, rising languidly to her feet to still the trembling of her legs. "There are times," she said, "when I hate you, and you aren't worth hating. But I warn you: don't keep this up . . . I have my pride, remember. . . . Perhaps this Corder has little money; perhaps he is a conceited oaf. I'll grant all that; but he comes from my home, from Suffolk; and that means much to me, more than you could ever understand. Or it did last night. I suppose I was drunk and drink can turn one sentimental. Aren't you ever sentimental?"

"Never," he said; then, with a sly glance at her opening *peignoir*, he added: "Except with you, my love."

"Don't be a fool," she said, realizing how impossible it was to explain what that meeting with Corder had meant to her in her drunken mood. She had wanted to escape, to be a girl again, to have the right to despise the painted women prancing with their one-night lovers. . . . Not Corder, but the memory of green fields, of earth like chocolate turning at the blade of the plough, of little villages amongst the hills, of oak-and-plaster houses, and of twilight pressing up to the window while tapers were lit at the fire and a violet mist turned the familiar garden into fairyland . . . such memories had brought her near to tears with longing to return to girlhood, to be again timid when men spoke to her, until that man, the only man she had ever loved, passed her on the road and then turned his horse and talked to her. . . .

Like this Corder, he had been a small squire, but she had believed he was a great gentleman until that morning when she

25

had awoken in a London lodging-house to find him gone and, insultingly—yet how useful they had proved—the five pounds on the table by the bed. That since that morning of remorse and tears she had taken rich revenge on men could never recompense her for the insult of that casual desertion; and she had sworn hatred, determined never again to bare her heart to pain. Yet memory of that smiling man could still make her tremble—with loathing, she swore—and her heart at times would quicken at the thought of meeting him again. Should that ever happen, she would make him suffer, she swore, as she had made other men suffer in his place for that crime against her youth, her beauty, her trust and her simplicity.

"My love," said the Corinthian, eyeing her with a dreadful suspicion, "you're not going to turn virtuous on me, are you?"

"Virtuous? Even God cannot raise a maiden after her fall, it has been written. You need have no fear of that," she cried impatiently, tossing back her heavy hair. "Just for this evening I want to talk of home. Besides, he might prove wealthier than you think. Hearing tales of London, these farmers are often cunning enough to pretend to be poor."

"Don't gammon yourself," he grinned. "That fellow's got no money. Or damn' little. And what little he's got he'll keep well buttoned up. And I don't believe he's a squire. I'd call him a little knave, a shop-boy who's robbed his master's till and has fled to hide in London. But let's not talk about him . . . If it's your wish, I'll bear with him tonight. But only for tonight."

"Thank you," she said, and kissed him lightly on the forehead.

Gripping her arms suddenly, he tried to drag her to him, but she stiffened and held back, chin up. The Corinthian was as startled as she by his unusual, unexpected passion; and while she commanded him to behave himself, he kissed her throat and breasts, the touch and perfume of her skin exciting him until he trembled.

"No," she said petulantly, "no," and wrenched herself away, flinging back her greasy uncombed hair. "You're behaving like a boy," she said with mock-severity.

"I feel like one," he giggled, half-ashamed.

"And I," she said, "feel like a mother who's discovered she has an incestuous child; and I can't say that I like the feeling. . . . It's time to dress."

Becoming uncomfortably selfconscious under his gaze, she turned and hurried to the bedroom, astonished that she should feel as awkward as a young girl before a man's admiration. For she no longer loved, if she had ever loved, the Corinthian. Too long had they lived together, their only bond the need to rob young fools at gambling, and for months lately she had gone wearily about her tasks, bored and melancholy, drink alone supporting her in the monotony of that existence. Was it, she wondered, the thought of Suffolk that made her feel like a maid again, for behind her eyes she could see the violet field and the moon, bright and round over his shoulder, and could remember her heart's fluttering with that mingling of longing and terror unable to sustain without dying which had made her shut her eyes and lie, limbs tense yet lax, in his arms, awaiting the moment of pain and ecstasy she had dreaded yet desired.

Impatiently, she tossed that memory into the past, swinging her long hair about her, as she closed the bedroom door and turned the key in the lock lest the Corinthian think to follow. Weary and sick though she was, she smiled; and she continued smiling after she had poured the water from the jug into the basin and begun to wash, although she dreaded the hours of dressing ahead while her limbs were heavy and she ached for sleep.

Below, in Bond Street, the lamps were lighted, their light gleaming on shop-windows blazing with the splendour of oil or gas, making expensive china twinkle as though washed in oil, the paintings shimmer and seem to live, and the various bodiless garments appear to breathe as if worn by invisible beings. This was Luxury Street to which ladies and gentlemen came in their carriages, where military men swaggered, their horses or tilburies in the care of grooms outside Steven's Hotel; where at night ventured only the more exclusive whores and where lived misses in the keeping of wealthy gentlemen. The cheaper mots paraded Piccadilly and rarely did more than peep to sigh at that stretch of wealth towards which they might aspire but which they rarely achieved.

Ignoring such cheap merchandise, save to grin waggishly into the painted faces of the more attractive or more persistent harlots plucking his sleeve, Corder trotted up from Piccadilly to stride into the blaze of Bond Street. Determined though he was to be impressed

27

by nothing, he could not stop his lips from shaping for a whistle when he saw the gay shop-windows. Being as yet early in the evening, passers-by were few, two gentlemen sauntering arm in arm and talking loudly of Lords This and That, while a carriage with blinded windows rattled past—a duchess off to an assignation with some low-born lover, thought Corder with a smile—and a singing errand-boy with a parcel on his back. Otherwise the street was deserted, but Corder found more to interest him in the shop-windows than in humanity. In particular, the jewellers' fascinated him, and idly he considered throwing a stone through the glass and making a grab and a run for it; but deciding that men who displayed such wealth were not likely to be such fools as not to have set a trap for thieves, he abused them for putting temptation in the path of the poor, while he dug his fists into his coat-pockets to keep them out of harm's way. Diamonds and pearls he recognized, his mother possessing a few poor specimens, but the other jewels were merely bright rocks to him, nameless though exquisite, and worth a tidy heap of money, he didn't doubt.

"Have you decided what you intend to buy your sweetheart, Mr. Corder?" asked a soft voice beside him, and he swung round, ash-faced, to see Bertram Marley smiling into his eyes.

"What d'ye mean?" he shouted, "creeping up on a fellow like that! You shouldn't do it. Might have had a weak heart for all you know."

"That," smiled Bertram, "I beg to doubt. There's nothing weak, I'm certain, about your heart, Mr. Corder."

"Perhaps there ain't," admitted Corder grudgingly; "only I don't like people creeping up on a fellow. You going to see Mrs. Lydia, too?"

"I am," said Bertram, "about to visit my friend, Mr. Thomas Barsett, commonly known as the Corinthian, and his wife, Mrs. Lydia Barsett."

"Don't tell me they're married!" scoffed Corder. "He's like Tom in the book and she's his Corinthian Kate. Thought so the moment I clapped peepers on 'em. Fine figure of a woman though, by God, true-blue Suffolk breed. Genuine Suffolk. That's where the prettiest women and biggest horses come from. Best men, too. Second largest county in England. And after all, Yorkshire's really three counties, only they call 'em ridings. Now, look here, friend, you know this couple well, don't you? . . . Well, what's their game?"

"Their game?" repeated Bertram indignantly, arching his brows.

"Don't try and gammon me," chuckled Corder. "I know I can be fascinating to females; no good being modest about what's obvious; but I also know that this Lydia didn't go nutty over me because of my handsome phiz. So what does she want?"

"That," said Bertram, "also puzzled me. I really can't understand it."

"Well," shrugged Corder, "you can't really tell with the Sex. There was a girl I knew in Ipswich——"

"Tell me about her some other time," said Bertram hastily. "We are already late."

After they had stumbled up the stairs, the front door having been left open, and entered the sitting-room, even Corder, determined though he was to despise these arrogant Londoners, caught his breath at sight of Lydia's beauty and blinked jealously at the Corinthian in his dove-grey coat and breeches and exquisitely folded stock. But, in her brownish-pink taffeta gown, Lydia seemed to draw all the candlelight to herself so that Corder had the illusion that the room was dark save where she lounged on the sofa before the dying fire, protecting her face from its glow behind a tiny fan. Corseted too tightly to bend, her waist appeared thin enough to have been snapped in a strong man's grip, while her breasts were squeezed up by the whalebone until they almost welled over the corsage. Hugely swollen at the shoulders by the wickerwork frame, her sleeves were drawn in at the elbows to meet the kid gloves that concealed forearms and hands. Below her bosom also was she concealed; only shoulders, throat and face were shown, while the skirt, swept out by the starched petticoats, flowed from the tiny waist bound in a red belt.

Even the pale dazzle of her shoulders could not hold Corder's gaze when he looked into the great blue eyes that seemed unnaturally enormous and intense in that high-cheek-boned face. Fresh from the country and crudely applied cosmetics, he did not yet know sufficient of a lady's boudoir to realize that those eyes were dosed with belladonna. On him, the effect was startling, almost frightening, and he thought that she must be feverish until he had drawn close enough to see that the brightness on her cheeks was the fire's reflection, and that her skin was actually pale enough to have been considered almost sallow.

"Charmed to meet you again, ma'am," he said, trying to conceal his excitement. "This is a comfortable crib you have here, particularly after the hotels I've been lodging in. This really is like home."

"Like your Suffolk home?" asked the Corinthian, stretching his legs to the fire while lying back languidly in the chair.

"Pah!" said Corder, "you'd lose all your rooms in one of ours. Place's actually too large. Difficult to keep warm, yet cosy enough at times. But as I'm always telling mama, one has to keep up appearances just to put the neighbours in their place. A squire's got a duty to perform, like the parson. Yet this is very snug here."

Gaping about him at the gold-papered walls, at the thick carpet on the floor and the gilt chairs and sofa, he sighed. For a moment, his audacious swagger left him and he appeared weary and envious, until he saw Lydia watching him. Then he smiled again.

"Until I met you, ma'am," he said, "I thought there were no beautiful women in London. But then, of course, you're Suffolk. That makes you different."

Seeing the cat's smile on Lydia's face and noting how the Corinthian's legs stiffened and his hands dug deeper into his trouser-pockets, Bertram said briskly: "Well, what's to be done tonight? Mr. Corder tells us he's no liking for wine, cards or dice, which rather limits our pleasures. I can only recall one other pleasure that might be offered him, unless he likes dancing."

"I want to see those places Mr. Egan wrote about," said Corder. "That's what you promised me. I know that book was written some years ago and things can't be quite the same now; but there must be some places like 'em."

"Things haven't greatly changed," murmured Bertram with a malicious smile, "and we can follow more or less in Pierce Egan's footsteps. But I'm afraid Mrs. Barsett could not possibly accompany us."

"Why not?" demanded Lydia, haughtily flashing at him her belladonnaed eyes.

Bertram shrugged. "Some of the cribs, of course," he said, "can be visited by ladies. Covent Garden Theatre, for example, or Vauxhall; but these, my dear, you must know *ad nauseam*. They may be fresh to Mr. Corder, but they'd only weary you."

"O, I've seen those places," said Corder contemptuously. "At least I've been to Vauxhall and I yawned all night. I was thinking more of places like the Sluicery, you know, and Tattersalls—I'm fond of horses: always had a partiality for mares—and All-Max's in the East, and the Cockpit, and the Holy Land, and . . . and, O, you know."

"I know," said Bertram. "But the haunts you want are often dangerous. No doubt you can use your fists, if necessary?"

Although he paled a trifle, Corder said truculently: "Never a man in all Suffolk could stand against me."

For the first time that day, the Corinthian laughed cheerfully. "So it's low haunts you want?" he said with relish. "You shall have 'em, my friend, you shall have 'em. I'll send you back to Suffolk, if you ever get there, with tales to tell of rookeries and slums that'll make the yokels think you must be Ananias. I'll be your Vergil into the filthiest of hells . . . But you, my love, can't come with us."

Holding the fan closer to conceal the flush of anger, Lydia said quietly: "I am going. You may leave the filthier places for some other night. I've been promised this spree; and I'm going with you."

The Corinthian looked at Bertram, and Bertram looked at the Corinthian, both raising their brows. They knew Lydia when she decided to be obstinate.

"All right," groaned the Corinthian, "if you must, you can come with us; but you'd better strip off that toggery and put on something plainer if you don't want it torn off your back."

"O, no!" cried Corder. "Please, ma'am . . . You look so beautiful, you mustn't change. We'll go disguised some other time."

Wrinkling her nose, Lydia turned her brilliant eyes scornfully on the Corinthian; then, gracious as a queen, she inclined her head to Corder. "Thank you, sir," she said, "I am grateful to have at least one gentleman for escort." And she gave him her hand that he might raise her to her feet, while, unblinkingly yet adoringly, he stared into her glittering eyes.

Chapter Three

WASPS IN COVENT GARDEN

BECAUSE of Lydia's determination to accompany them, the evening proved wearisome to the Corinthian and Bertram. Deprived of the opportunity to carry Corder to various low haunts where he would have been robbed, poxed and drubbed, they sank into a gloom which even large doses of brandy failed to dispel. Indeed, the drink merely intensified their depression, and after an hour or so Bertram asked to be excused and left his friend to contemplate alone the spectacle of Lydia and Corder chattering, laughing, and ogling one another. Now that he was fully at his ease in their company, much of Corder's bluster vanished and at times he even seemed to be prepared to listen and to learn from their larger experience of London life. Once or twice he even remembered to ask the Corinthian's opinion or advice, to be answered with little more than a grunt, but most of the time he conversed in a low voice with Lydia, and their conversation was closed to the Corinthian who knew no more about Suffolk than that it bred a horse known as the Suffolk punch.

As Lydia's expensive gown had ruined the intended spree, it was perhaps inevitable that it should dictate the evening's entertainment. Being a comparatively new addition to her wardrobe, she wished to flaunt it before the Cyprians in the Covent Garden saloon where she had spent her own novitiate. The idea enchanted Corder, recalling to him Cruikshank's print in *Tom and Jerry*, yet only after ruminatively tinkling the coins in his pocket did he, with a certain reluctance, agree to go, adroitly skipping behind Lydia when they were in the street so that the Corinthian would have the responsibility of calling and therefore of paying for the hackney-coach.

They alighted before the theatre, the dazzle of lights making the great building look pallid under the purplish sky a-flutter with stars beyond the city's smoke. Corder, to avoid paying the coachman, turned like any johnny raw to gape about him, while he squeezed Lydia's forearm. Jostled by the crowd, the fashionable folk stepping disdainfully from their carriages, beggars and pickpockets darting here and there, shouting that they would hold his honour's horse while slipping fingers into pockets, he stared at the great façade as though he had been turned to stone like the carved figures of Comedy and Tragedy between the pilasters.

Yet his excitement was not all a cheat to avoid paying the fare. Strive though he did to act the part of a knowing cove, he remained a countryman who previously had seen no towns larger than Ipswich, and now finding himself hustled by shrill-voiced fashion, with squeaking cold-eyed ladies elbowing him out of the way while their gallants quizzed him with curling lip, his heart lifted and he could have crowed his delight. This, at last, was life! a Tom and Jerry life at last! Even when the Corinthian, slipping his purse back into his pocket, scowled at him, he did not care. Amiably, he smiled back and shouldered a passage through the crowd that Lydia might follow without having her gown too badly crushed.

To him, they stepped into a wonderful palace of red porphyry pillars enclosed in white-veined marble walls, with a vast stone staircase ahead, and he tried to imitate the others shrugging forward with the air of kings and queens who had unexpectedly found themselves mixing with the *canaille*. Even for his effrontery, however, the effort was too great. He gasped, then reddened when he noticed Lydia smiling benignly at him as a mother might smile at her child at a treat; yet such was his excitement that for once he could not help speaking honestly.

"I've never seen anything so—so magnitudinous before," he gasped. Then hurriedly, he added: "Although we've got an excellent theatre at Ipswich, you know. Not as big as this, of course. . . ."

And to Lydia's surprise, his bucolic arrogance did not irritate but rather pleased her with its simplicity.

"O?" she said, widening her brilliant eyes at him. "You'll find it even more wonderful when we get inside. I'm sure it's better than Ipswich."

The Corinthian had believed that nothing could shut Corder's mouth for longer than two minutes, but he had failed to appreciate the effect of the blaze of lights, the vastness of the auditorium and, in particular, the performance of Mr. Charles Kean, looking as though he were about to die under his paint—he had been ill for some time: unkind folk tittered that he had been drunk—in the humpbacked part of Shakespeare's *King Richard III*. Mouth open, Corder sat and never moved after the curtain had risen. Sitting beside him, Lydia scarcely glanced at the stage. From the corners of her eyes she watched with fond amusement the effect of the great acto.'s performance on this silly fellow who was a simple country lad behind his mask of braggart. Even the Corinthian, biting his thumb as he calculated the expenses of the evening, relaxed and became tolerant with superiority at finding the hobble-dehoy exposed as a hobbledehoy. The evening was still young and it had proved damnably expensive. He had had to pay for every-thing since Bertram had left, including the seats for this box which, not being a private box, was one of the twenty-six that rose in tiers each side of the stage and held each a crush of ten persons: this inferior seating ruffled his pride. He felt that with his gentle-manly appearance and cultivated charm, the management should have been proud to present him with the key of a private box, for, save on important occasions, these were usually empty.

So captivated was he by Kean's ranting and bounding that when the lights went on between the acts, Corder blinked as if suddenly aroused from sleep, and he found it difficult to form a smile.

"I—I'd like a drink," he muttered to cover his embarrassment.

"I thought you didn't drink," said the Corinthian.

"Sometimes. . . . It's hot in here," he said.

"I feel," said the Corinthian, staring coldly into his shifty eyes, "that this time you had better pay. It would make it less embarrass-ing, wouldn't it? So far, you've paid for nothing."

"Nothing? Really, sir! Nothing?"

"Nothing," repeated the Corinthian, still staring at him.

"Then I will certainly pay for the drinks." Bustling to his feet, Corder seized Lydia by the elbow and, abruptly hoisting her up, pushed her ahead of him between the chairs behind. Bowing and apologizing for his companion's bad manners, the Corinthian slowly followed.

Upstairs to the saloon he went at the heels of the others, and he tried to look with indifference at the diamonds and gems against the women's skins. As often he had boasted, he was no thief, but there were moments, such as this, when he regretted his lack of education in the finer arts of picking a jewel, on pretence that it was a flea, out of a woman's bosom. Compared with the manœuvring of gulls towards the card-tables and the concentration needed in plucking them, the pickpocket's work seemed to him both simple and lucrative, even though the fence usually swallowed most of the profits.

Crushed amongst flesh, so much of it sweating diamonds, jewels hanging from ear-lobes nodding to be plucked, hands scabby with hard bright colours, his mouth grew dry and his eyes hot against the injustice of a world that gave wealth to so many who plainly did not deserve it—few were the attractive women present, few the handsome men—and who left unfortunate fellows such as himself no other resource save to use their wits.

Gloomily, he pushed his way to Lydia leaning back on one of the red pilasters that her gown might not be too crushed by the chattering horde of thirsty men and women all of whom seemed convinced that Mr. Kean was not the man he used to be. All talked loudly, tying to out-shriek the others, laughing with their friends, rolling up their eyes at the mention of Shakespeare's name, while groaning at the mention of Mr. Kean's whose amorous and drunken exploits had become the talk of the town. Some swore that he had never acted better, but the majority lamented that his days and nights were over and remarked how weak he seemed on his legs.

The Corinthian did not listen to such chatter. He could not blink from the jewels that blinded him at every move these elderly, unattractive women made under the bell-shaped lights with their lustres of glass tinkling above the hubbub. Squeezing down the stairs, protesting against the pressure of the iron rail, the fashionable women and their escorts struggled to reach the bar. Then, squaring his shoulders against the rush, the Corinthian saw Corder, his tall hat pushed forward almost to blind him, while delicately he held three small glasses of pale liquor.

"Thought I'd never do it," grinned Corder, giving a glass each to the Corinthian and Lydia. "Thought I'd smother in this crowd. What a stink of perfume! Rather be in a stable any day. . . . Hope you like your drink. Afraid I'd spill the lot, getting through that crush."

Glumly, the Corinthian took the glass and drank, noting that the measure was small, and he made no attempt to talk. His amusement at Corder's childlike excitement at Mr. Kean's performance had now left him and he felt savage at this wasted, expensive evening. Beside him, he heard Lydia and the bumpkin conversing in low tones as though they did not wish him to hear what they said; and he heard her laugh. That laugh set his teeth on edge because it did not sound like Lydia's. It was the laugh of an innocent girl shyly hoping for approval, and it took her from him into a world he could not enter, that world of her youth in Suffolk. And for the first time in many years he felt jealous, not of squint-eyed Corder, damn the fellow, but of her country-past and of that bucolic seducer whom he had heard her mention rarely, and then not so much with anger as with contempt for herself when a girl. Corder was too young a man to have been that rascal; he was much younger than Lydia, the Corinthian felt certain; but could he be some relation? That would explain much, he thought, reminding her of the man she must have loved with a passion she had never shown to him.

The crowd was thinning, glasses tinkling on to the wet bar, and many people were going back up the stairs. Sharply, a bell rang, peremptorily: irritable, it sounded; and there was a rush to return to the auditorium. The Corinthian had no desire to move. For this evening, he had had sufficient of Mr. Kean's shouting, and he would have preferred to remain where he was and drink, but Corder was impatient to return.

"Let's have another gin," said the Corinthian; and before the others could reply, he took their glasses and edged his way towards the bar.

With the departure of the audience, those women who had come to Covent Garden, not to see the play but to parade for victims in this saloon, that recognized meeting-ground called Mutton Walk where whores and whoremongers gathered to chaffer, wriggled away from the walls against which they had been crushed. The ladybirds and fancy pieces, the expensive Cyprians in fashionable garments hired by the night, with their bullies and their madams, and the fruit-women to act as go-betweens, shook free their skirts and pouted their bosoms and waggled their bottoms as they began to stroll for inspection, cards ready to offer likely customers. The Corinthian bowed and smirked when many of the harlots bowed and smiled to him, for he knew most of them intimately. Amused, he watched the parade, men inspecting the Venus-wares, openly arguing their preferences, and each mot showing off her particular bait—one lifting her skirts to display her sturdy calves, another waving her hands in the air to show her round white arms, others pulling back their shoulders to puff out their bosoms, others lifting their chins that their slim throats might be admired and caressed . . . and all of them rolling and blinking their eyes, swinging their hips, and tattling in shrill affected voices. . . .

While he was ordering the gins at the bar, the Corinthian heard a howl of fury that hushed all other sounds. As he might have expected, the howling female was Betty Blow, known as Black Bett because of her gipsy skin and dark hair, a tall bad-mannered beautiful whore with a vile temper which she never attempted to control. And to the Corinthian's delight, she was glaring murderously at Corder, crouching in front of him as though about to spring at his throat, her bottom appearing tremendous in the full skirt under the tightly gripped waist.

"You!" she squealed. "You dirty little bastard! you audacious bastard, to show your nose here! God Almighty, I tell ye now, you're not going out again except with a broken skull down the stairs unless you pay me the eight pounds you owe me; and two pounds interest I want, after the waiting and the worry you gave me; do you hear?"

Dislike Corder though he did, the Corinthian could not but respect his calm manner before this unexpected attack. His face had paled. Otherwise, he had not altered, his short-sighted eyes, save for the sinister squint, appearing innocent, a baby-blue, while, when he stroked his cloven chin, his hand was steady.

"My good woman," he began; but he got no further. Bett's shriek silenced every other sound and seemed to bounce from wall to wall.

"Your good woman!" she howled, "you good woman me, you dirty rat! Think I'm an old slavey, d'ye! I'll split your guts, by God, and you'll let no more women down. Your good woman! Did you hear him! And the dirty little bastard robbed me! Give me my rhino before I scratch your ogles out, you swivel-eyed bilking Greek!"

"Give her her money," said the Corinthian.

He saw that Lydia, usually so self-possessed, appeared more frightened than Corder; and he understood why. Since her rise from a night-house to the independence of a lady-sharp, her late sisters of the brothel detested her and were alert to insult or injure her in any fashion. Should Bett now begin a brawl, her nails were more likely to tear Lydia's than Corder's skin.

"Money?" mumbled Corder, fumbling for his pocket-book. "I—I've got no money."

"You'll give me my money," panted Bett, "or you'll not get out of the Garden 'cept as a cripple. So pay up, you cross-eyed lout. You had your money's worth of me. I'm never one to bilk an honest friend, no matter if his phiz's as ugly as yours; and I want my blunt. I want it now."

In their jealous hatred of Lydia, the other harlots were gathering behind Bett, urged on by their coves and procuresses, infuriated by the impudence of a bilking customer daring to invade one of their accepted haunts. If they allowed Corder to escape, it would encourage other good-for-nothings to enjoy love's apple without paying for the bite. Had Lydia not been present, gladly would the Corinthian have left him to his Bacchic-fate at the hands of these harpies, but once the brawl started she would probably become the first casualty, she might even be crippled by an expert kick, and would most certainly be defaced by sharp nails and thereby kept from work for weeks, or even months.

"I'm telling the truth," said Corder, beginning to stutter as he realized his danger. "I've no money; or very little."

"Let's see your reader!" shouted a squat, red-faced woman.

With trembling hands he pulled out his pocket-book, flipped it open and showed its contents. Bett seized the few pounds it contained.

"There's seven more pounds to come," she screeched. "You rotten little cheat to rob a poor hard-working girl! I hadn't left him for half-a-minute," she cried, turning to appeal to the others; "there was a friend waiting to be served, come unexpected-like, and I just hopped out to yell down the stairs I wouldn't be long, and when I mizzled back, he'd gorn! Outer the winder! Yere. Outer the winder. Him with his trousers in his hand and not forgetting even to leave his hat and boots, by glory! Even his boots,

I tell you! . . . I'll have that seven pounds, mister, if I have to strip you puppy-naked."

"Now, now," said the Corinthian, shouldering through the howling pack of harpies, "don't hit him, Bett. He's not worth your getting lumbered; and if you start a riot, you know you'll never be allowed in here again."

"Don't care!" snarled Bett, stamping her foot and pulling up her skirt that the hem might not be torn. "I work damn' hard for my money, don't I? And these screens I've took from him don't cover three minutes of my time, for I'm a busy woman, you understand, I'm sought after, I am, by lords and gents, and then to have him . . . I want at least seven more screens! And I want 'em quick."

Breathing hard, the Corinthian looked about him; and in that menacing crowd of women and their pimps he saw not a single friend. Yet most of these harlots liked him, some had even loved him a little, for he was one of the most popular swells in the Garden. But now all that was forgotten. Not only envy of Lydia who never could resist being ladylike before her old confrères, but professional terrors of having to work without payment had turned these whores and their coves to savages. In their expensive gowns—mostly hired for the evening—light glossing their nude shoulders and chests, at a casual glance they might have seemed a group of pretty women. That was until one looked into their faces. Their eyes cold, their lips tight-set or snarling, their fingers curled to scratch, their skirts lifted that they might kick their enemy in his most vulnerable parts, they were longing for the attack that future bilkers should be warned what to expect.

"All right," he groaned, "I'll pay"; and he pulled out his pocket-book.

The women relaxed, murmuring loud approval of such gentlemanly conduct while denouncing Corder and commenting on his appearance with words that would have made most men blush. He, however, seemed merely relieved at his escape, and, taking off his hat, he mopped his forehead with a red spotted handkerchief. At the same time, with eyes as avaricious as the whores', he gazed at the Corinthian's fat reader from which he was slowly counting pound notes into Bett's outstretched hand.

"Many thanks, my lord," smiled Bett with a curtsey. "I'll

39

always remember you're a gentleman, and we'll not quarrel over prices. . . . You must have my card."

"Nay, Bett!" said the Corinthian, managing a tender smile, "do you think I could ever forget where you lived?"

"It's the same address, near the Haymarket, and I'm always pleased to welcome open-handed gentlemen like you," she smirked. "But talking's dry work. You're going to have a drink with me. I insist on it. Hey, Moll," she shouted at the woman behind the bar, "fill 'em all up again. All except him, that cross-eyed cheating bastard over there. But give this gentleman"—she leaned against the Corinthian, rubbing her loose bosom on his arms, while leering up with kissing-mouth—"give him whatever he asks for. He can have what he wants of me any time of the month . . . I'll have some daffy: no water, blast you! give it to me stark naked."

Had it been possible, the Corinthian would have escaped, but he knew how mercurial were these women's moods, how tenderness within a flash could change to cruelty. Their pride was easily bruised and any look or word they might interpret as an insult was fast revenged.

"Thank you, pretty," he said, bowing when he took the glass which Bett, with a leer and a low curtsey, passed him. From the corners of his eyes he saw Lydia sink down on a golden chair, fanning her cheeks and chest with her hand; and, for once, Corder kept his mouth shut, although, now that immediate danger had passed, he quizzed the women with lewd eyes, smirking into their puffed-up bosoms and leering at their ankles. All ignored him, save to shrug their shoulders and lift their nostrils as though at a stench.

He did not seem to mind.

When at last he was able to make his excuses and escape, swearing on his honour to visit Bett again in the Haymarket, the Corinthian felt almost drunk, not because of the amount of gins he had been forced to consume without water—or stark naked, as Bett had it—but because of the near escape from danger. Not until he had Lydia safe in the cold street while a ragged boy ran for a hackney was he able to breathe freely again, shaking himself as if he would shake off the cloying scent of that almost airless saloon populated largely by indifferently washed and over-perfumed females in the shop-window of a gutter-Venus.

"We haven't seen the rest of the play," grumbled Corder.

Furiously the Corinthian turned on him. "Go back by yourself if you dare," he snarled. "And don't forget there's seven screens you owe me, apart from what else I've spent tonight."

Corder blinked and shuffled his feet. "I—I'm sorry," he muttered, "I've really little money on me at the moment. But I have Expectations. Indeed I have. I'm going to marry soon, a wealthy young woman; and there's money due to me from home, too. I'll pay you back. I give you my word of honour you'll get every farthing back."

"You'd better not forget," said the Corinthian between his teeth as he bundled Lydia into the hackney and slipped some pennies to the ragged boy, "because *I* won't forget," he added menacingly.

"Why! you're not going off now, are you, not without me?" quavered Corder. "The evening's young yet. You can't leave me here like this. What am I going to do with myself?"

"Do with yourself?" shouted the Corinthian through the window; "go back to Bett and have another evening on the cheap. Bond Street," he called to the driver and, breathing heavily, leaned back with folded arms as the hackney jolted forward.

In one corner Lydia lay as though in a swoon, her head bobbing against the greasy leather, and he felt her knee and thigh jolt against his, then swing back, then jolt back, then swing away, when the wheels bounced over ruts, as though her hip were jointless.

"Well," he said at last, "I hope now you're satisfied. You picked up the little rat and he's cost me over, at least, ten screens tonight."

"I'll pay you back," she moaned in a dying voice.

"Thank you," he said, "but I'm not like your Suffolk friend. I don't steal from the women who've favoured me. You can keep your bloody money. I only hope this evening's taught you a lesson and that we never have to entertain that swivel-eyed flame of yours a second time."

While he uttered that prayer, the Corinthian frowned, uneasily feeling that this William Corder was not the kind to disappear at so cheap a price. Even his satisfaction at having proved to Lydia that she had acted like a sentimental seventeen-year-old did not over-balance his dread lest, having evoked a demon, he would be unable to exorcize him at the mere cost of a few pounds. The fellow's skin was too thick and his vanity too great for him to feel humiliated by a debt. Besides, it was plain that he was nutty over Lydia; and Lydia, silly bitch, had so played up to him that he could scarcely be blamed for the delusion.

But, wondered the Corinthian with a faint shiver as he peered at her white face, eyes closed, gleaming momentarily, corpse-like, beside him when street-lights flashed through the windows, was that a delusion, after all?

Chapter Four

A LOVER'S TALE

WHEN days passed with no William Corder rattling on the door, the Corinthian began to breathe easily again and to hope faintly that, thick-skinned though he might be, this johnny raw was either too embarrassed to show his face again in Bond Street or was too mean to repay the money. And it was, he thought, money well spent if it kept the flat away from Lydia with her peculiar liking for the creature. Difficult though he found it, wisely he held his tongue from mentioning that name. Lydia had had her lesson. To salt the wound of her pride would merely have driven her away to revenge herself with some lover that she might uphold her self-respect. Therefore he was careful not to mention Corder, even when she most exasperated him; and he knew that she was grateful for his forbearance.

Back to the old life they went, seeking flats to fleece wherever laughter, drink and whoredom attracted young men from the city, St. James's or the country. Usually with Bertram, the Corinthian attended race-meetings and cock-fights, he strolled to Crockford's, looked in at Tattersalls to vaunt his knowledge of horseflesh; or he sweated out last night's drink in the fencing-rooms in St. James's Street, then poured it back into his belly at Long's or Steven's, the Cider Cellar or the Coal Hole. To such places Lydia, of course, did not accompany him. When not at her dressmaker's or gazing into shop-windows, she stayed at home, attended by the slavey, Nell, and reading the latest romances while dozing by the fire.

In the evening, she dressed and, escorted by the Corinthian and, occasionally, Bertram, visited theatres, dances or the Piccadilly Royal Saloon where she had first met Corder. Often, dressed less gorgeously, she went with him to other drinking-palaces, such as the Oyster Saloon in Bridge Street. This was a rowdier, more dangerous hell than the Royal. Open until dawn, under the pretence of selling shellfish and oysters it served its customers with expensive wines, coffee and supper. As the men were usually extremely intoxicated by the time they arrived, they were alert for insults, truculent or maudlin, whichever way the daffy had knocked them. To end the night, or to welcome day, it was usual to take final drinks in some Covent Garden coffee-house, such as the Finish in James Street, where whores and thieves gathered to yawn after their work, the whores slipping their purses from their stocking-tops or from under their stays to apportion the lion's share to their fancy men. Too weary by now even to brawl, the drunkards snored beside the Greeks who had robbed them; the fences waited for customers to sidle to them in a corner; procuress and pimp, ladybird and her captive, all were now in a state of semi-silence, faces bloated, eyes gluey and features seeming smudged from lack of sleep, still drinking if only because the waiters insisted truculently on serving them.

In such dens would the Corinthian often find his prey, Lydia tantalizing admirers with her artificially bright eyes and out-thrust bosom. Her emotions remaining undisturbed, she was able expertly to act the temptress, despising her adorers while languishing at their side, gazing from under heavy painted lids into their eyes. If the dupe had no inclination for cards or dice, she drew him back to Bond Street that he might be caught with her in *déshabillé* by an infuriated husband; and sometimes when the Corinthian had dallied, she found herself to her mortification on the edge of betrayal, unable to hold off the passionate fool.

So long had she been at the game that she was able to perform her rôle while most of the time thinking of other things; and she was beginning to tire of its savage monotony. Like an actress who has played the same part too often, she sighed at the tedium of acting the whore who rarely kept her bargain, or of leaning over the back of the flat's chair on the pretence of caressing him while she winked to the Corinthian the numbers of his cards. Greed kept her at it. Too many girls had she known who had enthusiastically embraced what was called a life of pleasure, only to end in a few years, diseased, disfigured or sottish, pleading to be taken for the price of a gin; and the thought of such a fate crinkled the skin on Lydia's thighs.

Some time, she swore, she would leave London and live quietly in the country; but always she pushed that time further into the future, telling herself that it would come upon her soon enough when her beauty crumpled into fat and wrinkles and her body became flaccid beyond the hope of stays' disguising. Whoredom had no appeal to her, and she submitted to her dupe only as a last resource when she had no other ways of cheating him, experience having taught her to despise men who, because of fleeting passion, could be cozened, robbed, even insulted and beaten. Indeed, she had found that often the more callously she treated them, the more eager they became to shower her with gifts and money. Only for the Corinthian had she retained a certain respect because she knew that he was unscrupulous and brutal and that he would abandon her without regret were she to fail as a partner or should a more expert female arrive to take her place.

With beauty such as hers she could have lived in idle luxury and have had her carriage in which to loll in Hyde Park, admirers riding beside and behind her, but the thought of remaining the property of one man, however wealthy, until he tired and she was passed into another's keeping, finally ending in a brothel were she not sharp enough to have had settlements signed and sealed, was revolting to her pride. She preferred this present partnership which gave her self-respect and protected her, save by unlucky chance, from unexciting embraces.

Yet, as the Corinthian noted uneasily, she was fast losing her enthusiasm for the game. There were nights when she plainly did not wish to go out with him and dressed only with reluctance, preferring to drink and doze in bed; and there had been occasions when, having hooked his flat, he had lost him because she had merely drowsed at the man's side, not bothering to stimulate him with fluttering lashes, panting bosom and the apparently casual resting of her hand on his thigh or knee. If this continued, he thought grimly, he would have to seek a fresh partner, somebody younger and more zealous; and the idea depressed him. There were not many women to be found as intelligent, as cold-blooded and as fascinating as Lydia. They were liable to frighten dupes by overplaying their parts or to take too enthusiastically to the seduction rôle.

"Ever since we met that cross-eyed flat she's not been the same," he grumbled to Bertram while they struggled amongst the crowd leaving the Westminster Pit after watching dog-fights and bear-baiting. Having lost heavily, he was in a bad humour, and the bad humour settled on Lydia. "D'ye know," he growled, "I really think she's nutty on the cove."

Bertram gave him a sharp glance. "I'm certainly surprised," he murmured, hunching his shoulders to keep as much as possible of his coat from being dirtied by those struggling about him towards the door, for to these pits came not only lords and other swells but dustmen, lamplighters, grooms, watermen, and all the sporting riff-raff of the town. "I'm certainly surprised," he repeated; "I'd always considered Lydia the only one of her sex able to master her feelings. At times, I confess, she's quite frightened me. A man likes a woman to be, in every possible way, beneath him. To tame a creature like Lydia one would have to be more than human."

"You're right," smirked the Corinthian, "perfectly right. She's not the goose for most men's plucking. That's what troubles me. Since that damned johnny raw met her, she's changed. She says that he reminds her of her youth—all carefree lecherous maids together, and that trumpery; but sentiment's as far from her leathery heart as pity's from a whore's."

"Are you certain of that?" asked Bertram, taking deep breaths of air to cleanse his lungs of the animal-stinks of the pit and its audience. "Perhaps this change shows that for all her sophistication and smugness she has a heart to be touched."

Surprised at the note of excitement in his friend's voice, the Corinthian glanced quickly at him. "Why!" he cried, "I do believe you're in love with her yourself!"

Bertram flushed, as though insulted. "I love no one," he said harshly; "but here's the truth," and he turned to stare into the Corinthian's eyes: "before God, if she'd not been your miss I'd have tried her long since! That's proof that there's honour even betwixt scoundrels!"

"You mean," said the Corinthian slowly, "that you'd have tried her had you had the spunk. Leave me out of this, with 'honour' and all that fine talk. You're afraid of her."

"Yes," said Bertram in a low voice, "I'm afraid of her."

The Corinthian laughed, delighted that his mistress should frighten so experienced a seducer as Bertram: that proved his own superiority in having mastered such an imperious female.

"Yes," growled Bertram, "there've been times when I've been

near it, but always I've drawn away. You're right. I was frightened, although I gammoned myself it was because you were my friend and I was acting honourably. I wasn't. O, I can't explain it! Even when I felt that she was ready, I've held back for fear of being laughed at. One night, yes, one night I almost did it. You were out and we were sitting by the fire, boozing. It was twilight before the lights were lit. Had I been sitting beside her on the sofa, I think I might have dared. But I was on a chair, far away from her and wanting her until it hurt, hurt like cramp. I made a gesture, leaned forward, almost touched her; and she looked up. You know how it is. I could see it in her eyes, in the droop of her mouth and her knees—you can always tell when a woman's ready, when her mouth goes loose and her knees relax—and I swear I could have . . . O, hell! how can one ever be certain? But then when you interrupted us, I've never been so relieved; and angry, too."

"I've often wondered," said the Corinthian, managing to conceal his fury. "I've noticed that cannibal-look in your eyes, but I'm used to seeing it with men and Lydia. Well! my friend, I give you *carte blanche*. Go to it, if you can, you bastard. But I know my Lydia! There's only one thing she cares about, and that's cash. Had you tossed your reader into her lap I don't doubt she'd have opened more than her arms. O, I'm not jealous about it. A man's a fool if he objects to his wife or his miss earning a little pin-money unless she happens to like the cove too much. It's only when she does it for pleasure that a man needs to look sharp."

"Do you mean to tell me," demanded Bertram, sweating in the cold, "that you don't care?"

"The devil a bit," smiled the Corinthian crookedly, "if you pay her well; and I might warn you, Lydia's a Jew for a bargain. O, don't think I'm afraid of losing her! It's this damned hankering after her maiden-innocence that I don't like, for that little swab did something to her. Stirred up the bawdy mud of her youth, as she tells me herself, and now she's got little heart for work. I tell you, I don't care if she sleeps with fifty men so long as she still brings flats to my card-table."

Smile though he did to show his indifference, he lied. He did care. On occasions, he knew that Lydia had been forced to act the lover against her inclinations; and that had never troubled him so long as her dupe was later delivered into his hands. But had she acted lovingly out of liking for the sport or had she taken to it as her sole trade, he would have kicked her out of doors. For then, his reputation as the bold Corinthian would have been tarnished, and women as well as men would have laughed at him as a cuckold; and what people thought about him was most important to the Corinthian. Airily he might dismiss Lydia into Bertram's arms, trusting not too strongly to her indifference towards other men, yet his heart beat painfully fast at the thought. If ever he caught her with Bertram, he swore, he would strangle her rather than let it be known in Piccadilly and the Garden that he'd been horned by a fellow-sharp.

Whistling to drive off his doubts, he bade Bertram a pointed good-bye and walked slowly up the stairs of his Bond Street apartment; then, at the door, he paused. A man was talking in there. And Lydia was answering softly, affectionately. The fact that they were talking did not reassure him, as ordinarily it would have done, silence being the cloak for lovers as well as for thieves; but Bertram's abrupt declaration of desire had frightened him with the realization that things could happen behind closed doors of which he was not aware, Lydia not having mentioned to him that scene with Bertram in the twilight.

Softly he turned the handle and tiptoed in. The candles had not been lit. In the amorous twilight, Lydia in a loose blue *peignoir* reclined on the sofa, her hair tossed back over her naked shoulders, one long disturbing white leg showing between the opening of the *peignoir*, and a slipper dangling from her toes. Facing her on the other side of the fire William Corder sat with his hands on his knees, grinning while he talked; and at the soundless approach of the Corinthian, both looked up— guiltily, he thought—and fell silent.

"You here?" he asked, turning scornfully on Corder. "You've come to pay me back, I hope?"

"Not exactly," said Corder, rising and offering his hand which the Corinthian ostentatiously ignored. "I've just been explaining my financial position to your dear lady here. Very shortly I expect to come into some money; not a great sum, just a small fortune, but, tee hee! more than sufficient to pay back the blunt you so nobly lent me."

Planting himself before the fire, hands joined at the back to toss up his coat-tails, the Corinthian glared superciliously down at him.

"What fortune's this?" he asked.

"Well," said Corder, giggling, "it's to come to me when I get married. . . ."

(Was the Corinthian mistaken or did he see Lydia start at this announcement?)

"I met a young lady, a highly respectable young lady," continued Corder, grinning and spreading his too large nostrils, "with a small yet useful jointure. It was by chance some months back when I was watering at Seaforth—a salubrious little place which I can recommend—that I encountered this lady: young, one would not say really beautiful, although most attractive, and unfortunately a trifle deaf. But she has a most devout and trusting disposition. Her attendance at church—thrice every Sunday, my friends, thrice every Sunday—impressed me deeply, for it proved she had a Soul. My interest being aroused in this virtuous young lady, I made enquiries, discovered where she and her mother lodged, and contrived to sit beside her in the pew on Sunday. I can assure you, it was no easy task to make her acquaintance. Useless with her any of the usual cheats to strike up a meeting. But that did not baffle me for long."

Complacently, he looked up at the Corinthian—for, while talking, he had returned to his chair—and was not disconcerted by the angry eyes shining in the shadows of that bowed head; then for approval, he turned towards Lydia who lay back, one hand shading her face as though the firelight's glare hurt her eyes, and he smirked at her smooth bare leg until, as if suddenly realizing that it was exposed, she drew forward the cloth to cover it.

"She was an innocent and lovely female who didn't attend dances or any of the public amusements of Seaforth," he continued, "and appeared to have no interests outside the Established Church. Having busied myself in discovering everything possible about her, including her address, I paid up my lodgings and took residence in the same house as herself. Here, without putting her out of countenance, I was able to attract her attention, discoursing on religion after dinner in the drawing-room, and great was the pleasure I enjoyed in her sweet, attractive company. In this manner I became intimate with this delightful female whose goodness and innocence appealed to my perhaps somewhat jaded palate the more I gazed on her. When the hour approached for her departure from Seaforth, as discreetly as I could I enquired her London address that I might wait upon her in the future. This she refused to give me, yet in so modest a fashion that it was impossible to be angry with her, for she told me to ask her mother. But her mother, I feared, did not regard me with a kindly eye, and I despaired of our meeting again."

The Corinthian snorted, then he turned and slowly spat into the fire; while Lydia seemed asleep, breathing deeply and now and then sighing very loudly.

"Nevertheless," went on Corder in the voice of one reading from a novel, "the young lady's simplicity came to my rescue. It was the very day of her departure and I was sitting in great distress when she sat beside me. She is no great talker, being deaf, but I believe she suffered the pangs of parting, and, to conceal her confusion, she chattered without thinking while the minutes ticked by that would part us, I feared, forever. So artless are the pure at heart, however, that she let slip that in London she often visited a pastrycook's in Fleet Street where the cakes appealed to her. I made mental note of this indiscretion, exulting in my good angel, and I was able to smile again, even after she had gone."

"Indiscretion!" laughed the Corinthian. "She hooked you well!"

"You would never say that," cried Corder indignantly, "if you knew the lady! She is the very soul of truth, a wingless angel if ever I have met one. Never had I believed that so heartless a fellow as myself, one who gloried in the debauching of helpless females, could be subdued by a maiden's blush. Yet I am her slave from now!"

"You seem very assured of her innocence, Mr. Corder," said Lydia wearily, her hand still shading her eyes. "There's only one certain way of testing a maid, and I doubt by your talk if you've attempted that."

"Of course I haven't! Not with such an angel! Nor will I until, at least, we're married; for this is the lady with whose small fortune I hope to recoup my temporarily empty pocket and to return to you, sir, that small sum I borrowed."

"You are really going to marry the woman!" cried Lydia.

"Most certainly," he said as though insulted. "Without

marriage, such a prize could never be boarded. Her jointure's not large but she's agreed that we invest it in a new school, for she has already a little school in Holborn and is a linguist, having been governess to some refined young ladies while on a visit to France. There's no detail of her past that I don't know. Incapable of lying, of even the faintest prevarication, she opened her heart to me, and her goodness, her sweetness at bottom——"

"Yes, yes," growled the Corinthian, "we've heard all that before. So now this chaste morsel, this nonpareil of maidenheads, turned up at the Fleet Street cook-shop?"

"And most amazed she was to see me there! Blushed to the roots of her very hair!"

"I really begin to admire this young lady of yours," chuckled Lydia throatily.

"When you meet her, you will adore her!" cried Corder. "Her fortune, as I said, is not large but sufficient to support us in a humble fashion, for she's some small personal property and money in the funds which could easily be converted into cash."

"Indeed?" jeered the Corinthian. "More than seven pounds, I hope?"

"Much, much more than seven pounds," said Corder earnestly, "so have no fear you'll not be repaid your debt. At present she has the lease of her house in Gray's Inn Terrace where she's opened a school and resides with her lady-mother. Her only other surviving relative, a brother, eats his meals there and maintains a workshop as a respectable working-jeweller. I've made enquiries, not that I suspect her of any little cheat, but just because I'm always a cautious fellow and like to do nothing in haste. I always plot everything most carefully. The great difficulty, which in Mary's innocent eyes seemed unsurmountable, I have surmounted and have managed to overcome her moral scruples into accepting the solution. This was how to explain to her mother and her brother how we'd met."

"I thought you'd met her mother at Seaforth," said Lydia, her eyes still hidden under the shadow of her hand.

"Of course, of course," said Corder; "but that introduction could not explain how Mary and I—her name, by the way, is Mary: Miss Mary Moore—how we could have met again; the chance of her having mentioned that she visited the Fleet Street cook-shop might have troubled her mother, a very good woman, though prim and of a highly suspicious nature."

"Doubtless," murmured Lydia, "she has cause to be."

Corder gave her a sharp glance but in his myopic vision she was little more than a voluptuous smudge lounging before the firelight that gleamed along the length of her leg under the robe. He decided finally to ignore her remark which, to him, appeared irrelevant.

"I therefore," he said, "concocted a harmless little subterfuge into which I don't mind admitting you, knowing you are my friends. It went against Mary's nature to lie, but after I had pointed out that there was no other way and that it would be less deceitful than our meeting in cook-shops without her mama's knowledge, reluctantly, with many a sigh, she agreed. She is All Soul, my friends, and hates untruths. The one imperfection in her is a physical one. She is slightly deaf, and courtship, I assure you, is carried on, particularly in a public place, under great difficulties when one has to shout sweet nothings." He frowned, shaking his head as though puzzled that God should have permitted even so small a blemish in one otherwise so perfect. "Though, doubtless," he added with a return to sprightliness, "I'll soon grow tolerant of such a little failing. It might even have its virtues. There are things at times which even the most devoted husband would prefer his wife not to overhear."

"Come, come," said the Corinthian, balancing on his toes while he tossed up his coat-tails to warm his breeches, "let's have no more of this jabber from a lady's novel. What's this devilish plot of yours to deceive the wench's poor old mother?"

Slyly, Corder peeped at him and chuckled. "A very simple one," he said. "I've advertised for a wife."

"You've what!" cried Lydia, lowering her hand that she might stare at him.

"Advertised for a wife," repeated Corder unctuously. "Indeed, if you had only read any other newspapers besides the *Weekly Despatch* for its sporting items, you might have spotted my little piece. It is excellently composed. I say so, although I wrote it myself; spent hours over it, I did. I have it here." From an inside-pocket of his grey coat he drew a newspaper-cutting and, gingerly unfolding it as though he feared it might crumble in his hands, he began to read, or rather, to intone the words in the voice of an elderly parson long drunk on port.

"'Matrimony',", he read, adding: "That's in capitals, you understand? Just to catch the female eye. Then I go on: 'A private gentleman, aged twenty-four . . .'"

"You look older," said the Corinthian.

"O, no, I'm not," snapped Corder. "I'm twenty-four years of age, having been born in 1803. Now, pray allow me to continue." Holding the paper so close to his eyes that he rubbed it against the tip of his nose, he began again to intone: "'A private gentleman, aged twenty-four, entirely independent, whose disposition is not to be exceeded, has lately lost the chief of his family by the hand of Providence'—my papa died two years ago, to be shortly afterwards followed to the grave by my dearly beloved brothers, James and John—that's not in the notice, of course, but I thought it might interest you. I now continue: 'Providence, which has occasioned discord among the remainder, under circumstances most disagreeable to relate——'"

"What circumstances?" asked the Corinthian.

Corder wriggled. "That's irrelevant," he muttered, "irrelevant. Kind of poetry. Besides, it sounds pathetic, what females like. After all, a man's not on his honour when he advertises, otherwise you wouldn't sell anything, would you?" Fearful of further interruptions, he rushed so hurriedly through the remainder of the advertisement that it was not until towards the end that he remembered his parsonical voice and began to read as though he had a sore throat:

"'To any female of respectability, who would study for domestic comfort, and willingly confide her future happiness in one very qualified to render the marriage state desirable, as the advertiser is in affluence, the lady must have the power of some property which may remain in her own possession. Many very happy marriages have taken place through means similar to this now resorted to, and it is hoped that no one will answer this through impertinent curiosity; but should this meet the eye of any agreeable lady, who feels desirous of meeting with a sociable, tender, kind, and sympathetic companion, they will find this advertisement worthy of notice. Honour and secrecy may be relied on. As some little security against idle applications, it is requested that letters may be addressed (post paid) to A.Z., care of Mr. Foster, stationer, No. 68 Leadenhall Street, which will meet with the most respectful attention.' "

" 'The advertiser is in affluence'," repeated the Corinthian. "Where's my seven pounds?"

"What I can't understand," said Lydia, still staring at Corder as though she had never seen him before, "is why you needed to write all that about property if you and this female are agreed to marry. Are you expecting other women to answer?"

"Well," drawled Corder, carefully replacing the cutting in his pocket, "one never knows, does one? One shouldn't be too hasty."

"But I thought you said you loved this—this person. Then why should you want other women to write to you?"

"I am interested in the female Soul," said Corder solemnly, "and any replies should make valuable reading about human nature. I'll bring them along and show 'em to you."

"You dare!" cried Lydia with an exaggerated shudder. "I'm only too aware of the stupidities of my wretched sex, and the last things I want to see are the pathetic outpourings of deluded creatures starved for a man. I think this is detestable of you!" she cried.

"I'd like to see these letters," grinned the Corinthian. "I might answer some of them myself. There's possibilities in this! Yes, great possibilities!"

"What do you mean?" demanded Corder. "You'd not take a base advantage of any of these poor females, would you?"

"No more than you, sir," said the Corinthian blandly, rocking himself on his toes, "no more than you."

"You are both disgusting!" cried Lydia, "and I'll not listen to such filthy talk. Pray move your chair, Mr. Corder, that I may pass."

Head high, cheeks flushed, she swung herself to her loosely slippered feet and, gripping her robe tightly about her hips, walked very erect out of the room; and when she slammed the bedroom door the noise was like a pistol-shot.

"Women," said Corder, scratching his ear, "rum coves, ain't they? What's she angry about now? I'm going to marry the girl."

"Are you?" asked the Corinthian.

Aghast, Corder glared at him. "Do you mean to say," he cried, "that you suspect some ulterior motive in this advertisement?"

"Apparently my wife does," smiled the Corinthian; "and in such matters of the heart, women usually know best. . . . But now, Mr. Corder, you must run along. It grows late and we have a dinner-engagement. . . . But seriously, I would like to read any letters you receive."

"If I've your word that you mean honourably," grumbled Corder, rising slowly to his feet, "I might perhaps read some of 'em to you. Just a lesson on the female heart, you understand?"

"I understand perfectly," said the Corinthian.

Long they stared at one another, Corder's crossed eyes blinking with the effort to focus the Corinthian's face that he might read its expression; the Corinthian smiling amusedly back at him, the perfect gentleman with nothing to conceal.

Chapter Five

POST-OFFICE CUPID

BEING experienced in the moods of women, after Lydia had finished dressing and had returned to sip gin before the fire, the Corinthian made no mention of Corder and his pursuit of a wife to maintain him in idleness. Eventually, she would have to speak of it, and he preferred to let her open the subject rather than give her the opportunity of abusing him should he speak first. Therefore, whistling very softly, he lounged before the fire, drinking brandy and soda-water, while awaiting the guests, two merchants' sons whom they had encountered on a spree the other evening and had invited to call for a friendly game of cards. Bertram was to make the fourth, it being Lydia's task to serve the drinks, making them as strong as their dupes could be induced to swallow. Then, leaning caressingly over the backs of their chairs, she would distract them with the pressure of her arm or breasts and the perfume of her hair, while she signalled what cards they held. Only the Corinthian feared, noting with dismay her sullen mouth and heavy-lidded eyes, the droop of her bosom and tenseness of her limbs, that tonight she might grow careless, her thoughts being elsewhere. Yet, even to distract her from her rancours, he would not mention Corder, knowing that she was hoping to hear the name that she might abuse them both as villains plotting to destroy poor innocent women.

He need not have worried lest she fail him. As though wishing to escape her thoughts, Lydia that night acted with a brilliance he had not seen her display for many months. Listening to her voice growing huskier when she whispered, he was himself almost deluded into believing that she was nutty over both lads while, pouting barren kisses, she coaxed them to heavier drinking and thence to wilder gambling. Once you looked into the dark blue depths of her eyes, you found it difficult to blink away; and if the Corinthian, who knew each inch of her and all her tricks, felt this fascination, the effect on the two city-lads was such as to bring them to a condition of quivering, gibbering emotional prostration so that they hardly knew what cards they used. Even after she had moved from the table, her spell distracted them. No longer deliciously tormented by her body's warmth, they became blind to all but the sway of the wide skirt fluting from the hips, the low-cut bodice between the bloated black velvet sleeves, and the gleam of the skin with a whiteness that seemed beyond whiteness, while her great dark blue eyes, dilated with belladonna, so held their gaze that, as though drunk on opium, they would have allowed the Corinthian openly to pick their pockets, and have made no attempt to stop him.

Yes, Lydia became the old Lydia again that night, each movement she made voluptuously exciting, her half-bared bosom seeming to pout for fingering and kisses, her lips drooping wetly with passion; and even if these youths had been experienced men of the town aware that they were being cheated, they would nevertheless have found it difficult to escape, like suicides drawn unresisting to the river's edge.

Not only on the innocent youths did Lydia's witchery have its effect but also on Bertram, so that on occasions he neglected to play the correct cards, to the Corinthian's unconcealed disgust. Having declared his admiration for Lydia which before he had been careful to conceal, Bertram now ran to the opposite extreme and, from discretion, became almost outrageous in his wooing. That the Corinthian had given permission for such behaviour and had therefore only himself to blame for this threat of cuckoldry under his own roof did not lessen his fury. He had told Bertram he might go to it, and Bertram was going to it with all the skill of which he was capable, and that was considerable indeed, delighting Lydia, not only because, like any woman, she was gratified at being desired but because she noticed how it affronted the Corinthian. To madden him further, she responded with smiling glances through her sooty lashes, and with studied postures to show off her chubby arms and bosom and long throat. Only the Corinthian remained outside her fascinations; or swore that he remained outside them, arguing that his shaking hands and hot blood resulted from exasperation with his partner and not from the fact that his miss's performance was exceeding even his bounds of propriety in the home.

And he should have been delighted with that evening's work.

After the two youths had been practically carried down the stairs and placed in the care of a well-tipped hackney-coachman, the sharing of the plunder produced over sixty pounds each with the promise of more to come. If necessary, the flats would rob their fathers, so hooked were they, so enamoured of Lydia. Despite the money, however, the Corinthian remained in a bad temper and he had almost to order Bertram out of the apartment before he could drag the besotted fool from fondling and kissing Lydia's lax hands.

Then he flung himself into a chair, and in the jerky light of the dying candles and the low fire, he wryly watched the collapse of the enchantress into a weary woman, as Lydia slouched on the sofa, and, no longer attempting to appear seductive, scratched her leg as though she were alone.

"I thought they'd never go," she signed, and yawned. "For pity's sake, get me a drink."

He poured out two glasses of brandy and added a little soda-water, then passed one glass to her. Not looking up, she stretched out her hand and he pressed the glass into her palm.

"Thank you," she whispered huskily, and drank. "Ah," she said, "now I feel almost human again."

"You were superb," he said, returning to his chair. "I feel quite madly in love with you all over again. As for those two flats, they'll be like flies at our door from now on. You even had Bertram twittering like a schoolboy. I must congratulate you, my duck. A great performance."

Silent she lay, gazing into the fire, and often sighed. Then in a low voice, very different from the husky voice she had assumed to simulate passion, she murmured: "Do you know, Tom, I was seriously thinking of giving up this life." She laughed without merriment. "I began thinking of home, of my father and mother and baby-sister. They might be dead by now for all I know and baby-sister's most likely got babies: she might even be a grand-mama! But I honestly thought of packing and running back to Lavenham like a fairy queen to distribute gifts to my poor relations, then settling down and living happily on good works ever after-wards! Me? Lady Lydia, the queen of the covesses!" The glass rattled against her teeth, and she coughed when she tried to laugh. "The silly thing is," she said, giggling, "that it was that ugly little devil, Will Corder, who set me thinking like that! I thought him rather pathetic, a small boy trying to be a man. And all the time he was a dirtier Greek than any of us. After all, we only fleece those who can afford it, and who come here for a good time. We don't go baiting for silly little girls to rob them of their miserable savings."

Delighted though he was at Lydia's return to sanity, the Corinthian nevertheless considered it good policy to defend Corder that her dislike might be strengthened by having to oppose his arguments.

"I don't know," he said with an air of impartiality, "he may be telling the truth and it's purely a plot to make his meeting with this woman look respectable to her relations."

"That advertisement proves the contrary," she said. "If it hadn't been for that I might have believed him, but if it were merely a plot between them why did he want to write so much about himself? All he had to do was to insert a few lines, just enough to give the girl an excuse for writing. No. That advertisement shows that if a wealthier flat appears he'll drop this silly bitch and grab the new one."

"After all," said the Corinthian, "I suppose even he has to live."

"O, stupid, helpless females! Ah, you're no better!" In disgust, she rolled on the sofa, showing him her bare back above the gown, and the dark curls clustered at her neck. "And what kind of a woman do you think this can be?" she said into her glass. "She's duped young Corder. She can't be any innocent, from the way she told him how to meet her in London, then agreed to this plot to deceive her own mother. No! she's a designing little bitch, probably more to blame than he is, and it'll serve her right when he robs her."

"Yet you pitied the woman!"

"No, not her. I meant the other poor devils who'll answer his advertisement. I'm most disappointed in the man and very sorry that we encouraged his visits."

"We?" repeated the Corinthian, and laughed. "You can't say that I encouraged the fool!"

"O, I'll take the blame for it. I was the flat. I just felt sorry for him somehow. I liked his Suffolk voice, reminding me of home. But now I'm sorry I did it."

"Because he's going to marry someone else?" asked the Corinthian with an angry snigger.

"What did you say?"

"Nothing, nothing," he muttered, airily waving his hand.

"O, yes, you did. You said that I was jealous because he's marrying this frump. But you're the one who's jealous. You'd have beaten me, wouldn't you, if you'd dared, teased me with your whip, only you're afraid I'll leave you? And you're right. I'd have left you fast enough if you'd dared touch me. Now, Tom Barsett, I want this understood—I don't care a fig for Bill Corder except as a son. I know your smutty mind'll never believe that, but it's the truth. He's only twenty-four and I'm ten years at least ahead of him. For once I'm telling the truth about my age. They say that there's a mother in every woman. I used to laugh at that, but now I'm not sure if they aren't right. . . . So let that finish with William Corder. I never want to see the man again."

"Amen," said the Corinthian and, turning to smile at her, he saw that she was close to tears. No longer the imperious woman who had frightened even Bertram and many another would-be seducer, she seemed a girl again, her body lax as though she had been beaten; and with sudden tenderness he went to her, knelt beside the sofa and kissed her hand. But when he would have kissed her mouth, she turned her head away and whispered:

"No, not tonight . . . I don't feel well. Please, dear, leave me. . . ."

Reluctantly, he stood up and replaced the hand across her stomach. Her head was turned away that he might not see her weep, but he saw her body tremble and heard the sobs half-strangled in her throat. Then, with a feeling of shame as though he had intruded on some personal thing, some feminine secret, he turned and tiptoed to their bedchamber that she might cry alone and as abandonedly as she wished, not troubling whether weeping made her ugly and washed the paint from cheeks and lashes. . . .

Neither mentioned that night again, yet continually they thought of it and it drew them closer together until they were almost as they had been before, affectionate comrades. Lydia's wish, so earnestly expressed, that they might never see William Corder again was, however—as they might have expected—not to be fulfilled.

The following week he was back, tapping on the door at his usual hour in the late afternoon when he knew that they would have breakfasted and be dozing in front of the fire before dressing for the night's work. At the sound of his voice in the hall speaking to the servant, the Corinthian raised his eyebrows enquiringly at Lydia, silently asking whether the fellow should be admitted; and she rolled on to her side on the sofa, faintly shrugging, as though the question was indifferent to her.

"Let him come in, Nell," called the Corinthian.

Trying in vain to conceal his excitement, Corder bustled in, bowing and grinning.

"Have you brought the letters?" asked the Corinthian in an indifferent voice. "Did you receive many?"

"Many? Dozens, dozens and dozens," chuckled Corder, with an enquiring lift of his brows towards Lydia's back.

"Take no notice of her," said the Corinthian. "She has a headache, that's all. Now let me see those letters."

With a cunning smile, Corder shook his large head. "You'll not catch me like that," he leered. "Honestly, sir, I suspect your intentions; but," he added, carefully sitting on the chair beside the fire and taking out a pair of spectacles which he hooked behind his large ears, "I've no objection to reading them to you."

"You will do nothing of the kind," said Lydia, not turning.

"What's that?" cried Corder, drawing a packet of papers from his pocket. "My dear good lady, you don't think I'd reveal their addresses, do you? or their names? I have, I hope, some honour left, and a little sentiment. Besides, even if I wanted to tell you I couldn't with most of 'em. Only a few have signed their real names. Most of 'em give initials and ask to have the answers sent to various post-offices. Others merely state that they'll be walking in so and so a place and tell what clothes they'll be wearing or ask me what I'll wear, so that we'll know each other. Nearly all of 'em are most discreet, except for one depraved creature here with a bastard child. Here's her letter. She blames the man, of course, and calls her sin—where is it?—'a deviation from rectitude, which was,' she writes, 'occasioned by the too easily listening to the flattery of one whose views I foolishly believed to be true, and I am entirely deserted by my family, and banished from society'. She says she's

61

two-and-twenty and has 'no pretension to beauty—quite the contrary'. Yet she has the face to write to me for a husband!"

"Poor creature," sighed Lydia.

Corder wobbled his head and raised his brows to the Corinthian to express his contempt for females who, in self-protection, defended their own sex.

"Well," he said tolerantly, "I'll speak no further of this 'un. Here's another what writes that her father's received an offer from someone she don't like, so she thinks she'll marry me. Must believe I'm an ass, the silly slut. And here's another what pretends she's recommending her sister, 'one of the most amiable and excellent of human beings', she calls her, meaning herself, of course. Some of 'em are as bold as polished brass writing as if they was duchesses, saying in a couple of lines that they expect me to answer 'em quick. You'd think they were the only women in the world, wouldn't you, when there's thousands of females nobody wants! The conceit of some of 'em, bless my heart! although most of 'em, I must say, are honest enough to confess they're no great beauties, not wanting to give me too big a shock when we meet, I suppose. Yet there's one damned conceited tit who says she has 'a tolerable person, perhaps some beauty, nineteen years of age, good-tempered, and of an affectionate disposition'. Might be worth meeting only she adds she's got no money. This one sounds a bit too pretty, don't trust her : says she's 'a merry-hearted as well as an agreeable companion' and thinks she'll make 'the identical little companion formed to constitute your felicity'—meaning me, of course."

"Poor unhappy wretches!" sighed Lydia, still not turning. "Why does God make them when they ache for love and can only hope to find it through a newspaper?"

"Well," said Corder, "from my reading of these letters, I'd say most of 'em have got no money, some of 'em are downright ugly— must be awful, otherwise they'd not confess they weren't beautiful, would they?—so what the hell else are they to do? Who's going to be fool enough to marry 'em when they've got no dowry, no looks, no shape? Now, ma'am, you can't blame the men, can you?"

"I blame you," she said, "for raising false hopes in their wretched breasts."

"False hopes! I like that, I do. Here, I've brought romance into dozens of homes, sent all these females nutty with the thought of hugging something better than a pillow at night. I'm a benefactor! It's philanthropy, that's what it is. Anyhow, most of 'em are liars. Ay, some of 'em even want me to pay the postage—would you believe that, now? Take this one here. She writes: 'Should the advertiser look for accomplishments or beauty an interview will be unnecessary.' You can imagine what she looks like! Born through a mangle, no doubt, hasn't a tooth in her head or a penny in the bank. Anyhow, if I'm not looking for beauty or rhino, what am I looking for? She must have a dirty mind, that one. And here's another who says she's the daughter of a clergyman with eight children—her papa's brats, not hers, 'Therefore you imagine,' she writes, 'I can have no fortune.' Why, here's another of 'em who says she's twenty-one and of the greatest respectability, and at the end she adds as though it weren't important: 'N.B.—I'm not very handsome.'

"But I'll not read any further. It's heartless to laugh at the poor heifers. Anyhow, I'll be getting a lot more soon. These are from the *Morning Herald* and I've put the same notice into the *Sunday Times*, except," and he squinted over his glasses at Lydia's impassive back, "I made one change, I hope you'll be glad to hear, ma'am. I took out that bit about the lady needing to have some property."

Slowly, Lydia turned, and her eyes needed no drugs to make them glitter when she glared at him.

"If, as you say," she cried, "this was a plot between you and that woman you picked up at Seaforth, why must you advertise in the *Sunday Times*? Didn't she answer your notice in the *Herald*?"

Corder shifted uncomfortably on his chair and blinked aside from the contempt in Lydia's eyes.

"Of course she answered me," he mumbled; "but I think I explained to you, ma'am, that I'm a serious student of human nature, and these here letters have been a revelation to me, showing up the female heart as they do. Yes, ma'am, a revelation! I never knew before that there were so many hungry, lying, treacherous females in the world, and all of 'em on the prowl. If they were good-looking, they'd be asking for trouble, if a fellow wanted to be unscrupulous. What an opportunity's here for a brothel-keeper! But, of course, the good-looking ones don't have to write for a husband, and who the hell'd pay for a female what can't even give herself away!"

"You are either the most abominable, abandoned wretch in the world," snarled Lydia, "or the biggest fool. I really don't know which."

"Because I'm honest!" cried Corder in an aggrieved voice. "I don't go round telling lies like these females here. I'm straight from the shoulder, I am. It's no use pretending. I like honesty."

"Have you answered any of these letters?" she asked, still staring into his evasive eyes.

"Well, no," he mumbled. "You see, ma'am, none of 'em's really worth answering. I can tolerate a woman who's not handsome, if she's willing, but none of these seem to have any dowry; and if she's got no looks, a woman has to pay to get a husband, particularly a young husband who, I can say without boasting, has had some good offers in the past. Don't you make any mistake. I'm not the kind of rascal who'd sport with the feelings of a young lady. Besides, I told you: I'm going to marry Mary."

"O," she said, "so you are really going to marry this Mary?"

"Of course I am, of course," said he with a show of indignation. "Why! I answered her letter first, before I'd even read any of these others. And was her mama surprised to see me! and was she furious when she learned that a daughter of hers had answered a matrimonial advertisement in the newspapers!" Corder laughed shrilly, like a boy. "She didn't believe us at first when we told her, insisted it must be a plot, that we'd arranged it all between ourselves, no matter how I swore that it was the strangest coincidence in all history. Only fear I had was that Mary in her innocence might put her precious foot through what I was saying. She's such Christian, I tell you, she can't even make up a lie. When I first asked her if she loved me, she asked me not to question her like that. 'I can't tell you the truth,' she says, 'modesty forbids it; and I can't tell you a lie,' says she. So when her mama asked her if this advertisement was really a coincidence, she hung her head. I went all cold, I tell you, and was too frightened to breathe until she whispered: 'Of course it is, Mama; have I ever given you cause for mistrust, have I?' says she. Even after that, the old bitch didn't seem to believe it was true. Then when Mary's brother came into the kitchen and found there was an extra plate laid, he made no end of a how-do-you-do. Said he should have been consulted first about anybody courting his sister, then he went off in a huff, saying he'd break my neck if I weren't honourable."

Still watching him intently as though to read the truth through his eyes, Lydia relaxed the rigidity of her posture and sank back against the cushion.

"You swear your intentions are honourable towards this woman?" she asked.

"Bless me!" howled Corder, punching his temples, "why should I tell you lies? We're putting up the banns and are going to get married in St. Andrew's, Holborn."

"So the brother didn't break your neck?" asked the Corinthian.

"Break my neck?" laughed Corder, wriggling his neck in the tall cravat. "Why! when he came back that evening he was so mild-mannered I could have patted him as though he was a dog. I was open with him, of course, I didn't conceal the purpose of my visit, told him how I loved Mary and hoped to make her happy as quick as the parson could make us man and wife. Told him how we'd first met at Seaforth and how I'd loved her at first sight but never thought to win such a precious burden; told him, too, about the singular circumstance that brought us close together again through advertising. He took it glum at first. Said he was most surprised to hear it and that he'd have enquiries made about me. Go ahead, says I; and I gave him my mama's address at Polstead so that he could write to her. All the while we talked, Mary sat at my side with her hands in her lap. Being a little deaf, she could only tell by our expressions what we were saying and later when I saluted her at the door she told me she'd never been so worried in all her born days. Her brother roared, far louder than he needed, the dirty beast, telling her he was going to find out the truth about me. . . . My friends, I wish you could have been there to see the wonderful look on her face, positively angelic, when she told him she was fully satisfied in her own mind and, being her own mistress, she'd use her own discretion, she said. Said she'd marry me to-morrow, she did; and that shut him up. Won't be long before I can give you your money back, my friend. That debt weighs on my conscience."

"Is that debt all that you have on your conscience?" asked Lydia.

"Please, ma'am," said Corder, "why do you mistrust me? I'm

marrying the woman, ain't I? What more would you have me do?"

Lydia could not answer. For all his coarse babble it did seem as though he intended to behave honourably towards this Miss Moore, but she could not believe that he was in love with her. Yet why else should he wed the creature? Her dowry appeared to be comparatively small and her prospects as a school-teacher not great.

"I'm getting her to leave where she is," he said. "Silly to pay her brother rent, as I told her, when she could be her own mistress and pay rent to somebody else. So she's looking for a school further out of London, in the suburbs somewhere. To tell you the truth, I'm sick of this city. It's probably all right for you two. You've a snug place here, right in the centre of fashion, but I'm living at the 'Bull' in Leadenhall Street and I'm looking for a home of my own, somewhere where her brother can't be jumping in and out when he likes. Besides, we could sell the lease of the Gray's Inn Terrace house——"

"I thought you told us that it was her brother's?" said Lydia.

"Well, yes; I suppose it is in law; but it's hers as well. . . . O, never mind about that! What I want to know is—will you come with me and meet Mary? or would you prefer I brought her here?"

"Why should I want to meet the woman?" asked Lydia, eyebrows raised.

"We're friends, ain't we?" he cried, opening his arms in a supplicating gesture. "You know, you're the only friends I've got in London; and I'd like the Corinthian to know that I'm telling the truth, for the moment I'm married he'll have his money back. Besides, you know, you'd like Mary: she's so good and sweet and innocent."

Lydia shivered complacently. "Then you'd better not introduce her here," she said. "My husband, I warn you, can't always be trusted with so-called innocents."

Corder laughed uproariously, slapping his thighs. "Think I don't know that!" he jeered. "Course he can't be trusted! What man that's a man can be trusted when he's alone with a pretty woman? But I know my Mary. She's as true as brass. He couldn't steal her from me!"

"Perhaps I mightn't want to," said the Corinthian complacently, looking down at his shapely legs. "Tastes often differ as greatly in women as they do in food and drink. Yet, I confess, I'd like to see this paragon. A truly virtuous woman's a phœnix that's not yet flown into my bed. Yes, yes. I'll go with you, my friend, and I'll honestly report to my lady here each feature I can see from the crown of her head to her toes."

"She's a modest female," frowned Corder. "You won't see much of her, I give you warning. Even I don't know what she's really like, she laces herself so tight it's like holding a piece of springy metal . . . O, hell, I can't wait for the parson!" He rolled his crooked eyes in ecstasy behind the glasses that made them appear to be double their size. "Then," he cried, "farewell to the wild joys, the roses and the blackberries of my youth, and heigh ho! for connubial bliss rocked in the arms of Hymen!"

"She might wear her stays to bed," said Lydia. "I know women who do. They're so used to having them on that when they take them off they just collapse in the middle and can't stand or even sit up straight."

"That's a lie!" yelped Corder, springing to his feet. "I'll see she doesn't wear 'em in bed, by God. No, no, ma'am. I'm the master and I'll see to things like that."

"Don't you be too certain," smiled Lydia, and pretended to fall asleep as a signal that he should go.

Even the obvious hint of Lydia lying, eyes closed, breathing quietly, on the sofa, could not get the ebullient Corder out of the apartment. In his enthusiasm for his new love and his determination to imagine an ideal future, he would have talked all night had not the Corinthian almost pushed him through the door.

"So," said Lydia in an icy voice when the Corinthian returned, "so you intend to inspect this scheming prude?"

"Why not?" he shrugged.

"And doubtless," said Lydia, infuriated by his smile, "you intend to ravish this miracle of modesty?"

"Perhaps," said the Corinthian. "You've scarcely been generous enough with me these last few weeks, my duck, to complain if I seek adventures elsewhere. This Corder! O, God, the rogue's so smug he deserves a kick. And, anyhow, I'd like to inspect the wench."

"O, men are hateful!" she snarled. "I only pray that she's as virtuous as that fool believes, not only to spite you, but that he might have hell in marriage. There's nothing like a true prude to drive a husband to drink or whoredom. But don't you deceive yourself: she's no real prude. . . ." Wisely, smiling, Lydia nodded her head. "She's a cunning little tit, the way she snared him, got him to follow her to London, got him to advertise . . . O, no! don't tell me who's the fool in that pair! She's made a flat out of him; and I only hope she makes as big a flat out of you, you damned conceited rooster."

The Corinthian laughed, staring at himself in the mirror over the mantelpiece, opening wide his eyes and arching his throat while trying to see as much as possible of his handsome profile. The sight of such peacock-preening was more than Lydia could tolerate. On the point of tears, she leaped to her feet and looked frantically about her, seeking something to throw at him; then on a sudden impulse she raised her foot and kicked him so hard that she almost kicked him into the fire.

"Let that give you your first taste of hell," she cried and ran into her bedroom, locking the door before he could scramble up and seek revenge.

But the Corinthian had no thought of revenge. Even while wincing as he tenderly fondled his bottom, he smiled.

"Ah," said he, rolling his eyes at his own reflection, "how greatly she must love me to be so jealous!"

Chapter Six

CUPID IS NOT ONLY BLIND

WHEN measured on a map, the walk from the bottom end of Bond Street to Gray's Inn Terrace was not far, but the Corinthian, who preferred above anything a horse or, next to that, a hackney-coach, found the way wearisome when Corder suggested that they use their feet. By avoiding Soho and Seven Dials, they kept for a time to the more orderly parts, and the Corinthian, being unsure of the way, let Corder lead him through Leicester Square which appeared miserably neglected. Abandoned by the gentry moving west, the garden behind its railings had become practically a wilderness clambering with weeds about the mounted statue of King George I, and the Corinthian was pleased to breathe the cleaner air of Long Acre, peering at the bright carriages being built and painted in the yards.

The fresher air, the almost country-smells, of Lincoln's Inn Fields induced him to dawdle as they turned north to cross Holborn. Even the cold and the wind with its tremor of rain could not hold lovers from meeting under leafless trees or from walking, warm hand in warm hand, along the paths beside the flowerless beds, while muddy beggars crouched in multitudes of rags, holding out scabby fingers at seeing two gentlemen approach. The Corinthian ignored their cries. He was never the one to give away a penny unless he could see a return for the expenditure.

All the long walk from Bond Street, Corder had not ceased talking. And his talk was all about Mary Moore. Almost it seemed that he wanted to sell the woman, for like a pimp pursuing a parson or a father attempting to excite a backward suitor, he rhapsodized about the beauties of her person and her character so minutely that the Corinthian—growing angry as he considered that it would have been quicker to have walked up Bond Street to Oxford Street— began to believe that he was being taken to visit some woman of the moon, a monster compounded of beauty and prudery. Not only, apparently, was this Mary Moore angelic, but she was also extremely practical; and while being otherwise the most perfect creature that God ever made, she was deaf, she freckled easily and her neck was too short; while possessing a Mind, she was no blue stocking; she was religious yet no bigot. In short, she was every man's dream on two legs—if so demure and bashful an animal walked on anything so solid and useful as legs, which the Corinthian had begun to doubt—and would have graced the board, if not the bed, of an archbishop.

While he yawned and with half-an-ear listened to these rhapsodies, the Corinthian was surprised to discover that his heart was beginning to beat unpleasantly fast. This was a sign of an emotion he had not suffered since youth, this confusion of fear, hope and excitement which he had known when being taken to an assignation with some strange wench by a young comrade who had wanted him to distract his mistress's friend from seeing too closely what happened behind the hedge. On such occasions, years ago, he had felt sensations similar, if more intense, to those he felt during this walk, and he had long since believed that they had died with his youth. But now, with Piccadilly and Lydia receding at every step, as he approached a more sober world and listened to Corder's incessant chatter, he found that he was raising in his mind the image of a lovely lady, passionate although of a far from easy virtue, the ideal of an understanding wife towards which he had aspired when young, one whom he could possess utterly and selfishly, glorying in the prudery that kept her concealed from chin to toes save when alone with him at night.

Most of his life had been spent far from such prudish oddities, at mention of whom he had always scoffed as exemplar for a sermon or for a dull book written to keep servant-girls virtuous, and, while he amused himself with Covent Garden ladybirds, he had begun to believe such women as mythical as Penelope.

To seduce a female like this Mary Moore appeared to be— if what Corder chanted about her puritanism were the truth, which the Corinthian doubted—would be the kind of titillating adventure he craved at the moment when he was wearying of the monotony of continual drinking and cheating. He needed, he felt, refreshment of some rare kind with which to revive his flagging interest in life. And what more enchanting, revivifying amusement could be offered a weary man than the tickling of a virgin into the bed of Venus? Ay, he smiled to think of it, to watch how under his expert handling he could fire an innocent into lewderies; to see a good woman tremble with horrified desire for what she dared not name . . . That would be something, he thought, to bring interest back to life. Lydia rejected him, or she took him at her whim, not at his. Soon she would learn that he had mastery over other, over better, purer, more God-fearing females than ever she had been. . . .

Besides, this wretch of a Corder needed cuckolding. His vanity, his conviction that any woman he honoured with a glance should be grateful for such condescension, demanded that he have his large-nostrilled nose rubbed in the dirt of reality. Swinging his gold-headed stick, his grey greatcoat buttoned to the chin against the cold, the Corinthian smiled as he savoured the prospect of teaching amorous gymnastics to innocent Mary Moore. That he would succeed, were the woman worthy of such exertion, he did not doubt. A creature such as Corder described, brought up in genteel poverty, whose knowledge of life's pleasures could only have been obtained by peering through keyholes of the great houses at which she had been the governess, or by watching undulating couples on the beach at places like Seaforth, should present no serious difficulties to a seducer as experienced as himself, one who knew the places where best to stroke a woman; besides, he was fashionably, faultlessly, dressed, and that meant a great deal in most women's eyes, for, may God be thanked! they rarely looked beyond the outer-skin or under the surface of compliments. Trotting beside him, Corder seemed puny, his brown tightly buttoned coat having been cut by no expert tailor. To ravish his beloved would be sweet revenge on this fool who had shouldered his way into his company, insolently daring to ogle Lydia; it would also be revenge on Lydia for having treated him in such a casual fashion. Only, he prayed, this Mary Moore might equal even one of Corder's hallelujahs.

Over Holborn they hurried, skipping out of the way of carts and hackneys, the cursing of the drivers pursuing them into the dusk, and the Corinthian felt most annoyed at such indignity. He had never been one to risk his life by hurrying across a crowded street. Always had he waited until there came a lull in the traffic that he might cross sedately, but Corder's grip on his elbows could not be resisted without a struggle, and before he had had time to protest he had been hurried over like a thief in the grip of the law.

"Don't do that!" he cried, shaking himself free.

"Don't do what?"

"Don't grab me when I'm not looking and hurry me over like that." Carefully, the Corinthian smoothed down his grey coat and squinted to see whether his cravat was ruffled. "It's foolish to risk one's life unnecessarily," he grumbled; then he added: "Are you sure I'm expected?"

"If I've told you once, I've told you a hundred times," grinned Corder. "Of course, they expect you. Mary said she'd pack the little scholars off early to bed; not that I care. I love the little ones. She loves 'em, too. And I love her for it." In the flickering flare from the Holborn shop-windows Corder turned and gripped the Corinthian's arm. "If I saw a fellow ill-treating an innocent child," he said ferociously, "I'd break his legs for him, I would. That's one of the things Mary and me have in common. We both love children. And we're going to have one about every year—she says so, too— and I'll call the first boy by your name."

"Thank you," said the Corinthian, disdainfully smoothing his sleeve; and he hoped that there might be a very good reason for that first boy to carry his name.

"Down here," said Corder, slipping to the left into Red Lion Street, crossing Eagle Street, then turning into a narrow way that ran, diagonally, from Eagle Street to Bedford Row. "This is it," he said with an open-handed gesture as though introducing the Corinthian to some wonderful palace of delights.

In the twilight, the dimly lighted street, blinds and curtains drawn in most of the houses, had a musty unlived-in appearance as though it had been pushed aside into this narrow space by the bustle of Red Lion Street and Holborn, and then left to decay in quietude. Before long, one felt, it would collapse out of sheer neglect. Red Lion Square and some of the other nearby streets from which respectable families had fled, surrendering them to men of commerce or to charitable societies, retained some spark of life, even if it were purely a daylit one, the premises being dourly shuttered at night, but Gray's Inn Terrace had not even this false vivacity to give it interest. The dejected inhabitants appeared to realize that no society or business-concern would ever want to buy their houses, and they continued living there from sheer weakness of will or the lack of money to buy their escape. Into it the night-mists seemed to crawl more dankly than into broader streets; here, one felt that it would be always damp, always neglected; yet here lived, if Corder spoke truth instead of poetry, a woman as fasci-nating as Cleopatra and as virtuous as Lucrece.

Beside the door of No. 6, the Corinthian noticed a small crudely painted plate:

MISS MOORE'S ACADEMY FOR INFANTS
PLEASE KNOCK LOUDLY

and below it, a yet larger plate announcing:

W. MOORE
WORKING JEWELLER
KNOCK THRICE

"That's her brother," explained Corder, rat-tatting with the knocker on the door. "Silly old buffer. Thought he'd make a fool out of me. Wrote to my mother. Everything all right, of course."

"Of course," said the Corinthian dubiously.

When he heard hands fumbling at the bolts, he braced himself for the appearance of Beauty, then he let his chest sag when a small, very erect little old woman peered at them through the dusk.

"O, it's you?" she said in a flat voice. "Well, you'd better come in now you're here. But don't forget to wipe your boots first."

While the Corinthian and Corder carefully wiped the mud from their boots on the wiper beside the steps, she stood aside, then grudgingly opened the door and watched them with a glittering grey eye when they entered as though she suspected they had come to pocket the spoons.

"Rum old girl," whispered Corder hoarsely. "Means well, though. Take no notice of her."

The hall was in darkness, apparently for reasons of economy, and they stumbled, groping against the walls, until the old lady flung open a door on their right.

"Wait in there," she snapped. "And don't eat nothing until I get back." Whereupon she darted across the hall and, opening a door opposite, bawled: "He's here again. Got another fellow with him, too."

Suddenly were hushed the voices of small children piping:

> *"Our days, alas, our mortal days*
> *Are short and wretched too;*
> *Evil and few the psalmist says,*
> *And well the psalmist knew!"*

Then the little woman was back in the parlour, closing the door firmly as though to protect those innocent children from possible contamination by Corder or any friend of his.

"Beef," she said. "And Ham. And cold Fowl. And Bread and Butter. And Tea for those that drink it. Not to speak of Pickles."

His hat in his hand, the Corinthian gaped at her, bewildered for the moment by this rapid list of comestibles, then he heard Corder smack his thick lips and noticed the food and drink placed ready on the table. The cloth was white and very clean; knives, forks, spoons and china were polished until they blinked in the lamplight. Everything in that smallish room gave an impression of almost over-cleanliness as though the women of the household toiled from dawn to dusk in pursuit of dirt. The wallpaper of golden fleur-de-lis on a pink ground showed not a fly-spot; the linoleum on the floor shone perilously as though greased; the stiff chairs with leather seats and backs seemed to reject all comfort, threatening rather than inviting the weary. The Corinthian, who preferred a more fashionable slovenliness, felt ill-at-ease and gave an abrupt bow when Corder introduced him to the little woman who, as he had expected, was Mary's mother.

"And what may you do, sir?" demanded Mrs. Moore with a bob of a curtsey, her large china-blue eyes watching him suspiciously while she took their hats, coats and sticks to carry into the hall. Like the furniture, she seemed over-washed in her black bombazine, the pink face scrubbed until it glowed and the tiny hands as white and looking as fragile as the lace at her throat.

"O, I do very well," said the Corinthian.

"I didn't ask How," said Mrs. Moore. "I asked What."

"What?"

"Yes—What?" she demanded ferociously.

"She means what work do you do," explained Corder from behind his hand. "Kind of mania with her. Asks everybody what he does. Tell her you're a governor of the Bank of England."

"I am a gentleman of means," said the Corinthian stiffly. "I don't have to work. '

"Another of 'em," groaned Mrs. Moore, jerking herself down on to a chair. "Might have known it, being a friend of him. He talks about his farm. Suppose he's got about three chickens and a donkey and half an acre of turnips, if you only knew the truth. If I'd ever thought my Mary could be so deceived, I'd . . . I'd never have gone near Seaforth. I'd have stayed here in Gray's Inn Terrace even though the school-children drove me to wearing ear-muffs. Well, my man, don't go staring like that: I'm no pane of glass. What have you come here for?"

"I—I believed I was invited."

"Not by me you weren't," said Mrs. Moore with great satisfaction, defiantly waggling her grey head. "Nor by my son, for he's an honest man and works too hard to mix with them that don't have to. I suppose it was my Mary again. That girl, mister, is too good and trusting for this world, and how she's lived to her age · without getting her throat cut, not to mention worse things that might happen to an innocent girl who ain't afraid of strangers as she should be, is beyond my understanding. Law! she went to France once. I did my best to stop her. I told her what Frenchmen were like and how everybody knew they'd no respect for the female modesty; but would she listen? Not she! Off she gadded and back she came and none the worse for it, so far as I could see. If her poor papa had been alive he'd have moaned himself into his grave, a daughter of his going to France like that as if it were any Christian country; and him a renowned breaker of blood-horses, too, in consequence of which he was employed by the best families, including noblemen, to train their favourite colts. 'My love,' he once said to me when our Mary was little more than an infant, 'I've broken in more blood-horses than you could count,' says he, looking at Mary who wouldn't eat her gruel, 'but the Lord save me from having to break in females,' says he, 'they're that stubborn that a poker can't bend 'em.' But the precious man, the Lord be thanked for small mercies, departed this sinful life before our Mary went to France, or his heart'd have been broken like a plate. Not that she isn't a good girl, mind you. She's all Soul and it's her goodness that'll prove her ruination, nature having made her so susceptible and given her such a tender little heart that she can't see wickedness even when it comes with a slimy tongue and cross-eyes and says it's got four hundred pounds a year, apart from property."

Corder laughed as though he had been complimented. "Will have her little joke!" he whispered loudly to the Corinthian. "In her heart she loves me like a mother, so take no heed of what she says."

So astounded was Mrs. Moore by this statement that for a moment she could neither speak nor move. Then slowly she rose to her feet and, stretching out her right arm, pointed one dainty polished finger, trembling with horror, into Corder's face and nearly blinded him.

"Reptile!" she squealed. "Blasphemer, insulting me under my own poor roof and after our Mary's taken all that trouble to get your supper! O, law! if only Mr. Moore were alive! but I'm a widow now, and well you know it, insulting me in my own face, and even my son don't come to my protection! But I'll tell him, I'll tell him; I'll tell our Mary, too, when she comes."

"Tell me what, Mama?" asked a low yet slightly shrill voice, and the Corinthian turned quickly to see the paragon enter.

Mary Moore stood in the half-opened doorway, the chatter of children's voices dimly heard from across the passage, and with grave affection she looked at her angry mother, and from her mother to Corder grinning at her, and from Corder to the Corinthian watching her speculatively.

She was small, like her mother, and looked as fragile and as well-soaped and scrubbed, her pale skin shining, her small hands so white as to give the impression of being transparent in their delicacy. Over many petticoats, her brown skirt stood out stiffly from the tightly bound waist, and was patterned simply with gold circles. The sleeves were full and loose, and a white collar covered her shoulders, being drawn down the front and tucked into the waist-belt. But it was not her dress, neat and undistinguished as it was, that drew the Corinthian's attention. He was intent on her face which, unpainted and unpowdered, was like a child's with its flower-petal skin and the gentle colour in the cheeks. His first feeling was of disappointment. He had not, he told himself, expected a beauty—and in saying that, he lied, Corder's enthusiasm having raised a Diana in his mind—but he had expected to find someone more—more remarkable than this young woman who seemed ordinary, scarcely different from hundreds of others whom he passed every day in the streets with barely a second glance. Certainly, she had fine blue eyes, the whites glistening, and a shapely mouth, and her features were regular, nose straight and neither too small nor too large, chin well-modelled, forehead wide, cheekbones high, and her luxuriant brown hair fell in natural curls about the round face. But he did not like the sound of her voice. Had she had complete hearing it might perhaps have been musical, but deafness made her unable to estimate its pitch, so that there sounded a sharp and irritating edge to it. And he wondered whether, after all, this seduction promised the delights he had planned.

"Well, Mama," she said again, gently closing the door on the children's shouting, "what is it you were going to tell me?"

"I've told you already," shrilled Mrs. Moore. "I've told you a hundred times over and over. This fellow's up to no good. I just now heard him telling his friend here to take no heed of anything I said. I know I'm only a widow and don't matter any more now your papa's in heaven, but I do think, if only as woman, not mentioning widow, that I should have some respect offered me at times. O, you can go your own way and when I'm in my coffin you'll shed a tear. Only it'll be too late then, my child. Just you mark my words. The worst thing you ever did in all your life was to shake that viper by the hand."

"Now, now, Mama," said Mary caressingly, with a timid smile at Corder and the Corinthian, "you mustn't get all worked up like this before supper with your digestion what it is. Have a little drop of cordial, just to please me. . . . Come, now."

"You know my feelings about strong waters," grumbled Mrs. Moore, greedily watching her daughter pour brandy into a glass, "and I had your unhappy papa as an example before my very eyes . . . but just this once. And I'll say no more. I may be your mama but you're not my child any longer. Him and his four hundred a year!" She tittered, rocking on the chair. "Four hundred *what* I'd like to know! O, the deceit of it; and after the careful way I brought you up, too, to throw yourself away like a bad sausage on . . . on that!"

Mary pretended not to hear the chatter, but the Corinthian noted her embarrassment in the way she squirmed her shoulders and the pleading look in her babyish eyes when she motioned him and Corder to be seated, then herself sat between them and offered the dishes that they might choose what they preferred to eat. Having licked her tongue around the brandy-glass, Mrs. Moore consented, after much cajoling from her daughter, to take the chair beside the Corinthian from where she could watch every morsel that Corder stuffed into his mouth. "Ugh," she said now and again with a genteel shudder; or she raised her eyebrows and shook her head as though made ill to see such greed. Corder smirked and took no notice of her while he chatted to Mary; and then it was that the Corinthian realized why the rogue wanted such a demure little wife. Her deafness made Mary the ideal listener. He could talk to her all day and night so long as he did not raise his voice, and she would not protest.

Silently, her brother entered to join them at the table. A tall cadaverous man with hanging jowls, he bowed stiffly and, with obvious distaste, took the chair the other side of Corder.

"Cold night," he murmured, rubbing his hands; "snow in the air."

"Fiddlesticks," said Corder, speaking through a mess of cold beef and pickles, "it's this street. Every time I come here I can feel it in my bones. It's damp, that's what it is. And if you had any real brotherly love for your poor sister you'd have left here years ago. She needs fresh air to bring some colour into those precious cheeks of hers."

Mr. Moore's face went purple, then it went white, while he clutched at his knife as though contemplating murder, and the Corinthian realized that this was an old quarrel between them.

"If, sir," muttered Mr. Moore, "if you think I fail in affection towards my sister, you are a liar, and a confounded liar. Do you hear me, sir?"

"Hush," hissed Corder, holding up his hand, "or she'll hear what you're saying and it'd be cruel to let her know what kind of a brother she's got."

"What is this?" cried Mary. "Are you angry about something?"

"No, no, no," shouted Corder. "Just saying you ought to get out of this miserable damp street. Can't have my precious better half coughing herself into her coffin. Ought to be living in the country. Only the other day I noticed an excellent little property, suit you down to the ground, make the perfect school, garden for the little

78

'uns to play in, and good clean air for the future Mrs. C. to breathe and get strong."

Mary blushed slightly when he spoke of his better half and of Mrs. C., and asked where was this property.

"Brentford," said Corder; "place called Grove House, Ealing Lane. Beautiful country. Rural surroundings yet close to London. And dirt cheap, I'm told. On the Hammersmith and Hounslow Road. Got the river at your back door and coaches passing all day. Great West Road, you know."

"What about Me?" roared Mr. Moore.

"Well," said Corder, "what about you?"

"This is my house, ain't it? Would you leave me here alone? What am I to do with My property?"

"Would you put your poor sister's health below your blessed property?" sneered Corder. "May the Lord be thanked that at last she's got someone to look after her. All you can think about's your rent, and I don't doubt she pays too much. Place is damp, no one would live here if they didn't have to; and you know it. And please know this, too. From now on I'm looking after my little girl. I'm protecting her. And I'll guard her against cold and chills as I would against any scoundrel who insulted her."

"What is it?" pleaded Mary, catching his hand and dragging him round to face her. "You mustn't quarrel."

"We're not quarrelling," said Corder, caressing her fingers, and the Corinthian noticed that now she understood each word the fellow said; then he realized that she was watching Corder's lips, reading the words while they were formed. "It's only that I'm worried about your precious health, my dear one. I don't like that little cough of yours; tears my heart-strings, it does, every time I hear it. And Brentford's almost country. There you could have the local gentry's children to teach, not the offspring of mechanics and shopkeepers."

"So that's your game?" squeaked Mrs. Moore with the delighted air of one who finds her worst fears justified. "Knew you were up to something underhand, I did, the moment I saw you sniffing after my poor darling at Seaforth. So you want to wrench her out of the bosom of her family, do you? Hide her from her unhappy mother who scrimped and saved after paying for her papa's funeral—not lost but gone before, yet a heavy loss to widows

79

—and away from her honest hard-working brother who's never had a thought but for her good! What's your game, young fellow? Mary's a respectable girl, I warn you, so don't you deceive yourself."

"I want to protect her," cried Corder, clasping Mary's hand and pressing it against his chest, "I want to give her fresh air and be her slave for life and . . . and all that kind of thing."

"Don't like it," growled Mrs. Moore. "Why, for all we know about you, busting in on us like this, you might want to cut her throat and boil her down for soap or do something nasty like what you read in the newspapers."

The effect of this muttered suspicion was startling. Corder's face went as white as the tablecloth he crumpled in one hand, then it turned a deep red, and he pulled at his collar as though unable to breathe. When he attempted to speak, he gurgled and his eyes behind the spectacles grew larger and rounder and the squint became positively hideous. Mary squealed and clasped his hand, while Mrs. Moore and her son stared at him with amazement not unmixed with satisfaction. Only the Corinthian acted. He tore open Corder's cravat and poured wine down his throat.

"Gug gug," said Corder, twisting his neck. "No air," he croaked, "gimme drink."

The Corinthian poured him a second glass of wine and Corder drank it in great gulps while health gradually returned to his eyes and cheeks. Then, with a sickly smile, he gazed at Mary and, raising the hand that grasped his, he pressed the knuckles to his lips.

"It's nothing," he gasped with a feeble return to his usually jaunty manner, "just my heart. Comes on me like this at times. Never could bear the smell of the city, you know."

"Then we will live at Brentford," cried Mary. "We'll go the moment we're married."

"No!" wailed both Mrs. Moore and her son.

"Yes," said Mary, staring coldy at them while nuzzling her cheek against Corder's hand. "If London affects poor Will in this manner, we can't possibly live here. Besides——" She coughed genteelly. "I do believe my own lungs are affected."

Against her placid determination, argument was useless, yet mother and son argued furiously, pleading with her not to desert them and Holborn, Mrs. Moore squeezing out tears and bringing Biblical threats to her aid. Mary remained firm, although, to keep her mother company, she wept, and she said she loved them dearly and no matter where she might dwell the roof would be theirs as much as hers. When her brother mumbled that he couldn't leave his work and what was he, a bachelor, to do with a house like this all to himself, Corder promptly told him to sell it if he could.

"I consider myself," said he, squeezing Mary's hand, "no longer Bill Corder but Bill Moore. When Mary assumes my name and takes me into paradise, I, more than she, will be the one to alter. I'll become Mr. Moore, her worser half, only praying that I might not shame her goodness, for she's a very angel."

"You serpent," panted Mrs. Moore, dabbing at her eyes with the end of the tablecloth, "we were happy until you pushed your way in here, pretending you met our Mary by chance in Fleet Street. Gad, sir, it was a suspicious chance that out of the thousands of lonely females in this city, Mary must be the only one to answer your advertisement."

"Are you suggesting," asked Corder with dignity, "that your own dear daughter deceived you?"

"The Lord only knows," sobbed Mrs. Moore. "All I know's that she was too good to be honest. I never could understand her, not since she was that high. Being deaf helped to make her secretive. She didn't have to hear unless she wanted to; and what she was thinking about neither me nor your poor father ever did discover. There she sits now, smiling like a stone angel blowing a trumpet on her papa's tomb in Willesden, and gloating on her poor mama's unhappiness; and for what's in her mind I only hope the Lord God will forgive her."

The Corinthian, who had sat in embarrassed silence during this family squabble—his sympathies lying with mother and son—now looked up and realized what had exasperated Mrs. Moore. Mary Moore sat with glowing cheeks and shining eyes, and her lips—untouched by any paint—were deeply red and curved at the corners into a smile that brought dimples to the plump cheeks. For the first time, he realized that Corder's enthusiasm had not been baseless, that there was a peculiar attraction, an unearthly beauty, in this woman; and he was astonished that at first sight he had dismissed her as ordinary. The pale-lashed lids were lowered over slanting eyes of an unusually intense blue, very bright in colour and with whites as clean as silver, while her mouth curled into a smile which on the face of most other women he would have marked as voluptuous. Indeed, he felt that there was a suspicion of lewdery in that smile, of some secret incommunicable delight which no man could penetrate, while the dimples, in contrast to that smile's goddess-like self-satisfaction, were the dimples of a romp, a roguish child. He who was used to women trained in all sensual diversions, he who had uncovered the secrets of all venerean cults, was disturbed by that unrevealing smile. It seemed to him a witch's smile on an angel's face, and he wondered what she was thinking behind the sealed ears that cut her off from general conversation. A female-Ulysses, she listened to the sirens' song in her heart, having been forced by her infirmity to confer with her own soul, secretive and self-satisfying, from which others, particularly men, must be excluded. And this Eden which suddenly he longed to enter must, he felt, offer a garden of profound sensations beyond body's delight, a virginal honeycomb of ecstasies such as he and other sensualists failed to appreciate, being too blunted by physical pleasures. While he looked at her, he felt the heaviness lift from his heart. Her pale face was an angel's mask protected by deafness, the mask of a precocious child dreaming of a wonderful future, and he wished that he and not this damned talkative Corder should be the man privileged to unlock the inquisitive spirit from the flesh.

In his absorbed regard for that pale mask, the Corinthian had almost forgotten about the others, loudly though they talked, and he was startled when suddenly Mary raised her eyelids and looked at him. Still faintly smiling, still dimpling, she looked into his eyes with the frank amusement of a child, and her eyes, he noticed, for the first time seeing them wide open, were large and slanting and most beautiful, being of an intense blue that was almost indigo, and sparkling with some secret amusement. It was as if they shared between them a jest from which these noisy others were excluded, and she gave the merest suggestion of a wink which embarrassed him, for he did not know what to do in reply.

"Will you have some more chicken, sir?" she asked in her low voice with its undercurrent of shrillness; and dumbly, still gazing into her eyes, the Corinthian passed her his plate.

The argument between Corder and Mrs. and Mr. Moore being apparently endless, the only thing to do was to leave as soon as possible; but the Corinthian found himself reluctant to go. No longer did he even pretend interest in Corder's quarrel about the proposed move to Brentford. Back in his chair he sat, twiddling the wine-glass in his strong fingers, while watching Mary. Lids lowered again, she sat primly erect with shoulders so stiffly back it seemed as though a board were strapped across them, her breasts out-thrust but so concealed by shawl and stays that their shape could not be even vaguely divined; only he felt certain that they were buxom by the formless swell of the cloth. This concealing of the body as a treasure to be kept for the husband alone excited him who lived in a world where women strove to reveal and not to hide temptations, and he could not resist speculating on what she would look like undressed. Beautiful he did not doubt; small and dainty and white yet plump in the right places, bashful, blushing, but bold in the dark; and it infuriated him to think that a country-boor like Corder should be given the privilege of undressing her.

Not since youth had the propinquity of a woman so disturbed him. It was as though he absorbed her sensuality through his skin, as though she radiated some odour too subtle for his nostrils but which his body drank. He strove to think calmly, scoffing at this extraordinary weakness that knocked his knees together, but by shutting his eyes he could not forget that she was close. Demurely, erect in her chair, pale hands folded in her lap, she sat, separated from them all by silence, a living statue against whose impaired ear-drums the thunder of argument became purely a meaningless whisper that could not divert her thoughts or actions. She had decided, because of Corder's alleged ill-health, to leave Gray's Inn Terrace. No matter what her mother and brother might say, her mind was made up and, if London air did not suit her future husband, she would carry him to Brentford or to anywhere else he wished to go. In this explicable love of an unquestionably good woman for that callous little monster there was, to the Corinthian, something not only perplexing but almost terrifying. It was the kind of love that a mother might have for a deformed child, based more on compassion than on passion, as he was soon to realize.

It was while he was preparing to leave and had gone into the hall in search of his hat, stick and coat, leaving Corder to shout at Mrs. and Mr. Moore, that he saw into Mary's mind. The hall was in darkness and she had followed him with a candle whose light gave to her pallid flesh a translucency like that of some old painting of a saint, as though the light shone from within rather than against her body, turning the flesh diaphanous. With this golden light beating up, marking clearly the line of lip, the dainty nostrils and slanting eyes with whites like mother-of-pearl, she whispered shrilly, gazing stealthily at the door she had closed.

"You are William's friend?" she asked.

"Why . . . yes," said the Corinthian, startled by her unearthly appearance in that narrow passage.

"Guard him well, I pray you," she whispered, and smiled. "He talks so grandly, so like a king, and he thinks he's clever"— tenderly, sadly, she shook her head—"and he's really only a child at heart. He needs someone to look after him, and he admires you so much."

Her hand rested on his arm so lightly that he scarcely felt the touch, yet his flesh tingled under even that faint pressure.

"You love him, don't you?" he asked.

The question was too crudely put for her to answer. "He is a child," she said again. "He needs somebody to take care of him. You will be our friend, always; won't you?"

"Friend!" cried the Corinthian, seizing her hand and kissing it; and cold it felt against his lips. "You can rely on me, ma'am," he muttered. "I am always at your service," and he let her hand fall because he did not know what else to do with it, so lifeless it felt in his grasp.

"Thank you," she said, her eyes intent on his lips.

Almost was he glad when, still shouting, Corder came from the parlour, slamming the door behind him. The situation had grown intolerable and the Corinthian had begun to feel himself a shy boy again in his first blundering love, not knowing what words to use to this enigmatically smiling woman who neither accepted nor rejected his admiration, as though she were blind as well as deaf.

"I told 'em," said Corder truculently. "I'm getting a special licence, for what's the use of wasting time when everybody's willing? We'll be married, my duck, before you can count fifty. Then we can snap our fingers at 'em. Never seen such mercenary people before! Money, money! Rents and money! All they can think about's money and rents. Look upon you as though you're still a baby who don't know what you're doing, 'cept that you're old enough to make a living and help keep 'em in idle luxury. We're going to change all that."

"Please," she said, wrinkling her nose and pushing out of his embrace. "You forget we're not alone."

"O, him?" laughed Corder. "You couldn't shock him, the kind of life he leads, not if you kicked your shoes over the moon."

"William," she said in a high-pitched scandalized voice, "how often must I ask you not to talk in that embarrassing fashion! Now, you must be off . . . No, no, I will not let you salute me again. . . . Good evening, Mr. Barsett. Do, please, visit us again if ever you should find the time. Most charmed to have met you. We will always be happy to welcome you, or any friend of William's."

"Always a chair at our table for my pal," said Corder, patting the Corinthian on the shoulder. "Told him we'd name the first-born after him. Thomas Corder! Sounds swell, don't it?"

Mary did not answer. Shielding herself within her deafness, she pretended she had not heard—yet her eyes had been on Corder's lips as though she yearned to kiss them, the Corinthian had winced to notice—and then stood back, holding up the candle while they walked down the steps into the street.

There, they turned for one last look at her, the swaying light giving her pale countenance an angelic appearance, turning her eyes to blind hollows while gleaming on the corners of her full mouth arched into that tantalizing, unreadable smile. From his fingertips, Corder blew her a kiss while the Corinthian bowed low.

When, at the corner of Red Lion Street, they turned to look at her again, she was no longer there. The house was now blank-faced, and they heard the grinding of the bolts shot home; and the Corinthian sighed as though finding himself locked out of Eden with the snake, cold and miserable in the misty street with Corder chuckling at his side.

"I put 'em in their place," chuckled Corder. "They'll find things mighty different now they've got me to deal with. Living on her. That's what they've been doing. Living on the poor girl, like fleas . . . And what do you think of her, eh, Corinthian? Corder knows how to pick 'em, don't he? And she's got a little egg of savings into the bargain. O, I know when I'm a lucky fellow; but what's the good of luck without initiative? She's absolutely nutty over me! You can see that, can't you? I've got her," he snapped his fingers, "just where I want her, by God. So you needn't worry any longer about that seven pounds you lent me."

"I was not worrying about my seven pounds," growled the Corinthian. "I was worried about Miss Moore. You really mean to marry her?"

"Of course I'm going to marry her."

"Even," asked the Corinthian, stopping in the glare of the Holborn shops to stare into his shifty eyes, "even if I paid you enough to clear out and never see her again?"

"What's this? what's this?" squeaked Corder. Then he slapped his leg and skipped in the air. "Stuff me full of marrow!" he cried. "Don't tell me you're nutty on her, too! Who'd have thought it! You with your Lady Lydia and all!"

"I don't care a damn about the young woman," growled the Corinthian, reddening with rage, "but I do respect her because she's decent and I'll not have you break her heart and doubtless rob her of her little savings and leave her in the family way without a penny."

"That's an insult! You can't say things like that to me!"

"I have said them," panted the Corinthian, still glaring into his eyes, "and I repeat them. I'll not have you robbing that poor innocent creature, then deserting her to starve on the parish. She's not your kind, any more than she's mine. She's honest and good, too good for you or me. So leave her alone."

"Jealous! Strike me dead, he's jealous!" cried Corder in a kind of ecstasy. "What would Lydia say if I told her?"

"Tell her what you like, you little bastard!"

Such was the Corinthian's rage that he trembled and he knew that if he remained a moment longer with this wretch he would have to beat him; and he recalled Mary's plea in the hall that he act as Corder's guardian. Swiftly, he turned on his heel and strode into the drizzle, jumping out of the way of the horses and not heeding the abuse of the drivers. For the moment, he was deaf and blind, maddened to think that he had acted so stupidly, letting his anger take command, for it seemed to him that with that outburst he had delivered something of his spirit and much of his dignity into the hands of one entirely unscrupulous, revengeful and dangerous.

Chapter Seven

THE PRICE OF LOVE

WHEN assured that Corder was not at his heels, the Corinthian slowed his pace and began to dawdle, roaming from public-house to public-house, not so much because he was thirsty as that he needed some excuse to keep him from returning to Bond Street. His elegant apartment with the golden wallpaper and golden furniture, the thick carpet and the polished walnut table, the bric-à-brac in the cabinet and the books in their case, appeared to him as lifeless and as unlived-in as a setting for the stage. The Moore home might suggest genteel poverty yet, in contrast to this luxury, it was bright and clean, and he longed to re-enter its warm security. He felt envious even of the cadaverous Mr. Moore who might that minute be seated with his newspaper by the fire while Mary read or knitted or sewed on a chair opposite. Although his brief experience in that room had been one of quarrelling, he put the blame for this disturbance on Corder who had destroyed the peace by talking of carrying Mary to Brentford. Brentford! miles away . . . The Corinthian faltered in his step and scurried into a public-house where loudly he demanded a glass of gin, followed by a glass of porter, and his hand shook while he drank.

Until that evening, Brentford had been to him little more than a name on the Great West Road, but now he pictured it as an enchanted village of sturdy farmers and red-cheeked maids with the Thames singing amongst the reeds at the bottom of Corder's garden. To this rural paradise the rascal intended to carry his beloved, hiding her there like some captive princess in the embrace of an ogre, away from her friends and relations for his sole lewd delight; and, groaned the Corinthian, that meant that he might never see her again.

The misery which succeeded that thought so surprised and frightened him that he carried his drink to a table in the corner and sat down, blind to the tentative ogling of two harlots fortifying

87

themselves with gin before venturing on to the wet streets in search of customers.

Absurd, he argued, to believe that he could fall in love with a commonplace little woman whom he had met for only a few hours and with whom he had exchanged barely a dozen words; yet more fantastic things than that can happen and love sprang, no one knew how or why, at a glance, at a touch of skin, at the sound of a voice. . . . In his youth, often had he adored many a girl glimpsed for a moment in the street yet never to be forgotten; and there had been nights of anguished longing for some pretty creature who had sat silent beside him in a coach or whom he had watched, pews away, in church.

Such incendiary times, however, he had believed were dead. He was in his late thirties and had been loved so often that he no longer believed in love. Indeed, he felt that one was well rid of an emotion which opened one's heart to little beyond suffering. Best, he said, never to demand too much, to accept women gratefully as capable of conferring a certain bliss for a certain time and never to worship them, never to demand from them, in the fashion of youth, perfections they were incapable of possessing. Yet already about this deaf little woman, his mind, a boy's again, was creating a dream of beauty. So long had he lived a life of riot, of whoredom, gambling and drinking, that he had begun to view the world through the fug of his own depravity, denying goodness to others and seeking it in women only that he might destroy it, as—God save him!—he had smugly intended to destroy it in Mary Moore. Goodness and ignorance had become synonymous in his vocabulary. If, because of careful upbringing, a girl should be prudish, it was, he had believed, a challenge demanding that she be ravished ruthlessly; and if a youth should be honest, he must learn the ways of the world via the brothel and the gaming-table. Otherwise, they remained flats, the destined prey of cunning sharps such as himself.

Those men who, when drunk, grew maudlin at memory of their neglected wives or who spoke with awe of the maiden they intended, when they found an attractive one, to marry, he had despised as clods ignorant of the world. Modesty he considered a deceit, a veil behind which to lure silly men. There was that lord, the mock of every pimp and bawd in London and Westminster, who would accept no sacrifice unless he believed himself the first

88

to chart her heaven. He retained a married couple, paying them five hundred a year, for the sole purpose of decoying virginities for his pleasure; and by a howling show of modesty and terror many a slavey had earned sufficient to set up shop and marry the man of her desire. This peculiar appetite had always seemed to the Corinthian a form of harmless lunacy, and he recalled having read that the great Dr. Johnson had once remarked that such painful labour was for ploughboys, a sentiment with which he had uproariously agreed. But now he was not so certain.

Was it her deafness that set Mary Moore apart, curtaining her in silence and giving her an air of tantalizing mystery? She was not beautiful. His first impression had undoubtedly been correct. Now that he could think, undisturbed by her presence and the sound of her breathing at his side, he could agree that, in person, she was nothing extraordinary. There were in London dozens, hundreds of women equally as personable; yet he could look into their faces with no twinge of longing, while the bare thought of Mary Moore set his senses tingling with desire. Once when she had suddenly moved, he had heard the creaking of her stays, and he had trembled at the sound as he had trembled when a boy at the rustle of petticoats approaching. The creak of most women's stays either irritated or amused him, they had never before thrilled him with a vision of nudity, suggesting skin creased red with tight-lacing.

As her deafness walled her from life, so did her heavy garments tantalizingly conceal her body and suggest so much. Doubtless she wore three or four petticoats and thick woollen drawers, not dainty ones of silk such as Lydia and other fastidious women preferred for important occasions. And this thought, instead of repelling the Corinthian, excited him.

O, he was weary of silks and perfumes and deceitful ribbons, of plumpers in the cheeks to make them round, of false curls and padded stockings. The smell of earth after rain, the scent of the rose, the honeysuckle and the violet, the salty tang of the wind rushing from the sea, and the singing of birds amidst the leaves—these memories from boyhood came poignantly to him as he sat in that Oxford Street public-house reeking of stale beer and spirits. At the nearby table, the two harlots stank of scent and sweat. Unwashed, with powder and paint to hide the dirt, with scent to disguise the smell, they drooped over their gins, reluctant to leave this snug bar to tramp the pavements; and suddenly the Corinthian felt that he hated them and their trade. He hated everybody in that sluicery from the prim woman in her lace cap polishing glasses behind the bar to the dirty fat creature with the baby in her arms— doubtless hired to assist her in begging—which she was trying to soothe with sips of gin while she chattered to the drunkard leaning against a huge vat labelled Old Tom. How he had managed to live contentedly in such haunts amazed and disgusted him. Yet where was he to go? He could never return home. . . .

For years now he had not written and did not even know whether his parents were still alive. Impossible now to go back, although clearly he saw again that small thatched house and the neat garden; and tears stung his eyes at thought of his little sister with the yellow-white curls and angelic appearance who could be a wild-cat when she chose. Deliberately, even merrily, had he shut the door on that unexciting past, exulting in wickedness while despising honest folk; nor even now in this remorseful mood did he truly regret some of the jolly times he had known. Only he wondered whether he had lost in peace of mind more than he had gained in experience.

Corder, who did not appreciate his good fortune, pointed the way to contentment; and it was extraordinary that a man so coarse and unattractive—one might even call him downright ugly with his squint-eyes and heavy mouth—could have attracted two females so dissimilar as Lydia and Mary Moore. The explanation probably lay in Mary Moore's whisper to him in the hall when she had asked him to father the scoundrel. He was a child, she had said, who needed looking after. It was this damned unreasoning maternal craving, not for a man, but for a child to be petted, protected and fed, husband and baby in one flesh, which drew them to him, his very imperfections becoming his attractions—the boyish vanity and exuberance which exasperated the Corinthian, and the complacency and craftiness mixed with simplicity.

For it could not be doubted that Mary Moore adored him: she so pure, so honest, so good, so pious. . . . And to think that he had set out that night intent on seducing her! How little he had known what to expect! Such women could never be seduced, their bodies being to them of small importance beside the sanctuary of their souls, and she would never be cheated into surrender. The peace of God was in her, in those great untroubled eyes, in the pale cheeks and glistening lips of innocence; she would sleep well at night, never disturbed with half-formed longings, with images of desire beside her pillow to turn her body at her own touch into a tense and aching instrument trembling with desire for a shadow-lover. . . .

Abruptly, he stood up, leaving his unfinished porter, and strode into the night, ignoring the fluttering eyelashes and the crooked smiles of the two harlots, feeling hot with disgust that he had ever thought to plunder Mary's innocence; and in the wet street he paused, not knowing where to go. Darkness; a moonless, starless sky and streets leading to smudges of yellow in the mist through which shapes scudded under the blurred lamplight. To go through Seven Dials was to ask to have his throat cut by the beggars and thieves lurking there in rookeries. It would be safest, and possibly quickest, to continue along Oxford Street; but he was in no hurry to reach home, not wishing to see Lydia while this depressed mood made him savage with the world. Little escaped her sharp eyes, and she would soon discover what had disturbed him; and the last thing he wanted was to be questioned about Miss Moore. What could he say to Lydia when she asked, as she would ask, for details of that evening? That a possibly stupid, highly respectable and not exceptionally handsome deaf woman had stolen his heart? Lydia would laugh, and rightly; but did she not love Bill Corder?

Perhaps "love" was too strong a word to use . . . yet who could tell what she was thinking, so cunning was she in veiling her eyes? The Corinthian laughed, and the snorting sound startled a harlot about to mince towards him out of the shadows, so that she shrank back in dread of a madman who might make love with a knife or a bludgeon. They were both bewitched: Lydia by a cross-eyed fool and he by a deaf prude. Who would have believed it? That the two who were feared and respected as the most callous sharps about Piccadilly should become the dupes of a dream of innocence would have made a jest to echo raucously in every gin-shop and saloon; and he shivered at the thought.

Well, he shrugged, it was unlikely that he would ever see either Corder or Mary Moore again. They were soon to marry and rusticate at Brentford, and that would mean good-bye; and he would return to the old life with occasional diversions when some pretty shop-girl showed her ankles in Regent Street or a chambermaid lingered too long while making his bed at an inn. And always he would be thinking of that quiet woman with the bright blue eyes seated by damned Corder's fire and sewing his shirts and knitting his socks.

Lydia was lounging as usual on the sofa when at last reluctantly he returned, and she was sewing no shirts, knitting no socks. In her careful posture she lay so that she might not crease the gold gauze dress with its bunched-up sleeves, open at the front to show the pink chemise that stretched across her bosom, the waist unnaturally high, pushed up by corsets and the red belt. Under the candlelight she looked beautiful, her carefully coiffured hair bunched in ringlets, and her fat arms naked; nevertheless she did not stir his blood. Not that pearl-white skin, the painted mouth and cheeks, the lustrous drugged eyes, the wide bosom, the firmly sloping shoulders and strongly rounded arms with dimpled elbows: he could look on such dispassionately as though she were a carven figure lying there. Yet thought of Mary Moore, of her small body concealed under layers of coarse cloth, tingled to his finger-ends.

"You're late," said Lydia, yawning. "It's well past seven. Was she so luscious that you couldn't leave her?"

He turned aside to pull off his greatcoat, glad to be able to hide from her sharp eyes, and said in as casual a voice as he could manage: "Ordinary enough. You need fear no rival there, duck. A mousy little creature with fine eyes—I'll give her that—and as deaf as an adder. She reads one's lips."

"O," said Lydia quietly, and poured herself a gin. "She sounds a dangerous woman to have at a party. She couldn't say No when she hadn't heard what was asked, could she, poor bitch? Well, I suppose it's what he deserves."

"She's not that kind. Most prim and proper. Wears her stays to bed with her, I don't doubt, in case there's a fire, and has leather drawers to the ankles."

"It didn't take you long to discover that. . . ."

"Pure speculation. I speak metaphorically." He tried to laugh as, after pouring himself a gin, he sat on the chair facing her, keeping as far as possible in the shadow. "It'd be a brave man who thought to investigate such secrets," he said lightly. "Hers is a very different world from ours. So quiet, somehow so safe. I can't see Corder settling into it; yet there's no doubt he's in love with her, or at least he thinks he is. Do you know, she asked me to act as his good angel, keep him out of trouble and all that! Said he needed a friend to protect him from his own folly. I always thought I understood women, but I don't know. . . . Here's as plain a rogue as a man could set eyes on, and with a damned ugly phiz into the bargain, yet he makes this modest mouse adore him; and you, too, pretty—forgive my reminding you—more than liked him for a time."

"I felt sorry for him," murmured Lydia huskily, staring into her glass. "Even now I feel sorry for him in a way. He think he's so sharp that he must end badly. Yes, I can see why that woman asked you to look after him. He does arouse one's maternal instincts; although, God knows, I thought that nonsense had been drowned in me ages ago."

"She's so innocent," sighed the Corinthian, warming his hands as he stared into the fire. "You should have seen the way she watched him, like a mother afraid her boy'll wet his feet. Why are women such fools with men! Are they blind that they can't see that he's selfish, unscrupulous and mad with vanity?"

"Yes," said Lydia, "I suppose she knows all that as well as you and I know it. That's why Cupid's always drawn blindfolded, I suppose. But he's not really blind: he can see through that bandage if he wants to; only he doesn't want to. A woman deliberately fools herself. She's got a silly faith in love, more than a man can ever understand, and she thinks it has power enough to subdue a tiger. After all, I suppose there's more satisfaction in marrying someone you doubt, and then conquering him. This woman probably knows her Corder, or thinks she knows him; and perhaps she loves him because of those very weaknesses that irritate you so much."

"Women are mad," groaned the Corinthian, "quite mad."

Over the rim of her glass, Lydia watched him closely, but she did not speak.

"Let's stay in tonight," he cried suddenly. "Let's sit here next to the fire by ourselves for once!"

"To turn the gin to tears?" she laughed, "to weep over our lost youth and dead hopes? No, my sweet, I had that mood for a while, but it's not one for our indulgence. We are going out. We are getting drunk to music and laughter. . . . So this little mouse has caught you, too, has she?"

"Me? Good God, no!" he laughed.

She shrugged. "Yes," she said softly, "you. O, I don't mean it's the woman herself, but she's set you thinking and regretting and wanting to save your soul before it's too late. I know the feeling too damned well. Don't lie about it, please. We've lived too long together to be lovers. That died long ago. But we remain jolly bedfellows, and no more, for fondness can linger even after love dies . . . and let's at least be truthful, for once. This monster of prudery has brought a little boy alive in you again, made you sentimental. I understand. We're both poor fools, Tom, craving after something we deliberately threw away. It wasn't this little rogue of a Corder that made me sad; and I don't suppose it's this woman who's made you discontented. It's what they mean to us that counts, what we think they're like. It was Corder's Suffolk voice reminding me of a boy I knew when I was a wee thing that made me want to howl like a silly heroine in a book; and I suppose it was the dull domesticity of this woman's house that plucked your heartstring. We're both too old, too tough for such regrets, my lad. If you were to marry her . . ."

"Good God, never!"

"If you were to marry her, you'd be yawning within a week. Once you'd stripped off her dozens of old petticoats and those leather drawers and found she was just an ordinary mock-modest female, you'd be chasing back to Piccadilly with a fire at your tail. I know you better than you know yourself; and I know all about this female although I've never met her. I was brought up in a highly respectable home and was taught all the tricks of modesty. Yes, tricks. Girls are told that unless they marry quick they're failures; and at the same time that they must do nothing immodest in front of men. There's this confusion from the start. Although we're told we've got to capture some poor devil or live in disgrace as old maids, we have to be careful lest we rouse his base instincts. Why! I've known girls to wear charms to protect them from being ravished, yet those same girls will steal out at dawn on Midsummer Eve to find if they can see their future husband's whiskers at the bottom of a well. Don't blame the wretched females, blame the way they're brought up."

"I blame no one," sighed the Corinthian. "And you're probably right about Miss Moore. Modesty may become tiresome after a man's swallowed the bait. But I confess I have been considering marriage. Not with this Miss Moore, of course—she'd never suit me as a wife—but of domesticity itself, the kind of life we can never find in Piccadilly. . . . Would you marry me, Lydia, and live quietly somewhere in the country?"

She laughed and swung down her legs that she might sit upright on the sofa. "I thank you," she said, "but, no, kind sir. We'd detest each other within a fortnight. Domesticity's not for us."

He saw that she looked almost happy, her eyes gay with a brightness not entirely due to belladonna, and her lips shining with a redness that had not come from a salve.

"Tonight," she cried, "we'll make merry, you and I. We'll not search for flats. We'll go on the spree and get drunk until we can't stand; and we'll pretend we're lovers again. Eh, my brave Corinthian Tom? We'll pretend we've just picked each other up, that I'm simpering sixteen and you're the hero to tickle my rib; I'll be a maid again, and I swear I'll be as coy as your Miss Moore, should that please you. O, I'm tired, tired of this life!"

"Can't we find another?"

"No, we know no other," she said, sighing and staring into the fire. "This is our personal hell, and we must live in it."

Both were silent, staring into the fire, seeing in the flames a youth long since ended, seeing a timid maid and a shy lad walk hand in hand along country lanes, longing while fearing to kiss.

"Come!" cried Lydia, springing to her feet. "This will never do! Out of your dumps, my bonny boy, and heigh ho for a flagon of jacky to wash away regrets!" She caught his hands and, as she pulled him out of his chair, gaily she sang:

"*This world was once deluged by water, drowning son and sire,*
 But when it is destroyed again, we read 'twill be by fire;
 And this must be the awful time, so prevalent is sin,
 As all the world do burn their insides out with gin,
   Gin, gin, sweet, sweet gin,
   There's no drops like gin!"

"Like gin, gin, gin!" he echoed, trying to play to her mood; and, sudden desire firing him at the touch of her hand, he caught her around her armoured waist and lifted her off her toes.

"No, don't," she laughed, twisting her face from his kiss. "Wait till we come home brimming with blue ruin. My mouth . . . you'll ruin its shape. . . . No, no! O!" she gasped, trying to swing away, "villain! I must to my paint-pots again! You have Ruined me!"

Faintly smudged were her scarlet lips as though his kiss had been fierce enough to draw blood under the chafed skin; and when she would have fled back to her paints in the bedroom, he lifted her in his arms and carried her there. Wailing and kicking, she pretended fright and squealed her protests, while crying for gin, gin, gin.

"Later," he growled; "we will celebrate later. This will be *our* wedding-night," and he pressed his lips on hers until at last she lay quiescent, her arms loosely about his neck, and permitted him to carry her without struggling, her eyes half-closed, her breathing rapid, as though make-believe had turned into reality and she had become indeed a maid again in the arms of her first lover. . . .

Make-believe it remained, although no less dear because of that. They acted a dream, and were happy in pretence, half-deceived and half-deceiving in their eagerness to be happy and to give the other happiness. Friends, seeing them laugh and drink and dance, holding hands under the table, wondered that two such cynical rogues could look and act as though they were youngsters in the first flush of desire.

The revelation that they shared a similar adolescent dream of peace in love drew them closer together than they had been even in the first year of meeting. As though after long illness, each was ready to soothe the other with sympathy and affection. By having revealed their secret weakness, longing for lost innocence and youth, she through Corder, he through Mary Moore, both as in a mirror saw their own sufferings reflected, their pity mingling with self-pity, so that when they sighed they sighed together, each in love with a ghost.

This mutual misery brought a certain happiness, and after the first wild riot, when, after rising from that passionate embrace, they had danced and drunk until dawn, they awoke miserable yet compassionate and kissed without excitement, like a long-married couple cushioned in the security of trust. They even seriously debated the question of marriage, Lydia mentally counting the years behind her and shivering with dread of lonely old age, and the Corinthian feeling assured that never again would he meet a woman so suited to his moods. They had saved more than sufficient on which to retire and live pleasantly, but not sufficient to continue their present expensive living without work. To retire would mean deserting Westminster for the suburbs or the country, and neither was certain whether such an uneventful existence could be borne. So long had they kept themselves active on the stimulus of brandy or gin, on the thrill of shuffling cards and throwing dice, of relaxing at a play or mingling in a masquerade, that they wondered whether they would be able to live quietly amongst quiet neighbours. Nevertheless, the idea for the time amused and pleased them and when alone they talked in low, happy voices by the fire, laughing softly, like children hiding from the world to dream gay mischief.

"I've always wanted a garden," said Lydia wistfully. "My father grew lovely flowers, And I adore birds, don't you?"

"I was once a strong walker," he said, "but I hate walking in the city. It's so different in the country."

"Yes, a different world. To wake to birds' singing!"

"To smell clean air and not this fog or mist!"

"I'll be a dutiful wife," she sighed. "I'll see you eat well and always have clean linen. And on Sundays we'll go to church with threepence for the plate."

"I've not been to church since I was a boy," he said, remembering that Mary Moore went to church three times each Sunday.

"Nor I," said she, "not since I was a girl"; and she sighed, recalling the tall youth who, when she walked demurely out of church, had always managed to get behind her and to touch her through the gown. That had been the rascal whom she had loved too well, the squire's son; and the memory made her restless on the sofa, for clearly in the twilight could she hear his voice, voice of Corder, slow Suffolk voice, telling her that she was beautiful and that he would love her until death, lulling her defences with sweet lies that she might not struggle when he slipped her gown over her shoulders. The grass had been damp and had tickled her back and she had feared she'd stifle, so intense had been that mingling of terror, pain and ecstasy which she had felt must stop her heart's wild beating.

"O, is it possible!" she cried, fiercely gripping the Corinthian's hand. "Or is it too late!"

S.O.T.R.B.—G

"Never too late," he whispered doubtfully, answering her caress while thinking that soon Corder would have Miss Moore in his arms . . . or they might be already married. . . .

"I pray not," she said, shutting her eyes to shut away thoughts of her youth and her Suffolk lover.

As they remained, hand in hand, before the fire, each sunk in dreams, they started as though caught in a guilty embrace when they heard a loud rat-tat on the door. Corder's knock. Questioningly they looked into each other's eyes, then Lydia suddenly cried to the servant whom they could hear moving in the kitchen:

"If it's Mr. Corder, admit him."

Furiously, the Corinthian tossed down her hand and sank back in his chair, while hurriedly she rearranged the folds of her thin nightgown.

As usual, seeming in a hurry, Corder bustled in; and the Corinthian, watching him with a jealous eye that missed little, noticed that he appeared ill-at-ease, that his greatcoat-pockets bulged each side, and that his face had a greenish tinge.

"Afternoon, good afternoon," said Corder. "This makes me envious, so loving, so domestic by the fire!" His eyes lingered admiringly over Lydia, for, without her stays, the shape of her broad bosom was plainly to be seen. "But I'll know the same bliss soon," the rascal chuckled, "or something like it with my own little Mary. We're getting married tomorrow. Special licence. At St. Andrew's, Holborn. Know the place? Fine church, looks like Solomon's Temple when you're inside, all gilded and the wainscot veined to look like marble, and it's got tremendous stained-glass windows. Most impressive, I can tell you. Just the place for a wedding. They've got the Last Supper there, and the Ascension, and St. Peter, and I don't know what else. The rector told me all about it when Mary and I went to see him about tying the knot. It's near the top of Holborn Hill, at the end of Shoe Lane."

As he rattled on with his usual air of impudent simplicity, the Corinthian, watching him with a jaundiced eye, felt that the man was not at ease, that something troubled him. In his eyes there was an unusual wariness; and in his stiff gestures while he pulled on the lapels of his greatcoat, and in the way he started and blanched when Nelly slammed the kitchen door, there was a hint of fear of— what? The Corinthian sat up, watching him more intently. Something extraordinary had happened, for beyond argument the man was frightened and had a hunted look. In the dangerous world in which he lived the Corinthian had learned to recognize fear, to smell its evil sweat, and Corder smelt of fear. And those bulging pockets. Could they contain pistols? Their shape suggested pistols; yet why in daylight should a man carry pistols?

"You'll come to the wedding, won't you?" said Corder, his gaze still on Lydia, and he licked his lips when he noticed how her nipples creased the cloth.

"No," said the Corinthian.

"Eh?" cried Corder. Then he looked from her bosom into Lydia's impassive face. "You will, my dear, won't you?" he asked caressingly.

"No," she said, lids lowered over her eyes.

"Now, now, please," begged Corder, "you're the only good friends I have in London; and Mary's dying to meet you, Mrs. Lydia, after all I've told her about you. She'll be most disappointed if you don't come."

"I presume it'll be in the morning," said Lydia in a weary voice, "and you know we never rise until the afternoon. It's quite impossible."

His thick lips working strangely, Corder looked from Lydia to the Corinthian, and his legs shook. For once he did not blink.

"What have you been hearing about me?" he cried suddenly. Cold though it was, there was sweat on his face. "It's a lie!" he shouted. "They tell these stories; I know they do; but they're all lies. It's my enemies, and they're jealous; they always were because I'm a big farmer and the women like me. And why the hell shouldn't I clear out of Polstead when I wanted to? What the devil's Polstead got to offer a man of my talents? Nothing, I tell you. Nothing. I had to come to London, hadn't I? Let the bastards talk, let 'em talk!"

"This," said the Corinthian, "would doubtless be most interesting if we knew what they were talking about. What bastards do you mean? And what are these stories? And who are your mysterious enemies? For the first time, my dear Corder, you begin to interest me. And why do you carry pistols in your pockets?"

"Pistols?" repeated Corder, his fleshy lips pressing one against the other. "What do you mean?"

"I'm not a police-officer, so don't be afraid, but I've lived too long in London not to be able to recognize the shape in a man's pockets. You're carrying two pistols, Corder: why?"

"They're not! They're bottles."

"Bottles! when you don't drink unless some fool pays for your daffy! Come now, my lad: empty those pockets."

Corder started back, his wet face darkening.

"I came here as a friend," he stuttered, "and you insult me! All right, Mr. Bloody Corinthian. . . . Do you know what, ma'am? The other night he tried to buy my Mary from me, he offered me cash down if I'd sell her to him."

"Then why didn't you sell her?" drawled Lydia, pretending to yawn. "Didn't he bid high enough? He never did know the price of a good woman, the conceited fellow."

"Aw, you make me sick, both of you!" almost screamed Corder. "There's no goodness in the world these days. And I thought that you, ma'am, had some honesty, some womanly sensibility in you; but, ah! . . . Sell my Mary! He'd never have enough money to buy such a woman, even if she was for sale, which she ain't. Ma'am, you astonish me! lying there with your bosom cocked up as if you as good as had nothing on . . . I wish you a very good afternoon, ma'am. And you, sir, a good day."

"Good day to you," cried the Corinthian; "and get out of here before I throw you out!"

His rage was such that he gripped the chair-arms to restrain himself from leaping up and kicking the rascal from the room; but Corder fled before he could move, and Lydia's cold hand on his thigh held him back.

"Let him go," she said in an icy voice as they heard the front door slam behind him; then she laughed. "How much did you offer him for his school-mistress?" she asked. "It couldn't have been much or he'd have taken it."

"I'll break his bloody neck," growled the Corinthian, lying back, trembling, in the chair. "What the hell does he want to carry pistols for?"

"Possibly to protect his wife's valuable little honour," said she. "But you haven't answered me yet: how much did you offer for this little Mary woman?"

"He's lying . . . But why those pistols?"

"How much?" she repeated.

"Do you believe his lies?" He tried to clasp her to him but she squirmed out of his grip. "Come here, damn you. . . ."

"How much?" she giggled. "Tell me that, my sweet," and swiftly she slid off the sofa. "No, my lad," she purred, "before you touch me, I want at least double what you offered for her."

"I tell you he's lying!"

"How much?" she repeated with an angry laugh, her hand on the bedroom door-knob.

"O, go to hell, blast you!" he roared; "to hell with the lot of you!" and he closed his eyes and pressed his hands over the lids; but he could not hide from Lydia's furious, mocking demands to be told how much. This would never be forgotten or forgiven, he knew; and he wished that he could have had Corder in his hands that he might have strangled him.

"For God's sake," he wailed, "leave me alone!"

At the door, beyond his reach, Lydia stood, flushed with anger, and parroted still her cry of "How much?" and even after he had thrown a cushion at her and shouted abuse, she did not go. Against the door she leaned, smiling venomously, eyes bright, repeating:

"How much, how much, how much? You bloody simple fool, how much?"

Chapter Eight

A CALL FOR HELP

NOW that they were rid of Corder, the Corinthian hoped that he and Lydia might snuggle back into their dream of youth and a future of connubial content, but the scoundrel had destroyed all hope of that by telling of his attempt to bribe him not to marry Mary Moore. Whenever now he sought to embrace Lydia, she either twisted out of his arms or remained comatose, eyes open and mocking, and snapped her fingers to demand: "How much?" He blustered, he raved, he pleaded, he cursed; and always, smiling cruelly, she asked: "How much?" He had offered to buy Corder's female, she reminded him, so why should he not pay her for her submission? Useless though he knew it was to argue, he argued. He swore that Corder was a liar, that all he had meant by that impulsive offer was to protect a silly woman from the misery she must know in such a marriage; and always Lydia faced him with that derisory smile, and asked: "How much?"

Christmas came, chill and dark, with waits shivering in the wet streets singing for alms, and with public-houses crowded with a brawling, roaring multitude drinking and dancing; and Boxing Day woke the houses with tradesmen's servants banging on knockers and ringing bells that they might be given gifts of money; and New Year followed with forced gaiety to ring the old year out and the new year in. Glumly, the Corinthian joined the dancing and the drinking, while Lydia, in contrast to his dullness, was the jolliest romp in whatever company they joined.

Deliberately, she taunted him, wearing few garments when they were at home and keeping them loose to swing tantalizingly to show for a moment a shimmer of skin, enough to madden him to action that she might laugh in his eyes with the cry: "How much?" Often in the past had they quarrelled, and she had treated him with cold cruelty after discovering him on occasions with her women-friends in postures no words could satisfactorily explain; but always before long she had shrugged off her displeasure as though he were not worthy of being hated. This time, however, she seemed determined on tormenting him, and he was aghast to see the deliberate way she set about his punishment, behaving as though he were not present when she dressed and undressed or washed herself, commanding him, like a mistress to her servant, to tighten the lacing of her stays while she gasped and clung to the bedpost. All that she did became deliberately tantalizing, and she who had previously affected a dignified modesty now sprawled beside the fire in chemise and silk drawers dangling with lace below the knees. All this was done, he realized, to tempt him that she might reject his proposals with hard eyes and that exasperating demand: "How much?"

He thought to take revenge through other women, but was too weary to pursue them far. The routine of seduction he knew so well that he yawned to consider the tedious hours in which he would have to pretend a passion he did not feel, harlots holding little interest for him. So often had he acted the part that now he craved for honesty, for frank desire between man and woman with no pretences; and this response Lydia would no longer give. He even contemplated cuckqueaning her with their slavey, Nell, but feared too much the aftermath; the wench had an astute eye and she made such crude overtures that she frightened him, sweeping out the apartment, when Lydia was absent, in semi-undress, and waggling her buttocks at him when on hands and knees she scrubbed the floor, the skirt pulled high to show her stumpy calves in woollen stockings. She wanted to have him in her power that she might bleed him of cash with threats of telling Lydia . . .

He did not desire the girl. He desired only two women: Mary Moore, the lost one, and Lydia who remained out of arm's reach and kept a pillow between them in bed; and yet it truly was not Lydia he wanted so much as the image of another woman he could clasp in his arms. And this, Lydia realized. And for this, she sought her revenge. All had promised so well until damned Corder had blurted out about his offer to pay to have Miss Moore left alone. His previous women had never troubled Lydia for long, and he had begun to believe her incapable of serious jealousy; but now this woman whom she had never seen had roused in her a demon of hatred, and always, whenever possible, she would bring up her name that she might spit it out. Continually did she jeer at this dragon of prudery, at this sly slut who had hooked not only Corder but him with a virginal lie; and she would rage against modesty, swearing that there was no such thing and that any woman who reached twenty without a lover must be deformed or heartless. This was so unlike the Lydia he had known that the Corinthian bit his nails in despair; and when they were in saloons together in search of flats he sat grimly apart while with the other women she sniggered at goodness, laughing at men's simplicity and at the tricks that were used to cheat them.

His one consolation was to see that Bertram was as distressed as himself, for he feared lest, in this rebellious, rancorous mood, reverencing nothing, her old pretence of fastidiousness abandoned, Lydia might, if only to spite him, betray him with his friend. Therefore he never left her by herself, remaining at home when she complained that she was weary, and gadding abroad with her whenever she wished to go on the spree. With ironic smiles, she mocked him; and no matter how drunk she might become—and almost every night she became so drunk that he had to undress her and roll her into bed—she repulsed his caresses, laughing until she choked while holding out her hand for money.

"How much? Aren't I worth as much as little Smooth-face?"

Her nudity became to him an affront when in the afternoons she staggered, puffy-eyed, from bed, vomiting, and drinking even while she vomited. Confident of her beauty's power and exulting in its effect on him, she drooped about the apartment in nothing more than a chemise and drawers which concealed little but seemed rather to accentuate her body's contours; and yawning, she would raise her arms and stretch her legs out to the fire.

"Lydia," he cried one late morning when they had been unable to sleep and had tossed in bed, groaning to escape their waking dreams, "why do you give me hell like this?"

"Give you hell?" She sniggered, complacently looking down her body's length under the blankets. "You flatter me, dear man. I thought you liked your women to be deaf and, O, so chaste! like Mrs. Corder. For she's Mrs. Corder by now you know, and you're too late again, poor darling."

"You're jealous," he snarled. "You blame me; you pretend

that I'm in love with Miss Moore—Mrs. Corder—but that's only to hide the fact that you're in love with him."

"What a clever man you are!" she laughed. "How did you discover my secret?" and she laughed again, rolling heavily on the bed until she dragged the clothes away from him. "I love the cross-eyed little Adonis," she hiccuped, being still a little drunk, "but I never considered buying him."

"I always thought you were a sensible person," he muttered, fighting to recover some of the bedclothes. "We can't go on like this much longer."

"Of course we can't," she simpered. "We're going to take a little cottage in the country, aren't we, and have a garden all to ourselves, and on Sundays we're going to sing in the church and put threepence in the plate? . . . Aw, you make me sick! So let me sleep. I'm tired."

He did not stir as, shaking the bed, she tossed away from him and the blankets and sheets again were wrenched off his legs. It was late in the morning and he was tired, after a sleepless night. In the darkness, the fumes of gin gradually evaporating from his mind, he had tossed in misery, wondering what the future held. For weeks now they had not earned a penny, Lydia being usually too aggressively drunk to act her part, and he had forced himself to remain sober that he might guide her safely home out of the hands of men like Bertram. Such a life could not continue, but he could see no way by which they might return to the old companionship. The revelation that he had attempted to buy Corder from marrying Mary Moore had had this extraordinary effect on Lydia, and her stupidity enraged him. Again and again had he sought to argue her back to sanity, only for her to giggle and to mock him with wriggling fingers begging money. Once, however, she had given him some insight into her feelings when she had cried:

"All men are bastards. You want silly girls to ruin, not women to love. You and Corder are a pretty pair, a pair of filthy debauchees, and I bet this fancy piece of his has queered you both and is no better than she should be; and serve you right, both of you bastards."

Of whom was she jealous? Of Mary and Corder? or of him and his desire for Mary? This problem the Corinthian could not solve, knuckle his chin though he did, while gazing at her bulk under the clothes—how much larger she looked undressed in bed than when she spread her bulk in petticoats—and wanting both to beat and ravish her. Or was she jealous of Miss Moore? of the girl's modesty and godliness, reminding her of her own lost innocence? Was she regretting her merry past and wishing herself a maid again like Mary? It seemed that she herself did not know, but raging, drank herself to greater rages against life that she might abuse him.

A knocking at the door roused him out of his black thoughts and he went cold with anger, thinking that this might be Corder again. No friend of theirs would think to disturb them in the morning, knowing that they rarely woke before noon. His impulse was to call to Nelly to let no one enter; then, with a grimace at Lydia's back, her posterior pushed up, it seemed to him, with a kind of challenging contempt, he decided that any visitor, even Corder, was preferable to his gloom.

"It's a Mr. Moore wants to see you," said Nelly, poking her tousled head, the greasy face unwashed, round the edge of the door. "Will I tell him you're asleep?"

"No. Tell him to wait." Out of bed he crawled and drew a loose robe about his nightshirt, then pushed his bare feet into slippers. The red-tasselled nightcap he retained, merely cocking it at a more jaunty angle. Lydia lay quiet, although he had felt her quiver at the mention of Mr. Moore, and he hoped, but doubted, that she was asleep. Mary Moore had caused trouble enough between them without her brother coming when he was hoping to forgot that she had ever existed.

Beside the cold grate, with its dust and burnt-out coal, tall Mr. Moore stood, awkwardly holding his grey top-hat in his hand and sourly staring at the dirty glasses and empty bottles on the table. At the sound of the Corinthian opening the bedroom door, he turned and gave a curt bow.

"Pray be seated," said the Corinthian, motioning to a chair while he lounged on Lydia's sofa. "Would you like a drink, or some coffee?"

"Coffee, please, for me," said Mr. Moore, not looking at him. "The hour's too early for me to touch strong waters."

"Nelly!" called the Corinthian, "pray bring this gentleman a cup of coffee. I," he added with a gracious smile, "find it never too early—or too late, for that matter—for a drop of my favourite poison. And what, sir, may I ask, causes you to honour us with a visit at this hour?"

"This hour?" repeated Mr. Moore, raising his thick eyebrows. "Why, sir, it's long past noon!" He peered with distaste at the careless luxury about him, snuffing the odours of that unaired room, the sharp smell of stale spirits mingled with sickly perfume. "I have come to see you," he said in a hurried voice, "as being, to my limited knowledge, the only friend that Mr. William Corder possesses, at least in London."

"He is no friend of mine," said the Corinthian.

For the first time, Mr. Moore looked him in the eyes. "But, sir," he cried, "he assured me on his honour that you were his oldest friend and would swear to his good character."

"I'll swear to nothing of the kind," said the Corinthian testily; "for all I know he might be thief, whoremonger or footpad. We met by chance a few months ago in the Piccadilly Saloon. Beyond that, I know absolutely nothing about him and I'll not take responsibility whatsoever for anything he might do." He raised his voice angrily, having heard the bedroom door squeak and noticing it open a crack. "The man's a total stranger to me, and, I might add, one who owes me money."

"This!" cried Moore, rising slowly to his feet, "this is what I feared!" He twisted the brim of his hat in his long fingers and gazed wildly about him, his eyes red-rimmed, his thin lips trembling. "O, poor unhappy girl!" he cried, "poor innocent! The villain! I suspected it, I warned her. Then when he tried to sell my house——"

"He tried to sell your house!"

"Yes, sir: my house, No. 6 Gray's Inn Terrace, which you've visited. He advertised it for sale in *The Times* newspaper and it was only from an accidental conversation with a friend that I discovered the fraud he intended to commit and instantly prevented the clandestine negotiation. Yes, sir, he would have robbed me behind my back; and when I taxed him with it, with the boldness of brass he said he'd believed the property to be my sister's, and as her husband, he said, he thought to act for her financial good. That was a lie, sir. He knew that the lease of No. 6 Gray's Inn Terrace stood in my name."

"And what did your sister say to that?" asked the Corinthian, delighted that Lydia should be listening.

"My sister, sir," said Mr. Moore in a quavering voice, "has the noblest soul alive; she is a perfect angel, too good for this gross world; and that is her undoing. She is remarkably attached to the Established Church and while living in My House she used to attend at Bloomsbury Church, St. John's Chapel, Bedford Row, and Clerkenwell Church, alternately, three times every God's day. Not only the sweetness of her disposition—positively angelic, I repeat—but this regular attendance upon divine worship distinguished her in the circle of her acquaintances more than any other feature in her character. This piety was instilled in her by her dear mother whom, sir, you met recently at My House, and who assists her in the holy task of teaching the young idea how to shoot. But, alas! like every human soul, my dear sister is fallible and in this hasty marriage she has acted with extraordinary imprudence and in opposition to the advice of her nearest friends. But before I and my dear mother are accused of lack of caution and carelessness of guardianship, it must be remembered that this delicate flower has arrived at a state of maturity and however imprudent might have been her behaviour, it by no means affects her moral character. This I must have understood, for I will not have her blamed for her husband's misdeeds."

"These misdeeds," asked the Corinthian, wishing Mr. Moore would be more explicit, "what are they?"

"He would have sold My House," said Mr. Moore grimly.

"Yes, yes; but what else?"

"What else! Is that not sufficient? Yet, there is more to tell." Sitting down again in the chair, he raised a moral forefinger, but before he could continue, Nelly pattered in with his coffee. With distaste, both men watched the young girl, noting her greasy hair, her puffy eyes, the dirty feet pushed into slippers that went flap-flap at every step, and the unlaced figure flopping in the loose gown. Although little more than a child in years, she had almost a matron's bosom, and the Corinthian wondered how she spent her evenings when he and Lydia were abroad. As he was rarely up in the mornings, he had never before surprised her in her present slatternly state with this evidence of a night's hard drinking—she was unsteady on her short legs and her eyes were glazed and swollen—and he decided that in future he would count his bottles and hide the corkscrew. Mr. Moore sat very erect and drew his knees away from the girl when she passed him his cup of coffee, shivering as though he didn't like the smell of her breath, and he shut his eyes when her gown flapped open. Not until she had pattered back to the kitchen did he open his eyes again. Then he resumed his talk as if there had been no interruption.

"Yes, sir," he said, balancing the cup on his thigh, "there is more to tell. My sister no longer resides under my roof in Gray's Inn Terrace. I am now a desolate man in a house of echoes, for our mother has gone with them to see that she comes to no harm and to assist her in her young ladies' seminary at Ealing Lane. This seminary is rather large and two females are scarcely sufficient to carry on the good work, but they have not the means with which to employ assistance. As yet, I have not visited there. I have not been invited by Mr. Corder, whose home it is, although both my mother and sister have pleaded with me not to neglect them. But a man has his pride, Mr. Barsett, his proper pride. Mr. Corder has seen fit to ignore my existence save to Laugh in my Face. Nevertheless, I am not entirely unaware of what goes on in that household. My mother writes regularly and I confess, sir, her letters trouble me. There is some hideous secret in the past of Mr. Corder. Why else should he carry pistols?"

"Pistols?" repeated the Corinthian politely, sipping his brandy and soda, and he remembered the bulging pockets and Corder's fury when he had asked whether they contained pistols.

"Yes, sir, pistols!" said Mr. Moore emphatically. "When he lived in London, as you probably recall, he behaved gregariously, but now he rarely leaves the premises and takes no active part in the conduct of the school. Although my sister is a pious lady, he refuses to attend divine service, no matter how she pleads with him to go. At home he remains and when he does venture out he always carries these pistols. When my dear sister remonstrated with him, he told her that having once been attacked by footpads, he would be prepared in future. I ask you, sir, as one whose feelings are not involved in the situation, do you not think this behaviour somewhat odd?"

The Corinthian shrugged. "I don't know," he said. "He's not the only man to carry weapons nowadays; nor is he the first husband who wishes to stay with his wife, at least during the first months of marriage."

"He never sees her, sir, save at meal-times. From early morning to evening, my sister is busy attending the young and supervising the household. There's nothing to detain him at home."

"Even now," murmured the Corinthian, "I see nothing criminal in this. Besides, what do you want me to do?"

"I would like you to call on him. You are a man he respects and . . . er, admires. If you were to question him, you might find what is on his mind; for he cannot sleep at night."

"That also," smirked the Corinthian, "is no phenomenon with newly wedded couples."

Mr. Moore stiffened his backbone and his long face grew red as though he boiled within. "This is no jesting matter, sir," he growled. "My sister's a virtuous woman, even though she is married, and no matter what her spouse might be. And I cannot stand aside and see her being made wretched. Our mother's distressed to the heart. She even believes, although doubtless she exaggerates, that he might murder them in their beds one night. She pleads my help, but what can I do? Mr. Corder dislikes and distrusts me and any interference on my part would make matters worse. Therefore I ask you, sir, to come to our aid."

"Even now," said the Corinthian impatiently, "I don't know what you expect me to do."

"Why, sir! to expostulate with him, to discover why he carries pistols, to find what lies on his conscience and will not let him sleep, and to learn what it is he fears so that he rarely leaves the house."

"No," said the Corinthian, "I can't. I won't do it. Your sister was misguided enough to marry a man about whom she knew nothing, and she must suffer the consequences. Even if she were to ask me herself, I would not interfere."

"But, sir, she *has* asked you. I have here," said Mr. Moore, drawing a folded piece of writing-paper from an inside-pocket, "a note to you which she enclosed in a letter to me. It was the receipt of this which prompted my visit this morning. Sir, I can assure you, knowing that modest woman inside out, as it were, that only the deepest distress would have induced her to write to a comparatively strange man, and in that letter to speak so plainly."

"You have read it?" asked the Corinthian scornfully.

"Yes," said Mr. Moore; "as her brother, I have read it."

To his annoyance, the Corinthian found that his hands were trembling when he unfolded the letter and saw, for the first time, the bold clear writing of this young woman whose memory he could not blot away.

Dear Sir, she wrote. *Forgive one who has met you only once that I should make any claim on your attention, but my dear William has so constantly assured me that you are his dearest friend from whom he keeps no secrets that I feel I am being neither immodest nor indiscreet in sending these lines, care of my brother. I am deeply troubled about the state of poor William's health and he will not see a medical man. His sleep is disturbed and in the mornings his nightcap and other garments are soaked with perspiration, which makes me fear he has a fever and which he denies in very strong and comical terms, laughing heartily at my natural distress. Most troubling to me is his aversion from attending church, although we have an excellent place of worship close to this abode, but I would add in justice to a man whose goodness of heart I could never doubt that he is no hypocrite and never pretended religion.*

All this, Dear Sir, must appear to you confused and foolish, the baseless fears of one who so admires Mr. Corder that her Sex's weakness makes her exaggerate what is perhaps the natural behaviour of all men. Knowing so little of that Sex, I remain perplexed. But if you would honour us with a visit, you would doubtless be able to set many of my fears at rest. I abhor deception, but on this occasion I feel, for his own good, it might be well not to warn Mr. Corder of our little plot. I would suggest you call in the afternoon—I have no right to ask it, and it shames me, but I know not where to turn—on Thursday, as on that day he has business in the City.

Burn this, I implore you, if you think my fears foolish, and I will understand.

Believe me,
Respectfully yours,
Mary Corder.

The Corinthian flattened the letter across his thigh and, frowning, looked up to see Mr. Moore watching him with a mingling of dislike and hope in his grey, heavy-browed eyes.

"Well," he said at last, "will you please inform your sister that I consider her fears quite groundless, and that there's nothing I can do about them. Besides, today's Thursday, and the letter gives me too little time."

"The fault there is mine," mumbled Mr. Moore. "I delayed delivery. I feared this letter to be indiscreet and my spiritual tussle was great before I could bring myself to show it to you. I see now that I was right. My sister's fate means nothing to you."

"Fate? fate?" jeered the Corinthian, lounging back languidly, happy to feel in a roundabout fashion that he was revenging himself on this woman who had been foolish enough to marry a rogue. "What fate do you expect? She has taken this fellow until death them do part and I can't interfere. That I distrust Corder is true, but my advice was never asked. And I'd not bother about those pistols and his lack of sleep and his sweats. He looked dyspeptic and he was incapable of honesty."

"Then you will not help?"

"I can't," yawned the Corinthian, joying to think that Mary Moore by now probably regretted her choice. "I met your sister only once and I was never a friend of Corder's. . . . Good morning, sir."

"Good morning to you, sir," said Mr. Moore, returning the letter to his pocket and reaching for his hat.

Before he could place that hat on his head, the bedroom door swung open and Lydia ran in. Annoyed though he was that she should thus display, not only herself in *déshabillé*, but her interest in the affairs of Corder, the Corinthian felt a smile twitch the corners of his mouth. Fearing lest Mr. Moore should go, she had not wasted time on dressing and the silk nightgown, unbuttoned, drooped to show her heavy shoulders, while her uncombed, unbrushed hair fell in greasy clumps down her back. Like an actress before the ravisher—although no actress would have dared stamp the boards in such undress—she padded barefoot into the room, her face smeared with old paint and powder that gave her skin an unearthly pinkish pallor save about the eyes where the black was smudged to give a bruised impression.

"You must go to her!" she cried, glaring at the Corinthian.

"I will not go," said he, raising his eyebrows disapprovingly at her near-nudity, while lounging back on the sofa. "You expose too many of your charms, my love. I am certain Mr. Moore won't be impressed by such provocative improprieties, become you though they certainly do. Mr. Moore, allow me to introduce my wife, Mrs. Barsett."

Mr. Moore bowed and made a squeaking noise while, impatiently, Lydia tightened her gown and ran her fingers through her damp hair.

"Sir," she said with dignity, "forgive my appearing before you in this state, but I was afraid you might go if I delayed in making myself decent. I promise you my husband will see Mrs. Corder today."

"O, no, he won't," chuckled the Corinthian.

"What! are you frightened?" she cried. "You heard he carries pistols, is that it? You pretend to love this female——"

"God bless me, no!" wailed Mr. Moore.

"You pretend to love her," repeated Lydia furiously, "yet you're afraid to see her again. Afraid of both of them, aren't you? Of how she might hurt you and how he might kill you? Come, this journey's only short, an hour at the most; and you must take it. Or would you rather I went in your place?"

"No," said the Corinthian, "you'd do only harm."

"Afraid I might corrupt the prude, is that it?"

The Corinthian laughed awkwardly. "Perhaps," he jested, "the prude might corrupt you, my dear, and I'd not lose so valuable and so immoral a partner. You may laugh, but goodness can corrupt just as evil can corrupt. All depends on the nature of the person. May God damn it, but she's set the poison in me! That's why I refuse to see her again."

Laughing, Lydia sat slowly on to a chair and, with shaking hand, poured herself a glass of brandy and drank with simpering motions.

"I must be going," said Mr. Moore, again reaching for his hat.

"Sit down!" cried Lydia, with an imperious glare.

"I will not sit down," quavered Mr. Moore. "I was mad to come here in the first place. I knew no good would come of it. That is why I delayed until the last moment before delivering poor Mary's foolish letter. This is an evil house and good folk are not wanted here."

"Don't be a fool," said Lydia with curling lip. "If you don't trust my husband—God knows, I can't blame you for it!—why not accompany him to Brentford? He's got horses in the mews——"

"With him? Never! Besides, I can't ride. . . ."

"Then he can hire a carriage, a phæton, a chaise . . . whatever you prefer . . . and you can keep your eye on him when he's with your sister. There," she cried, "all's settled!"

"Except that I'm not going," said the Corinthian quietly. It was obstinacy that held him on that sofa—obstinacy and fear—for with both body and mind he longed to look on Mary Moore again. To see her in daylight, to discover whether her skin was as soft and delicate as he remembered, her eyes so chastely, brightly blue, her mouth so red although untouched by paint . . . to stand before her, alone with her, staring into her eyes, his very pores absorbing the intangible essence of her femininity, making him drunk on her mere proximity . . . ay! he longed, he trembled with longing, to see her again. Nevertheless he repeated, smiling into Lydia's watchful eyes: "I am not going."

"Then," said she, taking a deep gulp of brandy, "that settles it. I'll go."

"You'll do nothing of the kind. I'll not permit it."

"I will go," she repeated with emphasis, "unless you go. This cry for help from an innocent creature, this little school-mama, cannot be ignored by a person of sensibility. If my husband has no heart, sir, his wife must prove that she, at least, is human. Pray, Mr. Moore, will you wait a little while I dress?"

"Hell!" groaned the Corinthian, between delight and fury. "O, stay here, you bitch. I'll attend Mr. Moore to Brentford. And I only hope we aren't behaving stupidly, at the whim of two females; and I thought that one of 'em at least was sane. Corder may be a dangerous fool, God knows, but it seems we're even greater fools to think that such a fool could be dangerous."

With dignity, he strutted to the bedchamber while Mr. Moore stood with downcast head, not knowing where to look, and licked his lips.

"Pray, sir, sit down," said Lydia.

He did not move. He dared not look at her. As though praying, his lips moved soundlessly.

"Sit down!" cried Lydia in the voice of a tragedy-queen.

Mr. Moore sat down, yet still he kept his eyes averted, and only when he thought she might not notice did he glance furtively towards her, blinking, and feeling his heart pound painfully until he was afraid he could not breathe.

That hour while the Corinthian washed and dressed and Lydia sat scornfully opposite him, drinking and stretching her legs that they might be glimpsed palely through the gown, was the greatest agony that Mr. Moore had ever suffered. He knew, he felt, what St. Anthony must have undergone; and when at last, beside the Corinthian, he stepped stiffly from that perfumed room, he sighed like a man escaped from battle.

Chapter Nine

IN THE FIRELIGHT

IN a hackney-coach with Mr. Moore, the Corinthian sat and folded his arms, keeping his eyes tight-shut. Despite the greatcoat, he shivered in the chill of early spring and pretended to sleep so that he would not have to talk. The very feel of Mr. Moore's presence irritated him. His air of decayed virtue, his silent condemnation, while through narrowed lids he had appraised Lydia's semi-concealed beauty, disgusted him. If the fool preferred austerity to love, morbidity to laughter, sermons to songs, it was his own dull affair and no one would wish to deprive him of such dark delights. Why, then, should he sniff at Lydia's lovely disarray, at the bottles and glasses on the table, and at the Corinthian's faultlessly cut coat and breeches? To the devil with such cant! He preferred, behind closed eyes, to recall the image of Mary Moore.

That he should have been affected by her innocence and charm was, he argued, a mightily different thing from Lydia's extraordinary liking for Corder, that vulgar little beast. While Corder was sly, Mary was honest; Corder was a devil, or he would have been a devil had he dared, but never had any female of the Corinthian's acquaintance appeared so angelic as Mary. On meeting most women, he pictured them undressed, sharp eyes calculating which was body and which was padding; but with her, he had not long considered any such intimate thing. Her garments concealing her as though she had been bodiless, he remembered only her pale round face, the brown curls shining with gold lights; and particularly he recalled her large blue eyes intent upon the movement of his lips. The fixity of that stare had given her a breathless appearance, as though she were a child fearful of missing something important; yet always her expression had remained placid, gentle and affectionate. And now Corder was husband to this divinity, slept with her, fondled her, could touch and caress and kiss her, holding her breathless in his arms, feeling her softness, feeling her back, her flank, her knees . . .

Groaning, the Corinthian opened his eyes. Then, seeing the bleak-faced man at his side, he groaned and shut them again. Better the exasperation of an adorable image than the reality of that sour Joseph.

"Wake up, sir," said Mr. Moore, poking him with a sharp elbow. "We have arrived."

Like a hundred others in that distant suburb, the house, her house, appeared characterless, the abode of soul-less folk who went to church on Sundays and, good tradesmen, spent the rest of the week cheating their fellowmen. Half-concealed by bushes and trees, it stood back from the wall as though wishing to hide from the dust and clamour of the Great West Road. A dull house, neither beautiful nor ugly, its garden lifeless in this early spring, the greyish bricks gleaming after recent rain, it depressed the Corinthian as being no Sparta for his Helen.

They had been expected. He saw the lace curtains shake across a first-floor window and, after bidding the driver to wait, they had scarcely left the hackney and begun to walk along the pebbled path before the front door opened and Mary hurried down the steps to greet them.

"Good sir," she said with a brief curtsey, "this is indeed generous of you."

The Corinthian felt his heart quicken and he feared he might blush. "No, please, Miss Moore—forgive me: Mrs. Corder—the honour is entirely mine," he stuttered.

"It was perhaps," she murmured, lowering her eyelids, "indelicate of me to write to you, but as my brother was the bearer I hoped you would understand that only my worry forced me to act in such a way. You are my husband's dearest friend, he assures me, and therefore I felt I might ask your advice. . . . But it is cold out here. Pray, will you enter?"

In the house, the front door shutting them in with an odour of dampness, the Corinthian felt uncomfortable. Many years was it since he had been invited to respectable homes and this atmosphere of gentility was alien to him, and disturbing. And the feeling of unreality, of entering some foreign and inimical world, was heightened by the fact that, the carpets having not yet been laid, the hall seemed denuded, and the wallpaper, being old and stained, appeared to drip gloom like grease. The staircase, facing him, reached up to darkness, grey in the centre where once the carpet had been, the wood having an air of splintery desolation, both piteous and aggressive, like that of a beggar arrogant in poverty. Nearby, he heard the chattering and laughter of children, but even that cheerful sound could not relieve the depression he felt in this lofty hall. Rather did it emphasize the cheerlessness, as of youth and loveliness locked out or—he watched Mary as she opened the sitting-room door—of beauty in a dungeon.

"Pray, be seated," she said, motioning him to an armchair with a worn tapestry-work back, "and forgive our lack of comfort. We have not yet properly settled in." A faint flush stole up her throat to tinge her cheeks. "All the furniture's not arrived," she added.

Almost empty was that room, save for a table and three decrepit chairs placed before the fire. No pictures hung against the faded wallpaper, and a little carpet isolated in the centre of the floor only made more plain the bleakness of its surroundings. Everything was old, except for the lace curtains over the windows. The Corinthian, who had long and loudly boasted of his hardness of heart, pitied this woman who, at Corder's prompting, had been induced to leave her brother's cosy home to rent this mansion that was plainly beyond her means. When, however, he looked at her, sliding into the chair she indicated as she sat down opposite, he knew that she desired no pity. Troubled she was, but not unhappy, and, after that first flush of embarrassment at the exposure of her poverty, she showed no other signs that she was ashamed of the bareness of the room.

"Mama wishes to see you," she said to her brother who stood indecisively on one foot, then on the other, as though reluctant to leave her alone with a rakehell like the Corinthian. His dismissal, however, was too firmly given to be ignored; and he bowed, lips pressed tightly together, before he strode off, loosely closing the door behind him. With no haste, yet swiftly, Mary went and firmly turned the handle, then she returned to her chair. The afternoon was dark; only the firelight, shining on the polished grate and the bare floor, lighted the high-ceilinged room, for the curtains were drawn; and in her heavy brown dress Mary seemed to glide rather than to walk, her shoes barely visible below the hem, as if she were a phantom of his desire, only the rustle of cloth reminding him excitingly of the woman concealed by the gown. When she was back in her chair, sitting erect but not stiffly, hands in her lap, the firelight flickered redly over her inexpensive skirt, gleaming amidst the ringlets of brown hair and turning threads to gold, while her pallid face showed with a silvered edge, a nimbus that revealed on her cheeks down so faint that generally it would not have been noticed.

"Mr. Barsett," she said, softly clearing her throat while smoothing the gown over her knees, "this is a very difficult subject for me to discuss and only my worry over Mr. Corder's health and state of mind has induced me to speak of it. Honestly, I am troubled, so great has been the alteration in William since our leaving Holborn. No, no! please don't believe that he has not shown himself as affectionate and playful a spouse as any wife could wish." The Corinthian wondered whether she had noticed the gleam of hope in his eyes, so swiftly and vehemently had she turned to repudiate what he was thinking. "No wife," she said firmly, "could ask for a better husband. That, please, must be understood."

Sighing, as he stared into her eyes, the Corinthian bowed to show that he accepted her word.

"I have no regrets for what I did. Far from it, indeed," she said almost fiercely, her fingers picking at her skirt. "We live in perfect amity. There have not been even the smallest of those matrimonial tiffs which are to be expected in most marriages. I would be an ungrateful creature were I to say otherwise, and I bless the impulse that led me to answer his advertisement in *The Herald*. He has shown me some of the other answers he received, forty-five all told, and although many of these women wrote in a style to make me blush for my sex, others were doubtless honest, good people who would have made him probably a better wife than I can hope to do. Yet, by the will of providence, I was the one he chose."

The Corinthian had placed his hand over his eyes as though to shade them from the fire, but actually he wished to watch her without her realizing how keenly he noted each change of expression, each gesture she made; and now he was glad of that protection. Otherwise she must have seen his startled look at this declaration, spoken with such apparent sincerity that for the moment he almost believed she was telling the truth. But Corder plainly had not lied about the point of that advertisement. They had met in Fleet Street —a meeting she had indirectly suggested herself—and she had conspired with him in using that advertisement to explain their renewed acquaintance. Much as he wanted to disbelieve it, the Corinthian could not twist from what were plainly the facts. Corder had mentioned the idea before her answer had been received; yet now, blandly, with the air of a Christian innocent before a Roman court, she said in her clear voice that the marriage had come about by chance. Often had he been amused by the ability of many women to believe what they wished to believe, like children convinced of the truth of their own fantasies, but with Mary Corder he had not expected to find such self-delusion. So unquestionably pious was she, so honest, so pure, that he had believed her incapable of telling a lie. But was it a lie? Had she managed serenely to blot out from memory what she did not wish to remember, affirming the fantasy to maintain her self-respect, until now she believed it to be truth? Certainly, conviction sounded in her voice and candour shone in her blue eyes. No, he told himself: this woman would never deliberately cheat.

"But I must not waste time," she said, "lest we be disturbed. My mama and brother might return at any moment, and Mr. Corder will not be late home. He has gone to London on business. I must therefore speak plainly to you. I am deeply worried. Something is preying on Mr. Corder's mind and he won't tell me what it is. A woman, Mr. Barsett, is notoriously an inquisitive creature. Alas for our Mother Eve! And I know I have no right to pry into my husband's secrets. A wife must submit without complaint to even grievous wrongs, being man's inferior; and her duties, I have always believed, are to console and tend him should he be in trouble, and to act as his helpmeet in all those affairs which have nothing to do with business. All the same, deeply though it runs against my inclinations, I feel that I must know the truth. Otherwise, how can I help Mr. Corder in his troubles, if he won't confide in me?"

"About what, ma'am?" asked the Corinthian, admiring from under his shading hand the play of light across her rounded cheek. He sighed to see how her mouth was wet, where, in her agitation, she had licked her lips, and how her eye when she turned towards the fire seemed to flare with liquid silver.

"That," she sighed, "is what he will not tell me. He laughs aside my questions; yet, Mr. Barsett, he goes armed. When there's a knocking on the door, I have seen him perspire and become most perturbed. At night he can't sleep and tosses and moans; and in the morning I have found his attire damp with perspiration. I know that he has probably been foolish in his young days . . ." Amusedly, yet sadly, she smiled at her thoughts, like a mother recalling her child's naughtiness. "Doubtless he has been led into some foolish extravagances," she murmured indulgently, "some boyish pranks which now weigh heavy on his conscience. That doesn't distress me. I would not like a husband who did not regret things he'd done before marriage, young men being too easily led astray by bad company. True penitence is loved in heaven, Mr. Barsett, above all virtues. I am only curious because, as his wife, I want to help him in his troubles. I suggested his visiting the vicar, but he would not listen, although he is a most understanding gentleman—the vicar, I mean. I am, however, determined to discover the truth. Need I assure you, sir, that my motives are ones of which I need not be ashamed? Not idle feminine curiosity, not common jealousy about any weakness that may have led him from the right path when he was young, agitates me now. The salvation of his soul, Mr. Barsett, is my only aim; and when that soul chances to be a husband's, it is a wife's duty to assist and console him."

More than the light from the fire twinkled in her eyes. With the rapt expression of a saint in a painting, she gazed up at the gloomy ceiling, eyes half-closed, lips parted, ecstasy shining on her face. Deeply moved, trembling a little, the Corinthian watched her, and his belly seemed to turn over inside with the longing to kiss her hands and comfort her.

"What is it you want me to do?" he asked, clearing his throat.

Slowly, she turned towards him, the holiness gradually fading from her look, and her eyes wrinkled at the corners as though she found it difficult to see him clearly.

"Pardon me," she whispered, "but I did not hear."

"I asked," he said in a louder voice, conscious of her gaze on his mouth, "what is it you would like me to do?"

"Ah," she said, and smiled, crouching forward over the fire, "I knew you wouldn't fail me. . . . I want you to go to Polstead in

Suffolk and to visit his mother, meet his friends, learn what you can about him. . . ."

"To act the spy!" he cried.

"O, never!" she said shrilly; "it's not spying when you're acting for his good, when you're assisting his wife in her wish to comfort him! I must know, I must!" For the first time, her composure failed her; her hands twisting together in the shadowed lap when she leaned forward; her voice, never quite in key, rising sharply, almost jarringly, she cried: "I must know, or I'll . . . Oh, I can't bear any more secrecy, Mr. Barsett! It is killing me. He has this secret, this strange, terrifying secret, hidden in his bosom; and although I've pleaded to be his confidante, he only laughs. I ask no treachery from you towards a friend. Whatever you discover we will share, and share with him alone. Even if—although I can't believe it—he might once have really sinned wickedly, gladly will I forgive him should he repent. Indeed, it would be heavenly joy to weep and pray at his side. He is young—younger than I—should I have told you that? But I'll not behave like any vain woman and commit the sin of prevarication: I'm five years his senior, and, although a woman ignorant of many things, in certain ways I am wiser than he. I could help him as no one else could help him; and that is a right on which I insist. And only you can do this for me."

Fascinated, he saw again that exalted look brighten her eyes and redden her parted lips that showed a flicker of white teeth; and her skin seemed to glow as though a candle were alight behind it, giving its texture a pearly, translucent quality. And he knew that no matter what she asked him, he would do it.

"All right, ma'am," he sighed. "I will go to Polstead for you."

"I knew it! God put the thought of you into my head!" she cried, her voice rising sharply in her excitement. "I was on my knees before retiring, and in deep anguish, not knowing what best to do, when I heard his step on the stair. Then, as I shut my eyes, imploring heaven's assistance, I remembered you. Deep then was my satisfaction. God spoke to me, I could feel His presence and it flooded all my soul with bliss. You would prove my friend in need, I felt certain. And now you've shown I was not wrong."

"Before God," he cried, "I'll never fail you, ma'am!"

"Hush," she whispered with a timid smile, "you must not take His name in vain. But I'm so grateful, my good friend."

In a diffident gesture, dimpling, she held out her hand, as though half-ashamed of the impulse, and he seized it and kissed it, pressing it tight against his lips even when she tried to draw it away. He heard her gasp and cry, "O no, sir, please, no! what are you doing?" but her cool skin was balm to his lips and he could not let her go, feeling the small bones move together in his grip.

"For the love of heaven, sir," she wailed. "O dear! . . . do let me go, please!"

He was mad for the moment. He did not care whither his madness led him so long as he could touch her; and he, who had considered any man a lunatic who attempted to seize from a female what he might enjoy comfortably with another woman, realized then that desire can destroy reason, caution and dread of consequences. Had he not been interrupted, he would not long have remained content with her hand; already his thoughts were climbing her arm towards her mouth. But then, like thunder startling him awake, he heard the front door slam.

"Heaven help me!" gasped Mary. "My husband . . ."

Not any fear of Corder but terror lest by his violence he had insulted Mary beyond forgiveness sent the Corinthian back into his chair. With trembling hands he sought to rearrange his cravat, furious because breathing had become difficult and he knew that his face was flushed. He dared not look at Mary but heard the rustling of her clothes as she settled into her chair, while from the corners of his eyes he glimpsed her in the firelight, her eyes staring at him with—was it horror, terror? Amazement? Or disgust? He dared not look to see.

Briskly, whistling, Corder entered, then stood stockstill at the sight of the Corinthian near his wife.

"Here's a rum go!" he cried pugnaciously. "What's all this, eh? You've both got faces like Dutch cheeses so don't try to come it over me that you've been talking about the price of cabbages. Out with it now and none of your lies."

"Lies?" repeated the Corinthian with an attempt at dignity.

"Yes, lies," said Corder, and he tapped his stick against his leg. "Here I go to the city on business, and it's not often I go out, and what do I find when I come back? Eh? What do I find? A nice sight for a husband, I must say! The renowned Corinthian who boasts that he's ruined more women than the king himself, and my good little wife, toasting more than their faces in front of the fire. Why! you burn a fellow just to look at your guilty phiz! Now, don't you try telling me that it's the weather, for I've just come in and it's cold enough outside to freeze the barnacles from a ship's bottom. What do you mean by it, sir? And who gave you the office I was out to bring you sneaking here like a cat at a mouse-hole? If I didn't know my wife's innocent heart, I'd be thinking the worst, I would. I can trust 'er, I know that, but I'm damned if I can trust you. So what have you been up to?"

Mary did not answer and still the Corinthian kept his back towards her, afraid to meet the contempt in her eyes. "You've a low mind, sir," he said coldly. "How was I to know that you were out when I called?"

"Of course you didn't know! Mighty rum though you should sneak here on one of the few days I ain't here."

"Pure chance, I tell you. . . ."

Corder laughed till he shook and the Corinthian realized that the man was almost insane with rage. Always had he considered him a weakling, a garrulous coward, but now he saw that under that façade of foolishness there watched a wild creature capable of ferocious moods; and he trembled to think that, should the fellow become really suspicious, he might ill-treat and even thrash Mary. The words of anger that rose to his lips he therefore forced himself to swallow for her sake and to say in a mocking, offhand manner:

"My dear fellow, such thoughts are not only an insult to your lady, whom I don't doubt is most virtuous, but they make a mock of her modesty. Do you seriously believe that we had an assignation and that you've caught us in the guilty act? Look at us now. Look at your good lady and see if any of her garments be disturbed, if so much as a curl on her head be ruffled. Come, come, sir. This is unworthy of both yourself and her. I came here because by chance I met Mr. Moore——"

"Ah," said Corder, and the released breath blew loudly through his curled nostrils; "so that's it! I might have known! The kind of thing the ungrateful cur would do! Bring you here, hoping to make me suspect my precious lady. Where is he?"

"With his mother, I believe," said the Corinthian, relaxing as he saw suspicion flicker out of Corder's eyes.

"I'll ferret him out of there; I'll not have him coming to my house with his tricks, trying to make me doubt poor Mrs. C." He turned and strode to the door, then stopped with his hand on the knob and smiled shrewdly at the Corinthian. "Want to get me out of the room, do you?" he chuckled. "Clever of you, but I ain't that kind of a flat. Anyhow, if everything's innocent, why were you both hot in the face? Tell me that."

"It must have been the reflection from the fire. . . ."

"Pooh," scoffed Corder. "Think of something better than that, can't you?" His restless gaze moved from the Corinthian to his wife, seeking signs of disturbance in her gown. Realizing by her trim appearance that whatever the Corinthian might have attempted, he had been foiled, he became suddenly merry and laughed, tossing his stick on to the table. "Thought to sneak to her behind my back?" he grinned. "He tried to buy you once: did I tell you that, Mrs. C.? Offered real money, he did; and you can guess what I told him to do with it. Well, now he knows that there's at least one woman he can't buy or steal. . . . My love, you've not yet saluted me!"

The Corinthian would not watch them. Into the fire he stared, and he could dimly see beside him the ghostly shape of Corder lean over the ghost of Mary. Minutes passed and Corder did not shift his posture, although by the ruffle of cloth he knew that Mary was trying delicately to protest at the kiss deliberately prolonged to torment him. At last, becoming breathless, Corder drew back, his lips making a juicy, smacking noise.

"There's nothing like wedlock, old boy," he said, rubbing his hands and warming his back at the fire. "There's nothing like having a good woman waiting for you when you come out of the cold. You should try it, Corinthian, old fellow. What's the Holy Book say about pure love being more precious than rubies? Why! I tell you, there's nothing like it. Don't know how I could have wasted all those years with a warming-pan or a hot brick at my feet. When we have our little ones about us, life will be bliss indeed, images of my darling and me growing up at our knees and making the house bright with innocent mirth! Nothing like it, nothing in the world."

A stab of hot jealousy made the Corinthian blink. Children! He had not considered that she might be already the envelope for this scoundrel's child; his breeding-machine. . . . The thought made

Mary's physical presence so real that he had no need to look towards her. Clearly in the fire he saw her pale round face and the great grave eyes watching him, and he remembered the startled horror with which she had looked when struggling to take her hand from his. . . .

"I must be going," he said, standing abruptly to his feet. "Will you kindly call Mr. Moore and ask if he wishes to return with me?"

"He's staying," said Corder. "I want to talk to him, so don't you worry about what he's up to. I want to know what his game is, bringing you here like this. Here's your hat and coat. You'll find the hackney waiting outside. Or it was when I came in. Thought it was some doting mother come to fetch her child. . . . Aren't you going to say good-bye to Mrs. C.?"

Not to say good-bye to her would confirm Corder's suspicions, yet the Corinthian dreaded to meet her glance. Slowly he turned and looked down at her, and sweetly she smiled as though he had never attempted to ravish her hand. Bewildered with delight and grateful for her magnanimity, he bowed low; then he saw that she was offering her hand, the pale hand he had gripped so fiercely that he must have jarred the bones and pinched the skin. Here was Christian charity! Not so much turning the other cheek, as offering the same cheek to the sinner! Gently, as though she might bruise at a touch, he held her fingers and was moved to see how the nails were broken by work.

"Good-bye," he said huskily, and he noticed her pale brows rise as though to question him. Faintly he nodded in reply that she might understand that he had not forgotten his promise to visit Polstead.

"No," she said, smiling, "not good-bye. Farewell, sir."

"Come on," grumbled Corder, rattling the door-knob. "You must owe that rattling-cove out there a pretty penny by this time; but of course you don't have to worry about the price of a hackney-fare, you've not got a family to think of and can throw your rhino about as you like. Wait till you're properly married and the inevitable little strangers come along. . . . O, come on now, come on."

Shining beside the fire she sat, her hair fluffy with light, her eyes glittering, smiling friendlily, at him; and all save face and hands and hair was concealed under the stiff armour of her gown.

Then was the Corinthian certain beyond any doubt that he loved her and he longed to remain and look at her.

So intense was this desire that he shivered in the cold air outside when Corder had pushed him through the door and down the steps into the garden.

"Look here," said Corder, gripping him by the lapel, "we're friends, ain't we? And you can't blame a fellow for being jealous of his own wife, can you now, particularly when a handsome swell like Corinthian Tom's around? So let's be honest, cards on the table and all that. Why the bloody hell did that bastard want to bring you here?"

"We met by chance. . . ."

Corder made a spitting sound through his pursed lips. "Don't come that over me," he said. "Anyhow it don't matter because I *know*. That fool hates me like poison, and he thought he'd entice you here to debauch Mrs. C. when I was out. There's a brother for you, by God! Ruin his own sister, he would, just to spite her husband! And I don't suppose you were shy when he suggested it." He leered. "Nice little partridge, ain't she? Now, I give you this advice 'cause you're a friend of mine, I hope. If you want to know real loving, marry an innocent woman. She's sharp to learn and always willing to oblige. O, I should be such a happy man! Doesn't *Tom and Jerry* say that the three finest sights in the world are a ship in full sail, a field of corn and a pregnant woman? And I know which of 'em I like best and it won't be long before I have it, too. Women like her what have had to wait a long time soon make up for it and have a family like in the Bible. Begat and begat and begat . . . Hey, don't go yet! There's something else I want to say."

The bantering manner suddenly left him and, still clutching the Corinthian's lapel, he drew closer, his cross-eyes roving so that it was impossible to know in which direction he was looking.

"Has anybody been asking after me?" he whispered.

"Asking after you?" growled the Corinthian. "How the devil should I know?"

"You go to the same places as I used to. Wondered if you'd heard whether there'd been any questions. That's all."

"What kind of questions? Are the duns after you?"

"Yes, yes, that's it," said Corder eagerly. "The duns. That's why I wanted to live out here at Brentford. London gets a bit warm for a fellow when his pockets aren't too full. You'll tell me, won't you, if you hear anything? Give a fellow time to bilk 'em in the moonlight?"

"Yes, I'll tell you," said the Corinthian, remembering Mary's fears. So the rascal did have some secret from which he had mizzled to skulk out here. And plainly it was something more dangerous than debt.

"You're a pippin," cried Corder, slapping him on the shoulder, "a real out-and-outer!"

Yes, it was something far more important than debt. Forgery, perhaps. At any rate, something that frightened him; perhaps, like forgery, a hanging matter. And that thought lightened the Corinthian's heart as he watched Corder walk jauntily up the steps and open the front door, turn to wave his hand in farewell, then close the door behind him.

Twilight was misting the earth with violet, shadowing the house with its blank windows; and as he moved on heavy feet to go back to London, the Corinthian saw lights suddenly flame behind the lace curtains of the room he had recently left, and he gritted his teeth at thought of Mary by the fire raising her mouth for that dandiprat to kiss.

For the first time, he began to look forward to his mission. He would ride to Polstead as Mary had asked and, if there was anything shameful in Corder's past, with delight would he track it down and dig it up to stink in her nostrils. Then, perhaps, in disgust from Corder she might seek consolation elsewhere. . . . Even the best of women having once tasted love must afterwards become lonely on warm nights; and angelic though Mary might be, she was, after all, a woman, and therefore built of flesh and blood; and being a woman, she would need a man to protect her if only he could get Corder transported or hanged. And he did hope that he might get him hanged.

That prospect kept him comfortably warm during the long drive back to London in the twilight.

Chapter Ten

A BROKEN DREAM

AS he turned the key in his Bond Street door, the Corinthian felt quite merry. Like a warm ghost whose presence he could sense in the gloom, Mary Corder walked beside him, smiling her secret smile, offering with Christian charity the small hand he had bruised. There was proof, he encouraged his dream, that she was far from indifferent towards his person; otherwise, so demure a wife would have spurned him out of the house. Instead, with a lift of pale brows she had asked him not to withdraw his promise to travel for her to Polstead. And to Polstead would he go. Into the spring countryside, he would ride from the smoke and stinks of London; away from cards and dice and whores and nocturnal living, he might regain his youth's illusions; and there would be to him the added delight of digging into Corder's past. The man was obviously afraid of something. Good. He would become even more afraid, grinned the Corinthian, when the truth, whatever it might be, was discovered; and he wondered whether this truth, should he discover it, might not prove more valuable if kept to himself. With such a weapon he might have Corder his slave and the pimp to his own wife—an intoxicating idea that made the Corinthian whistle like an errand-boy. Corder sending Mary to him, her beauty heightened by the shame in her cheeks, by the sorrows in her eyes, while, like the wife of some old tale, she offered herself to save her husband from the gallows. . . .

Even when, on entering his apartment, the Corinthian found Bertram seated by the fire, his good humour did not vanish. Sharply he glanced at Lydia on the sofa, a glass of brandy resting on her stomach to rise and fall with every breath; but as she had not yet dressed for going out, it was impossible to detect what pranks she might have been performing with his best friend. A yellow dressing-gown was loosely corded over her nightgown, and her hair was hidden under the cap with its lace border. She might have that moment got up from bed; she might have been up for hours; and she might only a few minutes since have risen out of Bertram's embrace. That Bertram looked miserable gave the Corinthian some satisfaction, for that dark frowning face did not seem that of a successful lover; yet one could not be certain. Bertram was a skilled amorist and would know how to act a part to divert suspicion.

In the thought of his Suffolk journey, the Corinthian was, however, too happy to allow doubts of Lydia's fidelity to disturb him. Still softly whistling, he took off hat and coat and poured himself a glass of brandy, watched in silence by the others; then, pulling forward his coat-tails, he took the chair between them and warmed his hands at the fire.

"You are very merry, sir," said Lydia, leaning forward to sip her brandy. "So your visit, I presume, was highly successful?"

"Successful?" he repeated, stroking his chin. "I don't understand, my love. It was certainly a very domestic *tête-à-tête*."

"You know what I mean," she sneered. "Did you find the paragon not quite the dragon you expected? Judging by your smug appearance and that silly noise you made, I suspect she was as willing as most wives when they find themselves alone with a rake. Farewell virtue and welcome joy, for the door's locked and if I scream I'll lose my reputation—— O, don't protest! What you do is no affair of mine. Have your suburban tits if they amuse you; only I confess to being curious about what the trouble was that brought that miserable-looking brother of hers here. Or did he just come as the pimp with the key to her bedroom?"

"My dear," chuckled the Corinthian, "you have the most appalling mind. I don't suppose it's any use my assuring you that Mrs. Corder is one of the most modest, saintly women I have ever met. You despise your sex too much, my love, ever to appreciate it."

"I know my sex and I know yours," said she darkly, "and I trust neither. But come, sir. Was all this mystery of that fool's just to make an assignation for you with his sister while her husband was out?"

"Indeed, no!" said the Corinthian. "I saw Corder as well as his wife; although I confess I was alone with her a little time before he arrived. Yet all we did, although you'll never believe it, was talk. Yes, yes, snigger if you like, but that's the truth. We talked.

We talked about Corder; and I promised her that I'd leave London for a time."

"What?" squealed Lydia, so startled that some of the brandy jerked out of the glass. "With her?"

"Will you pray keep your mind off your own sex," said the Corinthian severely. "She is not coming with me, unfortunately. I'm going alone, if that's any satisfaction to you." He tried to hide his smile behind his fingers, chuckling silently at being able to grill Lydia on suspense; then he heard the squeak of Bertram's chair, the fellow starting back, undoubtedly excited at the prospect of having Lydia alone in Bond Street. . . .

"Come, sir," cried Lydia, "we've had enough of riddle-me-rees: who is going with you, and where?"

"I told you, I'm going alone, to Suffolk."

"Suffolk?" She sank back on the sofa, breathing heavily, the brandy rippling in its glass at every breath. "So you are going to be a pig?" she said at last with loathing in her voice; "you who always hated the traps! You're mizzling to Suffolk to see what you can dig up about his past so that his good little, treacherous little bitch of a wife can hold it over him! God forgive you! I never did believe you had a decent instinct in you, but I never thought you'd sink as low as this; you an informer!"

"This is a private matter," growled the Corinthian, "and it's nothing to do with the traps. Good God! Do you really believe I'd be a nose! How little you understand me!"

"I understand you well enough," she snarled. "Give me another drink to wash out my mouth."

It was Bertram who took her glass and refilled it with brandy and warm water. She did not look at him, but stared at the Corinthian, and she did not trouble to thank Bertram when the full glass was returned to her. With a savage air, she drank, muttering to herself.

"I tell you," cried the Corinthian, exasperated by her scorn, "I'm going purely to set her mind at rest. The scoundrel's got her worried; he can't sleep and sweats all night and goes around with pistols. The man's frightened of something and he won't say what it is. He asked me if I'd heard of anybody chasing him and pretended he was only scared of duns. This is something worse than duns and I'm going to find out what it is."

"Why?"

"Why? Because she's worried and she asked me to."

"You're a bastard," said Lydia coldly. "You want to dig up dirt to ruin him so that you can steal her. Don't take those noble attitudes with me. I know you to your rotten backbone, but I never thought even you'd sink as low as this. If you're going to Polstead, I'm going with you."

"I go alone."

"I go with you," repeated Lydia. "Besides, I'd like to see Suffolk again. And you can't stop me going. If you won't take me, Bertram will."

"With all my heart," said Bertram, bowing. "Suffolk, Sussex, Norfolk, Essex, all are the same to me. Any of 'em would be paradise if you were there, my love."

"Fool," said she. "Then that's settled."

"It is not settled," said the Corinthian angrily. "If you really insist on this silly escapade, I suppose I'll have to take you." He glared at Bertram. "I don't know what you two have been doing behind my back," he growled, "but I don't need much imagination to hazard a guess. Anyhow, I won't have the pair of you running off together and making me the talk of the town. If you must come, damn you, you can come with me."

"Thank you," smiled Lydia. "And when do we leave?"

"Tomorrow," snarled the Corinthian.

Delight now had left the journey. His return to youth in balmy country-air had been only a dream, after all. With Lydia at his side, he carried London with him and remained Corinthian Tom, the sharp, the cheat, the city-swell; besides, she was Corder's ally and, whenever possible, would frustrate him in his search. But he had to take her or let Bertram take her.

"I might go, too," said Bertram suddenly.

"You will not!" cried the Corinthian.

"I like the country," smiled Bertram. "And I believe Suffolk's good hunting. Yes, I think I might do worse. . . ."

Murderously, the Corinthian glared at him while Bertram laughed, twirling the glass of brandy in his fingers. On the Corinthian's other side, Lydia slouched on her back, smiling down at the glass rising and falling gently with each breath. And he felt himself enclosed in scornful enmity, by the mistress who despised him and the friend who mocked at his cuckoldom. Trapped, he could not escape to Suffolk save by surrendering this woman to that man, for, the moment he rode off, Lydia would take the fellow, if only out of malice; and his pride forbade such a solution. And Lydia was too valuable an asset to be carelessly surrendered. Should he let her go, later, he realized, he would regret such romantic weakness. The dream of Mary Corder might be sufficient for the moment, but only for the moment. When a boy, he had managed to remain content with a dream of beauty. Now that he was a man, he required more than a pretty wraith for a bedfellow, and his present passion could not last unless Mary became his mistress; and he knew that she would never become his mistress. No. She would have to remain the unforgotten unpossessed to be embraced only within the bodies of others, so long as Corder lived. So long as Corder lived. . . .

Sharply he drew in his breath. In Suffolk lay the evil heart of the mystery, and if he could unearth some monstrous wickedness, so virtuous a woman as Mary would surely turn even from her husband in disgust? Then would open his opportunity. Then . . . He smiled again, the glass clinking against his teeth, as he stretched his legs to the fire. If only he could get the rascal lumbered or hanged . . . If . . . if . . .

He heard Bertram shuffle on his chair, and he frowned at this disturbance of his dreams. He wanted to be alone with the ghost of his desires, yet he dared not leave these two together; then foolishly —while he spoke, he cursed himself for an undiplomatic idiot—he suggested their staying at home that night.

As she had not yet troubled to wash or dress, it was evident that Lydia also wished to remain at home; the suggestion, however, coming from him brought immediate opposition.

"What!" cried she, "our last night in London before we rusticate! Most certainly I am going out. You may do what you like."

Setting her glass on the floor, slowly she rolled off the sofa and slowly stood to her feet, the gown falling open to show her body's outline through the thin nightdress. The Corinthian caught his breath with rage that, before his face, she should thus display herself to another man. Was this proof, he wondered furiously, that he had been already betrayed, that Bertram was now her lover?

Sharply he glanced at the man and saw the amorous grin, the greed in the dark eyes, and almost he crushed his glass in his fingers.

"All right," he croaked, "get dressed. At once."

Standing before the fire, lazily she smiled down at him, torment-ing him with the beauty he might never know again, while coquetting with Bertram. And he was astonished that, possessing so well-fleshed, so tall a human goddess, he should yet desire Mary Corder, a little thing who was doubtless thin under her many garments. Such stupidity maddened him. No other man would have paused had the choice been his. He would have laughed at Mary and kissed the feet of Lydia. But he no longer wanted Lydia, save to possess her that Bertram and others might not possess her, taking her in jealous spite, out of hatred more than love, with the image of prim Mary to urge him to kissing. Undoubtedly, he was mad. Only a fool would have preferred the kitten to the tigress, the deaf little simpleton to this intelligent, bold and beautiful woman.

"Get dressed," he growled. "You aren't in a brothel now. And we aren't customers."

"No?" Lightly she laughed and showed her teeth. "My price now, my dear, would be too high for you to pay," she said, "yet I might give freely to somebody else what you'll never have again, no matter how high you bid."

"What do you mean by that?"

She shrugged and, stepping over his legs, strolled to the bed-room door. "You know what I mean," she said. "Women, yes, even women like me, have pride, you know. Or call it vanity, if you wish. You're in love with Mrs. Corder, and, to get her, you'd ruin her husband. I can't stop you doing that, although I'll try, of course."

"Don't blame me! It was you that went nutty over the little rat. Any man would have taken his revenge."

"Revenge?" Deep in her throat she chuckled, languidly open-ing the door. "We shall see who's revenged on whom. And whatever happens, I can't see you getting any satisfactory revenge out of that little prude, my poor fellow. You're too vain to realize it, of course, but don't you think it possible that she might love her husband?"

"Of course she loves him! Who ever said otherwise? And you love him, too, God only knows why. What the hell do you women see in him?"

"What do you see in Mrs. Corder?" she asked, and swiftly, before he could answer, glided into the bedroom and shut the door.

"Women!" howled the Corinthian, stamping his heels. "They'd drive a man to Bedlam. To think that two such women, and two such different women, should like a jumped-up johnny raw like him! Can you understand it?"

"I've long since given up trying to understand their motives," said Bertram quietly. "But then I don't pretend to understand even myself. Often, my own behaviour appals me. Why! I really shock myself at times, the things I say and do which I don't really mean. Some of the women I've loved . . . I'd be ashamed to talk about them. And look at yourself and this Mrs. Corder."

"Don't you start talking about Mrs. Corder," growled the Corinthian, giving him a vicious look. "I've had enough of this. She's not the kind you all seem to think. You're so used to handling demireps that you've forgotten what a good woman's like. You make me sick with your dirty minds. She's pure and good and modest. She's not like these others."

"There!" said Bertram. "What did I say! You don't understand yourself any more than I understand myself. You and your purity and goodness and modesty! That's not what you've ever wanted a woman for, and don't try and come it over me. Aw, well, if you want to gammon yourself, there's nothing for me to do except to say: I thank you kindly."

"What do you mean: thank me kindly?"

"Lydia's a very beautiful woman," smirked Bertram. "And I repeat: I thank you kindly."

"Have you and she . . .? Tell me now. What were you doing before I came back?"

"Unfortunately, nothing that need worry you."

"I'm not so sure about that. You had a guilty look in your eye and there she was lying down with practically nothing on. . . . You'd better remember that she belongs to me."

"But you gave me permission . . ."

"I was only joking; and you know it. If I catch you with Lydia, I . . . I'll . . . I don't know what I'll do."

"Surely," smiled Bertram, "the important thing is not what you, but what Lydia, will do? And I hope for the best."

Growling, the Corinthian sank back into his chair. "You'd

better look out," he muttered; but he knew that he was defeated. He might shout and rave and threaten; and it wouldn't matter a twopenny damn to Lydia what he said. She was a determined, ruthless woman, a dangerous woman, and at heart he was afraid of her because he was never certain what she might do next. The true Lydia had always evaded him. Even in their embrace, he had felt, no matter her submission and passionate response, that something was withheld, that she remained contemptuous of her body's weakness and of him.

What he wanted was to possess both women, to keep Lydia as his mistress and partner in fleecing flats, and to have Mary Corder as his wife, obedient, affectionate, faithful and uncomplaining. But life permitted no such compromise, save to a Turk, and the damned laws of England were against him, not to speak of the spiteful, possessive, adulterous souls of women who expected too much from a man and would never meekly share their husbands, as a true helpmeet, thinking only of his happiness and peace of mind, would surely gladly do?

Chapter Eleven

POLSTEAD

HAVING to drive the chaise, the Corinthian was relieved from the embarrassment of sitting beside Lydia on the long journey to Polstead. After they had roved with Bertram through Covent Garden until the early morning, she had rarely condescended to speak to him, save curtly, while lolling on Bertram's arm and allowing him without protest to squeeze her through the stays. Far from each other that night had they tossed in bed, backs turned on the pillow between them; but sleep had brought reunion, and in the morning the Corinthian had opened his heavy eyelids to find Lydia's hair across his face and her hot cheek close to his, her breathing convulsive as though she were half-strangled. Long had he stared at her desirously, her face greasy with rubbed cosmetics, the pores enlarged by over-painting; and he had groaned at his stupidity in preferring the ghost of a woman to this creature of flesh and blood. Never again, he realized, would they know the old fellowship that had been close to love, for never would she forgive him his spiritual infidelity. Other women whom he had taken she had despised too greatly even to mention, only keeping him from her for weeks afterwards, both to torture him and because, she would say, she would not risk infection. Mary Corder was different, a rival she could not scorn and a woman of whom she was jealous because also she was loved by the cross-eyed scoundrel she herself desired. For, strangely, exasperatingly to the Corinthian, Lydia was nutty on the fellow. Looking at her closed eyelids, glossy with black paint, the lashes glued together by sleep and gin and brandy, he sighed to think that, like himself, she was haunted by a ghostly lover. And these two ghosts, as though to spite them both, had united in marriage.

By God, he had sworn, watching the shuddering rise and fall of her bosom under the disordered silk: by God, he would ruin the fellow before he was finished; he would degrade him not only in

Mary's eyes, but also in Lydia's, revenging himself on both women for their blindness in preferring such a creature to him.

That resolution kept him warm during the long drive to Suffolk and he ignored Lydia's ill humours. Since waking in the afternoon, she had scarcely spoken a word; and, after being noisily ill, she had dressed slowly, deliberately delaying their departure while he fretted and watched the clock. The only discussion they had had was about the servant, Nelly, whom Lydia had insisted must accompany them because, as she loftily told him, she could not be expected to dress herself every day. Reluctantly, and only to stop the argument, had he agreed to the girl's coming; and he had merely grumbled under his breath at the bags and boxes she had insisted on taking with her. Late in the afternoon had they set out, to stop after nightfall at a tiny inn in a tiny village—Lydia protesting that she was too bruised to continue—and as the one bed to be provided was a narrow one, they had spent a cramping night in which knees, feet and elbows seemed inescapable.

Glad were they to avoid one another in the morning, bruised and flea-bitten, and to continue through the thin rain over rutted roads to Colchester. Soaking, and feeling ill, Lydia refused to continue that day, the quantities of gin and brandy she had consumed having been so tossed inside her that she was unable even to look at food. Demanding a room for herself and Nelly, separate from her "brother", she managed to find a good night's sleep; but the Corinthian, unused to a bed to himself, with sheets warmed only by a warming-pan, spent a restless night, for he had no Nelly to clasp in his arms against ghosts.

Irritable and tired, he ate his breakfast and glared out of the window at the rain slashing on the cobbles; but when Lydia, with a sigh that was half a belch, suggested that they remain where they were for the day, he had the malicious satisfaction of refusing to listen.

"Stay if you like," he said. "I'm going on."

Not wishing to be left in a strange town with only Nelly for companion, Lydia had again to crawl into the chaise, sitting down gingerly and with many a sigh and groan. Only Nelly appeared to enjoy the adventure. A Cockney, this was her first vision of England outside London and she giggled and chirruped and bounced as though her bottom, moaned Lydia, were of leather, exclaiming at everything she saw and clapping her mittened hands. Approvingly, the Corinthian noted that Lydia had taken some trouble with the girl's appearance, making certain she was washed and forcing her into tight stays and a clean gown, so that she looked almost attractive and, in her gurgling rhapsodies, even innocent.

Polstead, the Corinthian had been told, was a bare nine miles from Colchester, yet he managed to get lost in the rain, and it was almost three hours before he crossed the Stour into Suffolk, and, at last, saw on the hills the plastered houses that were the village he sought. The country hereabouts was well-wooded and the ploughed fields between the trees showed the gentle green of newly risen corn; while, glittering in the feeble sunlight, the spire of a church gleamed above the foliage, a finger to beckon them on.

"Thank God," groaned Lydia, dragging herself upright and tossing the empty gin bottle into the hedge. For the first time that day, she fully opened her eyes, as the chaise bounced up the steep incline into the village street and drew up before a whitewashed inn with, swinging over its gate, a crudely painted rooster lifting its claws and crowing. From the stables at the side, an ostler lounged out, dung on his hair and shoulders.

"May we have accommodation here?" asked the Corinthian.

"You can have a bed and something to eat and drink," said the ostler, peering, huge-eyed, at Lydia who, although thickly cloaked and bonneted against the weather, remained beautiful and queenlike.

"Thank you," said the Corinthian, tossing him sixpence. "See that the horse is well watered and fed."

The man touched his bare wet head with his forefinger when, after springing out of the chaise, the Corinthian helped Lydia to alight. At his touch on her forearm, she shivered, and the Corinthian wondered whether that was because of the cold as she glanced furtively up and down the road with its bordering of plaster houses amidst the trees; and he saw her lick her lips and heard her sigh. Was it the cold, he wondered, or memories of her youth in Suffolk that made her shiver? Or was it because this was the village in which Corder had lived?

The thought angered him and he turned away to hurry into the warm parlour; and he heard her hurry after him, squelching in her thin shoes through the wet, plainly terrified lest he order a double bed. The Corinthian grinned with rage at the vanity of women.

"Could I have three separate bedrooms?" he demanded loudly, striding into the bar.

Apart from a melancholy landlord, there were only two men there, both very old men, brooding over their half-empty pints of ale; and from under their thick brows they watched him with deliberate unconcern.

"*Two* rooms, please," panted Lydia, pushing in at his heels. Then when he turned with a grateful smile, she added superciliously: "One for my brother and one for myself and maid."

The landlord, who had been polishing an already polished pint-pot, turned slowly and looked them up and down. In that dim room there was silence of a kind to which neither the Corinthian nor Lydia were accustomed. Instead of landlords bowing in welcome, waiters running to brush invisible crumbs from tables, these people watched them with barely concealed suspicion.

"Any luggage?" asked the landlord.

"Of course," said the Corinthian. "The ostler is seeing to that. Good heavens, man, do you doubt if I can pay?" From his trouser-pocket he dragged a handful of gold, silver and copper. "Why! I could buy your public-house if I wanted it! Let's have your best bedrooms, please; and we're hungry. In an hour's time we would like supper."

Even with the coins winking at him, the landlord eyed him doubtfully, but at last mumbled: "Sir, we ain't used to gentlefolk coming here without warning. You must forgive our country manners. But if you and your lady——"

"My sister," growled the Corinthian.

"Your sister," said the landlord with a distant bow, "if you and your sister——"

"And her female servant."

"And her female servant would speak to my wife, she'll attend to your wants. The bar alone is my concern," he added bitterly, and turned his back on them.

"But where's your wife to be found?" asked the Corinthian.

The landlord did not turn. He nodded towards the back of the bar. "Don't ask me," he said. "I'm just a married man, that's all I am. Yell for Clara and she might listen to you. I don't count outside this bar. So just you go outside and yell for Clara, my lord."

The Corinthian went into the narrow passage that smelt of

cabbage and shouted for the landlady, not daring to call for Clara, and a barefooted slattern sidled in through the door at the back and opened her eyes at the sight of his fine coat.

"Your mistress, child," he said: "I wish to see her."

"You want to see her?" asked the girl, her mouth falling open. "You'd better find her then. Last time I saw her she was walloping Henry for plucking the fowls without putting 'em in hot water first. I ain't looking for her, sir: no, for nobody, I ain't."

"But we've come all the way from London," said the Corinthian, speaking slowly as though talking to a foreigner, "and we must have somewhere to sleep."

"O, beds!" said the girl. "You can have all the beds you want, so long as you behave clean and take off your boots. Missus don't mind whether you're married. You've only got to say that you are and her conscience's satisfied."

"Here is my sister," said the Corinthian, breathing heavily; but from force of habit he could not help noticing that, if only she would allow herself to be bathed, this little savage might prove an excellent substitute for a warming-pan. "And this is her maid, Nelly," he added. "I want a room to myself. They sleep together."

"O, law!" squawked the girl. "But the missus will be pleased! Them together and you by yourself!"

"That is our wish," said the Corinthian coldly.

The slattern smiled and rubbed her leg through the cloth. "Up here," she said, ogling him as she pressed by, pushing hard against him, to the stairs. "Don't know what the missus'll charge you, coming all the way from London, but being a gentleman, most like she'll leave it to your generosity."

Up the stairs, creaking, she trudged as though she had a dislocated hip, and on the floor above she opened a bedroom door.

"Take what room you like," she said. "We ain't got no other travellers."

"This'll do me," said the Corinthian, edging past her. "Will you see to my sister and her maid, please?"

To his surprise, the room was clean, although the bed had not been aired, the mattress being rolled up under the white curtains; but it did not have that sour smell of previous sleepers which made many inns offensive. The floor was swept and in the grate sticks and coal awaited kindling. And suddenly, being at last alone, he felt dispirited and wondered why he had undertaken this journey. What did it matter to him whether Corder were a rogue? He did not like the man and he would never be able to seduce his wife. In that moment of weariness, his spirit flagging, he saw the truth. He was a fool, a doubly damned fool, the pawn of a woman who was not so simple as she pretended. Mary Corder cared not a farthing for him, she was using him for her own ruthless ends that she might master her husband. Ay, Lydia, as always, had been right. It was Corder, Corder, continually Corder; both Lydia and Mary cared only for that four-eyed rat. He did not count. In their different ways, both women were using him in their passion for that bastard.

Exasperated, the Corinthian decided to wash his face and hands in the hope that cleanliness might refresh his soul with his body, only to find that the jug was empty. This seemed to him the inevitable end to such a journey after the dead-weight of travelling with two women who did not love him. He could not even wash the smuts of London and the mud of the journey from his skin. And he wondered why he had been such a fool as to come to Polstead. In Mary Corder's seductive presence the idea had offered a wonderful escape from boredom and he had pictured himself as the patron of country-bars and the god of country-wenches as clean as a poet's dream of a milkmaid. Instead, he had found suspicious drinkers and a servant as smutched as any London slavey. And in his heart, he hated the country; since boyhood he had hated it, for there was nothing to do in this empty green world except to get swine-drunk in dull company or to embrace some muddy wanton under a hedge.

"Hell," he growled, glaring through the window at the rain; yet, having come so far, he could not abandon the quest. Memory of Mary Corder was already blurred. Hers had now become a face confused with other women's faces; nevertheless the thought of her, the memory of her soft voice frilled with shrillness, and of her pale face with huge eyes, stirred him with the need for action. For what action?

He went to the window and stared into the roadway. Oak and plaster, oak and plaster, which he had hoped never to see again save occasionally in an old London street. Standing on high ground, the inn gave an excellent view of the village, and he could see the tall-spired church and the oaks of somebody's estate. Further from the village were little houses and sheds and barns on which, god- or bird-like, he could look. About everything there was a feeling of decay, of neglect, as though the village had been forgotten in this green pocket of the country while the nineteenth century rushed forward after wealth.

"Dead," he muttered, "dead. Nothing could happen here."

That even such a dandiprat as Corder should have wanted to leave this deathly place he understood, and he regretted the sentiment that had weakened him into accepting this mission. Had he been alone he would have driven immediately back to London; but Lydia being with him, pride forbade the retreat. Corder was just a johnny raw whose greatest sin in such a place could only have been the begetting of a bastard or two. In such a little village, everybody watching one another, true wickedness was impossible, he felt. But he had given his word to Mary Corder. What was to be unearthed, he would unearth: but how? And where to begin?

Having set out on the task, it was impossible to withdraw, and his investigations might start, he realized with a wince of dislike, through the servant-girl. The men about here would doubtless be suspicious of strangers, but the women would probably be dazzled by his well-cut coat and trousers. Therefore he had best rely on his manly charms; and he groaned, wondering how he might tactfully suggest that the girl first have a bath.

While he winced at the thought, the wench slammed open the door and stared at him.

"Got to make the bed," she muttered, with a toss of her bottom under the pink cotton skirt as she bent over the mattress to roll it down. "Mrs. Gordon'll be back soon and she'll tell you what she wants you to pay. Ain't for me to say. Or poor Mr. Gordon neither. You talk to her polite and she'll treat you like you was a gentleman. Married beneath her, she says; but don't all women?"

Over her shoulder she smirked at him, her matted brown curls falling to half-hide her face and making her appear perversely attractive. She had washed herself a little and, unfortunately, had added rouge to her already red cheeks, but her figure, he noticed, was firmly plump.

"What is your name, child?" he asked.

She giggled, banging the feathers in the mattress. "Lucy, sir," she said.

"Why," said he, "that was the name of my first love! And she was very like you, Lucy."

"Now, now, sir," she smirked, "I may be only a country girl but I'm fly to gentlemen. I've had my own experiences, although I'm a good girl for all that; so don't you think otherwise."

"Of course, I never would!" said the Corinthian, forcing himself to go to her and lift the greasy curls that he might kiss the nape of her neck. "My love," he whispered, "you're wasting time in making that bed; a princess in disguise like you: your task should be a different one. . . . Here, pretty." On to the crumpled sheets he tossed the half-sovereign he had ready in his hand. "Pick that up," he whispered, "if you dare."

She looked at him; she looked at the gold; and he felt her tremble under his hands. Then she licked her lips.

"This is a new game," she giggled.

"New?" he laughed.

"I mean no gentleman . . . I mean . . . I don't know. . . ." With open mouth she turned to smile at him knowingly. "I think I can trust you," she said, and wriggled under his caresses.

"Of course you can trust me," he said, kissing her. "Take it in your teeth and slip it under your tongue."

"That'd be silly. . . . " She stretched forward towards the coin, giggling and looking backwards at him, then she squeaked mild protests when he lifted her off her feet. "Oh, sir," she gasped, "there's Mrs. Gordon coming and the door's not locked, and she's a tartar, I tell you."

But the Corinthian was not one to be foiled in so naïve a fashion. He took the half-sovereign before she could seize it; after which, he locked the door. . . .

The money was not wasted. Once her lips were opened, Lucy gabbled as though she could never stop. With eyes closed, the Corinthian lay and listened, perfunctorily caressing her when she fell silent. On and on and on she talked—about her mistress's meanness and baseless suspicions; and about her master's humiliating cowardice in never answering his wife back; and the Corinthian did not interrupt, hoping that amidst the chatter might emerge something about Corder. She mentioned Mrs. Corder, and he stiffened, but she merely said that the woman was an old bitch who deserved what she'd got.

He asked why she was a bitch and what it was that she had got. "Why," said Lucy with the scorn of the inhabitant towards a stranger who does not know the village-tattle, "ain't she lost her husband and children? There was Tom died, him that got Maria Marten in the family way, poor bitch, for you can't bring affiliation orders against the dead or make 'em marry you. John and Tom both died of the consumption."

"Wasn't there another brother, William?" he asked casually, fondling her to lull suspicion.

"You mean Foxy? Ay, there was Foxy Bill, too. But he's gone."

"Gone? Where?" he asked.

He felt her shrug against him, her shoulder pushing up his chin.

"God knows," she said, "or the devil, more like. He was a one, he was, with his squint-eyes and all his promises of what he'd do for a girl if she were a fool. No fear, says I to him, my name ain't Maria. For he was no real gentleman. 'Tis said he robbed Maria. Ay, after all she'd done for him, carrying his pup and all! For it was no use her pretending otherwise. She might fool the men but not me. I knew at once, for all she might wear the stiffest busks to keep it from showing. She was far gone, and serve her right, the airs she gave herself with her new bonnets and laces because of the bastard some London cove gave her and was fool enough to pay her for her pleasure afterwards. She was a bad lot, she was."

"Was?" repeated the Corinthian. "Where is she now?"

She shrugged and yawned. "God knows," she said, "but I don't suppose He cares. Went off with Foxy, so they said, but no one believed that. That's only her father trying to pretend she's become an honest woman. Foxy was too fly to marry her."

"And Foxy—where's he?"

"He's gone, too, went after the harvest. He's been blamed for taking her away, but I can't see how. She'd gone some time before him, but it's only old Marten's talk, trying to cover her shame. Doesn't like to think his darling daughter's a sixpenny bit on the corner. She never was much, for all her ladyish ways and the silly voice she put on because she could read a book. I don't need books to tell me what to do and the parish has never had to worry about my goings-on." She caught her breath and hurriedly added: "Please God."

"She was Corder's wench?" he asked, to bring her back to the subject.

"One of 'em," grunted Lucy. "You can never trust a fellow what don't drink. I've stood by that all my life and no one can say a thing about me. There's something wrong with them that don't drink. But it was no good telling that to Maria or the other fools. They thought they'd trip him into marriage but he weren't called Foxy for nothing. Got what he wanted, he did, and then off he danced. He was a nasty fellow and I hope he's no friend of yours."

"Certainly not," said the Corinthian, "but you make me interested. Tell me more about him."

She told him a great deal more, but nothing that explained why Corder should carry pistols and live in fear. He had once robbed his father, he learned, and had been suspected of having been a partner in a robbery committed by one Beauty Smith shortly to be transported, and he had seduced any wench simple enough to listen to his lies. Beyond these peccadilloes, the Corinthian discovered nothing. That Lucy disliked him was evident, but that was possibly because Corder had preferred this Maria Marten to her. One could never take women's rancours seriously, for they were usually too personal. Disappointed and annoyed that he had wasted time on a drab unworthy of his skill, he was relieved when he heard a woman shrieking her name.

"Coming, ma'am," squealed Lucy, bounding off the bed. As she had not taken off shoes and stockings and wore no stays, she had only to drag her gown over her tousled head to be ready to face her mistress, and this took less than a minute.

"See you tonight, love," she hissed and turned the key in the door. He heard her bawling in the passage: "I'm coming, I'm coming," and he sighed and closed his eyes and wished that he could sleep.

Sleep, however, he could not, and action was preferable to remaining with his thoughts. Lucy had told him nothing of value, nothing that he had not already suspected. Corder was a thief and a lecher, yet apparently he had not been caught at any crime. In this

S.O.T.R.B.—K

inn Lucy would have heard all the local gossip, and if this were the extent of her knowledge, it seemed unlikely that he, a stranger, could unearth anything further.

Having journeyed so far, however, he must, he felt, continue. Unfortunately, having lived long in London, he had lost the art of talking at his ease with simple folk, as he realized after he had strolled into the bar and ordered a brandy and soda. The two old men still sat at the table, one tall and hollow-eyed, the other small and crouching as though some heavy weight pressed his head forward; without apparent interest they watched him until he asked whether they would like a drink. Instantly, their pots were emptied and passed to the landlord to be replenished, but, except to wish him good health, neither man spoke.

"Pretty little village you have," he ventured at last.

"Ay," said the tall man.

"Very quiet though, I suppose. Nothing much happens round here?"

"Tom Silver's daughter's in the family way again," said the small man after long thought, "and she don't know who to blame this time. Although that ain't unusual."

"Bill Webb's old woman fell down the well and some folk say he pushed her," chuckled the tall man. "Oh, there's rare doings in Polstead, mister. She thought it was the devil got her at last and now she stops at home without him having to lock her hair in the chest when he goes out."

"'Tain't so quiet as you might think," said the other. "Is it, landlord?"

"Quiet enough," growled Mr. Gordon, leaning both fat arms wearily on the bar. "Nothing much does happen here. Girls in the family way, wives falling down wells. That ain't Life. That goes on everywhere. You're right, my lord, this is a dead-end of a hole and trade's bad; but we've got the cherry-fair coming in a few months. You'll be staying for that, sir, won't you?"

"I don't know," sighed the Corinthian. "I really have no plans. My sister and I grew weary of London and thought we'd see rural England. A fellow we met by chance one night suggested Polstead, fellow called Corder. Do you know him?"

"Know him?" rumbled the landlord. "Old Foxy? He was never the one to come here often, 'cept during cherry-fair when the gipsy girls might push in to warm their insides with a dram. He was too mean to drink, he was."

"Too cunning," said the tall man. "I've heard him say many a time a man's a fool to fuddle his wits for he never knows what he's saying until he's laughed at in the morning; and many a fool's been hanged for that, so he says. I don't know if he were right; I ain't never had enough."

The Corinthian took the hint and had their pots refilled. "I only met him casually," he murmured. "Can't say I really know the fellow. What's that you called him? Foxy?"

"Ay, Foxy," said the tall man, "and foxy as a snake he was. Never could trust him one minute from another. When he weren't pinching the lassies he was up to some other silly trick. Never doubted he was with Beauty Smith the night Harry's pig was stole. Why, Constable Ayres himself says to me that if he'd had a warrant he'd have nabbed him for it, and Beauty used to say that he'd be damned if old Foxy wouldn't get himself hanged some day."

"Stole from his old father, he did," piped the small man. "Stole his dad's pigs and said they was his own. And when old man Corder seen his pigs in Baalham's sties, he claims 'em as his property. 'That they ain't,' says Baalham. 'Yes, by God, they are,' says old Corder. Almost come to blows over it they did afore Baalham lets on that he'd bought 'em off young Bill. Old Corder had to pay after that."

"Always was paying for Foxy's doings. If it weren't him, it were Mrs. Corder who, in the daft way some mother's will, liked him best of all her children 'cause he was bad. There was nothing they could do with the boy. Old Corder thought to ship him overseas and got him a place aboard an Indiaman, but when he took Bill to London, never a captain would sign him on 'cause of his eyes. So back he comes to Polstead, bold as brass, to get poor Maria Marten into trouble again."

"Her!" said the small man, snorting. "As hot a piece of dirty meat as ever disgraced the name of daughter. I said to the constable many a time, I said, 'Look here, Mr. Baalham,' I said, 'why don't you take her up for having all them bastards; she's a wicked example to every silly little bitch in the village,' says I, 'and a constant temptation to the men.' But it couldn't be done, he tells me, not unless she asked for parish relief; and she did too well out of her naughtiness to need ever do that. There was the London gentleman what sent money every quarter to feed his baby with."

" 'Twas said that Foxy stole some of the money, copying Maria's name at the post-office, and the gentleman never sent no more afterwards."

"He'd do anything, would Foxy," grumbled the other. "Well named he was. Never trust a man what don't drink and a woman what does. There's always something wrong with both of 'em. Did he have a youngish woman with him when you saw him, sir? A brazen hussy with ribbons, a fat chin, a wen on her neck and a nose that curved a bit at the end. Did her hair in curls, browny hair, it was."

"He had no lady with him," said the Corinthian.

"Wouldn't expect him to have," grunted the little man. "But he'd have some female hanging on his arm, I dare say. And if it weren't Maria, it'd be another like her. They ain't so difficult to find, if a man ain't particular."

"Why? Did Maria go off with him?"

"Ay, that she did; or so her dad tells us. But what's a man to believe? She was a fly-by-night; and fly she does with old Foxy; then Foxy comes back and says she's well and happy and with friends. But do you know what I think?" He raised his heavy brows and nodded fiercely. "She's gone and left him. That's what I think. Used him to take her to London, likely enough, where a girl what ain't got no morals can get paid for doing what she likes best, and I'd not be surprised if she don't come back some day with ribbons and silks and powders, showing herself off in her sins and flaunting her wicked wealth and tempting other silly bitches to go and get ruined alongside her. That's what I'm thinking."

"Likely enough," assented his comrade, "but even Londoners wouldn't be such fools as to pay for what they can get for nothing. Ain't there no other females in London? And although Maria were a plump partridge, she weren't so attractive, 'cept that she was easy game, of course. And I never could abide that wen on her neck. Remember my grandma saying that things like them were certain signs of a witch, and the only way to find out was to stick a needle in, deep, and if it drawed no blood she was a witch for sure. I never had no chance to get close to Maria with a needle, but I often itched to try."

"You and your needle," chuckled the other. "It was something else you was itching to use, only those days have gone for the likes of us. Can't say a wen or two ever put me off when I liked a young woman. And she was a saucy minx with a rolling eye, and for all the bastards she dropped, she kept her figure wonderful well."

"Why!" said the Corinthian. "How many bastards had she?"

"Three," said the tall man, "to our knowledge. One by Foxy's brother, Tom, him that's dead, poor fellow, of a consumption. One by this Mr. Matthews what lives in London. And one by Foxy himself. Tom's baby didn't live long. Lived only a few weeks, if I remember right. Then she had the one by Mr. Matthews which is living to this day in her dad's house; young Thomas Henry he's called; and then the one by Foxy which died. O, she ain't wasted her time, I'm telling you. They say she had two other bastards. Slipped off on the quiet to hide her shame, then came back to make some more of 'em. And she not twenty-five or -six when last I seen her."

"A most energetic lass," smiled the Corinthian.

"That she was," nodded the small man. "Scarce a young villain in Polstead what hasn't used her. You was stumbling over her, even in foul weather, for she'd be sneaking off to a barn or some such place. Kept the lads from drinking, though; all their pennies went into her placket and it was bad for trade here."

"Trade," said the gloomy innkeeper, "is always bad here, 'cept in cherry-fair time."

"Better though now she's gone," chirruped the tall man. "None of the other wenches be as shameless as her, whatever they might like to be doing. And once they get a taste for sin there's no stopping 'em with salt on their tails. Father, mother, husband, brother, nay, the very babe at her breast, won't keep a woman at home when she itches. I've seen too much of it, children left dirty and starved, homes broken, husbands on the drunk, and all because a female's been cooking more than her dinner. Weren't old Mother Eve a woman? And look at what's become of us because of her."

"Ay," nodded the thin one, absently tapping his empty pot on the table, "'tis a sinful world, thanks to the women in it."

The Corinthian had the pots refilled, but he was weary of this chatter about a girl with the morals of a sparrow. And he felt tired after the bumpitty journey and the fatiguing embrace of Lucy.

This Maria Marten was probably like Lucy, coarse, envious and stupid, lewd and calculating, a whore without the experience or the ability to make a living at the game. He had heard sufficient of her gallivantings, he felt; besides, his search lay into Corder's past, not into hers.

Bidding the landlord a curt good-bye, he strolled into the yard to see whether his horse had been fed and rubbed down. The moon was rising over the treetops, casting heavy shadows about the white cottages, and he groaned at the thought that on a chivalrous impulse he had been led to undertake this mission which, it seemed, would lead nowhere beyond Maria Marten's bed. In a village like this, everything a man did was quickly tattled; and had there been a truly dangerous secret in Corder's past it would not long have remained a secret with so many gossips watching from behind windows, trees or hedges.

Tomorrow, he decided, he would speak to Lydia and suggest going back. No. Should he suggest it, she would be certain to insist on staying. He would have to wait for her to ask him; and he did not doubt that it wouldn't be long before she also craved the lights of London.

Chapter Twelve

OVER THE TEACUPS

A FURIOUS knocking at the door awoke the Corinthian in the morning. He blinked in the pale light, uncertain for the moment where he was, while the angry rat-a-tat continued. Beyond the curtains he saw the sunlight as a blur of gold; he saw the washing-stand, the table and chair and the faded carpet on the floor; and the unfamiliarity troubled him. Then suddenly he remembered. This wasn't Bond Street. This was the Cock Inn, Polstead, and that slovenly wench was banging for admittance.

Grumbling to himself, he crawled out of bed and unlocked the door, and as though she had been leaning against it, Lucy sprawled forward. Fortunately, she did not drop the jug, although the water flew out, and when the Corinthian sought to steady her, she knocked his hand violently away.

"What you frightened of?" she jeered. "Locking doors as though you'd something valuable to lose."

The Corinthian yawned and pushed forward his tasselled night-cap that he might scratch the back of his head. Unused to these early hours, he was not yet fully awake, and he felt cold in the nightgown, the floor like ice to his bare feet.

"Sorry," he mumbled, crawling back into bed, "force of habit, my love. Had too many drinks and forgot where I was. Always lock my door in London. Thieves about."

"Don't you apologize," said Lucy, poking out her lower lip. "I never knew it was locked till I tried it just now. Don't you go gammoning yourself that I come here last night, 'cause I didn't. I ain't that kind of a girl although you might have made a fool of me yesterday. Oh, you're a fine London gentleman, ain't you, to tell lies to poor country lassies! That's why Maria Marten was such a fool——"

"Hey," said he, his senses returning at sound of that name, "why was Maria Marten a fool?"

"You can find out," said she. "I was never the one to talk, and look what it did to Maria! 'Why,' says she, 'I could have old Foxy hanged, I could; and he knows it.' So she makes him marry her, the fool; men ain't worth marrying."

"How could she have had him hanged?" asked the Corinthian, now fully awake.

"You'd better ask her, if you can find the bitch," she grinned. "For I ain't got nothing more to say to a fellow like you who ain't no gentleman——"

Shrieks from downstairs for *Lucy*! robbed the Corinthian of further revelations. Back against the pillows he lay while the wench hurried out of the room, and he tried to sleep again, but couldn't. For the first time, he had heard of something mysterious in Corder's past, something sufficiently threatening to force him to marry, or at least to run off with, a girl he had apparently no longer liked. . . . And if he had married this Maria Marten he could not now be married to Mary Moore. That thought sang in his blood and he smiled when he opened his eyes again. Yes, Mary would be a free woman if this were the truth; and no matter how, in her religious enthusiasm, she might be prepared to forgive a knave, she could surely never forgive a bigamist who had seduced and made a public mockery of her with lies?

His first call must be on this Marten family. From what he had heard last night in the bar, the second Mrs. Marten had disliked Maria and therefore, possibly, Corder as well, while her husband was obviously a chucklehead. He must see Mrs. Marten alone if possible; and he grinned to think of Lydia in her bed nearby, plotting to frustrate his investigations. Being a woman, she would not have his sources of information. She could never have gone into the bar and talked to the yokels and, no matter how strong was her wish to help Corder, she would scarcely have slept with the groom to learn secrets. Being a man, after all, did have certain advantages.

Hours later, he crawled from bed and cursed because the water was cold and shaving painful. After dressing carefully, he strolled down to the bar to await dinner. Complacent he felt, although still tired, while he speculated on the various crimes Corder might have committed. Apparently, only Maria in the village knew about them, which suggested she might have been an accomplice; but an accomplice, unless she turned king's evidence, could be hanged with the criminal. The only possible hope of learning the truth was from Mrs. Marten, he felt, and he would visit her later. Meanwhile, Lydia was in bed; and that thought made him laugh.

While leaning against the bar and inwardly laughing, he saw through the window Nelly pass towards the front door, her face red as though she had been running or laughing, and one hand pulling up her flowered skirt to keep it from the mud. Behind her raced the ostler, and when Nelly skipped through the door, he stumbled as he tried to stop his speed. The Corinthian stiffened with disgust at the sight. He had warned Lydia not to bring that dissolute girl with them, and there she was already disgracing herself with country louts. He would, he told himself, speak seriously to the wench and have a talk with Lydia about such behaviour. One had a certain dignity to maintain, damn it, if one wanted to be respected . . . and a servant's behaviour reflected on the master.

His indignation remained throughout dinner which he ate alone, carving the boiled beef as though he were sawing into Nelly's rump. And after dinner, having consumed many gins and water during the morning, he dozed in his chair until disturbed by Lucy bouncing in, crashing open the door, to clear away the plates.

With a reproachful look, he slowly got up and staggered into the passage, yawning and stretching his arms. It was time, he supposed, to visit Mrs. Marten; and on enquiring the way from the landlord, he set out to find what he had been told was the last cottage in the village before reaching what they called the Red Barn. "Ain't much red left on it," the landlord grumbled, "most of it's peeled off. But you can't miss it."

About a mile beyond the church, the barn showed clearly enough with outhouses running from it to form a half-rectangle; and, roughly half the distance between church and barn, stood a small thatched cottage with oak-and-plaster walls. Beyond the hedge with its crumpled wooden gate, this cottage stood in a garden with cherry-trees in the orchard on one side breaking into a froth of buds.

Slowly, the Corinthian opened the gate, pondering how to begin the conversation, as he strolled along the path between the rose-bushes. He felt half-ashamed of his mission which, by raking up old scandals, might bring misery to this pretty little house's occupants. Unhappily he stood, hand raised to knock on the door under the porch, which was covered with a climbing rose, a ladder hooked overhead below the thatching. Then suddenly he stiffened and tiptoed to the tiny window, for he had heard a voice he recognized.

Before a bright fire in a small dark room, Lydia sat talking to a little woman whose back was towards him. Lydia! Then he remembered Nelly and the ostler. That had not merely been Nelly at amorous sport. Lydia had sent her amongst the inn servants to spy, and doubtless the ostler, or some other man, had told her tales similar to those which he had learned from Lucy. . . .

Furious at such a base trick, he knocked firmly on the door.

"Mrs. Marten?" he asked with his most winning smile, bowing and taking off his hat. "My sister, I believe, has already visited you. Would I be intruding to ask if I might also be your guest?"

"O, no, sir," said the woman, dipping into a low curtsey. "I'd be proud to have you both under my roof."

He had expected somebody old and bent, wrinkled by the sun and bowed from work, but Mrs. Marten looked comparatively young, scarcely more than thirty. She was small and, for a country-woman, dainty, her hands well cared for, her skin untanned, and her round blue eyes watched him with a child's simplicity, fearless yet inquisitive, and her manner, although respectful, made him feel that she was not in the least impressed by his city clothes and gentlemanly bearing. Indeed, there was even a suggestion of mockery in the faint smile on her unpainted mouth and in the way her nostrils curled to make the tiny nose more pointed.

"My love," said he, bowing in the raftered parlour to Lydia where she sat erect before the fire, face hidden in her bonnet, "I thought you might like me to call to escort you back to the 'Cock'."

"I've scarcely arrived," she drawled, not looking at him, "and unless Mrs. Marten is already weary of my company, I have no wish to leave."

"Indeed, ma'am, no," said Mrs. Marten, "you mustn't think of going yet. And, sir, would you kindly sit down while I brew the tea?"

"So you followed me here?" hissed Lydia in a low voice, darting at him a glance of hatred, after Mrs. Marten had glided into the kitchen.

"You do flatter yourself," he yawned, drawing forward his coat-tails before sitting on the chair beside her. "You're the last person I expected or hoped to find here. I suppose it was that slut Nelly who discovered this abode at the price of her long-lost maidenhead. I saw her with the ostler."

"I did not see you with that filthy slattern at the inn, but I was told about it." She shuddered and closed her painted eyelids. "Really, sir, there are times when you make me positively ill. Some of the dreadful creatures you've pawed in London I thought degrading enough, but this is the lowest. . . . Really, it is too much!"

He shook with rage, being unable to find a retort, but he resolved to be revenged on Nelly in some fashion. From the first he had been against bringing the girl. Now he realized why Lydia had been so persistent. Even before they had left London, she had determined to use her as a spy.

The return of Mrs. Marten saved him from further embarrassment, and he leaped up to help her set the tray on the table. With a slight bow, she thanked him and began to pour the tea. The woman was surprisingly young and graceful, he noted with approval, and she appeared to have come from a better class than her agricultural husband whom he had seen last night in the "Cock"; or was it that, being a woman, she sought for improvement and tried to make herself act like a lady that she might feel superior to her husband and her neighbours? On a shelf against a wall he noted a few tattered books, and glanced at the titles. *The Lady's Magazine, or Entertaining Companion for the Fair Sex*, an *Annual Register* or two, a well-thumbed pamphlet on the interpretation of dreams, and a few sentimental novels—surprising literature for a labourer's wife; but then he remembered having heard that Maria was able to read.

"You are a great reader, Mrs. Marten?" he asked pleasantly.

"I would be if I'd time for it, sir," she said. "But most of those books were Maria's. She was a fine scholar, sir; always reading, she was. She got the habit when she was young and was in service to the reverend gentleman at Layham; and after that, Mr. Marten has told me, there was no stopping her at the sight of any piece of print. I used to say to her father that it would bring her to no good, just putting grand ideas into her head; but he never was the one to

155

interfere, liking his comfort too much. And not being her mother, I couldn't say nothing, of course. . . . Sugar, ma'am?"

Lydia took the cup she offered and refused the sugar. The Corinthian took both sugar and the tea, surprised that so poor a family could afford these genteel luxuries. Then he sat down after Mrs. Marten had settled into the third chair in front of the fire. For a while they remained in silence, sipping cautiously at the hot drink; and of the three, Mrs. Marten seemed the most at ease. As though it were nothing unusual to have a lady and gentleman visit her in the early afternoon, she asked no questions, accepting their presence in her lowly cottage; while both the Corinthian and Lydia felt uncomfortable. He revealed his awkwardness by humming loudly to himself and smiling stupidly, sitting very upright; and Lydia, lounging gracefully in her chair, showed by the tapping of her foot that she was troubled. Loudly sounded the ticking of the clock on the wall and the Corinthian found himself seeking tag-ends of talk he might produce.

Then, after clearing his throat, suddenly, almost desperately, he spoke. "I called, as I was about to tell you, ma'am," he said, "because a friend asked me to do so to enquire after you and your family's health.

"A friend?" said she, raising her colourless brows.

"A Mr. William Corder, ma'am."

The cup rattled on its saucer as Mrs. Marten for the first time betrayed emotion. The round eyes gave a blink—was it fear, anger, or merely surprise?—and faint colour darkened her cheeks; yet when she spoke, she spoke quietly, and gently smiled.

"It was very kind of him to remember us," she said; "very kind indeed. Did he mention his wife?"

"You mean the late Miss Moore?" asked the Corinthian, eyeing her shrewdly.

Now there was no doubting her agitation. Hurriedly she placed cup and saucer on the floor beside her that their tinkling might not betray her feelings, then she dabbed at her mouth with the back of her hand, saying in a toneless voice:

"Miss Moore? Who is Miss Moore? I am afraid we have not met."

"She's a school-mistress, ma'am, with a small fortune."

"A very charming lady—I am told," added Lydia.

"O," said Mrs. Marten, pursing her lips together in a pout of disapproval.

"Yes," said Lydia, "quite a profitable marriage, I believe, and so much love on both sides! It does one's heart good, does it not, Mrs. Marten, to see young couples entering bliss so trustfully together? They adore one another in a most romantic fashion. Indeed, they go beyond good taste, and keep so much to themselves that they deprive their friends of their company. Rather selfish . . . yet, I suppose, understandable when young people are so very much in love."

"I'm pleased to hear it," said Mrs. Marten primly, dabbing again at her mouth, "although I confess to being rather surprised. It would be foolish for me to pretend that Mr. Marten and I did not expect Mr. Corder to marry Mr. Marten's eldest daughter, Maria. You've probably heard the gossip. They left the village together many months ago."

"And where's Maria?"

Mrs. Marten raised her hands in a supplicating, helpless gesture. "That is all I know," she said. "She left with Mr. Corder."

Casually though she spoke, there was anger quivering in her voice. This revelation of Corder's betrayal of Maria had evidently come as a cruel surprise, cleverly though she strove to conceal it. Her rosebud mouth tightened and showed creases, while her hands worked together in her lap; yet her blue eyes stayed blank.

Lydia becoming silent and lying back in her chair with eyes half-closed, the Corinthian considered that this was his opportunity to talk. He did so, exerting all his charm, delighted at the exposure of Corder and hoping to unearth more of his callousness to Lydia's discomfiture. He leaned towards Mrs. Marten in the firelight, smiling encouragingly, enlarging his eyes in their lids, and speaking in a soft cajoling voice.

"You've not heard from your step-daughter lately?" he asked.

"O, we had letters: yes; but they weren't in her hand. Bill— Mr. Corder said that she'd a gathering at the back of her hand and couldn't hold a pen. He said that they were very happy. And that's all I know."

She knew more. That was evident in the precise way in which she spoke, carefully choosing each word, and in the twisting of her narrow shoulders and the deliberately dull stare of her eyes.

"You've not seen him since?" persisted the Corinthian.

"O, yes, he came back," said Mrs. Marten in a lifeless voice. "Most surprised I was to meet him in the village. He said he'd found her a place in Ipswich with a Miss Rowland, the sister of some old school-fellow of his. He told me not to worry about her. He'd changed a cheque for twenty pounds, he told my husband, and he'd given her the money. 'I treat her like a queen,' he said. He said he had a licence to marry and had to go with it to London, which meant, he said, they couldn't wed for a month or six weeks."

"He was lying; he always was a liar; that's why they called him Foxy," said a soft voice in the gloom, and they turned to see a young girl with bright grey eyes gleaming from the shadow of a pink bonnet watching them. Slowly she walked into the firelight, and the Corinthian, a connoisseur in femininity, noticed that under the faded cotton frock she had a noble figure. He sat erect and smiled at her.

"This is my step-daughter, Maria's young sister," said Mrs. Marten. "She has the same name as myself, Ann, which makes for confusion at times. My dear Ann, this is Mr. Barsett and his lady-sister, Mrs. Atherton. And you should not say such thoughtless things about other people."

"I said 'em and I meant 'em," said Ann, swinging from side to side with her thighs squeezed together. "And I told Maria often enough; but she'd not listen. What was he doing, carrying her green umbrella at his brother's funeral?"

"He explained that, my dear," said Mrs. Marten gently. "He said that Maria had made him take it on account of the weather."

"No, he didn't!" chuckled the girl viciously, swinging her hips and pretending she wasn't looking at the Corinthian. "That's what he said afterwards. You know! At first he said Deborah Pryke had left it behind and he was going to give it back to her. It was only the next day that he said he knew it was Maria's. Now, why did he say that? And why haven't we heard from Maria, I'd like to know?"

"She has a wen on her hand and can't write."

Young Ann sniffed, shuffling her hips. "I never did trust that four-eyes," she said. "Maria got what she wanted, but she was always a fool and didn't know when to stop having sport, and I bet he's left her in such a horrid place she's ashamed to tell the truth. You know that's right."

"I know nothing of the kind," gasped Mrs. Marten haughtily, "although I must confess that I'm most surprised that Maria hasn't written. Her poor father is deeply grieved and when I see Mr. Corder again I shall speak to him very seriously about it. I will, indeed."

Above Mrs. Marten's disapproving head, the girl wrinkled her attractive snub-nose. "O, yes," she jeered, "you'll speak sharply to him *if* you see him again, I don't think!" She sniggered. "I've heard you speaking sharply to Foxy Corder before now," she said, and stalked, on stiffly disapproving legs, out of the door.

"Young girls these days have no respect for their elders," fluttered Mrs. Marten, fanning herself briskly with her hand. "I really don't believe that Ann cares what might have happened to her unfortunate sister, and her poor father is really most distressed. Most distressed, indeed. Not a word from her after all these months, just as though she were dead and murdered. And there's little Thomas Henry to look after. A dear boy, but such an enormous appetite. Mr. Matthews—and I can't say that I can condemn him for it—has refused to continue supporting him. There was . . . Well, we'll not talk of that; all's forgotten and forgiven; but it was his noble nature that restrained him from starting proceedings that might have turned very serious."

"You mean," said the Corinthian, "when Corder stole the money intended for the child?"

"So you've heard of that!" she sighed. "There's no hiding anything in a little place like Polstead. Very foolishly and thoughtlessly, William took the five pounds, going to Colchester and signing for them. Naturally, Mr. Matthews was most annoyed when Maria asked why the money hadn't arrived. We had the post-mistress herself come over here to ask what had happened to it, and William got Maria to say that she'd been mistaken and that she had had the money. She never got any more. Mr. Matthews was furious, and it's difficult to blame him really. That was so like William! He was never one to think of the future. . . . But now you say he's married."

"To a Miss Moore of Holborn," said the Corinthian.

"And he wrote to tell us he'd married Maria!" said she, taking a deep breath. "O, he is a villain!" she cried suddenly, striking the arms of her chair. "A very villain and a liar!"

As though ashamed of her outburst, she sat back, her eyes half-closed. "Forgive a mother's feelings," she murmured, "for dear Maria was like my own daughter to me, although, of course, I'm far too young ever to have been her mother."

"No word's been heard from her?" asked Lydia suddenly.

"No word," said Mrs. Marten faintly, "except in William's hand."

The Corinthian regretted that Lydia was present. Her coldly suspicious nature rejected sentiment, and he felt that Mrs. Marten, grieving for the bad behaviour of her romp of a step-daughter, needed consoling. Although no lady, there was a certain refinement about her which suggested a noble soul and appealed to his pity. Besides, it would have been charitable to have acted gallantly to a woman hidden in this dull corner of the world with only dreams on which to feed her vanity. It was plain to be seen that she had been the mother of more than one child, but the thought of a bucolic mother, the helpless breeding-machine of some crude yokel, appealed to him to pity her. All women, he thought, deserved some happy memories of love to light them through dull nights with their husbands. Only Lydia, watching with those sharp, cruel eyes, kept him in his chair; and he hated Lydia, he told himself.

"You have been most kind, Mrs. Marten," he said, rising to his feet, "to have wasted so much time talking about a mutual friend, but the hour grows late."

"Wasted?" said she. "Nay, sir, it has been a pleasure to talk with learned folk for a time. Whenever you be passing, pray call in."

He took her hand and kissed it, lingering over the crusty skin while giving her a languishing glance to keep her warm after he had gone. Compared with his, Lydia's farewells were perfunctory. She bowed faintly, then, shrugging on her heavy blue cloak, touched Mrs. Marten's fingertips with hers, and slouched out of the house.

"We will meet again, I pray?" said the Corinthian.

"I hope so, sir," curtseyed Mrs. Marten.

Not until he and Lydia had walked some distance along the muddy road did the Corinthian speak. Then, hitting a stone with the ferrule of his stick, he said pleasantly:

"A delightfully unspoiled rustic creature! How refreshing it is to leave predatory Londoners and be able to talk soul to soul with a simple person! I have really enjoyed this afternoon."

Lydia snorted, not condescending to answer while worrying whether this rocky road would tear her satin shoes.

"It is strange," he continued, determined to be friendly, "that Corder should have deserted these pastoral surroundings for the city. Maria Marten, it would appear, was not particularly faithful, and why should he run away with her? I think we can safely set aside the idea of marriage. That was mere talk to gammon her father. Doubtless they plotted it together, for a girl can scarcely announce to her family that she intends to earn her living on the streets; and to keep her father's mind at rest, that lie was told. Having conducted her probably to some brothel, Corder leaves her to her chosen profession for which she seems to have had a born aptitude. I think we can accept all that."

"You may accept what you like," said Lydia, watching her feet and peering ahead for stones.

"Of course, I feel sorry for the father," continued the Corinthian. "But it's the fate of all fathers to be lied to, particularly by their daughters who have much to lie about. And that dear, poor Mrs. Marten! Obviously married far beneath her. And still attractive in a coarse fashion. I don't suppose she can be much older than her naughty step-daughter. I must confess I was really sorry for the woman."

"Sorry for her!" cried Lydia, turning to glare into his eyes. "That bitch! Pah," she almost spat, "men are such fools! I don't know why we women bother with them! Sorry for *her*!"

"Yes," said the Corinthian, very dignified, "I was sorry for her."

"You make me tired of life," she groaned. "Couldn't you see that she'd have liked to have killed us both?"

"Not *me*!"

"Both of us. When we told her he was married, were you blind? I'll say this for the bitch: I respect the way she kept her composure. O, she's a clever one! Don't ever tell me again that country folk are fools."

"What the devil do you mean?"

"Didn't you see it? That girl, Ann, her step-daughter, made it plain enough: she wasn't fooled. O, for God Almighty's sake—" She held her side while she laughed and grimaced at him like a madwoman. "For God Almighty's sake," she cried, "the woman's in love with him, you fool!"

Chapter Thirteen

THE HEART OF EVIL

THAT night the Corinthian again locked his door and when in the morning Lucy's fierce banging woke him up, he crawled from bed, turned the key in the lock and crawled back to bed, digging himself under the blankets and taking no heed of her grumbling. The wench no longer had any value to him. All that she knew about Corder, he had learned, he was certain; and after Lydia's startling assertion, his interest now lay solely in Mrs. Marten. At first he had dismissed Lydia's remark as being the outcome of natural jealousy—for Mrs. Marten, although indisputably the mother of three children, was yet youngish and attractive in her stays—towards a woman whom he had shown admiration; then he had begun to wonder whether it might not have had some truth in it. Mrs. Marten had plainly kept a restraint on her tongue while pretending an indifferent air, and her step-daughter had treated her with contempt and had hinted that her relationship with Corder had been more than friendly. Women with that appearance of stupidity were sometimes, as he had learned to his cost, more artful than the brazen kind. Under an assumption of near-idiocy they concealed cunning, vindictiveness and, often, murderous anger. Yet he found it difficult to believe that prim Mrs. Marten was not a good woman. Knowing her own sex best, Lydia would naturally conclude the worst. Being a man, he was more chivalrous.

Nevertheless the doubt remained. It was not often that he had found Lydia mistaken, particularly about other women, and she had spoken with conviction. Mrs. Marten, she had said, was in love with William Corder. An extraordinary error of judgment, to the Corinthian's thinking; but then, both a woman of the world like Lydia and a shy little mouse like Mary Moore also loved that cross-eyed dandiprat. Therefore it was impossible to dismiss the idea, greatly though it outraged him. Besides, if Mrs. Marten was in love with the rogue, she might prove useful. "Hell hath no fury like a woman scorned," he recollected having read somewhere; and Corder had certainly scorned her, running off with her step-daughter and marrying a third woman.

Carefully did he dress and, after a lonely breakfast served by a snorting Lucy, he strolled down to the Marten cottage. On this second visit he was not fortunate enough to find Mrs. Marten without her family. The pretty step-daughter, Ann, he regretted to note, was absent, but the cottage seemed crowded with small children in various conditions of nudity and bad temper. The uproar was beyond his bearing, although he managed a ghastly smile, and he would have withdrawn had not Mrs. Marten, without haste or embarrassment rearranging her dress to tuck in her breast, placed the baby in its cot and suggested that he might walk with her in the orchard.

The day was cold but the scent of the grass and young blossoms was invigorating, and the Corinthian took deep breaths, feeling himself a man again in this green world with a pleasant, smiling little woman walking step for step beside him.

"This," said he, "is a good life. The thought of going back to London sickens me."

"A good life?" said she without bitterness. "For a man, perhaps. You have seen my children. They give me little peace. Not that I am complaining. When I married Mr. Marten I knew that he was a widower considerably older than myself and that I must be mother to his first wife's offspring; and I also knew, of course, that, once married, it would be my duty to add to their number. Go forth, saith the Lord, and multiply. But there are times . . . O, one grows weary. Yesterday you were more fortunate. My sister took them into the garden when Mrs. Atherton called. Today is, alas, too cold to send them here. So we, in our turn, are driven out."

"Yet," said he, sighing, "what more can life offer the human heart than these green fields, your humble cot and those dear pledges of affection at your knees? Mr. Marten is indeed a lucky man. I envy him; with all my heart, I envy him. . . . But I've not come to talk about myself: a dry subject, I assure you, Mrs. Marten, but I confess to an inexcusable curiosity. Call it, if you will, an impudent curiosity. But since meeting Mr. Corder I've grown mightily curious about him; my sister, in particular, yearns to know

163

something of his history. I was wondering if you might be good enough to help satisfy that curiosity."

"In what way?" she asked casually. "What does your sister want to know?"

"I can't really tell. The man's such an odd fellow. For example, there's this hurried marriage with Miss Moore after he'd run off with your step-daughter."

She laughed without merriment. "Shed no tears for my step-daughter," she said. "Maria was well able to look after herself, and if she's met with disaster . . . well, I don't doubt it was her fault. If you want me to speak plainly, sir, I'd say that Bill Corder, rather than Maria, was the victim in that matter. He didn't want to marry her. Nor, to be honest, did she want to marry him. But time was passing, and girls past twenty—Maria was twenty-six or -seven when last I saw her—grow frightened when they look in the glass. No, Bill was no enthusiastic wooer, and she was weary of him. Besides, she was frightened. There was an order sworn against her. She was to be taken up by the parish because of her children born out of wedlock."

"That, I have been told," said the Corinthian, "was untrue."

"True or untrue, it scared her to a jelly. Bill told her about it. That's all I know." Lightly she shrugged, not looking at him but staring at the hem of her gown wet from the grass. "And he made a great to-do about it," she said, "until he had Maria too afraid to poke her nose outside the door. That was why there was so much secrecy about her going."

"What secrecy?"

For a while she did not answer. Ringleted head down, she walked as though thinking deeply, her skirt dragging wetly behind her. Then suddenly she looked up and laid her hand on his arm and her great expressionless blue eyes seemed as innocent as a child's.

"Yes," she said, taking a deep breath, "you have an honest face and I can trust you. The moment I saw you yesterday I knew that you would be my friend and that I could talk to you as to no one else. Have you noticed, sir, that one can often be more open with strangers than with those one knows intimately—not that I consider you a stranger, of course, but I feel as if . . . as if we'd known each other many years and you were an old friend of the family." Those round candid eyes watched his with such trust that, scarcely aware of what he did, he leaned forward and kissed the worn fingers resting on his arm.

"Ma'am," said he with a catch in his voice, "you can trust me until death."

"I pray it doesn't come to that," said she, and gave a faint titter, without haste withdrawing her hand while continuing to walk under the young cherry-blossom, he keeping in step at her side.

When she did not speak again, the Corinthian began to grow exasperated. She had aroused his interest by promising to tell the truth, and now she lapsed into baffling silence. A feminine trick, doubtless, to keep him in a fever that she might enjoy a woman's power, having a man to dangle in suspense. When he glanced down at her, however, and saw how childlike was the expression in her blue eyes, how soft the pouting rougeless lips, and how smooth the brow and healthily reddened cheeks, he was ashamed of his suspicions. So long had he sojourned amongst artful harlots that he had begun to mistrust all women, and London now was far behind him with its fogs and misery and crime. This was the well-washed countryside, the grass a glittering green after rain, the cherry-blossoms pink and delicately shaped, distilling a pellucid glow on Mrs. Marten's cheeks and chestnut curls; and the sky was of God's blue of innocence with little puffs of clouds. He must put behind him the dark world in which he had lived too long and try to feel young again, trusting and trustworthy, in this snakeless Eden with a good woman at his side.

Memory of Lucy jarred his sentiment. But she was an exception, corrupted by life at an inn where unscrupulous city-travellers lodged. And thinking of her, he recalled how she had said that Maria Marten had pretended to have some secret with which she had menaced Corder.

"I've been told," he said, "that your step-daughter used to threaten Corder. That this proposed marriage was of her begetting."

"Maria was a wicked girl," said Mrs. Marten without emphasis. "She did threaten Bill Corder. Often I heard her at it, but what the secret was she held over him she never said. Probably it was nothing of any importance, just something that he didn't want his mother to hear. But a mother, Mr. Barsett, is the very last person to know what her children are doing; and I looked on Maria as my daughter, although there were very few years between us. No, I don't think she really wanted to marry Bill, but I've heard her say that she would marry him; and some girls are like that. They want the holy state of marriage more than they want a husband. Besides, she was afraid of being taken up because of her children."

"All this is most confusing," said the Corinthian. "Would I be requiring too great a favour if I asked you to tell me the tale from the beginning?"

Again was Mrs. Marten silent for some time until the Corinthian began to wonder whether she had heard what he had said. Then she sighed and looked up at him with those placid round eyes, her rosebud lips trembling a little.

"I said that I believe I can trust you, sir," she murmured wistfully, "and after all, there's nothing to conceal. The whole village knows, or suspects, much of what happened. I'll not be hurting the girl's reputation if I tell you of her doings, for doubtless you'll soon be leaving us again for the big city. There are a few things which, perhaps, are not known to everyone; yet her sister was here when she left, and, knowing Ann, I'm sure she's not kept her lips sealed. What is it you want to know?"

"Everything," said the Corinthian. "From Corder's first meeting with Maria."

"That would make a long tale," said she, pausing to lean on the ivy-covered hedge while staring at the hills fading into the sky. "Yet," she said, "I'll tell you what I can. When first my step-daughter and Bill became intimately connected I can't say for certain. She had been his brother's wench before him and he gave her a son who died. Then she was kept by a London gentleman who was connected with Polstead Hall. His son remains healthy and, God be praised, is still with us, although we find it no easy matter to feed our own babes, and now that no money's sent for his support I do wish Maria had been more careful. But you want to know about her and Bill. O, that went like her other foolishness until her sin couldn't be concealed any longer. She had the babe at Sudbury, and when she came back from her lying-in she brought it with her, an infant of about a month old; then it died. They took it away, Bill and her I mean, and had it buried at Sudbury; or so they said. But Maria was not always a truthful girl, Mr. Barsett, and I can only repeat to you what she and Bill told me. There were, of course, talks between them I chanced to overhear, for the house is small and full of echoes, and high words they had at times, she being vain and haughty and ever demanding; and he would silence her in the end by saying that the constable had a warrant to take her up on account of her children. That always made her afraid, because, of course, she wasn't married and allowed to have babies; and then she'd grow impatient and want to get out of Polstead. They made attempts to go, but always something seemed to stop them. Once he said she was to go to Ipswich early the next day and must sleep first at his mother's house; but back she came about three or four in the morning. They'd quarrelled, of course; they were always quarrelling."

The softness was beginning to fade out of her slurred Suffolk voice. Pressing against the hedge, heedless of the prickles under the ivy, tearing at the young leaves with quick fingers, she looked into the sky, but plainly did not see it, her thoughts being inward.

"Then one day," she said, "Bill came to the cottage in great haste and hurried upstairs. I was in the bedroom with Maria, making the beds, and he hurtled in on us in a great sweat, crying, 'I've come, Maria, make haste, for I'm going.' Had he not been an abstemious young man, I'd have thought him drunk, so excited did he look, yet anxious and bustling. Maria was never the one to be bustled. 'How can I go out at this time of the day,' says she in her impudent manner, 'without somebody seeing me?' He'd not listen to her objections. She'd been disappointed before, he says, several times, but this time she'd not be disappointed. While they talked, she making the bed and talking off-hand as though it were nothing important, I stayed quiet. 'You can go to the Red Barn,' says he, 'and wait for me there while I bring round the horse and gig.' That's the Red Barn," she added with a weak wave of her hand, and he saw in the distance the wooden structures grouped roughly in a half-rectangle—a tall thatched barn with sheds and outhouses thrusting from it on either side. In that soft light it looked the palest pink against the green. "Most of the paint's peeled off," she said. "It was red once."

Again she lapsed into one of her long silences while she stared towards the barn, a faint line creasing her forehead; and with a start of surprise he noticed that her eyes which he had considered expressionless had become bright, their corners wrinkling.

"In there," she said in a low, almost angry voice as if both exulting over and defying something, "in there they were to meet. He swore that there'd be no risk of her being seen by Baalham, the constable. None of his workmen were in the fields, he said, and the coast was clear. He'd brought some of his dead brother's clothes and these she could wear while he carried her dress to the barn. There he'd join her and she could change back again into a woman and he'd drive her to Ipswich and marry her. She didn't want to go at first. She was always like that, wanting too much; she wanted to get married and she wanted her freedom, too. Her love for Bill had long since died. Not that you could ever have called it love. They'd met and were lonely: that's all . . . but for the order against her and her wanting a husband to make her respectable, she'd have been glad to be quit of him. And I know he was bone-weary of her and her tantrums and complainings and greed and general foolishness; and then she had this threat she'd throw at him. . . . I don't know what that was, of course."

"Of course not," said the Corinthian uneasily. His first impression of her as a childlike creature was vanishing before the spite in her voice when she spoke of Maria; and he saw again that almost vicious look in mouth and eyes when she turned towards the pink barn. Perhaps Lydia had not been mistaken; perhaps she did love Corder. . . .

"He put her things in a brown Holland bag," she continued, smiling. "I helped her pack. There was a reticule wicker basket, a black velvet reticule, two pairs of black silk stockings—she was a dainty one—a black silk gown, and a black cambric skirt; and several other things of that sort. After we'd finished packing, he came and took the bag away; and I remember thinking this was not how true lovers should behave. Nothing but nasty words and sulky looks, and never a kiss. Then after he'd gone, Maria dressed herself in the man's brown coat, striped waistcoat and blue trousers belonging to his dead brother which he'd brought. They were too big for her, but that didn't matter because under them she wore her flannel petticoat, a pair of white stays, an Irish linen chemise which she'd made for herself, and a green-and-red handkerchief in which to hide her face. I helped her into the things and I remember that the day before she'd put an ashen busk into her stays instead of the bone one that it might be firmer and hold her figure in more tight. She looked a comical sight, I can tell you." Mrs. Marten giggled. "Fat as a ball with all those clothes on, and on her feet, she was that vain, she wore her shoes of Denmark satin what had leather foreparts, and to see 'em poking from under the trousers . . .! I had to stuff a handkerchief into my mouth for fear I'd laugh and ruin everything, for in her vanity she would keep two little combs in her hair—although the man's hat covered 'em when she went out—and there were earrings in her ears.

"I saw Bill coming back and slipped downstairs to speak to him." She licked her lips and her knuckles showed white as she gripped a branch of the hedge, while her eyes darkened. "Maria was upstairs when we talked, and he said that all would be well, that he'd marry her in Ipswich, and all that." Again she giggled. "Then Maria came downstairs," she continued, attempting to speak evenly, "and she asked me to go into the yard to spy if any-body was about who was likely to see her. The coast was clear, so she came out by that back door while he went out of the front. I watched her trot away, wobbling at the back as big girls do, the green cotton umbrella in one hand and the man's topper over her hair. He went up the road towards the Red Barn, across that field and fen, and they met at the gate near the road. I saw them meet, and they both got over the gate and walked together in Harefield. Since that moment I've neither seen nor heard from Maria."

"What! Not a word? Not a sign?"

"Not a word, nor sign, except the letters Bill wrote for her, saying she'd a sick hand. When they went, Bill had a gun with him and he told me in the kitchen that it was charged. What he should want a gun for I don't know, but he warned my little boy not to touch it. He seemed strange that day, in high spirits as though drunk, and he never drank but little. Yes, he was strange and very merry and full of pranks, and I . . ." She sighed, pressing against the ivy-covered hawthorn. "Later, my little boy, George," she said, "saw him coming from the Red Barn with a pickaxe on his shoulder. What should he want with a pickaxe, do you think? And a gun?" Smiling, she looked into the Corinthian's eyes, her own eyes gay and mocking. "When Maria went off," she said, watching him unblink-ingly, "she had a silk handkerchief with her with yellow flowers on it which belonged to her little boy. It was put over her chin, over the green striped one, to hide her face. When I saw Bill again I asked him for the child's handkerchief, as he'd promised to bring it back, and he told me it was lost. How? He wouldn't say. Then at his brother's funeral I saw him with Maria's umbrella. I knew it at once. It was of green cotton and had a crooked bone handle, or hook, and a button. And when I taxed him with it being hers, he said it was Deborah Pryke's—this before all the mourners with long ears—and I says to him: 'No, William,' I says, 'it's Maria's.' 'No, it's not,' says he, his eyes more crossed than ever, 'but it's one just like it,' he says. Later when I spoke of it again, he'd forgotten the lie, for he said he'd been to Ipswich and it had rained when he came away, and so Maria had lent it to him or he should have been dripping wet. He showed us all a gold ring, which he said was hers, and also a brace of pistols. It was very strange, don't you think, Mr. Barsett?"

While she talked she had edged closer to him, still smiling tightly, and her eyes seemed to him to expand, laughing at him; and he was amazed to think that at first he had believed her a simple creature. In almost every carefully chosen word she used there had lain a sinister implication, not stated, barely suggested, yet indubitably there; and, despite the cold, he sweated, while, over her narrow shoulders and small head, in the distance he saw the Red Barn, palely pink against the green. To that barn had Maria Marten walked that May day, stepping high in her dainty shoes, Falstaffian in her many garments, the earrings bobbing from her ears under the rim of the male tall-hat; then she had vanished. Since then, no one had seen her or heard from her, Corder always writing in her stead, saying that her hand was sore.

He felt that the day had darkened, although the sun still shone, turning the cherry-blossoms diaphanous, an odorous bright canopy for the bees sipping, like shining snow along the branches; and he shivered. This was something which even in the depths of his loathing for Corder he had not expected. The girl had become a nuisance to him, not only because he was amorously weary of her flesh, but because she had held some threat which might have damaged him. Had he therefore murdered her? . . . And was this woman, this dainty little country-woman with the well-washed face, his accomplice? She hinted much, she knew more than she told; and she had helped dress Maria for her flight; possibly she had forced the reluctant girl to go to that fatal meeting. She might well be lying and, for all he knew, she might have accompanied Maria to the Red Barn, holding her hand and drawing her through the door to where Bill Corder waited with his gun. Lydia was no fool and she had insisted that this creature loved the rogue. Did that mean that he had betrayed both women, lover of both and the murderer of one? The thought seemed impossible, a nightmare in the sunlight.

"She wasn't seen again?" he asked through dry lips.

Still smiling, still staring at him with that taunting gaze, slowly she shook her head.

"Mrs. Marten," he cried, "you've not told me everything. There's something more, something you're afraid to tell me. You loved him, too!"

He had intended to startle her, hoping to surprise her into an involuntary admission of guilt, but he had not expected the look of hatred she gave him, and the pursing of her mouth as though she were about to spit at him.

"I hate the man!" she cried. "I hate him, and I hated her!"

"Hated?" he said quietly. "Past tense. Is Maria dead?"

No longer was she smiling. In those eyes now there shone a suggestion of madness such as he had seen in the eyes of women frantic at their failure to hold him after he had begun to weary. Too well he knew that look. The look of despair and fury, of vanity roused towards murder, of self-esteem broken and tortured by loss of love. She stepped yet closer to him, those eyes which he had thought expressionless now wise and blank, and the unshaped nostrils distended. So close did she come, silently stepping, that he could feel her breath on his lips.

"Why did you have to come here?" she asked.

"Eh? I didn't have to come. I . . . I was curious. That's all."

"To tell me he was married to some London good-for-naught? You know too much, or you're a liar."

"I'm no liar, and he is married—to Miss Mary Moore of Holborn, and he's taken a house for her at Brentford outside London. O, he's forgotten you and all you did for him, abandoning you as he's abandoned so many other women once he'd had his fill and found no further use for them. It's no good lying to yourself, ma'am. He killed your step-daughter to get rid of her; and he mixed you in the crime to make certain you'd not talk. Then he skipped to London to have gay nights with the women there. He's made a fool of you as he made a fool of Maria."

The rosebud shape had left her pale mouth. The lips seemed thin, and he noticed how swiftly she breathed, her hands twisting together. The control which had impressed him at first meeting, making him feel that she was an honest woman with a serene and sinless spirit, could only have been maintained by an iron will; now that it was broken, she showed her torment, a desperate, passionate creature living a lie.

She said in gasps: "You think you're cunning, don't you? You thought to trap me. But I've got nothing to hide, nothing to be ashamed of. Bill Corder didn't mean a penny to me, and I'm glad he's gone. I'm glad Maria's gone, too. She was a wicked woman, a cheap whore who shamed us with her bastards, and what she got she deserved."

"What did she get?" he asked.

She shuddered. "I don't know," she moaned, "I don't know anything. You've no right to torment me like this."

"You know sufficient to hang him," he whispered. "Let's no longer lie. He killed Maria, and you helped him kill her."

"No, no!"

"You dressed her for her murder in a dead man's clothing; you urged her to go and you knew he had his gun with him, and you knew what he meant to do with it. He wasn't after rabbits that day; at least, not after a four-legged rabbit. You might even have helped him get rid of the body afterwards. And yet you never got your reward, did you? And you can't tell the truth for your own sake. That's the jest of it, from his point of view. How he must laugh! You've got to stay here and sit mum while he's living with another woman; and for your own sake, you've got to keep your mouth shut."

"That's not true!"

"He made you his fool all right. You're still young, you're still attractive, you could have men love you if you had pretty clothes like Maria had, ribbons and things like that. You're wasted in Polstead, a mole-catcher's wife, and it's eating into your heart, isn't it, to think of the good times you should be having, that Corder's having without you?" He gripped her elbows, holding her lest she run away, and he noted with delight how agitated was her breathing, how blind appeared her stare. "Are you going to be the jest of a man like that?" he cried. "The woman he used and tossed aside?"

"I—I know nothing."

"You know everything. You know how he killed her and where he hid the corpse. Did he bury her in that barn?" She shivered but did not answer. "That's why you twitted him about her umbrella in front of everybody at the funeral. That was a threat, wasn't it? But a threat he knew you daren't use; as he knows now you daren't use it. Why was he frightened of Maria? Why did he have to kill her?"

"I tell you, I don't know." Weakly, she struggled to escape. "For the love of God," she wailed, "let me go."

"Why did he have to kill her? O, I can see why you wanted her out of the way: that you might have Corder to yourself without her spying on you and stealing him from you. But why did he want to murder her? It wasn't because of the baby: that was dead; it wasn't because he couldn't get away from her. He had only to leave Polstead and she couldn't have done anything. But he didn't run away. For some reason she had to die, and you helped him kill her. What was the threat she held over him?"

"How do I know?" she stuttered. "There was nothing. He was nothing to me. He was nothing whatever to me."

"But you know why he killed her. Why?"

Helplessly, she looked about her at the young blossoms in sunlight and at the bees singing as they tumbled in and out of the buds.

"I don't know anything," she whispered. Then suddenly she added breathlessly: "But I heard her threaten him, often. I don't know, but I think, I think it was about the child, their child, the one he took away and buried. He didn't register the birth. I know that. He buried it secretly. At least that's what she said."

"So he killed the child, too, did he?"

"No, no; you mustn't say that; I'm sure it died naturally, but he didn't want any talk. I heard him say it was buried at Sudbury. They put the poor wee thing in a box and went off with it. She said he left her at his mother's place and took it away with him. I don't know anything else; before God, sir, I don't."

"So that was it!" The Corinthian sighed his satisfaction. "If he didn't murder it, he buried it secretly. A crime, not to register a birth. So that was why he had to shut her mouth? We're getting near the truth at last."

Sobbing, she tried to drag away from him, and the tears rolled down her cheeks. With fear and embarrassment, she blinked and lowered her head, whispering in a babyish voice:

"Sir, you're hurting me."

He would not let her go. Still gripping her elbows, he said: "And you'd let him make a fool of you! Where's your woman's pride? He's got his bonny young bride and a big house near London while you're left here, too scared to speak. Have you no wits, woman? Must you sit and suck your thumb and let him crow over you? There are surely ways in which you can let out the truth, yet not confess your own part in it? If she's buried in that barn, can't you get someone to dig her up?"

"It's his, his mother's; it's not my barn. . . ."

"But there are surely ways? Haven't you a dog, and can't you claw the earth and set the dog to digging for you? If you can't find some trick, you are no woman, by God."

"I don't know what you mean."

"You know well enough. Set those woman-wits to work. Are you going to remain tamely here, a labourer's wife, looking after her child with your own, and the dead wife's children, too, driving you old before your time, and let him laugh at you? What we've said today I have forgotten; but I leave the epilogue to you."

He dropped her elbows and she sank back against the prickly hedge, taking deep breaths of air as though she had been near drowning. Childlike she looked with those heavenly eyes and un-rouged mouth, and childlike was her body, flat-breasted, thin-hipped. The shadows of the cherry-blossoms gave her skin delicate colouring, smoothing away wrinkles and the dryness of age. She was not old—scarcely more than thirty, he was certain—but her troubles, her poverty and her worry about Corder had made her peaked, giving her an ailing look.

"You must be the Devil," she moaned, and shut her eyes.

"I am your friend," he whispered. "Before God, ma'am, I'll respect your confidence. Now get to work. There must be ways. Or would you leave him to sport with his young wife in London, leaving you to watch over the thing he killed?"

"For the love of God!" she wailed, and hid her face in her hands.

He was about to speak, then shut his lips, realizing that there was nothing further to say. The tale had been told at last, and now he held the truth of Corder in his hands; but it was worthless to him. This woman alone could prove the facts, and that she dared not do because she would have to confess herself his accomplice. Often must she have brooded on revenge and most likely she had written threateningly to London, only to find that threats were useless. That would explain why he had taken to carrying pistols and had insisted on leaving Gray's Inn Terrace for faraway Brentford, fearful lest, in a moment of spite, she denounce him.

The Corinthian understood her dilemma yet could not pity her. Cold-bloodedly had she helped to destroy her step-daughter, and her present sufferings were judgment on that sin. A stupid murder it seemed to him: Corder afraid lest the girl tell the authorities he had not registered the birth of his bastard—possibly, he had murdered the child: that seemed most likely, giving strength to Maria's threats—and Mrs. Marten unable to confess to the deed without implicating herself. Looking now at that frail body, the face hidden behind the delicate work-worn hands, and seeing how she shuddered when she sobbed, he could scarcely believe this was not a dream. The countryside which he had thought so innocent was darkened by adultery and murder; and, in the distance, the pink barn showed against the hills, softly coloured as though it blushed.

He turned away and strode out of the orchard, not happy with that morning's work. Hate Corder though he did, this pursuit of a man to the scaffold went against his principles as a good scoundrel; but when he recalled Mary, he felt justified. At least he would have saved her from a villain; and for that she must prove grateful in the end.

Chapter Fourteen

THE SECRET OF THE BARN

THAT night the Corinthian went very drunk to bed, disliking himself for having acted like a thief-taker; and his sole consolation was that, however revengeful she might feel, Mrs. Marten could not act without accusing herself, for she had been Corder's accomplice both before and after the fact. With a woman's clearness of vision when examining another woman, Lydia had sensed immediately that she loved the cross-eyed dandiprat: a thing he would never have believed had not Mrs. Marten herself indirectly confessed it. She had conspired with him to get the disguised girl out of the house, dressing her in coat and trousers so that any passer-by might be deceived into thinking that it was a man trotting over the fields. She had sent her to her death—for dead she was: that had been too strongly implied in Mrs. Marten's talk to be doubted—that she might enjoy her lover undisturbed without a step-daughter to betray her. And Maria had held two secrets with which to threaten Corder: the secret burial, if not the murder, of their child, and the liaison with her step-mother. The madcap, smug in her mastery over a man, not to have foreseen the dangers in that situation! No doubt, Corder had appeared to her a weakling, obedient to her in most things in fear of scandal, but she had failed in her vanity to read his arrogant heart that would never tolerate remaining the plaything of a woman. He and little Mrs. Marten had dressed the wretched girl for murder in an old suit of his dead brother's; and with earrings to dance from her ears under the tall hat, she had trod on dainty shoes to the Red Barn, never to be seen again save by one man alone; and he had carried a loaded gun with him to that meeting—scarcely, one would think, the natural thing to carry to a wedding.

But, having set vengeance afoot, the Corinthian was ashamed of himself. Never before had he been on the side of the traps, and much as he disliked Corder he felt like a traitor, and his only hope was that Mrs. Marten would be unable to act without betraying herself as the murderer's accomplice.

This hopeful mood strengthened when the days passed and he heard nothing further from Mrs. Marten, and he began to console himself with the illusion that she intended to stay silent. When he recalled how he had deliberately poked the woman into jealous fury, tormenting her by insisting on Corder's betrayal, he felt— an emotion rare with him—distinctly ashamed. He even began optimistically to believe that he had misinterpreted her words and looks, and that her distress had been the natural reaction of any good woman at the suspicion that her step-daughter might have been murdered. Almost he grew cheerful again, when he could avoid the glowering presence of Lucy; and as the early spring passed into full blossom-time, he felt no urge to return to London. The peace of this little village amidst the hills enchanted him, and even Lydia unbent sufficiently to appear gracious during meals. Unless it rained, he spent the days walking or riding, often seeing Lydia and Nelly abroad with baskets in search of primroses and violets, and his evenings he lounged away in the bar, listening contentedly to talk of crops and cattle and the weather.

Occasionally, Tom Marten entered for a pint and a chat, and he looked many years older than his wife. His shoulders bent, a handkerchief wound about his throat, he sat in moleskin breeches and torn jacket, sagely nodding at the talk, and only now and then joining a discussion. Usually, he stayed silent. His square face under thinning tangled hair had in repose a melancholy look, the eyebrows arching sharply into points, the eyes light blue and steady, the nose firm-beaked and well-fleshed, the mouth wide and tightly set, and the chin small between broad jaws. He would grunt and drink and spit, staring abstractedly up at the ceiling, and at times he sighed heavily. The other drinkers respected this melancholy and rarely roused him with a question; and after he had lumbered out into the night, they would nod their heads and tell about the grievous change there was in him since his daughter had run away.

"Think he'd have been pleased to get rid of her," said a wizened old man one evening. "Nothing but terrible trouble she ever brought him."

"Ay," said a burly fellow at his side, "I'd have belted her had she been mine; and him with her bastard to keep and all, and she no doubt selling herself for a tidy price in Ipswich or London. We'll not be seeing her again, I'm thinking."

"And now his missus seeing visions and waking him up in the middle of the night with the horrors. He's had no sound sleep, he tells me, for many a night." The tall man in a stained frock tapped on the bar with his pot to have it refilled. "Always thought she was a sensible little body," he grunted, "but there's no telling by women's outsides. You've got to live with 'em before you know 'em; otherwise there'd be no weddings, would there?"

"Visions?" asked the Corinthian, feeling suddenly cold. "What kind of visions has she?"

The tall man shrugged. "Visions of a dead 'un," he said with melancholy relish, "of her step-daughter, Maria, lying in that there Red Barn with her gizzard slit open. I had a peep into the place the other morning through a break in the slats, just being curious, you know, but there weren't no corpses there. And how the hell could there be, I ask you, when it's been stacked with corn? I was there when Foxy had the corn brought in and put into the upper-bay. Not much left there now, of course, just a bit of litter that was put down to keep it from the damp."

"Does she say the girl's body's in the barn?" asked the Corinthian, trying to speak carelessly.

"Ay," said the tall man, "that she does, according to what old Tom tells me. She says she dreamed of it afore Christmas last but didn't like to tell him; and now she keeps on dreaming it. It's on her mind something dreadful, she says, and she hopes he won't think she's superstitious. What else could a man think?"

Sitting back, the Corinthian rubbed his hands on his trousers, for they had become suddenly damp. From Mrs. Marten's dreams, the talk wandered to women in general and their peculiar superstitions; and he no longer listened, remembering that dream-book he had noticed on the cottage shelf.

Cunningly had Mrs. Marten set to work, indirectly revealing the truth, as, when talking to him, she had hinted but never definitely stated that Corder had murdered the girl; and it would not be long before, for the sake of peace, Tom Marten gave way to her persistence and began to dig. That the girl's body lay in that barn the Corinthian did not doubt. He was as assured of it as if he had been present at her murder. Not only had Mrs. Marten practically confessed to it, but Corder's own suspicious behaviour, his carrying of pistols, his lurking at Brentford, his nightmared nights, his sudden sweats, all pointed to a conscience in agony. Conscience or fear of discovery? That did not matter. He had become a haunted man with the threatening image of Mrs. Marten to drive away sleep even in the arms of innocent Mary.

Deeply did the Corinthian regret his part in the exposure. Too late, he realized that so long as he lived he would be ashamed to think that he had helped send a man, much as he disliked him, to the gallows; and once caught, if vindictive Mrs. Marten gave evidence, Corder assuredly would hang. And there was nothing he could do to save him. To warn him would have been useless. The fellow knew too cruelly the sword hanging over his head and he should long ago have fled abroad. The one hope was that Tom Marten might continue to ignore his wife's alleged dreams; and that was a frail hope indeed. In time, if only to earn a night's repose, he would go with a spade to that barn.

Unable to remain still, the Corinthian got up and strode into the moonlight. Ghostly seemed the plaster houses amongst the trees, yet all looked so peaceful that it was difficult to believe that a murdered girl lay in that old barn nearby.

Along the lane he went, drawn by the Red Barn, until he could see it, dark against the hill, behind its tall fence. Within those decaying walls a dead girl rotted, and soon, it seemed, her spirit would be appeased, if it were true that the slain lusted after the slayer. He tried to picture her as she must have been in life, a bigger, more alluring image of her young sister, Ann, but with the same chestnut curls and laughing grey eyes. He could see her in those shadows trudging to her death with the cotton umbrella swinging on its hook from her finger: a bulky shape in padded male coat and trousers, but with dainty shoes on her feet. How had she been killed? Corder had carried a gun, and Mrs. Marten had hinted that it was the weapon used; then, later, her boy had seen him carry a pickaxe from the barn. What would one want to dig in a barn, except a grave?

The Corinthian had lived a violent life, he had witnessed many a hanging and had seen dead men enough; and their ghosts had not troubled him as did the ghost of this girl he had never known. A silly wench, vain and lecherous and ambitious, wanting both her lovers and a husband as well; too stupid and reckless to avoid the consequences of her love-making, too conceited to realize that she could arouse fear and hatred in a man sufficient for him to kill her. He could understand that, however. One never did believe in death. One felt that some other, less fortunate fellow might be killed while oneself would remain curiously immune, immortal. And Corder did not look like a murderer; although, of course, murderers rarely did look like murderers. With his boisterous ways, his ingratiating manner, his childlike conceit and cocksureness, he would arouse terror in no one; and to this girl it must have seemed incredible when she encountered him in the gloom of that barn and saw his gun levelled at her breast. Whatever might have been her wickedness, she had paid for it then; that moment of terror and horror with the barrel glinting in her eyes would have been sufficient to atone for any villainy; and, after all, she had behaved no worse than hundreds of girls whom lads afterwards thanked for their generosity. Had she not held that threat above him—for unquestionably Corder had killed their child and buried it secretly —and had not her step-mother been set on her death, she might have been alive to this day. Those threats, with the urging of jealous Mrs. Marten, had given him the terrible courage to do the deed. The Corinthian wished there might be some way to make Mrs. Marten suffer with her lover; but that was not possible. So carefully had they behaved that no one suspected their liaison; and he had only suspicions to offer.

Wearily, back to the inn he trudged to a sleepless night; and in the morning he rose and dressed with reluctance, relieved that Lydia never got up for breakfast. She would quickly have detected his bad conscience and have made him confess to the doom over Corder, and he was too disgusted with his own part in that to want to suffer her contempt.

Peaceful seemed the countryside, the neat thatched cottages and houses, the smooth sensuously rolling hills ridged by the plough and divided by trees, bushes and hedges. Not caring whither he went, he strolled along the road and followed paths, often unknowingly returning on his own tracks, yet he could not tire himself. On its ridge, Polstead could be seen from most of the points he reached, the spire of the old church piercing the leafage. The blossoming cherry-trees gave the village a fairy-like quality with their gentle pinks and whites, so that one thought of clean and jolly peasants, of maypoles and innocent laughter, of honest lads and blushing maids, and not of lechery and murder.

Beyond its fence, he saw the Red Barn. Looking old in sunlight, the thatching glossy as though with spittle, it stood within outhouses, and only with an effort did he restrain himself from strolling over to investigate its secrets. Let Mrs. Marten and her cuckold, he decided, bear the responsibility of hanging Corder. Already was he involved further than he liked.

Then he noticed that two men were walking up the narrow lane by the thatched cottage at the foot of the hill, and he realized that they were making towards the Red Barn. One carried a pointed stick over his shoulder, while the other slouched beside him. Squinting to shut out the dazzle of sunlight, he gradually recognized one figure as being Tom Marten's, while the other man, he believed, was a fellow he had seen often at the "Cock" named Bill Pryke, Mrs. Corder's bailiff. Yes, it must be Pryke! If, to quiet his wife, Marten intended to dig inside the barn, he would have had to borrow the key; and the Corinthian remembered having heard that since the last harvest the place had been kept locked, the key being taken home by Corder.

The high gate swung open and the two figures, small at that distance, vanished from the Corinthian's sight. With both hands he clutched his stick and leaned on it, breathing fast through his nose, while he waited, it seemed to him, many hours, although scarcely more than ten minutes had passed before he saw the men again. Pryke carefully closed the gate behind them as though it guarded something valuable, and turned the key in the padlock. Then briskly he set off towards the village, Marten lagging at his heels.

Maria Marten had been found! There could be no doubt of that. In Pryke's fast walk there was a serious purpose; and there was misery in Marten's slow stumble and bent shoulders. She had been found and the thought of her decaying body rising out of earth into her wretched father's sight choked the Corinthian with horror and pity. It was foolish to grieve for the dead. With her unimportant sins and vanities, Maria Marten was no more; but the living, her father, her sister, her child, would suffer remorse for past quarrels and would mourn her dreadful end. By God, he thought, Corder deserved to hang; and he no longer felt shame in having helped to snare him for so senseless, so brutal, a killing.

Turning his back on the Red Barn, he strode off down the road. Had he remained, he would not have been able to resist the impulse to look upon the dead. For a reason he could not understand and which disgusted him, he longed to see her, even though, after almost a year, she would have proved no pretty sight. So many, however, had been the tales he had heard at the inn about her amorous escapades, so clearly had he conjured her into flesh from Mrs. Marten's talk, imagining her in her dainty shoes and male trousers, that he was curious and wished to see her face. There would be little to see, he told himself: only putrefaction; yet, had he remained staring at the barn, he would have had to go and look. Therefore he fled from that horror, walking swiftly down lanes and along roads and narrow paths, fearful of returning to the noisy inn, fearful of seeing Lydia when, by now, the village must have rung with the tidings.

Not until afternoon did he limp back into Polstead to find, as he had expected, people at their doorsteps or gathered in groups, all chattering about the discovery. No signs of horror or grief did he find. Excitement made these creatures cheerful; their eyes sparkled and they licked their lips, while shaking their heads that there should be such sin in the world. Into their tedious lives had come this drama, and they wasted not a moment while they talked of it and gloated on the details.

In the "Cock", the bar was crowded. Men and a few women were pressed around Tom Marten and Bill Pryke, goggling at them as though they were strangers. Dejected, Marten sat on a chair, a mug of untasted ale in one hand, and looked at nothing. Now and then he moved his lips as though speaking to himself, while tears ran slowly down his wrinkled cheeks. Pryke, however, appeared almost merry, strive though he did to look solemn.

"Ay, Mrs. Marten dreamed well," he was saying. "No mistaking that wen on her neck and those two gap-teeth; and what man is there that don't know what she looked like? There was a handkerchief around her neck, and until we untied it we couldn't be sure it was her. She was lying down, not stretched out decentlike, but with her legs curled up and her head pressed down to her knees. We hadn't far to dig. She weren't more than five inches down. I tell you, it was no choice sight, and the smell was disagreeable."

"How big was the hole?" piped a woman.

"About three feet," said Pryke, "or three and a half feet long, I'd say. Eh, Marten?"

Tom Marten did not hear. Head bowed, he muttered to himself, and the tears still flowed.

"Let the poor man be," said another woman. "He's got troubles enough without you tormenting him. I always did say that Maria'd come to no honest end."

"There's the hand of God in this," cried the lean school-master, blinking at them through his spectacles. "Murder can't be hid, as Eugene Aram learned. And here's God Almighty Himself pleased to depart from His usual course of procedure to expose the iniquity of man. Let sceptics sneer. We've proof in Polstead to refute their ignorance and I doubt not but we'll have a most edifying sermon on Sunday about the working of God in devious ways. There's a passage in Job that will come in wonderfully useful here."

"Ay," said a toothless old man with the complacent air of one who, being ancient, was in heaven's confidence, "even from the mouths of babes and sucklings, it is writ; and now out of the head of a silly woman comes the truth in vision. If this were a popish country we'd have pilgrims by the million coming here, we would, and no doubt foolish Ann Marten would be made a saint."

"She was always a good hard-working soul," said one of the women, "and an honest wife and mother. So why shouldn't God speak through her lips, loving good women like they say He does?"

"Well, God or the devil," chuckled the old man, "it matters little. 'Tis equally as wonderful and mysterious. For her to dream a thing like that! Knowing where to dig, too. 'Tis indeed a miracle for these sinful times."

"Ay," said the others solemnly, nodding their heads.

The Corinthian could listen to no more. That little Mrs. Marten, Corder's mistress, should be considered practically a saint because of the cunning with which she had betrayed her lover horrified him. The longing to shout the truth had grown so strong that he had to bite his lip to keep it shut, and he dared listen to no more such blasphemous nonsense. Besides, it was past one o'clock and he was hungry. . . .

Lydia had already started her dinner when he entered the parlour, and he noticed that her hands shook and that she merely nibbled the food; she gave him a dull glance as he sat in the chair opposite, then she turned back to her plate.

"You've heard?" he asked.

She nodded, not looking at him.

"It was Maria Marten's body," he said, and his hunger suddenly went when he saw the vegetables and cold mutton on his plate. "They knew her by the wen on her neck, and her teeth. Corder murdered her. No doubt of that."

"You've no right to say such things!" There were tears in her eyes when she glared at him. "The girl was a dirty little whore. She had dozens of other men. Any one of them might have killed her. She gave them all cause enough, God knows."

"Yet Corder did it," he said quietly. "And you know he did it. The evidence against him is too strong. You didn't hear what Mrs. Marten told me."

"I don't want to hear, and I wouldn't believe a word that woman said. She probably did it herself."

"A little thing like her, when Maria was a strapping wench?"

"If not her, then someone else did it. Why must he be blamed for everything? Your malice is unforgivable. One can understand it with silly country-folk and their prejudices: they're always envious of the squire; but I thought you'd know better."

"There's the inquest tomorrow," he said, determined to ignore her rage. "Thank God they'll not want us to give evidence. After that, we'll know the truth."

"Yes," she murmured, "after that, we'll know. . . . Until then, it's not your or anybody's place to act as judge."

"I'm judging nobody," he said, trying to restrain his temper. "I merely wanted to warn you that it won't be long before we're questioned."

"Questioned?" she repeated haughtily. "Who'd question us?"

"The law, pretty: the law. We're known to have been his friends. Our coming here has caused talk; everybody's naturally curious that a lady and gentleman should have visited this dead end. We've asked questions about Corder. We've not denied we've been intimate with him. Unless the local constable is a bigger fool than most of them, he'll seek us out. For one thing, they'll want to know his address."

"But he's not charged; it's only suspicion; they can't do anything until after the inquest."

"They'll not wait till then, my love, giving him a chance to mizzle off. I don't suppose they'll swear out a warrant yet, but you may be certain that the constable's been warned and is collecting all the evidence he can. Naturally, he'll come to us."

Leaning her elbows on the table, she gazed at him with dark-rimmed eyes, her skin unnaturally pale. "What will you tell him?" she asked.

"The truth," said he.

"By God," she cried, "would you tell him where he is? You're even baser than I thought! I knew you hated him because you're jealous, you're in love with his wife and you're frightened of losing me, but to betray him, to give him up to the traps—that's something I can't believe, even of you."

"He killed that unfortunate girl."

"If he did, and I don't believe it, she doubtless deserved all she got. O, like all men, you're on her side because she was a hot little piece, the way you like them. All you know is what that hypocrite of a Mrs. Marten told you and the dirty stories you've listened to in the bar; I've heard different tales. Mrs. Gordon's told me one or two things, and Nelly's learned a lot from the other servants. That Maria was wicked right through. I don't mean only because she had lots of men; the poor slut probably couldn't find any other amusements in this wretched hole; but she was not above squeezing them for money, threatening to tell their wives and pretending her babies were theirs. That's a part of her history you wouldn't have heard, the men'd be too damned ashamed to talk about it; but the women knew."

"And how," he asked, "did the women know if the men didn't talk?"

She drew in a long breath, shuddering with rage. "O, you are a beast!" she cried. "You sit there grinning when a man's life's at stake. If you give him away you'll be a murderer, a worse murderer than ever he was. He killed the girl—if he killed her—in a moment of anger after she'd tormented him beyond bearing: anybody might do that: you or I, anybody; but to give him away cold-bloodedly, out of malice and jealousy . . .! What will your London friends say when they hear of it?"

"I don't care a damn what anybody says," he growled. "There's justice to think of, and that unhappy girl . . ."

"Justice!" she sobbed with unhappy laughter. "You talk to me of justice—you, a dirty thief with crooked dice and cards! If there were any justice you'd have been whipped and hanged long ago. A fine, noble fellow you think yourself, and you're a cowardly rat at heart. . . . O, for the love of God, Tom, you can't do it, you mustn't!"

He did not answer, gazing into her tormented eyes, puzzled that such a man as Corder could mean so much to such a woman. And as they sat thus, she leaning on the table with a hand stretched supplicating out to him, and he frowning, perplexed, the door opened and Lucy bounded in.

"Finished?" she snarled. " 'Cause there's a visitor for you. Mr. Ayres, the constable from Boxford, wants to talk to you."

"Take them away," said the Corinthian, nodding at the plates.

Still gazing imploringly at him, Lydia sank into her chair, then she pushed it further into the shadows that her back might be towards the window.

"Tom," she whispered coaxingly, "for my sake, for the sake of old times, don't do it."

He sighed and poured himself a glass of brandy.

"Tell Mr. Ayres," he said, "that we are ready to receive him now."

Mr. Ayres, a big man in a brown coat that seemed too small for his bulk, entered respectfully, hat in hand, bowing and grinning.

"Forgive me, ma'am," he said, "and you, sir, but I've been instructed by the coroner, Mr. Wayman of Bury, to make certain enquiries into the remains of a young female that's recently been disinterred. You must have heard tell of it?"

"I've heard talk of some such thing," said the Corinthian carelessly. "Will you join us in a glass of brandy, Mr. Ayres?"

"I'll not say no, sir, thanking you kindly. Your good health, sir; and yours, ma'am," said he, taking the glass the Corinthian offered and sipping the drink with relish. "That's the poison for a cold day," he said, rolling his bloodshot eyes; "but we mustn't forget

186

business. And a bad business, too, sir; a very bad business indeed. A murdered corpse is an uncommon rarity in these parts."

"So the girl was murdered?" asked the Corinthian. "There can be no doubt of that?"

"Well, sir," Ayres chuckled, "seeing as how there was a wound in the neck from something sharp, like that knife there, and another stab into the right eye, and a handkerchief tight enough around her throat to stop her breathing or hollering, I don't see how we can come to any other conclusion, now, can you, sir? And how did she come to bury herself if she weren't dead first?"

"Thank you for this information," murmured the Corinthian, "but I really don't see why we should have been told, as we're strangers here."

"Well, sir, it's like this, sir," said Ayres, taking a deep gulp of brandy, "there's strong suspicion—only suspicion, mind you, sir, and perhaps I shouldn't be talking about it—but there's strong suspicion that William Corder might be able to explain one or two things that puzzle us. And seeing as how you're a friend of his——"

The Corinthian raised his brows. "He's no friend of mine," he said.

"Well, call it an acquaintance then. I know you've been asking questions about him, as well you might, for curiosity ain't no crime, and that you've had a talk with Mrs. Marten, step-mother of the dead 'un. So I wondered whether you mightn't have a little information for me. Just a hint's all I'm asking. It's like this, sir . . ." Confidentially, he leaned forward, coughed and lowered his voice. ". . . We've had information that William Corder was seen going with her to the Red Barn during May of last year, she in man's toggery, too, and she ain't been seen since then until they dug her up today. I'm not suggesting that William Corder done it, mind you. Never for a moment. He's a gentleman like yourself and I don't doubt he's got a very good explanation of what he was doing. Always was good at explaining things, was Bill Corder. But it's important that I should see him immediately; and if you'd like to have his good name cleared—there's ugly rumours about, you know—you ought to help me, sir, 'cause we'll get him anyhow."

The Corinthian heard Lydia catch her breath and he twiddled the glass in his hands. Now that the moment had arrived he knew that he could not act Judas. Much as he disliked Corder and loathed his crime, all his training as a sharp cried out against telling the truth. The traps were his enemies and on no account were they to be helped.

"I'm sorry," he said, "but I can't assist you. I knew Corder slightly; we met at the Piccadilly Saloon and such places in London; once or twice, without invitation, he called on me. Beyond that, I know nothing whatever about him. He never gave me his address."

He heard Lydia sigh and resisted the impulse to look at her. Instead, he gazed into the constable's sceptical eyes.

"That's all you've got to say?" asked the constable.

"That's all I know," said the Corinthian.

"Well, sir, I can't say I'm not disappointed." Ayres licked the last of the brandy from his glass. "It would have helped, you know," he said, "but we have other means. The law, sir, is not to be laughed at. We have our methods; and if William Corder don't come forward after the inquest, we'll have to find him, that's all. You'll be staying in the village, I presume?"

"For a time, yes," said the Corinthian.

"Thank you kindly," said the constable, bowing low with a mocking smile. "We'll meet again, no doubt."

"No doubt," said the Corinthian quietly.

He said no more until the door had closed behind Ayres, then he leaned towards Lydia in the shadows.

"Thank you, Tom," she said quietly and squeezed his hand. "Now we must be off!"

"Off? Off to where?"

"To Corder, of course," she said. "He must be warned."

Sadly, the Corinthian smiled at her and shook his dark head. "If you want him hanged," he murmured, "go to him, my love. That Ayres is no fool, for all he put on the johnny raw act. He knows perfectly well that I'm lying. The village has talked of nothing else but us for weeks, and what we wanted here, and why we've asked about Corder. And they've tumbled over themselves to tell Ayres everything they've seen or suspected. I always thought you a wise woman, my duck, and I'm surprised you can't see that. From now, there'll be a hundred spies at our heels. A hundred! Why! I'm told that there're nine hundred inhabitants in this village, and every one of those inhabitants has two eyes with which

188

to watch us. We'll not be able to move an inch without Ayres knowing where we've gone. And if we went to Corder, we'd not ride there alone. We'd merely show the way to Ayres or one of his fellows."

"Then I'll write," she said.

"Who can you write to? Not to William Corder. Take the letter as far as Bury and once the postman sees the name he'll open it. I tell you you can do nothing that won't help to hang him."

"I want a drink." She tried to speak evenly but when he had passed her a glass of brandy, she spilled much of the spirit down her chin and throat.

"So we must sit here and wait and wait!" she cried. "Just wait and go mad!"

Sadly he looked at her, noting the flushed cheeks, the eyes fierce with angry impatience, and he wondered at his own stupidity in not loving her with all his heart. Love her he did, in a way; but it was with a rebellious love resentful of her assumption of superiority and the casual manner with which she had accepted his caresses.

"Good Lord," he said with a shaky laugh, "what fools we are! We're a fine couple, Lydia. Wherever we go, men and women turn to look at us, you so shapely and me so tall and strong. You'd think God had shaped us especially to live happily together for ever afterwards. But, no! . . . you go nutty on a cross-eyed little cowardly whelp, and I dream of a deaf little creature you could crush in one hand. We're both mad, of course. I never realized it before, but I can see it now. In a way, it's like a god and a goddess mating, and that's why those heathens were always stepping out of heaven to sleep with human beings: Venus and Adonis, Jupiter and Circe—no, not Circe! she turned men into swine, didn't she? and I don't suppose that was difficult—well, it doesn't matter. But I used to think those were just silly tales. They're not. They've got a true moral. And we're the proof of it. We're both too strong, too handsome, for one another. You don't want to marry a man: I mean a real man like me; you want to be the man yourself and to keep a mistress in breeches who has to shave every morning."

She flashed him a bright glance. "You are sometimes wiser than I thought," she said.

"That's it!" he cried exultantly. "You want a husband you can both bully and cosset; and, by God, so do I a wife! It's not Mary

Moore as a lovely woman I want. It's her shyness, even her deafness, yes, even her deafness, that attracts me. And what's the result? The two weaklings, the children, are yoked together; and we, the strong, are helpless to win them."

"Really," she said, pouring herself another brandy, "you quite surprise me with your brilliance. And I suppose you're right, in a way. I've never thought about it like that, of course; I never do trouble to think about what I'm doing; but I suppose you're right. Not that it makes any difference or makes us any happier."

"Come," said he, fondling her hand. "We were happy together once, and we're still deeply fond of each other, and the battle of wits will always hold us, for you'll not submit to me and I'll never submit to you. Let's start again, my lovely. It's only a silly dream that's separated us, nothing that's real."

"Yes," she said bitterly, "but dreams are often tougher than reality. I feel closer to you now than I've felt for years . . . but, no! It's all finished, my dear. Let's stay brother and sister . . . for a time, at least. Later perhaps . . ."

"As you wish." He filled both his glass and hers. "To our future," he said, "and may it be happier than the present, please God."

Both drank, then wryly smiled at one another, squeezed hands like good comrades, and sat back in their chairs, each sighing to think how uncomplicated life should be and how stupidly muddled it became because of that unhappy, never satisfied demon which lives in all of us.

Chapter Fifteen

THE FETTERED MAN

THE following day the inquest on Maria Marten was held at the "Cock", the dining-room being cleared for the jury and the coroner from Bury St. Edmunds. An elderly gentleman with a flushed face, he sipped a glass of often replenished alleged water throughout the proceedings and unquestionably he must have needed something to take the taste out of his mouth, having, with the jury, inspected the body which remained in the barn. As the inn's most important lodgers, Lydia and the Corinthian were given comfortable seats and faced the coroner at the end of the table, the jury shuffling on hard forms that ran along one side of the table, on which lay various parcels and pieces of rotten cloth.

Maria's sister, Ann, was the first witness, and she identified the corpse by the clothing, by the hair and by two missing teeth. Gently, the coroner questioned her, leading her on to tell how Corder had said that Baalham had had a warrant for her sister's arrest because of the bastard child, and how they had decided to go to Ipswich to get married; how on that fatal day, Maria had left her home disguised in man's coat, waistcoat, trousers and hat; and later how Corder had attempted to explain that they had not got married, after all.

In a low, sweet voice she gave her evidence, looking down at her hands in her lap, now and then licking her lips with the tip of her tongue, her eyes dulled with embarrassment at being watched by so many people.

Her father followed her to the chair and his evidence was equally unexciting. He told of Corder's wooing, of the birth of his and Maria's bastard, and how Corder, whenever he was asked, evaded any explanation of why Maria had not written after her flight. He told of the baby that had died and how Corder had carried the body away, wrapped in a napkin and placed in a box. When he spoke of the discovery of his daughter's remains, he began to falter; then, setting his lips, he continued without apparent emotion.

When his wife took his place, Lydia and the Corinthian watched her narrowly, being curious to see how she would behave when, always pressing on her tongue, must have been the knowledge of her own guilt. She gave no sign of being ill at ease. With slow steps, head down in her bonnet, she walked to the chair and bowed to coroner and jury. Only pity showed in those bright blue eyes, and without other expression, she looked timidly about her, glancing at Lydia and the Corinthian with never a glimmer of recognition.

She identified Maria's clothing, speaking in a gentle melancholy voice, and dabbed her eyes with her handkerchief. At the coroner's prompting, she agreed that Corder had alleged that Baalham had a warrant against Maria because of her bastard child, and that he had sworn to marry her at Ipswich. She told of Maria's change of clothing, of Corder's promises, of his later lies about her not having written, and how her little boy had seen him carry a pickaxe out of the Red Barn.

"She changed her clothing there?" asked the coroner gently. "I mean, she, ahem, became a woman again?"

"So Mr. Corder told me," she said primly.

"But why the disguise in the first place?" mumbled the coroner, rolling in his chair. "It was surely just as dangerous for her to be seen leaving the barn as your house?"

"He told me he kept his coat over her dress till they got into a by-lane," she said in a voice so low that it was scarcely heard.

"Ahem," said the coroner, "and, hum, there have been peculiar rumours, hum, about how you brought your husband to search this barn."

"It was a dream," said she, looking up, her eyes shining. "I dreamt it once before, and just before Christmas, too. I dreamt that my poor daughter was murdered and buried in the Red Barn. Hearing no tidings of her, I became so very uneasy that I entreated my husband to make a search; and he did it."

"Ahem," said the coroner, scratching his chin, "ahem. Next witness, please."

With the same rapt expression, eyes seeing beyond this cloddish world, Mrs. Marten left her chair and walked noiselessly to the back of the court; and although Lydia stared ferociously at her, she took no heed.

"The bitch," said Lydia under her breath, while the Corinthian squeezed her hand to caution silence.

The next witness, one George Gardiner, had little to say. Mumbling in his embarrassment, and tugging at the red spotted handkerchief about his neck, he deposed that after May 18 he had asked Corder what had become of Maria Marten.

"What did he say to that?" asked the coroner.

"Well, your honour," groaned Gardiner, sliding on the chair as though the seat were hot, "he says to me, he says, 'She's all right,' he says. 'I suppose she's in keeping of Mr. Matthews,' he says. And I don't know nothing else, sir."

The coroner would listen to no more evidence. Rapping his knuckles on the table, he announced that the inquest was adjourned.

"Doesn't want anything to come out about that old goat Matthews," grumbled Lydia when they were in the fresh air again. "Probably a friend of his, and it was really disgraceful the way he stopped the evidence once that name was mentioned. Perhaps he was the man who killed the woman."

"Who? Matthews?" The Corinthian laughed uneasily. "No, pretty," he said, "it's useless trying to look for scapegoats. From all I've heard, Matthews behaved very well. He allowed the girl five pounds a quarter to support his child, and it was only after Corder stole one quarter's allowance that he refused to pay any more. He had no reason to kill the girl. Corder did it. Come, my dear, you know he did it."

She did not answer immediately, but dug into the road with the point of her parasol. "Truthfully," she said at last, "I really don't care. I didn't know the woman and from what I've heard about her I wouldn't have liked her if I had known her. But I do know Corder, and I'm sorry for him. I'm sorry for any young man trapped by an unscrupulous female. There are occasions, whatever the law might say, when murder's justified."

"Perhaps I'm biased because I don't like the fellow," he murmured, "but my pity stays with the victim. Bitch she might have been, but bitchery doesn't merit murder. Look, my love." They were close to the church, and he caught her arm to detain her, for he had noticed people, men, women and children, walking slowly amongst the larches and sycamores. "They are going to pray for Maria Marten," he said, and took off his hat.

"I don't want to see the fools." She struggled to shake her arm from his grip. "Hypocrisy!" she cried. "Liars! They'd have stoned her alive, and now they weep at her memory; the parson'll give a sermon; they might even raise a monument to her dirty memory; and she, who was no better than any Piccadilly bunter, might become a saint. It's a rotten, lying, canting world. O, give me Covent Garden and St. Giles where no one's ashamed of the truth. Christ," she moaned, "that man, Ayres, left. I saw him go. He'll be on Corder's track and then they'll hang him."

"They must find him first," he said gently, leading her from the churchyard; "and if he's got any brains he'll be in France at the first whisper he hears."

She did not answer immediately but walked on grimly, frowning. Then she said: "That Mrs. Marten'll not get away with it. I'll see to that, if it's the last thing I do. I'll have her shown up for what she is. Corder must tell the truth about her."

"And hang himself?" asked the Corinthian.

"O!" she sobbed. "Is there nothing to be done?"

"Nothing," said the Corinthian; "unless he's been cunning enough to skip the country. The fool, not to have gone before when this was hanging over him! But that's so like him, smug and self-satisfied; when all the while that body was only a few inches under the soil and any chance spade might have dug it up."

"He is a child," she whispered, "he doesn't think."

She wanted no supper, she said, and went straight to her bedroom. The Corinthian followed her upstairs, but he could not sleep. Anger at the crime had fled, to give place to pity. His dislike of Corder had not lessened, while his compassion for Lydia had grown. That afternoon the thought had come to him as a revelation when he realized why he and she had failed as partners. They were too alike, both self-possessed and passionate; both wishing for mastery and resenting domination by the other. It was not Corder the man who had drawn Lydia, any more than it had been Corder's wife that had drawn him; it had been an image in flesh of their own desires after which they had yearned, seeking a union of opposites, their likeness to one another making true love impossible between them. To triumph over her, to prove that he was not her slave, he had taken other women without desire, feeling that in their embrace he somehow humbled Lydia.

Now that they had this understanding he wondered whether it would be possible to begin again. Each would be aware of the desire for mastery and should therefore be able to subdue it. But he doubted. In a way, the truth had widened their separation, making them selfconscious, and he felt towards her now the affection he might have felt for a sister. Love-making would only embarrass them, each trying not to be masterful, each striving to appear submissive.

The future seemed very black to him when he went to bed that night. If their partnership were finished, he would lose interest in the old life, for he would never have the patience to find and train another woman to take her place. Few were as swift to learn as Lydia, or as clever as she in duping flats; and if that life were finished, what was he to do? Marry someone and settle into quietude? That he would have liked, but there was only one woman, he felt, with whom he could live peacefully: Mary Corder. By helping to hang her husband, he had hoped to win her; but would she be the kind to grow quickly out of mourning? He doubted it; yet he hoped; and when at last he slept, he dreamed of her.

As he had warned Lydia, they were watched. When the following day he strode far from the inn, he noticed a man dawdling some way behind him. Wherever he went, no matter how he turned and twisted, that man remained. They were making certain that Corder would not be warned. Ayres had left with a warrant for his arrest, it was said in the bar, and it would be only a matter of time before he sniffed the track to Brentford. Then, unless the fool had fled abroad, there would be no escaping the scaffold save by a miracle.

Wherever he went, talk of hanging Corder greeted him. People could speak of nothing else, it seemed, exulting in the thought of his execution and weeping at mention of the murdered girl whom, when living, they had despised. The tale had spread for miles and many were the new arrivals in the village, and men were bidding high for a bed. It was the dream that had excited them, not the murder, which, after all, was commonplace enough. But the tale of a miscreant brought to justice through a woman's dreaming was something to be tattled in every tavern and at every dinner-table in the land, and it grew fabulous in the telling. About the little Marten home crowds gathered, pushing through the broken gate to peer into the rooms in the hope of glimpsing the woman who had been visited by heaven. Unperturbed, Mrs. Marten went about her duties, humbly curtseying to the wealthier folk and gratefully accepting what they pressed into her hand. When further prophecies were expected from her, she firmly refused to oblige, saying that she had been but a humble instrument. . . .

Even more to be adored than Mrs. Marten was the Red Barn. The old wooden building, timbers rotting, the paint cracked and ready to snap at a thumb-nail's pressure, was assailed by sightseers; and not content with examining it and staring into the shallow grave, they tore down pieces of the walls to take away with them as precious relics. Hundreds came from the surrounding towns and counties to stare into that empty hollow. Mostly in silence, reverently as though in church, the men taking off their hats, they trod the dirty floor, and women sobbed, crying: "Poor Maria! . . . Poor thing! . . . Ill-fated girl!" while weeping noisily. Men gripped their sticks and pushed out their chins. A fierce light in their eyes, they growled of what they would like to do to such a rascal who could destroy so virtuous a maid. "Cold-blooded villain," they said, holding their women protectively on their arms. "Cruel wretch," sobbed the women, clinging to their escorts.

Sickened by the show and hoping only that the uproar might reach London to warn Corder, the Corinthian rarely left his room for the remainder of that day, and from his window he gazed down at the festive crowds. For once, Gordon could not complain about lack of custom and he had even dared to suggest that the Corinthian might oblige by sharing his bed with strangers; the Corinthian had said "No!" and given him such a basilisk look that he had fled without another word. Soon he was sending for fresh supplies of liquor to quench this gigantic thirst and not until early morning, when even drunkards could drink no more, and the wenches were sore-footed from dancing, was he able to stumble to bed for a few hours' sleep. All was riot, boozing, brawling and lechery, the singing of lewd ballads, for pedlars and mountebanks had joined the throng, with pickpockets by the dozen. Suddenly, Polstead had become famous and the villagers were never a moment sober, each man being ready, at the price of a pot, to tell sweet lies of a virtuous Maria Marten and of a wicked profligate young squire, pursuer of village maidens, who had not only plundered her of her maidenhead but had stabbed and shot her for thanks.

"O, the villain!" sobbed the ladies, almost swooning.

"Miscreant," said the men and swelled at their chests because they were, it was plain to see, so very different from the monster.

The attack on the Red Barn had been such that a guard, too late, was placed to protect what splinters remained; but a few coppers slipped into his hand, and he turned his back and another piece of the barn went into some gentleman's pocket or a lady's reticule. One man, a hatter from a distant town, who wished to carry home a tale to strike wonder in the hearts of friends and customers, slid into the grave when the barn was momentarily empty. Lying snugly curled where Maria Marten had lain in her sack, he was surprised by the arrival of a lady and gentleman. Seeing something move in the dark hollow, the lady shrieked so violently that the hatter was convinced that only a ghost could possess such a voice. Too paralysed with terror to stir, he shivered in the earth, while the lady swooned into her husband's arms.

When he heard the tale, the Corinthian did not join in the others' merriment in the bar. He could see nothing amusing in a fool lying in a grave and a stupid woman thinking him a ghost. The authorities, he felt, should never have permitted these sight-seers who had already tried and condemned Corder. His only consolation was that the tale of the ghost having become the talk of England, Corder by now must have heard of it and have seized his opportunity to run to hiding. There were many rumours telling where he lurked, and it was confidently asserted that he had already been arrested and was on his way back to Polstead; but nobody seemed to know the truth, the authorities remaining silent.

Then, three days after the adjourned inquest, while he lounged at the inn door, cynically watching the jolly people pass, the Corinthian was surprised and delighted to see Bertram ride towards him through the dusk.

"Good Lord!" he cried, running to hold his stirrup-leather. "This is a welcome sight! Come back here, to the stables."

Not until the horse had been surrendered to the ostler did Bertram speak.

"They've got him," he said, and added: "Where's Lydia?"

The Corinthian had never expected that Corder would be able

to escape; nevertheless, now that he knew that he was nabbed, he felt a trifle sick.

"The poor little bastard," he growled. "O, Lydia? She's in her room. You'd better share with me, for there's not a bed to be had for miles around. Luckily, mine's big enough for two."

Leaving Bertram in his bedchamber, he hurried to knock at Lydia's door.

"Bert's here," he whispered through the panels; "and they've nabbed Corder."

Quickly, the door swung open and she stood framed before him, a solid shadow with the light from the window behind her tinselling the edges of her gown.

"Where's Bert?" she stammered. "Take me to him, at once."

She had been dressing and her hair was uncombed. It fell over her shoulders in thick coils, and with a swift gesture she tossed it down her back and hurried after the Corinthian into his bedchamber opposite hers.

"Lydia," whispered Bertram, and he took a deep breath of joy mingled with pain at seeing her again, the Corinthian closing and locking the door behind her, "you're even lovelier than I remembered. I like you with your hair down."

"They've nabbed Corder?" she cried, impatiently tossing her heavy mane at his compliments.

"Ay, they got him," said Bertram, sighing while he stared at her. "Mrs. Corder told me all about it."

"You've seen Mrs. Corder? Did you see him, too?"

"No. Let me tell you what happened. God, I'm tired! I've been riding hell-for-leather to get here before the newspapers." Groaning, he sank down on the bed and stretched his legs. "I slept at your place," he said, "as you suggested. Cosier than that bleak room of mine; besides, your things were there and I liked to touch them and look at 'em and smell 'em . . ."

"Please," cried Lydia, "what about Corder?"

"All I know is that his wife came bounding up the stairs. Didn't know who she was, of course; at first, thought she might have been your dressmaker or something. Little wee thing, she is, common enough, with a white skin and deaf as a newt. She wanted to see Tom, she tells me. It was important, she says; and when I told her you were up here, I thought she'd swoon. So I let her in and gave her a glass of sherry, and it wasn't long before she was as calm as a bloody statue. You'd never have thought her husband had just been nabbed for cutting another woman's throat, the way she talked about it. She said the police officer had pretended he'd come on business but her brother soon had the truth out of him. She said she couldn't believe it at first, but then she remembered how worried he'd been and she felt there must be some truth in it; not that her Willy would murder anyone, of course. . . . Very brave she was about it all, except when she first came in; and she told me she hadn't been able to eat since he'd been boned; otherwise you'd never have thought she cared a damn."

"Cold, cold!" said Lydia with a shudder.

"No, brave!" said the Corinthian. "That was how I'd expect her to act. Not wasting time in useless lamentations, but seeing how she could help her husband. And she came to look for me!"

"I don't know what she expected you to do," said Bertram, "but she said she'd no one else to turn to, and she thought you might think of something to help the little bastard. Not that she called him bastard, mind you. It was her dear Willy, her poor Willy, all the while. And never a tear neither. She said that the police officer took him to a nearby inn and then came back for the keys. She gave 'em up, but she wasn't certain what he found. He took away some papers and letters, she said, and some books, and some pistols. Then she went with him to this inn and they all had supper together."

"Very sociable," scoffed Lydia. "I suppose they all sang comic songs."

"She didn't say," grinned Bertram. "Anyhow, she asked me to see what I could do to help the scamp; and she particularly wanted me to tell the Corinthian. Seems to have a peculiar trust in you, old fellow, thinks you'll be able to save the little dandiprat. Anyhow, she hopes to be up here soon as she can, after she's arranged about leaving her school and settled a few other things."

"Of all the heartless monsters," cried Lydia, "worrying about her school and money and things at a time like this! Now be truthful, Bert. What does this paragon really look like?"

"I've told you. Insignificant. Mousy. And almost stone-deaf, but I must say it's clever the way she reads your lips. So long as you're facing her, she doesn't miss a word. But, as a woman," he shrugged, gloating on Lydia, "why, pretty, she's not the same species as you. Looks as though she'd lived in a cellar somewhere. Clothes just cheap and buttoned-up to the chin; and as for tight-lacing, you can't see what she's made of! And she's small enough as it is without trying to hide inside whalebone. A little church-mouse who smells of cheese and vinegar. That's what she is."

White-faced, the Corinthian glared at him, but, with Lydia watching, he decided that silence would be safest. Any argument would only make Bertram more contemptuous and Lydia more spiteful.

"Where have they taken Corder?" she asked.

"They're bringing him back here to the inquest. That's all she knew."

"Here?" She looked about her and wrung her hands, as though expecting to see him suddenly thrust through the door or a window. "He'll be given no fair trial here," she cried: "feeling's too high against him; and that Maria Marten was a whore. Why don't they try him in London or somewhere where he might have a chance?"

"Aw, I don't suppose they'll try him in Polstead," said Bertram. "They've got to finish the inquest first, and if the verdict goes against him, he'll be sent to the assizes, probably at Bury."

"They'll be no less prejudiced at Bury. Is nothing to be done for his defence?"

"That's why his wife's staying in London. She's got to raise the rhino. She said she'd spend every penny she has to get him defended by the best man. Even if she's got to sell all she's got, she said."

"She said!" mimicked Lydia. "Well, we'll see."

"Ay," growled the Corinthian, glaring at her, "we'll see."

His annoyance with Lydia had returned. It was not so much that she made no attempt to conceal her love for Corder but her jeers at Mary infuriated him. And he could gladly have kicked Bertram downstairs for having said such foolishly insulting things about the woman. He knew that Mary was not beautiful; in many ways she appeared insignificant; she did not dress fashionably and she did conceal her shape under bone and metal. Bertram had told the truth, as he saw it, and the fact that it was at least half the truth, as he saw it himself, exasperated the Corinthian. It was not Mary's exterior that he loved, although he trembled at the possibility of holding her in his arms: some subtle, unexplainable attraction drew him to her. Beside Lydia, she appeared helplessly feminine, fragile and easily bruised, needing a strong man's care; and he had lived so long with a woman as arrogant and as domineering as himself that he craved to possess a lover who would worship him and never ask questions nor doubt his omniscience.

The other day at dinner, he had realized that truth. He wanted her for the same reason that Lydia wanted Corder. Their partnership had become irksome and they were both weary of cards and dice and constant drinking. To both of them had come a longing to escape while they were yet young, and escape remained possible; and at that unhappy moment William Corder and Mary Moore had appeared. Had they met them even a few months earlier, the pair would have meant nothing to Tom and Lydia; but, just when they were needed, they had come to chime with their disgruntled moods, bringing a glimpse of a contented dream which, in their hearts, they knew was a dream they could never achieve.

Even if Corder was hanged, Mary would never accept him, at least not until after many years, more years than a man of his humours could wait. Hers was the nature to take to mourning as a holy rite, to feed on memories and to be appalled at any suggestion of a second husband. Nevertheless, he hoped. Lightly he stepped and smiled when he thought of her as Mrs. Barsett, imagining a cosy firelit home with doors and windows locked on a pagan world. After all, with women one should never dogmatize. Once Corder lay buried in quicklime, she might in revulsion from his crimes wish to forget him in a happier marriage. Frail seemed that hope, yet hope it was, and it helped smother his irritation at Lydia's haughtiness and Bertram's open wooing of her which, to annoy him, she encouraged. Although his vanity was ruffled by her purring antics, he was not jealous, no longer feeling desire for her, and knowing that she acted purely from pique. Besides, he felt that she should be pitied. While he might possibly marry Mary, there was little chance of Corder's escaping the gallows to become her captive.

The news of his arrest was soon known in the village, and the rioting grew ever noisier, more turbulent and lecherous, as hundreds came to see what remained of the barn, sightseers arriving from Ipswich, Bury, Cambridge, Norwich and London. Details of the prisoner's progress reached them almost by the hour, messengers riding to say what he looked like, where he and his guardians had stopped, and even what he had eaten for dinner. Almost was it like the triumphant approach of a hero rather than the dragging back of a criminal to the scene of his crime.

In Colchester, the governor of the jail had refused to admit him, arguing that the warrant mentioned no specific jail, that the offence had been committed beyond the jurisdiction of Colchester, and that he would not accept the responsibility lest Corder should commit suicide. So they had to lodge him at the George Inn. Handcuffed to Ayres, he had lain in no easy bed. One wrist locked to Ayres' wrist, the other to the bed, he must have tossed all night, unable to sleep at the near prospect of the gallows. Yet it was reported he had been most cheerful during the coach journey, telling such obscene stories, and laughing uproariously while he told them, that the other passengers had loudly complained of his conduct.

Mary's brother had followed and had spoken to him at the "George".

"The waiter told me about it," said a dusty traveller in the "Cock's" bar. "He was outside the door and he heard all they said. This fellow—Moore his name was, I recollect—went for Corder hell-for-leather, wanted to know what the devil he meant by cutting other girls' throats when he was married to his sister, and why he wrote them letters to old Marten about how happy he was with Maria when all the time he was living with this fellow's sister. Married to her, too, by the Lord! But Corder wouldn't say nothing. 'I'll not answer any questions nor say anything about it,' says he; and very haughty he was, the waiter tells me. And that's all the satisfaction the old cock got out of him. This constable fellow, Lea, turned him out for making too much row. Said his questions were improper, or something, and off he went, red as a carrot, swearing he'd have the law on him yet."

Now that Corder was trapped, fate struck at him again. He was recognized by representatives of a Manningtree bank as the man who had presented a forged cheque for £93. Even should he wriggle from the murder charge, he would most likely hang for forgery.

"The waiter told me about it," said the traveller. "He was there when the chief clerk arrived in a chaise. He could see by the look on the fellow's phiz, he said, and by the troubled air of the cove with him, that something was up. This other cove, it turned out, was the landlord of the 'White Hart' at Manningtree, and Corder had got him to say he had a good character or something. How he did it, only the devil knows, for I've never seen a fellow with a more villainous phiz with those squint-eyes and all. Anyhow he'd got over ninety goblins out of that bank, saying his name was Cooke and that he was a farmer who'd got a cheque from another farmer for a herd of cattle he'd sold him. And the bank—would you believe it, fellows!—the bloody bank paid him out in solid gold! And here's me, a respectable merchant what can't get a penny out of my bank without going on my knees and lying like a politician! How they do it's beyond me."

"When did this happen?" asked the Corinthian.

"During April, I was told," said the stranger.

April! That was following his marriage to Miss Moore. He must have required money with which to impress her after his grand talk and her need to begin again at Brentford. Yet how had he managed to cash a cheque in a strange town, when all that the landlord of the inn knew about him was that he had occasionally dropped in for a drink? It seemed that his mysterious charm did not operate only on women, but that men—and hard-headed bankers, too—could be trapped by it.

"That beat him," chuckled the traveller. "Until then he'd been grinning and making jokes and talking about all the women he'd had, but when he saw the bank clerk and the publican he shook in every joint, the waiter tells me, and went as white as paste. The clerk had the cheque in his hand and he rubbed it under Corder's nose. 'Pay me the £93 you received on this,' he says, and Corder was struck dumb with terror and hung down his head. 'Come,' says the clerk, 'why don't you look me in the face like a man?' says he. And still Mr. bloody Corder could say nothing. He hung his head as though his neck was broke, as it'll be broke soon, sure enough. Then he threw himself into a chair and hid his face in his hands. It was rare, says the waiter to me, to see how he shook and choked. Why! he had to run out of the room, says the waiter, for fear he'd bust out laughing, the banker's clerk looking as though he was going to explode with rage like a frog with a straw up its bottom, and there Corder was shivering and blubbering like a child going to be whipped."

"When's he going to get here?" asked one of the crowd.

"Nobody knows," growled the stranger. "They ain't telling for fear of a riot. They want to sneak him here without nobody knowing. And, by God, if I could get my two hands on him, I'd teach the bastard not to go murdering unfortunate females, the swine. . . ."

"Ay, ay," said the other drinkers, nodding vigorously. . . .

"There's no escape for him now," said the Corinthian after supper that night with Lydia and Bertram. "If he wriggles out of one noose, he's in another."

"He forged that money for her," said Lydia, and bit her trembling underlip. "If she hadn't taken that big house at Brentford he wouldn't have had to do it."

The Corinthian said nothing, realizing that argument against a woman's prejudice was a waste of time. Not Mary, but Corder, had urged that removal from London when, apparently threatened by Mrs. Marten, he had become afraid of remaining in the city. Lydia, however, was determined on Mary taking the blame; as she also blamed Maria for having got herself murdered. And he was shocked that a woman otherwise so intelligent and sane should behave so blindly; yet when he looked at her, he realized that this defence was put up, not out of conviction of Corder's innocence, but because she was determined not to be jeered at. When Bertram had called Mary a mouse he had felt as Lydia must feel every time Corder was insulted, knowing that what was said was the truth while refusing to admit it.

In fellow-sympathy, he took and squeezed her hand. "He's not dead yet," he said with false cheerfulness. "And he's no fool. He might have a good defence, for all we know."

"I'll pay for it," she said. "He'll have the best man money can buy."

Of all the expressions of Lydia's fondness for Corder, none astounded the Corinthian so much as this offer of paying for his defence. Always had she been mercenary, squabbling over farthings, refusing to share with him even the cost of a meal, and now to say that she'd spend money to keep Corder alive proved to him, as nothing else could have proved it, that she was no longer sane about that cross-eyed dandiprat.

"We'll see," he said, patting her hand. "The inquest's not over yet. Anything might happen. . . ."

Nothing could happen to rescue Corder, as both well knew. The man must die unless a miracle intervened, but Lydia was grateful for this encouragement, and she squeezed his hand in thanks. Bertram sat silent, gazing into his brandy-glass and fearing that Lydia, now that she was no longer the Corinthian's mistress, was further from his arms than ever she had been.

That night the Corinthian could not sleep. He never had liked sleeping with a man and the effort of keeping away from Bertram, lest by chance he touch him, made him restless. Besides, he had caught something of Lydia's optimistic mood and in sympathy hoped that Corder might yet be saved, although he could imagine nothing that could possibly save him. At last, restlessly, he slid out of bed and poured himself a drink of brandy.

It was very dark and when he drew his repeater from his fob-pocket and, pressing down the catch at its side, it chimed twice, he felt distressed because it was not later. So many hours of darkness, of loneliness left before the dawn, with Bertram snoring under the sheets and blankets.

He gulped down the brandy and was about to return, shivering, to bed, when he heard the sound of wheels approaching.

Arrivals after two o'clock in the morning at a country inn were far from common; and then suddenly he realized that this must be Corder coming home. To avoid the possibility of a hostile demonstration, they had decided to bring him in the dark. . . .

He threw open the window and looked out. No one, nothing, was to be seen save the trees and houses in the moonlight. The wheels he had heard had stopped turning, and he began to wonder whether, weary yet sleepless, he had imagined the sound. Or had the chaise or cart stopped at some house further down the hill? At Corder's mother's, perhaps? He turned, and was about to close the window, when he heard men walking, the crunch of stones under heavy boots. Then, up the hill, he saw three men approaching. One man by his bulk he knew to be Ayres. The other man, stocky and broad, he did not recognize. But the third man, crouched between these others, he knew was Corder.

Into the inn-yard they walked stealthily, and Ayres stepped forward to tap on the door. The other man kept his hand close to Corder's and it was not until they moved and the heavy Spanish cloak which Corder wore fell open that the Corinthian realized that, by metal links, they were bound wrist to wrist. The sight of those handcuffs came to him with a shock of horror, yet he should have expected to see them. Until then, the thought of Corder in custody had not seriously disturbed him. This reality, however, those steel links rippling in the moonlight, made him understand, as he had not understood before, that this poor wretch was death's ordained victim soon to be cut off forever from his fellows.

Quickly he drew back lest he be seen, and as he did so he heard a rustling nearby and noticed that something white had gripped the ledge of the window close to his. Lydia's window. Clearly, he heard her sob, then heard her window softly close.

He did not look out again to find whether Corder, too, had heard, lest the fellow believe he crowed over him in his distress. He tiptoed back to bed, his heart heavy at the thought of Lydia in her misery, as he crawled in beside the snoring Bertram.

And he wondered where and whether Corder would sleep that night.

Chapter Sixteen

THE TRUTH OF A LIE?

THE next morning, the inquest was resumed at the "Cock", Lydia, Bertram and the Corinthian, as residents at the inn, being allowed seats; but the uproar outside was such that they had to strain to hear each word. In and around the inn, the crowd drank and shouted, sang ribald songs and howled for Corder's neck. Women squealed merrily when pinched and slapped and kissed, men laughed at a word, all determined to enjoy every minute of this hangman's festival. In the room next to that in which sat coroner and jury, a merry party had gathered to bellow and blaspheme, clapping, stamping and singing.

The Corinthian tried not to listen to the bawdy squeals and curses, and he saw how white Lydia had grown when above the murmur of the court some drunkard called for a quick hanging to woman-killers, and the women hissed and blurted and shrieked their approval of such a sentiment. The public, it seemed, had condemned him already, and this inquest was a farce.

Corder was not present, and the first five or ten minutes were wasted by an argument between the coroner and representatives of the public press, the coroner ruling that no notes were to be taken and insisting that they return their books to their pockets. As these reporters had travelled from Bury, Ipswich, Chelmsford, Colchester and London, they were naturally indignant; but the coroner would not listen to their complaints. He would permit no notes to be taken, he said, and that was final. Muttering, the reporters put away their books and pencils and sat back, arms folded, determined to remember what they could, so that their public should not go unsatisfied.

Suddenly, a heavily built man dressed in wig and robes strutted into the court and, giving a brief bow to the coroner, demanded, on behalf of the prisoner William Corder, that his client be present during the proceedings. This started another wrangle, counsel producing precedents which the coroner dismissed, until it was finally ruled that Corder should not be allowed to hear what was alleged against him, but that the depositions should later be read to him. Sniffing and wobbling his dark jowls, which looked as though they were in need of a shave, counsel sat down with a truculent air and crossed his legs, glaring with disdain at this bumpkin court.

Little George, Maria's eleven-year-old half-brother, was the first witness, and with no sign of timidity, almost unctuously, he told how, on the day that his sister had left home, he had seen Corder go from the Red Barn across two fields with a pickaxe over his shoulder, walking in the direction of his own home.

Then came a shy female, Phoebe Stow, with a shrill defensive voice, as though she were refuting insults to her character. She lived, she said to the coroner's prompting, in the cottage nearest the Red Barn, and one day last year before the dinner-things had been cleared away, Corder had come to her house and had asked her to lend him her husband's spade. "I replied," said she, with a watchful look, "that I had an old one which was good for but little. He said, 'Anything will do for what I want it for.'"

"Did he say what he wanted it for?" asked the coroner.

"No, your honour," said she, curtseying, "but I fetched him the spade; and when he came back he asked me how I did. I told him, very weak and low. He said, 'I'm in a hurry and can't stop to talk with you.'"

"Was he," asked the coroner, "confused in his manner? was he, ahem, different from usual?"

"No, your honour. I didn't notice nothing different."

"When did this occur?"

"I don't know, your honour. I was in no state to notice the calendar, for I was very poorly, as I tell you, and on the next twenty-ninth of April I was took with the pains and confined, and I went to church that day four weeks, and it happened in the interval."

"Was the, ahem, spade returned?"

"I don't know, sir," said she, plainly astonished that anybody should want to talk about spades when such fascinating subjects as her confinement might have been discussed.

Her husband followed her to take the oath. He had not missed the spade, he said, and he had helped last harvest to fill the bay in the barn where the body had been found. Corder, he said, came in soon after they had begun work and had said to him in a joking manner: "Frank, there's a constable coming for you."

"What did he, ahem, mean by that?" asked the coroner.

"Don't know, your honour," mumbled Stow. "I told him I didn't care for any constable, and that's that."

"Was anything further said, anything, ahem, suspicious?"

"Well, sir," said Stow, biting the brim of his best hat, "one day when we was at dinner in Thatley Lay, Corder comes up to me and he says: 'I'll give you a pound to cut my throat.'"

"He said what!" cried the coroner.

"He said he'd give me a pound to cut his throat. I thought it was a joke; and Towns, he's our foreman, asked him how he could run on so."

"And what did he say to that?"

"He was laughing as he said it, your honour."

When the next witness strode forward confidently to take the oath, the Corinthian straightened his back. This was the burly fellow he had seen last night in the moonlight and whom this morning he had been told was James Lea, a police officer from Lambeth Street office, the man who had arrested Corder at Brentford.

With almost a sailor's roll he walked, his brown coat seeming too small for him and ready to burst at the seams. He was going a trifle bald in front and, to cover this, he brushed the thinning hairs up and forward until they stood on end, thinly covering the temples, although his whiskers curved luxuriously in half-moons. His long pointed nose seemed to have been sharpened especially to sniff out secrets; the brows were drawn over the alert eyes as though years of disbelieving whatever he might be told had made him suspicious of everything and everybody; and his small mouth was tight-set above the pudgy jaw between the high white tips of his collar.

Glibly he recited the oath, staring from screwed-up eyelids at the faces about him, as if he knew the secrets, particularly criminal secrets, of everybody present; and he answered the snuffling coroner in a sharp, faintly derisive way, like a man whose mind is made up and who is impatient of wasting time when the prisoner should be instantly hanged on the nearest tree.

He gave his evidence briskly, in abrupt sentences, as though repeating from memory, and now and then he glanced at a small notebook to remind himself what next to say. He was a police officer, he said, and "in consequence of an application at Lambeth Street office, by the constable, Ayres, I afterwards apprehended William Corder at a boarding-school called Grove House situate in Ealing Lane, Brentford. When I went to the house, Corder came out of a room to me in the hall; I told him I was come on some business I had with him, and he asked me into the drawing-room. I then told him it was a serious charge I had against him and he must consider himself a prisoner. He replied, 'Very well'. I then told him it was respecting a young woman named Maria Marten, with whom he formerly kept company in Suffolk, and who having been missing a length of time great suspicion existed respecting her. The prisoner said: 'I never knew any such person even by name.'"

"Fool," groaned the Corinthian, "the bloody fool!"

"I told him to recollect himself," continued Lea, "while I repeated the enquiry twice over; and I said, 'Did you ever know a young woman by that name?' He replied: 'No, I never did.' I then told him I would put no more questions on that point. I took the prisoner to the 'Red Lion' public-house at Brentford and left him in the custody of Ayres; and then returned to search the house where the prisoner lived. In a desk which I unlocked with a key taken from the prisoner, I found a passport for France, dated December the twentieth, and four letters, all of which I produce. In the dressing-room I found a black velvet reticule containing a pair of detonating pistols: maker's name: Harcourt, Ipswich; a flask with powder and bullets, and a bullet-mould. The prisoner told me he bought them when he was ten years old."

"Ha!" said the coroner, cocking an eyebrow. "The detonating pistol is a recent invention. The prisoner must be, ahem, a very small boy still, if that's the case."

Lea gave him a professional smirk and the audience sniggered; then he continued in his singsong voice: "On the way to the 'Red Lion' I told him that the body of Maria Marten had been found. He made no reply at first, but when we had gone about twenty yards he asked me when it was found."

After such damning evidence whatever else might be said must come as an anticlimax, and the Corinthian nestled back in his chair; he noted the intensity with which Lydia was staring at Lea, how heavily she breathed through wide nostrils and how her fists were clenched. Now she could scarcely pretend that Corder was innocent. Twice had the fool given himself away: first by stupidly denying any knowledge of Maria, and then by pretending that he had had the pistols since he had been a boy when they could have been on sale for only the last seven or eight years. The idiot had helped to hang himself with senseless lying. And when he had had that passport for France, why hadn't he used it? Had he found it impossible to break from Mary and the peace of Brentford?

Mrs. Marten was again taking the oath. Demure, pale-skinned, she stood and took the oath with uplifted hand, swearing to tell the truth, the whole truth, and nothing but the truth. Even before Lydia's accusing glare she did not shrink, but sadly smiled and in a low voice answered the coroner's questions.

When the reticule which Lea had found at Brentford was passed to her to identify, she burst into tears, sobbing: "O, yes, this was my daughter's! This was poor Maria's! I saw her put it into her bag the day she went away."

Before such grief, the court shuffled into an uncomfortable silence, the coroner stroking his chin and gazing at the beamed ceiling, while several women began to sob in sympathy.

"Bitch," muttered Lydia.

From the room next door came a hoot of laughter and a girl's giggle ending on a choking noise. Someone began to sing a bawdy song to the scraping of a fiddle, while others stamped, clapped hands and loudly joined in the chorus.

"Can't anything be done about that, ahem, indecent uproar?" growled the coroner.

From the back of the court, the landlord rose to his feet. "I'm sorry, your honour," he said, "and I tell you I'm quite disgusted with the nuisance which it is impossible for me to abate, much less to suppress. They are out-of-hand and unlawful, your honour."

The coroner shrugged and turned again to Mrs. Marten who, still clutching Maria's reticule, gazed at him with round wet eyes.

"I'm, ahem, sorry to press this, ma'am," he said gently, "but we must find the truth, no matter what people's natural feelings might be. You say you saw the, er, deceased take this, er, reticule the day she left home? Was there anything important you remember about that day—any, hum, quarrelling, for example?"

"No, sir," she whispered, "I heard no words between Bill—between Mr. Corder and Maria of any angry nature; but she was very low."

"Very low? Why, er, was that?"

"When Mr. Corder told her that the constable had got a warrant against her, she cried very much."

"Was this, ahem, their only quarrel to your knowledge?"

"O, no, sir! I've often heard them dispute about a five-pound note; and Maria used to say to him: 'You've taken away the bread which belonged to me and the child.'"

At this example of Corder's callousness the listeners groaned and moaned, and some cried: "Shame on him! Shame!" while Corder's barrister glared ferociously into their faces.

"On one occasion when they were so quarrelling," continued Mrs. Marten between sniffles, "I heard Mr. Corder say, 'Pray, Maria, don't tell me of that note any more; you shall have a shilling as long as I have one; and your child, too.'"

"Ah," said the coroner, "then these quarrels were not, ahem, all of his making?"

"Far from it, sir," said Mrs. Marten with an appearance of great honesty, as though determined to be fair even about a villain. "I've often heard my daughter say to him: 'If I go to prison, you shall go, too!' She often said that: about once a week at least before she went away with him."

While the court growled ferociously, the shifting on forms and chairs with the frou-frou of women's dresses sounding like the hissing of angry birds, Mrs. Marten walked slowly back to her seat, and many were the compassionate glances given her. Lydia stared down at her own hands in her lap, sucking in her lips and not daring to look up lest in her fury she denounce this female, who, with each cunning word, had tightened the rope about Corder's neck.

William Towns, foreman to Corder's mother, next gave evidence, describing how last harvest the wheat had been stacked in the Red Barn, and how, since his brother's death, William Corder had managed the farm.

Then Mrs. Marten was recalled to identify the dead girl's clothes which she did with particular care, as though determined not to be hasty, lingering over the filthy, smelly rags. The handkerchiefs, she said, she recognized as being those which Maria had worn the day she left home. Also the bonnet which Corder had carried in his bag. And also the pieces of shift. The shoes, too, she was certain had been Maria's because they were tipped at the heels. She added that she had seen Maria put an ashen busk under her stays the night before she went away, but she made no attempt to explain why; and as the coroner asked no questions, she ventured nothing further.

A servant-woman from the Corder household next told how, while cleaning Corder's room, the lid of a box had fallen off by accident. Inside it she had found a pair of kid gloves and a pair of high-heeled boots of Denmark satin calashed with leather.

She was followed by a cutler from Hadleigh who alleged that Corder had entered his shop with a short sword that had had a curved blade about twelve inches long. It had, he said, an ivory handle and was mounted with brass.

"He wished it to be ground," he explained to the coroner's prompting, "and to be made as sharp as a carving-knife."

"Did he say for what, ahem, purpose he wished it ground?"

"Sir, he told me he had a cousin going to be married, and that he should sit at the table to carve with it. I did as I was directed and he called for it the same evening and paid for it."

Even more loudly than they had applauded Mrs. Marten did the listeners titter and groan and hiss at this evidence. A short sword with a curved blade to be used for carving! For carving what? . . .

The tall stooping surgeon, John Lawton, next was sworn, and he peered over his glasses as though he had mislaid something and had both forgotten where and what it was. Like Lea, he needed little prompting, the coroner allowing him to gabble his evidence with the aid of notes; and all were hushed that they might not miss a word.

"I was present," he said, "when the body was viewed by the gentlemen of the jury, and I made as minute an examination as I could. I first took off some pieces of sack which covered it; the body was lying upon the right side, with the head forced down upon the shoulder. There was an appearance of coagulated blood upon the cheek, and there appeared to be blood upon the clothes and handkerchiefs. The green handkerchief round the neck had been pulled tight, so that a man's hand might be put between the knot and the fold, and under it there was the appearance of a wound from a sharp instrument, but that part was so decomposed that I can only say that it had that appearance. The internal bone of the orbit of the right eye was fractured, as if a pointed instrument had been thrust into it, and the bone dividing the nose was displaced; the brain was in such a fluid state that I am unable to say whether it had sustained any injury or not."

"Would such a stab penetrate the brain?" asked the coroner, looking owlishly wise.

"It might and it might not," said Mr. Lawton, plainly put out by the interruption and this demand to be precise. "I found no injury in any other part," he continued hurriedly; "but there were two small portions of bone in the throat which might have passed thither from the nose or orbit of the eye. I think the handkerchief was drawn tight enough to have caused death; the neck of the deceased appeared very much compressed indeed. The sack had evidently been tied after the deceased had been put in head foremost."

This surgeon was the last witness. After he had returned to his seat, the coroner coughed for silence and announced that there was no one else to be called. Whereupon Corder's defender rose, tossing his gown like feathers behind him, and said in ringing tones: "Sir, as the evidence has been gone through, I propose that my client be permitted to come into the room to hear it read."

The coroner scratched his chin and closed one eye; then, with the air of a king conferring knighthood on a scavenger, he agreed. "Let William Corder be brought in," he said.

Everybody turned to look towards the door. Even those who had known Corder since babyhood stared with excitement as though expecting that during the months of his absence he had sprouted horns and goat-feet.

"I can't look," moaned Lydia, gripping the Corinthian's large hand and squeezing it. "I can't. It'd kill me."

Uneasily, he glanced at her, troubled to see the torture in those large eyes, red at the corners, and in the tightly compressed lips. This was a new Lydia, one whom he could understand and sympathize with; stripped of her feminine defences of ridicule and scorn, she had become a frightened girl, and with distended nostrils she took deep breaths of the foul air. Had she always shown herself so ill-assured as this instead of as an imperious woman, how happy might have been their partnership, he thought; and he marvelled, as so often he had marvelled, that a cross-eyed hop-o'-my-thumb like Corder should have been the one to awaken her motherly womanhood.

In the next room, the drunken crowd still sang. From ballads of murder they had swung to sentiment, and with slippery voices were bemoaning the fate of some lass dead of having loved unloved. The Corinthian tried not to listen, but the sound could not be shut out. He would have preferred cries of moral vengeance to this sugary sentiment in which love was made sacred by drunkards who were mostly thieves and whores. That the authorities should permit such behaviour was scandalous, and he considered writing to the newspapers to complain about it. One could not blame the publican, making good money for the first time in his life, and it would have been inhuman to suggest that he should refuse to alchemize the king's silver into beer and spirits; but the inquest, he felt, might have been held elsewhere, in more suitable surroundings. Justice could not be expected in this place with savages weeping and howling maudlin nonsense in the next room.

So silently did the door open and Corder enter, Lea at his heels, that it was some seconds before it was realized that the hero, or villain, of the drama which the audience had come to witness stood amongst them. Tightly did Lydia grip the Corinthian's hand, as, face shaded by her bonnet, she squirmed on her chair.

Muffled in a huge Spanish cloak, Corder stood beside Lea, his head down. No longer was he the impudent young fellow complacent in his cunning. His cheeks were white and drawn, and he shivered as though feverish. Had it not been for Lea's support, he would have fallen; and when he moved, the handcuffs clinked between his wrists.

"Bring the, ahem, gentleman a chair," said the coroner. "Pray, sir, be seated while I read over to you the evidence that has been already deposed."

It was plain that Corder did not hear a word, for when the chair was brought him he looked around dazedly, as if not understanding that it was for his use. Only after Lea had whispered to him did he sink down, drawing up the black cloak to hide as well as he could within the folds of cloth. His counsel went and leaned over him, whispering, but it seemed by the blank look he gave that he did not hear, and while in monotonous stutter the coroner read through what the witnesses had sworn, he took no heed. One moment he was deeply agitated, shivering and sweating, and the next he sank into a miserable reverie, eyes half-closed.

"Sir," said the barrister, "my client is indisposed. I very much doubt if he's capable of appreciating what you are kindly reading to him. I would ask your permission for him to retire. I will attend to everything and explain it to him later."

Delighted at the chance of escaping those accusing eyes, Corder sprang to his feet and would have pushed his way out of the crowded room had not the coroner, reluctant to lose this opportunity for an oration, said sternly:

"William Corder, you are charged with the, er, wilful murder of Maria Marten, and I shall be, ahem, very happy to hear anything which you have to say, or to listen to any, er, evidence which you can adduce in proof of your, ahem, innocence. You have heard what some of the witnesses have, ahem, said against you, therefore you are at liberty to, ahem, invalidate their testimony if you can, or be silent, as you, ahem, may think proper."

Shaking, Corder gaped at the coroner, then turned to his counsel; and, at that moment, he saw Lydia. Until then he had stared mainly at the floor, as though ashamed or afraid to meet the threatening looks of strangers or of those who had known him since childhood; but when he saw Lydia amongst them, he started back and leaned against the wall. Incredulity was the first expression in those crossed eyes, then pride and pleasure sparkled in them, and he gave her a faint bow. She acknowledged the bow, and smiled graciously. And immediately, Corder seemed to lose his terrors. He even gave the illusion of growing in height, colour returning to his cheeks and lips, and almost perkily he looked about him, as though reluctant now to leave. But already Lea and his counsel were escorting him to the door, and he could not dally.

"That man," said Lydia in a voice of profound conviction, "is as innocent as you or I."

The jury had a different opinion. They refused to waste time in listening to the coroner's recapitulation of the evidence, and, after an hour's retirement—the Corinthian felt that they delayed out of decency's sake and to swell their own self-importance by maddening the court—they returned for the foreman to answer the coroner's usual question in echoing tones:

"Yes, unanimously. We return a verdict of wilful murder against William Corder."

"Disgraceful. Pure prejudice," hissed Lydia as the Corinthian led her from the crowded inn into the clean air. "A woman understands such things by instinct. Corder's absolutely innocent."

"Innocent!" stuttered the Corinthian, scarcely believing he had heard correctly.

"Yes," said Lydia fiercely, "it's only prejudice against him . . . and that woman. She did it. I'd swear on a mountain of Bibles that she did it; jealous of her step-daughter, that's what she was. If there's a God in heaven, this tragedy must be stopped. You mark my words. We've not heard the end of this, and truth will out in time. . . . Corder will not hang."

Chapter Seventeen

SURPRISE FOR LYDIA

THAT night nobody slept in Polstead. Sober folk lay sleepless in their beds while drunkards roamed the streets, singing, fighting, quarrelling, making love, and shouting execrations on the name of Corder with obscene details of the things they would like to do to him. By morning, most of the rioters had collapsed in slumber, lying in the chilly spring air separately or in couples, clothes muddied and torn, in outhouses, sties, hen-yards, stables, or on the roadway itself. A cold dawn crawled through the Corinthian's window and he was glad to rise after a miserable night.

The first act of the drama was now ended, and he felt restless, impatient, both desiring and dreading the climax. Whatever Lydia might say, Corder would hang. The evidence against him was too damning and his defence, if he had one, would have to be, to say the least, ingenious. Women fortunately did not sit on juries, or twelve Lydias might have acquitted him because they felt that Maria had been a mercenary slut who deserved to be murdered. Twelve men, however, would put their thumbs down beyond question.

The Corinthian had not seen Corder since the inquest. Such a meeting would have embarrassed them both, and there was nothing to be gained by talk. Several of the jury, for some peculiar reason, had waited on him—a wonder he did not throw bottles at them after their verdict—while he had kept his head under the bedclothes. Even a glass of rum had not inspired him with sufficient courage to look into his neighbours' eyes. Old Towns, who had given unimportant evidence about the barn, and Pryke, who had helped discover the body, also came to offer condolences, Pryke talking to him in whispers for some minutes, possibly about the management of his mother's farm. Nobody in the bar last night had pretended to know what the two had said, but Towns had made no secret of his conversation. Weeping into his beer, he had related how, sobbing like a woman, he had clasped his young master's hand. " 'O, Master Bill!' says I to him," he had piped. " 'O, Master Bill, I'm sorry it's come to this.' And I exhorted him to act like a Christian and to read the scriptures and to consider them as the best instructor in his day of trouble. He listened, solemn, to what I said, and I saw him shake under the blankets while he wiped the dew of sorrow from his eyes. He said nothing, but he nodded his head, and I knew that he understood my meaning. ''Tis never too late,' I told him, but he said nothing: he only groaned. Ay, he feels it bad. I told him I was sorry for being forced to bear witness against him, for he was always a good master to me; and again I exhorted him to find consolation in religious exercises."

Now that he had been charged, hatred against Corder seemed to have lessened, at least amongst these villagers in the bar—the hordes of strangers still screamed for his death—and the Corinthian had been happy to sit amongst them while they retold old tales, mostly pointless, about Foxy in his youth.

Even when Corder had been brought downstairs to be taken to Bury jail, the Corinthian had made no attempt to see him. In the deserted tap-room he had remained while, outside, men and women had howled and cheered, and he had heard Lea shouting back at them, telling them to give way before him and his prisoner. There was something bestial in man, it seemed, that liked to sniff at blood. In London, thousands ran to watch a hanging, and the country was no better. The man they had known since babyhood had suddenly become a monster, a thing to be feared and loathed, yet, strangely, reverenced. Yes, in a way they reverenced Corder and his deed, carrying away with them chips of the Red Barn as though they were the precious relics of a saint, and struggling to touch him, to stare and spit and yell at him.

By now he would be safe in Bury St. Edmunds jail, for a time, until the assizes came and, later, the hangman. The Corinthian shivered to think what must be his thoughts, and moodily he went downstairs to breakfast, leaving Bertram half-shaved and grumbling at the stale booze in his belly.

After their debauch, both villagers and visitors looked blear-eyed and sallow-skinned. Many were leaving Polstead, riding off or travelling in carts or chaises, but a few lingered to wander around the remains of the Red Barn, piously rolling their eyes at man's depravity and sighing above the shallow grave, titillated at the vision of violent death, of a girl wounded and hacked and shot and bleeding in her lacerated finery.

Under the cherry-blossoms in her garden, the Corinthian saw Mrs. Marten playing with the children; and although she curtseyed as he passed, plainly wanting him to enter, he pretended not to see her. Already he was managing to half forget that it had been at his suggestion that she had betrayed her lover, and he thought of her treachery with disgust and horror. Corder might have been a villain, but even villains, he felt, should not be betrayed by their mistresses.

There was no longer any reason to remain in Polstead, and had he seen Lydia he would have suggested their return to London; but she remained in her bedroom and did not come downstairs until supper-time. Then, despite paint on cheeks and lips, she looked ill, her eyes feverish, and her gestures meaningless and erratic. Nevertheless, she managed to smile and, when she talked, her voice took on a shrill note of desperate gaiety.

"I am going to get drunk tonight," she announced. "Has the landlord any passable wine? I'd like to start with a clean drink."

The Corinthian went to enquire, and as he stepped into the passage he saw Mr. Gordon with a strange woman who yet appeared oddly familiar. Heavily cloaked, she wore an immense bonnet, and it was not until he noticed her gloved hand in the air as though she were asking the landlord to be silent that he felt his heart falter. At first, he refused to believe it, then he stepped closer and, as he touched her arm, she turned.

"Mrs. Corder!" he cried. "What are you doing here?"

Mary Corder gave him a wintry smile and held out her hand.

"I'm so relieved to see you, Mr. Barsett," she cooed shrilly, pretending not to notice how amorously he squeezed her fingers. "I'm completely unchaperoned and, although of course I'm now a married woman, I really can't altogether feel like one when I'm with strangers; I get quite frightened. And now the landlord tells me that my husband's left here."

She spoke as though Corder might have been any traveller who had departed a trifle earlier than had been expected; and, fondling her gloved hand while gazing into her blue eyes, the Corinthian felt that he would like to kiss her skirt-hem to honour such restraint, such magnificent sang-froid.

"Yes," he said, "he left for Bury yesterday."

"O, dear!" she sighed, raising her eyebrows comically. "So I'll have to go on there, I suppose; and travelling is such an expense. Every penny's needed now to help poor William. I've sold whatever I could, and I hope to sell more things, and I grudge every farthing given to any other cause. The law is so expensive. But if we can only save him, what does anything else matter?"

"Indeed, no," said the Corinthian, unable any longer to hold against the gentle pull of her fingers and letting her hand leave his. "But, ma'am, you must be hungry. Would you honour us by sharing our supper? Pray, don't be alarmed. I am not alone. My, er, sister, Mrs. Atherton, is with me, and a friend whom I believe you have met, Mr. Bertram Marley."

"I should be most grateful," she said, showing her shining teeth, "but first, if you'll excuse me, I'd like to attend to my toilet."

"Of course," he mumbled, "of course," and stood aside that she might pass to walk up the stairs, the landlord holding high the candle. "Mr. Gordon," he cried, "will you fetch me the finest wines in your cellar?"

He almost ran back to the parlour and at sight of his laughing eyes and flushed cheeks, Lydia and Bertram looked up, startled.

"You'll never believe it," he cried, dancing about the table, "but we've a guest for supper. Do you know who it can be?"

"By your infantile behaviour," said Lydia coldly, "I can only presume that it must be a female, and . . . Good God, not Mrs. Corder!"

"Yes, Mary Corder," said the Corinthian, a trifle dashed that she should have so quickly opened the secret. "Mary Corder herself galloping to Polstead with gold for her husband's defence. I knew that woman'd never desert him. She's been selling everything, she told me; and she's convinced the scoundrel's innocent!"

"Haven't you even considered the possibility that he might be innocent?" asked Lydia darkly, gazing at her face distorted in the glass decanter. "Not that this woman can know anything about it, as she wasn't there to see how that hypocrite, Mrs. Marten, lied in court. She's acting purely on impulse, because she wants to believe what she wants to believe. Anyhow, I must confess I'm curious to see this paragon. There must be something really extraordinary in a female who can not only turn the wits of a half-exhausted dirty old man like you but can make a young spark like Corder become domestic."

The Corinthian did not reply. He dared not reply. Being called a half-exhausted dirty old man made him quiver with rage, but he did not wish to begin a quarrel. When Mary Corder entered he wanted to appear at his best, as a suave man of the world.

"There's nothing extraordinary about her," mumbled Bertram, staring hungrily at Lydia's bosom. "She's just an ordinary little woman, the kind you see by the thousands every day: the grocer's wife, the butcher's wife; you'd not give her a second glance in the company of three. Besides, the creature's deaf; and how the hell can you bellow love to a deaf woman?"

"I'd have thought it rather an advantage," said Lydia. "She can pretend not to understand what you're asking, so that she can nod 'Yes' with a good conscience. But, of course, dear Mrs. Corder would never say 'Yes' under any circumstances, would she? . . . She's taking enough time over her toilet, however. Can she be a coquette, your little prude?"

"She asked time to wash after her journey, and doubtless there are other things to be attended to. . . ."

"Doubtless," said Lydia with a twisted smile; "however angelic she may appear to be, she has her human weaknesses. . . . Do you know," she added brightly, "I think I'm going to enjoy this evening."

When the door opened, all turned expectantly, only to sink down into their chairs as Mr. Gordon entered with four bottles of claret.

"Supper will be ready in a moment, lady and gentlemen," he said, producing a corkscrew from his apron pocket.

"We need a fourth plate," growled the Corinthian. "We expect a guest tonight."

"I know, sir," said Mr. Gordon, "and I have brought it." From inside his jacket he brought out a plate which he placed on the table, while out of his pockets came knife, fork and spoon. "There's nothing else you require?" he asked, drawing the cork and placing it and the opened bottle on the table.

"For the moment, no," said Bertram, pouring the wine. "Later, we'll probably want some brandy."

"Of course you will, sir," said the landlord, backing suddenly from the room and straight into Mary Corder who was about to enter, so that he almost knocked her off her feet.

"You clumsy oaf!" cried the Corinthian, pushing him aside and grasping Mary's hand. "You're not hurt, my dear, I pray?" he asked anxiously.

Lydia and Bertram raised supercilious eyebrows at one another, then Lydia leaned back negligently in her chair, and waited to receive their guest with the greatest possible insolence. Although she did not wear her most expensive gown, she was nevertheless trussed in a rich dress of green silk, and her hair, as always in the evening, was carefully curled and oiled.

Timidly, Mary Corder entered into the candlelight, smiling and blinking, and her gown was of unadorned black—as though, thought Lydia contemptuously, she already mourned her unfortunate husband—her brown hair carelessly curled and falling in slight disorder down the nape of her neck. Intently watching the Corinthian's lips, she curtseyed at each introduction and did not seem in the least disconcerted by Lydia's icy bow.

"We have some claret," said the Corinthian, after seating her between himself and Bertram. "You must need a stimulant after that long journey."

"Very little," she whispered, "and a lot of water with it, please."

Bertram coughed to cover his chuckle and glanced maliciously at Lydia; and even he was startled by the basilisk glitter in her eyes as she stared at this insignificant little woman, fluttering her hands in protest at the largeness of the glass the Corinthian filled for her.

"Drink it," said the Corinthian: "it will do you good; and you'll need all your strength for the ordeal before you."

"Ordeal?" she repeated as though puzzled. "O, you mean about poor William! But that'll come out all right. I know it will. I prayed many hours and the gladness that filled me afterwards could only have come from heaven. No matter how black everything may seem at the moment, we are under the protection of heaven and must not despair. I only wish I could share his troubles, for he must be as lonely as poor Robinson Crusoe without even a footprint in the sand. But it'll not be for long. Such things are sent to try us, and poor William may become even a better man, if possible, once this ordeal's behind him and he is free again."

"How do you know that he'll be free?" asked Lydia harshly.

"Why, ma'am, I just know it." She smiled at Lydia as though they were old friends. "You're a woman, too, so I'm sure you must understand," she said coaxingly. "We feel things, don't we? O, you gentlemen can laugh at us, of course; but we *know*, don't we, my dear? In our hearts, we *know*. I see that you're married, too. . . ." Lydia clenched her left hand, furious with herself for not having taken off that lying ring she had bought to make her alliance with the Corinthian appear respectable. ". . . so you can understand what I feel," continued Mary gently. "There are more things in heaven and earth than are dreamt of in our philosophies, as the great bard wrote, and the union of souls, which is true marriage, remains a holy mystery. Yes, a holy mystery. A sacred sacrament. I *know* everything that my husband feels and does."

"A most embarrassing gift," muttered Bertram. "In that case, I will most definitely not get married."

"O, I don't mean it like that!" she shrilled, with a faint titter. "Of course I don't know what he's doing all the time, but I do know when he's telling the truth or when he's been guilty of some little thing. I can sense it—here!" she whispered, staring round-eyed from face to face, as she tapped her stays above the left breast. "William's been a foolish lad, most men are, and it's not for wives to complain about the past, seeing that it's usually bad women who lead men astray in the first place. There's this Marten creature, for example"—she wrinkled her nose—"I've read all about her in the newspapers, and poor William would have been clay in such hands. O, she tempted him, and because he was young and silly, the devil led him on. I've forgiven him all that, and I swear I'll never speak to him about it so long as we live. Never. When all these troubles are over, I've decided just to forget everything as though it were a bad dream."

Before that calm assurance even Lydia remained silent, although she breathed more deeply while watching Mary with suspicious eyes; and all fell silent when Nelly shouldered open the door and splashed the soup-plates on to the table.

While they ate and drank, no one spoke, the Corinthian watching with tender admiration this little woman so confident in her faith. That Corder might be hanged, she refused to believe. He was her husband and she wanted him to live, and God, being a fatherly old gentleman, could scarcely deny her that small portion of legal happiness. It was Lydia who showed herself worried, with the violet stains under her eyes and her convulsive gestures; and with wonderment and dislike, she stared at Mary, as though as yet uncertain what to believe about this extraordinary animal. Only Bertram showed indifference, eating grossly and looking at the company with a certain impatience from under cocked brows.

Daintily, birdlike, Mary ate, pecking at the food with knife and fork as though this were a rite that really should not be acted publicly, and she scarcely did more than press her lips on the rim of her wine-glass. Lydia ate almost nothing, but she drank heavily, silently passing her glass to Bertram to have it refilled whenever, as was often, she emptied it. The way she lounged in the chair, displaying her almost naked shoulders to shine glossily in the candlelight, and puffed out her bosom, lolling her legs loosely within the skirt and petticoats, made the Corinthian uneasy. He knew these dark moods of hers, and he feared them.

"So," said she, after the table had been cleared and the door closed on the servant, "you are quite convinced of your husband's innocence, ma'am?"

"Why, of course!" said Mary, opening wide her eyes. "Do you know, ma'am, when I came in here—I don't often get these feelings, but I do at times—I felt that you were on my side and would be my friend. I thought that at least you'd understand, whatever the men might think. William could never do such a dreadful thing."

Confounded by the woman's *naïveté*, Lydia licked her lips and took another drink.

"You didn't hear the evidence at the inquest," she said gruffly. "I did. And there were things sworn to that couldn't have been lies. He left this woman's house carrying her clothes and he met her at the Red Barn so that she could take off his brother's coat and trousers and put on her skirt again and run away with him to Ipswich. And she was never seen again afterwards until her body was dug out of the earth the other day."

"A horrible story," said Mary with a shiver. "I read all about it, and that dreadful female in those immodest garments! I do declare it made me blush for my sex when I read it. I know she was a bad lot, but she appears to have had no shame whatever!"

"Her reticule was found in your house," continued Lydia,

staring into her eyes, "with other things of hers. How do you explain that?"

"William could explain it, I'm quite sure, if people would only listen to the truth instead of jumping to the worst conclusions. Most likely that horrid baggage put it in his pocket while she was changing her garments and he forgot to give it back to her."

"If Corder didn't kill her, who did?"

"I haven't the faintest idea." And by the way she tossed her head to set the curls rippling into one another, it appeared that she did not consider the question of any particular importance. "A tramp, possibly," she said. "Why, it might have been almost anybody with a woman like that. That kind asks for it."

"Asks to be murdered?"

"Of course not, my dear lady. I meant that, being immoral, she must accept the consequences of anything that happens to her. God works in devious ways. But it really is disgraceful the way people talk about this creature. Why! you'd think she was some good little maid whom my poor William had led astray! As if William could ever lead anybody astray!" She tittered faintly. "He hasn't the cruelty to kill a thing, even blackbeetles, and he's *so* fond of children. But I knew when I married him that life would not be easy. It has been my profession, ma'am, to teach young children and I think that's what made me so fond of William. He seemed just like a naughty little boy."

"He was more than a naughty little boy with this Marten woman," muttered Lydia, but it was apparent by her heavy breathing and her low voice that she was losing the battle.

"Not in the least," said Mary. "If I were to tell you the dreadful things some little boys do you wouldn't believe me, my dear. It is really shocking at times, and usually I pretend not to notice—my affliction has its uses on occasions—but when young Master Bobswell, for example, pushed the nib of his pen—not even cleaning it first—into poor dear little Minnie Cowbell's anatomy and said he only wanted to find out if the female—er—anatomy was as tough as old boots, as he'd heard his father say, I had to take notice, of course. Even I could not fail to hear her shrieking. But they do far worse things than that. I have to watch whenever they ask to leave the room, because I noticed that a boy often followed a maid rather too quickly, and vice versa; and I caught two of them with the door bolted. Of course I had to expel them both, much as I needed the fees and disliked the fuss. But I had my school's reputation to remember. I tell you these unpleasant stories, which I hope you'll forgive—when we're alone I'll tell you something far worse, something you'll never believe, and the little thing not eleven years of age, too!—because I want you to have some understanding of William. He has never really grown up."

"Why!" cried Bertram, "does he stick pen-nibs in little girls and lock himself in the bog with them?"

Steadily smiling, Mary gazed at Lydia, and it was possible, the Corinthian hoped, that she had not heard Bertram's ill-mannered comment, for which he was grateful. Like an angel, she sat behind the bottles, her eyes a heavenly blue, her pink mouth showing a flicker of teeth when she talked, and all her body concealed from him under cloth and steel and bone.

"Doubtless," said Lydia in a heavily ironic manner, "you have had very intimate dealings with small boys, Mrs. Corder. I have had dealings only with men, and their habits, I agree, are deplorable at times. I could tell you tales of the Corinthian that would drive you blushing out of the room, but I'm too affectionate a sister to do any such thing. Nor would dispute your peculiar knowledge of your husband's habits, small-boyish or otherwise. I would only like to point out that somebody murdered Maria Marten and if it were not your husband it must have been someone remarkably like him."

"O, but we all have doubles!" cried Mary eagerly. "Surely you know that! I remember such a kindly old gentleman stopping me in the street when I was quite a small girl and giving me an apple and insisting that he knew me; but it was my double, of course. It must have been; he was so certain that he knew me and it really made me embarrassed when I had to refuse his pressing invitation to dinner. But of course I couldn't take advantage of a mistake like that, could I? It wouldn't have been honest."

"At least it wouldn't have ended honestly, you may be sure of that," grumbled Lydia, plainly baffled before such innocence. "But to return to your husband, ma'am. What is it that you intend to do for him now that he's in jail?"

"That dreadful word!" She rolled her eyes and groaned. "I really can't believe it, even yet. Poor William in prison, and he did so like his comfort! But what am I going to do, you ask? Why, ma'am, I am going to him, of course. A wife's place is beside her husband in prosperity or adversity, till death us do part. I shall see the governor of that horrid place and I'll insist, I'll insist that I be locked up with him. William's such a helpless person really and never remembers when to change his linen or things like that. And I'm sure he won't eat properly. At a time like this he needs all his strength. The trial—should it come to that—will be a terrible experience, and after what the wretched newspapers have been saying, all the country seems to have gone mad. I know these men must earn a living and newspapers have their uses——"

Bertram laughed and she turned her startled, enquiring look upon him.

"Did you speak, sir?" she asked.

"No, no," he said hurriedly, taking a glass of wine.

"As I was saying," she said, turning with dignity back to Lydia, "newspapers have their uses or we wouldn't know what other people were doing, would we? But this time they really have behaved very badly. You'd think my unfortunate husband must be guilty, the things, the lies, they write about him, and it will be difficult to find a jury not already corrupted. By what they say, you'd think this horrid little—trollop"—she flushed at the word— " had been a model of chastity, when from what I've heard she was no better than—than . . . She was a bad lot. And that a man should stand in danger of his life because of such a baggage as that will make justice a laughing-stock. He may be unfairly judged by sinners here below, but there's One Who'll pardon him if he repents his sins and tells the truth. And so I've told him often."

"You have extraordinary faith, ma'am," murmured Lydia.

"I have prayed," said she, "and God is a wonderful Being."

Lydia sank back in her chair, her fingers tapping on the table, and the Corinthian was delighted to see with what perplexity she stared at Mary. No longer antagonistic, she was puzzled, unable to decide whether to take the woman for a hypocrite, a fool, or a saint. Having long since concluded that she was a saint, the Corinthian was amused by this dilemma, and he watched Mary as though he had invested a large sum in her morality and was delighted to find that the dividends had arrived. Only Bertram remained the swine before this angelic Circe. He drank his claret, grunted now and

228

again, yawned rather often, and openly sneered at the Corinthian's infatuation.

"To be honest," said Lydia abruptly, frowning and staring into the glass in her hand, "I, too, have felt that there's a strong danger of vulgar prejudice obscuring the truth. I've talked to the dead woman's step-mother, an unpleasant sly little woman—my brother, of course, thought her charming: for all his wide experience, he's a fool with women, who have only to look as though they smell of sugar to have him swear that they're as honest as rice pudding——"

"That's untrue!" cried the Corinthian.

"It's perfectly true, my dear," said Lydia, giving him a sweet smile. "You like to think you're strong and ruthless, but you've a sentimental heart."

"I'm sure he has!" cried Mary, gazing admiringly into his reddening face.

"Yes, he's quite a child, really," confided Lydia, as though he were not present. "When you were telling me about those little boys at your school, it did remind me of my Thomas! Just the way he goes on. And he thinks he's such a swell, quite irresistible to women, my dear. And they take advantage of it, of course; they've only to look languishingly at him and he'll give them anything they ask. You should have seen him with this spiteful Marten creature. He believed everything she told him!"

The Corinthian writhed on his chair, glaring defiance at Bertram lest he dare to laugh, and he was unable to retort to these insults without revealing himself to Mary as a scoundrel. To hide his confusion, he drank and choked, while, placidly ignoring him, Lydia continued, leaning close to Mary over the table.

"I can assure you, ma'am," she said, "that she's a sly puss whom I'd not trust with a maypole. You and I are women. *We* know our sex."

With a tight-lipped complacent smile, Mary nodded. "*We* know," she repeated, screwing up her eyes, and gave a compassionate glance to the choking Corinthian.

"The creature was in love with your husband," said Lydia.

"Of course," said Mary, nodding energetically, her eyes sparkling, "they all are, the poor things!"

Lydia flashed her an angry, challenging look. "This woman," she said with emphasis, "this Mrs. Marten, was his whore. She and her draggletail step-daughter were both his whores, and probably his bastards play together in that filthy little cottage. Her evidence was all lies. She's so mad with jealousy that she'd say anything to revenge herself on the man who deserted her. Possibly she was the one who really killed her step-daughter. Then when your husband left Polstead and didn't come back, she took the only possible revenge. She couldn't confess the truth, of course, so she pretended to dream it. She's the guilty person, not your husband."

"O, my dear!" cried Mary, rising suddenly to her feet and, before Lydia could fend her off, kissing her on her painted mouth. "How completely right you are!" she said, sitting down again. "We must tell the authorities at once."

"They'd not listen to us," sighed Lydia, sucking in her lips at the unaccustomed flavour of a woman's mouth. "They've got their victim and that's all they care about. If you'd seen that woman at the inquest, looking so demure and telling such outrageous lies . . . O, I wonder how I managed to keep my hands off her, I really do! And pretending all the time that she loved her Maria when it was obvious that she hated her to hell."

"I know. Some women are such liars," said Mary. "I understand what you mean, my dear. But now she's got two women to deal with; and I think we'll manage her, don't you? Even if we've got to beat her till she tells the truth."

"No," said Lydia. "You'll get no satisfaction out of that cat. She's set on having William hanged. He deserted her, and her filthy little pride can't forget it."

"We can leave her safely to providence," said Mary with a genteel yawn behind her knuckles. "For the wicked shall not prosper, you know, and it's an eye for an eye and a tooth for a tooth. We have that on divine authority. . . . But I'm really very tired, not being used to travelling. . . . Would you please excuse me if I retired? And, dear lady, I can't tell you what it's meant to meet such a sympathetic friend when I believed I was all alone. Tomorrow I'll go to Bury to see poor William. Perhaps you might come with me, would you? In a few days I shall have to go back to London to see about selling the school. But before then, I must visit William. I'm sure he will be most anxious about me."

"I will gladly help, if I can," said Lydia and she did not shrink from the kiss which the Corinthian groaned to see wasted on another woman.

"Good night, good friends." At the door, Mary dipped into a slight curtsey and, rising, the men bowed low. Then when the latch clicked back into place, Lydia glared at them both, drinking with a desperate air as though the claret was poisoned.

"You're a fine couple," she growled. "Here's Bertram who tells me she's just a stupid little mouse; and there's your talk about her as though she were Venus in a flannel petticoat! You make me sick, both of you. She's just as much a child as Corder, in her way, and two such innocents shouldn't be let out together. I felt as if it was my own daughter talking to me—not that she's that young, but she's innocent and babyish in her ways—and all that you men can see in her is either a plain-faced female or a possible bedmate. I never really did like men, and now I know I hate 'em!"

There was murder in her eyes which appeared black by candlelight as she turned from one man to the other, the glass at her lips which moved soundlessly as though she were mouthing insults. Bertram slouched in his chair, staring at his hands in his lap, and the Corinthian sat up straight, glaring back at her haughtily.

"That poor woman," she said, after pouring herself another drink, "has no idea how rotten men can be; and I'll make it my duty to see that she never does find out. I don't think Corder killed that girl, I think her step-mother did it, and I don't care a damn whether he did or not, but she would never believe it even if it's proved to the hilt. Not if she lived a hundred years and he were gibbeted at the end of her street. And you'll never get her, Corinthian: don't you fool yourself. She's too good for such as you. Bah! You've only got one idea about a woman in your dirty heads, both of you, you never think of anything else; but women have souls. Do you understand me? I said Souls! God forgive me, mine's a bit bedraggled by now, thanks to you, Corinthian Tom, and other bastards like you, but from now on I'm living decently; and if there's a God in heaven, you'll regret what you're thinking."

"I'm thinking of nothing," yawned the Corinthian. "I am too bored to think."

She threw the glass at him and he dodged just in time. Nevertheless some of the wine, to his annoyance, splashed his coat.

"Salt," he cried, "where's the salt?" and, bounding out of the chair, ran into the passage, howling for salt.

Muttering to herself, Lydia waited until his return with his coat over his arms, the wine stains heavily crusted with salt.

"All you think about's your bloody clothes," she said. "Glad I've ruined your coat. Serve you right."

"That was a silly thing to do," growled the Corinthian, tenderly placing his coat on the table and dribbling salt on any wet mark he could find. "I really don't understand you nowadays, Lydia. First you hate the very name of Mary Corder; now you talk about her as if she were a saint; and in the meantime you try to ruin my coat."

"Damn your coat," she growled, seizing Mary's scarcely touched glass and swallowing its contents in a gulp. "I know what I'm going to do," she cried. "I'm going to protect this poor creature from bastards like you. You want that poor devil of a Corder hanged— of course you do!—so that you can debauch his widow; and there's that sly fox Bertram hoping to stir up trouble because the fool thinks I might drop into his arms in a pet. Bah! Bah to both of you! And may you both rot in hell. I'm going to bed."

Pushing back her chair, she staggered to the door, half-opened it, then suddenly lurched back to the table, gazing at the men with a defiant leer, and seized an unopened bottle.

"Goo' night," she hissed.

"Good night," groaned the Corinthian, watching the salt turn pink.

When the door had slammed behind her and shivered under the latch, both men sighed and looked at one another.

"She must have managed three bottles on her own," said Bertram with raised eyebrows.

"Which means that we shall have to order more," grumbled the Corinthian. "Women can be the very devil when they want to."

"Indeed," said Bertram, rising to seek for further bottles, "they *are* the very devil. I often thought that when I was a small boy and mother used father's belt on my backside, and now I know it for certain,"

Chapter Eighteen

SHADOW OF THE PAST

NOW that they were to leave Polstead, the Corinthian realized how he had grown to love the place. Thoughts of grimy London, of sleeping through the days for sleepless nights, of flats and sharps and whores, repetition of gambling, boozing and the dull round of forced merriment, so depressed him that when in the morning he strolled into the bar, he was pleased to find it empty save for one man. This man was hidden inside a coat of shoddy grey, a tall hat on his head, and he was leaning over the bar that he might whisper confidentially to the landlord. At the sound of the Corinthian's entrance he turned a suspicious brown eye, but did not speak. Indeed, his abrupt silence was in a subtle way insulting, and it angered the Corinthian before he recognized the man, by his long thin nose and quivering nostrils, as James Lea, the police officer.

"Mr. Lea?" he said. "I remember noticing you in court. Will you join me in a glass of wet?"

"If your honour wishes," said Lea, smiling with cocked eyebrows. "A rum. Hot." He spoke with an aggressive familiarity which annoyed the Corinthian, for it was as though they shared some dirty secret; but eager to learn what he could about Corder, he pretended not to notice.

"Unless I'm much mistaken," he said, "I believe you are the gentleman who arrested an acquaintance of mine, William Corder."

"Saw you in court," grinned Lea. "Don't miss much, I don't. I see and remember what others forget to notice. You was with a very handsome bit of muslin who seemed distressed by what she heard."

"Correct," said the Corinthian, wishing Lydia was there to hear herself called a bit of muslin. "You refer to my sister; and, just between ourselves, I don't mind telling you that I'm interested on her behalf. Personally, I never did like Corder. Unfortunately, my sister felt otherwise."

"Woman, woman! lovely woman!" said Lea, shaking his head. "There's no accounting for their tastes, sir. In my work I come across things that would surprise you. Some of the lowest ruffians unhung with honest-to-God gentlewomen thinking they could save their lousy souls!" He laughed. "Souls! they've even got holes in their boots! That's the kind of souls they have. What any woman could see in this fellow Corder's more than I can understand. Would you believe me, sir, when I tell you that on searching his house I found such books as would make a goat sick! There was *Fanny Hill*, of course—they all have that—but there was other books that made little *Fanny* read like a Sunday-school kiss-me-hands. I'm not one to blush, I tell you, but even alone I felt ashamed of myself when I read 'em. There was one tale about a girl what's got a broken spine and a fellow ties her down so's she can't wriggle—he's a medical man, you see—but if she moves sudden she'll die, understand? So he ties her down tight so's she can't move, and then——"

"I'm not interested in smutty books," said the Corinthian hastily. "You found these in Corder's house?"

"Yes, sir. And the drawer weren't even locked. Why, his lady-wife could have read 'em any time she wanted. And perhaps she did," he added, rubbing his bristly chin.

"Never," cried the Corinthian. "If you knew the lady you'd know that that was quite impossible."

"I agree. I felt real sorry for her, I did, the way she took it. Game she was: game, I tell you. Never a flicker of an eyelash. All that bothered her was whether he'd catch cold or not. There are times, sir, when I don't like my work. If a man's a villain, it gives me a particular satisfaction in nabbing him, but then there's almost always his womenfolk. It's hard on them. This Corder now. You'd think he was a Sunday-school pet, wouldn't you? but then there's these filthy books of his. After I'd read 'em I couldn't look Mrs. Corder in the eye, I was that embarrassed. To think that a choice female like her's married to a foul-minded beast like him. . . . Ah, women are simple unless they're bad. When they love a fellow, they're blind to everything about him. Why! if she'd read those books most likely she'd have thought the dirty words was Greek or something and not known what they was all about. And hers was a school, too, with young girls there; and if there's anything on earth more inquisitive than a young girl I'd like to meet it. What if they'd come across those books? Just think of it, sir, just think of it!"

"Disgraceful," murmured the Corinthian, trying not to think of dozens of young girls in starched petticoats reading *Fanny Hill* aloud together. It would most certainly have completed their education in a way not intended by either the school or their parents.

"Not only that," grumbled Lea, "but his talk! When we was taking him in the coach, he behaved something awful. Now, it's a queer thing, sir, but I've known it happen often. I don't know why it is, but fellows what have murdered their wives or other females carry on laughing and talking fit to burn your ears off once they've been nabbed. They will talk smut and think it's funny. And the things this fellow Corder said. . . . Well, I'd not repeat 'em, even to you."

"He behaved bravely, though?" asked the Corinthian. "He didn't whine?"

"Not at first," said Lea, after a moment's thought. "He was merry, he was, until that banker's man showed up at Colchester about the forged cheque he'd passed at Manningtree. That settled him; he weren't the same fellow afterwards. Why! as we was coming into this village in the early morning, he was dreadfully agitated when we passed his mother's house. Until then, he'd slept heavy, but he suddenly woke up and began to groan. He talked about how his family had been cut off by death within the last fifteen months, and he blubbered at it, showing us the pond where one of his brothers had been drowned. Two of his other brothers had died since then, he said, and he was the last of the family. And the last he will be, too, if there's any justice in the world."

Lea drank and twirled the empty glass in his fingers until the Corinthian, realizing that he must pay for further information, ordered that it and his own glass be refilled.

"Well," he said, "I'm pleased to hear that he suffers some remorse. I never thought him capable of a tear for anybody but himself."

"That's it!" cried Lea, hitting his fist on the counter. "You've got it, sir! He ain't crying for nobody but himself. I know these blackguards too well. O, they'll weep and call on Jesus after they've been nabbed, but they've got no true religion in 'em and no more real remorse for what they've done than the flea what's bit you on the neck. Let 'em loose and they'd do the same tomorrow. I know 'em. O, he's very sorry for himself, Mr. Corder is; and who wouldn't be sorry for his bloody self when he knows he's going to swing in a month or two? He's having bad dreams and he talks of fortune-tellers what told him he had bad times coming ahead. You see? He can't blame himself. It was the fortune-tellers, it was the stars, it was fate, or just damned bad luck, and he can't really be blamed because he sliced up a woman what was a nuisance to him, can he?"

"So you think he'll hang?" asked the Corinthian, nodding to have the glasses refilled.

"Think?" Lea choked on laughter. "Now, sir," he said, "you heard the evidence. If that don't hang him, there ain't no justice. Hang him? I'd hang the little bastard myself. By God, I would! I'd hang him with my own hands, given half the chance. Why, he spends the whole time now moaning that the coroner weren't fair, and when he had the witnesses's evidence read over to him he said it was all my eye. He alluded particularly to the evidence of Mrs. Marten—and if ever I've seen a good, hard-working, honest body, it was her: and I know 'em—but he won't have it and says he had no gun when he called for Maria. What's that matter when we know he stabbed the young woman? But he makes a hell of a to-do about it, and calls Mrs. Marten horrid names. Won't even have it that she ever spoke to him afterwards about his going to the barn. He don't help himself with that kind of talk."

"I suppose not," said the Corinthian and drank because his throat was suddenly dry.

"Well, I can't stand talking here all day," said Lea, hitching forward his coat with a hunch of his shoulders. "I came to get one or two things I left behind. And I'd like a word with Mrs. Corder if she's anywhere about."

"Good Lord! You don't think she had anything to do with it!"

"Of course not," said Lea, smiling at him with that fascinating yet slightly insulting smile which, while admitting the Corinthian as a comrade, also seemed to accuse him of being a liar. "I've a message for her from the prisoner. He wants her to come and sleep with him. Now, would you believe that, eh! thinking of things like that when he ought to be worrying about his soul! When we was getting near the jail, he says to me that the world don't mean anything more to him, he says: all he wanted was to have his wife, for she'd do him more good than twenty parsons. 'She can contribute so much to my comfort,' says he, weeping down his shirt, 'for she's a truly pious woman,' says he. Of course I knew he couldn't have her. That's against regulations, you understand. But I tells him I'll see what can be done and that Mr. Orridge—he's the chief jailor at Bury—was a very humane person who'd give him every help he could, but the visiting magistrates were terrors, I says to him, and Mr. Orridge was scared out of his trousers about what they might say."

"Do you mean to tell me," cried the Corinthian, "that Mrs. Corder's going to live with him in prison!"

"Of course she ain't," laughed Lea, poking him with his elbow. "That's what I'm telling you. It ain't allowed these days; and a mighty cruel law it seems to me, too. If a fellow's going to be hanged he might as well have what fun he can before he's turned off. But, no: it's all Bibles and sermons nowadays, with damn' little booze and no female company, until a poor devil's so worked on by the parsons that he don't care what he says and is bloody pleased to be strung up to get away from 'em all. Ain't human, sir: that's what I say. . . . But I'd better be seeing Mrs. Corder."

"What have you got to see her about?"

"Don't fret yourself, sir," said Lea with a swift, understanding smile. "I ain't going to lock her up or anything and she ain't likely to sleep with her husband again this side of hell. That ain't moral. He's got to keep his mind on a very different kind of heaven from now on, a place where nobody ain't got no legs, if what the preachers say is true. But I promised him I'd tell her that he wants to see her and won't be happy till he does."

"She's in the parlour," said the landlord, "having breakfast with the other lady."

The Corinthian would have followed, but Lea waved him back.

"I'd better see to this alone, sir," he said, "having had more experience in such delicate matters than you, if you'll forgive me saying it. Some women carry on something dreadful, and others are so glad they kiss you, although that ain't often. Usually they're too

237

worried about where the rent's coming from to do anything but howl. And by thunder, some of 'em can howl! It's the gin that does it."

"You won't find Mrs. Corder weeping," said the Corinthian. "And she doesn't drink gin."

Depressed, he lounged against the bar after Lea had gone stealthily from the room, and he wondered what kind of questions the man would be putting to Mary, doubtless trying to trap her into an admission of some sort. Had she been an angel out of heaven, to a fellow like that she would have seemed merely a suspicious character without an address he could verify. When talking to him, the Corinthian at times had felt as guilty as a small boy with a stolen cake in his pocket; such was Lea's manner after years of consorting with criminals that it was impossible for even an honest man to feel at ease under that accusing eye. Outwardly genial, he looked as though he was always ready to pounce.

Bored with his own company, the Corinthian lounged out of doors into the sunlight and looked to right and left; he strolled this way, he strolled that way, then he stood stockstill and he yawned. There was nothing to do; there was, thank God, nothing he wanted to do. But soon, hustled by the women, he would be hurried from this refuge to visit Corder, and the last thing he desired was to see Corder again.

Sighing at the beauty of these oak-and-plaster houses and the cherry-trees in blossom, he wished he had never left his boyhood home. He should have remained there and married some sturdy, sensible country lass and lived blisfully with pigs and cows and bullocks, under cherry-blossoms, with dozens of fat babies at his feet.

Good-bye to Polstead! Slowly he walked the roads and lanes and plodded over fields. Under the greed of souvenir-hunters the Red Barn had become a ruin, yet he stepped amongst the fallen beams and heaps of rubbish until he saw again that small hole in the earth which had once held Maria. Crowds had trodden the ground about it until it had become hard, flat underfoot, and the grave itself had been enlarged by those seeking to carry off a handful of mould. No longer could he feel anything eerie in the place now open to the sky. This had become merely a hole in the ground, giving no suggestion of a grave. With the arrest of her murderer, it seemed that the girl's spirit was appeased and she no longer haunted here.

He wondered whether that spirit might haunt a cell in Bury St. Edmunds jail; and he shivered at the thought.

From the Martens' cottage, when he passed, he heard a woman singing prettily, and he stopped, surprised at the sweetness of the voice. Then he saw at a window, staring at him, the pale face of Mrs. Marten, her nose pressed to the glass, formless, twisted, like a smear of putty. The song died when he looked at her, and she smiled and raised her brows as though in invitation. For some reason, the effect on him of that face was startling. Perhaps it was the bloodless blob of a nose, perhaps the mockery in the round blue eyes, perhaps the raillery of her tight-lipped mouth, or perhaps a combination of all three, but she seemed to him to be evil beyond words, a satyress tempting him to obscene rites through a witch's glass. She said nothing; she made no gesture, no sound; she only stared at him; yet that was enough to frighten him. He turned and strode on, feeling chilled in the sunlight and no longer in love with the country.

All was bustle when he returned to the inn. The women had packed and the post-chaise was ready. Impatiently, with resigned expressions on the bonnet-framed faces, they looked at him feelingly when he entered, and they said nothing while he settled the bill and gave gratuities to the servants. When he pressed a florin into Lucy's hand, he feared she would throw it in his face; but her parsimony was stronger than her pride. Her fingers closed over the coin while, with the insolent look of a great lady, she scorned him with slowly lowered eyelids.

"You're very generous, I'm sure, my lord," she sneered.

"No man can be so generous as a woman, child," he said. "The gratitude lies in my heart and money couldn't express it."

"It could help," she muttered; but he pretended not to hear.

No longer did he regret leaving this village. Lucy's disgruntled manner and lowering eye, and the self-satisfied smile of Mrs. Marten behind the glass, had made him dislike the place. Gladly did he take up the reins and turn the horses down the hill towards Bury St. Edmunds. . . .

At Bury they lodged at the "Angel" nearly opposite the entrance to the abbey, the two women taking a room together and almost entirely ignoring the men. They had, they made it appear, some secret understanding too delicate to admit the presence of males, and they conversed not with crude words but with sighs, with rolling eyes, raised eyebrows, puckered lips and clasped hands, enraging the Corinthian and Bertram almost to murder.

"This is a pretty go," grumbled Bertram as, after being quietly dismissed by the women, he and the Corinthian strolled to view the town. "Here I come all those bloody miles to have a sniff at Lydia and she doesn't even seem to know I'm here! I'm going to have it out with her, by God. I don't know how you stand for it, letting a woman make a fool of you like this. If there was another man, you could do something about it, call him out or something, but to see a pair of females snuffling together and whispering and holding hands . . . I tell you, Tom, it's more than body and soul can bear!"

"I know, I know," said the Corinthian. "Only it's worse for me. What the devil do you think Lydia's been saying about me to Mrs. Corder? Get two women together and you never hear 'em say a good word about anybody else. She'll make my name stink."

"Pooh," said Bertram, too engrossed by his own troubles to have sympathy for his friend's, "women never believe what other women tell 'em about men. The more Lydia abuses you, the more interested Mrs. Corder'll get. But look at me! . . . I don't think Lydia's said a dozen words to me for days, except to tell me to fetch her that or this or to get out of her way or to pass her a drink or something. You know, the trouble is I'm in love with the bitch!"

"Are you?" growled the Corinthian with no attempt at interest. That Bertram should be tormented by a woman with whom he was himself no longer passionately involved seemed to him not only foolish but in poor taste. At least the fellow should have found somebody else to babble about her to. If for the moment the Corinthian's feelings were detached from Lydia, she nevertheless remained his property and he had no intention of surrendering her without a struggle. So long as she, however, kept her senses and ignored Bertram, he would not interfere. At the same time, he did wish Bertram would shut up.

"Yes," said Bertram miserably, "I'm in love again! I started as a fellow usually does: you know: Here's sport! Pretty face, trim ankles, jimper waist, fat shoulders: altogether, a fine piece of fancy-work. Then before I knew what was happening, I was nutty over her. Can't think of anything else; I'm eating her and drinking her and dreaming about her; and I can't sit still or hold a deck of cards without spilling 'em. I lose all interest in my work. If the easiest couple of flats were to come along now begging to be fleeced, I'd have to let 'em go. I'm finished, Tom, and all because I can't get a woman to say 'Yes'."

"You're not the only one," muttered the Corinthian, spitting into the Ouse as they passed along its bank. "It's the same with me and Mrs. Corder. Look here, Bert, something's got to be done. Unless we break this damned conspiracy between the pair of 'em, we're sunk."

"How're you going to do it? You couldn't shift 'em apart with a chisel. There's birdlime on their hips and fingers. And just think of the kind of things Lydia used to say about Mrs. Corder before she met her!"

"The trouble is, of course," growled the Corinthian, "that they're both nutty over the same little bastard, and if he weren't in jail and safe from both of 'em, they'd be tearing each other's eyes out. The only way to break this damned love-bird conspiracy is to get him out of prison; and that's not possible. Yet if we ever want to sleep in peace again, we've got to prize 'em apart somehow."

Prizing the women apart, however, proved no easy matter. With sighs and ogling, both men declared themselves the slaves of passion, and the women either took no heed, being too fascinated by their own soulful conversation, or they looked at them reprovingly, then turned again to talk together in hushed voices. Not being able to hear her own voice clearly, Mary had less control then Lydia over her tongue, and now and then her words rose shrilly. To the Corinthian's disgust, these words almost always referred to her husband, to the injustice of the law, the barbarism of the time, the insensitivity of most men, the goodness of God and the hope of a pious future with her husband, purged of sin by his ordeal, meekly settled at her side.

In this delusion that Corder must be acquitted, Lydia openly encouraged the woman, and they behaved as though, being on visiting terms with God, they had His positive assurance that the verdict would be Not Guilty. When they were told that Mrs. Corder might visit her husband, they became as excited as if she were getting married, and they dressed with extreme care, Mary, for the first time, wearing a recent purchase, a leghorn bonnet fashionably adorned with green ribbons; and, as she disliked being stared at by strangers—everybody in the town, of course, knowing who she was —she hid her face behind a long black lace veil.

"Give him my love, won't you?" jeered the Corinthian.

"Of course I will," said Mary, leaning on Lydia's arm.

From the inn window, he watched them walk down the street, people drawing aside to stare after them. With her veil, Mary remained a faceless enigma, but boldly Lydia looked about her, seeming to challenge strangers to speak rudely.

"O, hell," groaned the Corinthian, "I love 'em both; and, by God," he cried, "I hate 'em both!"

Had he known any women in Bury he would have sought a suitable revenge on this indifference; but he knew no one and he lacked sufficient energy to begin courting a stranger. The mere thought of the chase depressed him: of having to act the desperate lover until the pursued fair one condescended to notice his existence, the sending of gifts and notes, the following her in the street, the passing of *billets-doux*, and so until, when her husband chanced to be out, she slipped him her bedroom key and he slipped in for a scampered embrace with one ear open for the husband's return. . . . One had to be very young to enjoy such nonsense. He was old enough to require comfort and leisure in his amours. The only approachable female within reach was the chambermaid, and after his experience with Lucy he kept his eyes averted whenever she dawdled past him in the passage or bounded into his bedchamber with broom and brushes.

Such casual tumblings were affairs of the past. He wanted to settle down. He wanted a house in the country and he wanted Mary Corder to share it with him. But until Corder was hanged, it would be no use, he realized, attempting such a courtship. Both women were so enthralled by the romantic situation of loving a man in jail that they had no time to think of anyone else; and he wondered whether their feelings would change once it was indubitably proved that Corder had murdered Maria Marten. For the time being they were able to prop up their baseless faith by abusing Mrs. Marten as a liar; and although the Corinthian knew that she was a liar, he didn't doubt that her tale was substantially correct. At the inquest she had told the truth, only suppressing her own part in the deed.

Corder had dressed Maria in his dead brother's clothes and he had sent her to the Red Barn; he had carried a gun and had been seen leaving the Red Barn afterwards. The links were too strong to have been welded merely by Mrs. Marten's spite. Besides, since the inquest, further evidence had come to light. Medical argument over the cause of death had resulted in the corpse being dug up in Polstead churchyard and a more expert examination had revealed that, in addition to strangulation, a sharp instrument had been used to stab her between the ribs on the left side, and this stab had pierced her heart. Re-examination of her stays now that they had dried had shown the marks of the stab. Injuries on the neck proved that a pistol-ball had entered above the jugular vein and had taken an oblique course to the eye on the other side of the head. In the neck also there was a stab wound.

With bullet, knife and rope, Corder had been determined to make certain of completing his work. But did this discovery trouble the women? Not a bit of it! They had blanched a little when told, then they had loudly reasserted their faith in the rascal's innocence. As he hadn't murdered the girl, they argued, it didn't matter to them in what way she'd died; and, weeping copiously, Mary had read aloud a maudlin, hypocritical letter from her husband. Justly calling her his "much injured and afflicted wife", he had moaned about his present misery and his solitary state and how he had relished a sermon he'd heard. "Yes, my dear wife," he wrote, "I feel persuaded my sins are more in number than the hairs of my head." Even this admission had not bothered Mary and Lydia. Mary had continued to read until the end, then she had folded the letter, kissed it, and returned it to her reticule.

At first, she had been refused admittance to the jail, but later it had been agreed that she might make brief visits; and this, her first visit, the Corinthian hoped would knock some sense into her head. Once faced with shifty-eyed Corder again, she would surely have to admit his guilt?

The Corinthian had underestimated the strength of a woman's faith. When, with Lydia, Mary returned from the prison and, in the room that had been set apart for the four of them as dining-room and parlour, took off her bonnet and veil, he saw that she had been weeping, and that her eyes shone as though they had looked on some holy vision. Even more emotional than she was Lydia who, the moment the door closed, fell on to the sofa and burst into noisy tears.

"What's all this?" growled the Corinthian. "What are you crying for? What did he say to you?"

"Poor Lydia was not permitted to see Mr. Corder," said Mary in a cold, flat voice, carefully seating herself in the easy chair. "I was allowed to go to him alone and it was altogether unsatisfactory. I was given merely a few minutes and was watched all the time by a warder, while I was not even permitted to salute him, although I am his wedded wife, after all. We had to stand some distance apart and shout at one another. If there wasn't such disgraceful prejudice against my poor husband, I'd write to the papers and complain about it."

"But what's Lydia crying for?"

"And the horrid clothes he has to wear," continued Mary, not heeding, or perhaps not hearing, his interruption. "You know how fastidious William was about his appearance, and how neat he liked to look. But they've taken his own garments from him and made him wear the costume of the prison, a most unbecoming jacket and trousers of coarse grey frieze, striped, at intervals, with a yellow bar, bordered by two narrower bars of black. He looked such a fright that I almost screamed when I saw him, and he seemed so uncomfortable, poor dear. It made me realize what he must be suffering, to see him dressed like that, like a criminal; yes, just like any common thief. . . ."

"Hey!" cried the exasperated Corinthian, shaking Lydia by the shoulder, "what's all the to-do about? What's the matter with you? I don't understand, but you're not the same woman nowadays; you've lost your will, your wits and your courage. The whole world's mad!"

Her face made ugly by weeping, mouth loosely contorted, cheeks glistening, she gazed up at him, gulped and gasped, then stuttered: "Tom, O, Tom! She knows. I told her everything."

"What do you mean, she knows?" He felt cold in his belly and a prickling of his skin.

"About us," gurgled Lydia. "She knows we're not brother and sister and that I'm Miss and not Mrs. Atherton and that I've been living with you for years. When she saw Bill and told him we were staying here with her, he was most upset and told her the truth;

and of course I couldn't deny it when she asked. I told her how we'd been cheats and how we'd lived by robbing drunken young fools, and the wicked way we'd lived together."

"You did, did you?" he said viciously. "That's the kind of dirty thing one'd expect from Bill Corder but not from you. I thought you'd have sense enough to keep your trap shut. Not that it matters. That kind of life's finished for us now."

"I'm very glad to hear you say that," said Mary. "I knew that it must have been only thoughtlessness, and although you might have led poor Lydia astray when she was a girl——"

"Lead Lydia astray!" he howled, and crowed like a cock.

"Such levity is sadly misplaced," said Mary, becoming again the prim school-mistress and sitting up straight in the armour of her stays. "I'm beginning to believe that my poor husband was not mistaken in his estimate of you, Mr. Barsett. I thought it pure heedlessness on your part, and because you had not been properly instructed in good works, but it seems that at bottom you are a wicked man, after all. Your unhappy partner in sin has repented and the angels in heaven rejoice, and all you can do is make a noise like a rooster that's laid an egg. Lydia is now under my protection, and she is coming back to London with me."

"Back to London!"

"For a day or two, yes. My husband implored me not to desert him, but finally, after I had explained my situation, he agreed to permit me to go. A good counsel must be briefed for his defence, the best we can afford. I'll sell my lease of Grove House and certain other property that's in my name. I'm also writing to William's mother, although I've been informed that she's rather a mercenary old lady. But I must first go to London."

"You'll need a man to take care of you," said the Corinthian. "And I've a good head for business."

"So also, I believe, has Lydia," smiled Mary, "and I'm not exactly a fool about money, even though I may be merely a woman. We will leave by the London coach in the morning. Meanwhile I will pray for you; and with all my heart, sir, I beg you to think seriously about your future."

"I have thought about it, I think of nothing else," he cried, gazing at her passionately.

Closer she stepped towards him until, tantalizingly, he could have kissed that pale mouth had he dared, while her eyes were soft and affectionate, gazing into his.

"You are good at heart, sir," she said. "I know that. God would not have entrusted me to your care had you been otherwise. In my hour of trouble, you and darling Lydia appeared. And please don't feel that I'm not grateful. It is of your soul I think, of that immortal part of you which belongs to God. Lydia has seen the light, may heaven be blessed, and she's repented her evil living. Will you not try to pray? I've tracts in my room, if you'll only promise to read them."

"I promise," he said hoarsely.

"Read them with care and ponder their message. I'll bring them down to you this evening. Now, please," she said, and her gloved fingers lightly touched his arm—yet that frail touch of kid sent the blood fluttering up his arm. "Now, please, leave me with poor Lydia. We must pray together. Until supper, leave us in peace."

He kissed her gloved hand and she did not attempt to deny him the caress. With sad and almost loving eyes, she watched him, pityingly, and sighed. Then, blind with hope and happiness, he turned and stumbled into the passage, pressing to his lips the hand that had touched hers; and he felt that he had no need for her religious tracts. Already, under her influence, was he a different man, washed almost clean of sins and aching for the opportunity for self sacrifice to prove he was her slave, on his knees to God through her in the hoped-for salvation of her arms.

Chapter Nineteen

LYDIA GROWS AFRAID

WHILE Mary and Lydia were continually busy, plotting Corder's defence, hurrying to London to raise money or to consult with a Mr. Humphreys whom they had engaged as lawyer, or visiting Polstead to lament with old Mrs. Corder about her son's misfortune, the Corinthian and Bertram had little to do save read the newspapers and drink. At times they announced their imminent return to London, but they did not go. Both lingered in hope that the women might falter in their faith in Corder's nobility of character, and they waited impatiently for the trial which, they felt, must destroy these idiotic delusions. Almost every day Mary visited her husband and returned with tales of his courage and his piety. When any tactless person doubted his sanctity, she gave a melancholy, forgiving look and would say: "Mr. Corder is a misunderstood gentleman and could not possibly be guilty of such a horrid offence." That sufficed for her and, to the Corinthian's amazement and disgust, apparently also for Lydia. Because they loved the rascal they refused to believe he was not innocent, and they shut their ears to any evidence that might batter down their faith. Some evenings while the men drank their brandies—Lydia, under this new influence, bravely confining her thirst to tea or coffee—Mary would talk of the situation as though Corder were one of her pupils who had been naughty in class.

"When Mr. Lea first took him away," she said, "I thought it was only for bigamy. For some time I deceived myself into thinking that. The other thing seemed so absurd."

"You would have forgiven bigamy?" asked the Corinthian.

"Well, not exactly, but it's not like this other thing, is it?" she said with her gentle smile. "And God didn't seem to mind very much about King Solomon, did He? After all, he's only young and young men can behave very foolishly when they're in the hands of a designing woman. If he'd gone through some form of marriage before he was old enough to know what he was doing, he could scarcely be blamed for it; then, when he met me . . . He might have thought the woman was dead or something."

"She was dead all right," growled the Corinthian, "slashed, stabbed, shot and throttled."

Mary sniffed, and turned away, and would not speak to him again, save when good manners demanded it, for the remainder of the evening.

Such arguments, however, were not common between them. Usually, the Corinthian managed to control his jealous temper and to listen without blaspheming to talk of Corder as though the rascal were a holy man captured by Turks. And he was always most respectful towards Mary, on tiptoe to anticipate her smallest desire, that he might be rewarded by a charitable smile. She was becoming far from indifferent towards him, he realized. Had it not been for the baleful presence of Lydia who, when she was abed with Mary, doubtless spat her poison, he believed that he might without great difficulty have succeeded in winning her even to accept him as a future husband. As yet, no word of love had been spoken between them. Wordlessly, he wooed her on a sigh and a languishing glance, and often she, too, would sigh and he caught her watching him with sorrowing interest. So pious a woman could not be easily untrussed of her whalebone; only marriage might unlock her, and she would be sure to insist on a long widowhood that she might know that luxury, so precious to many women, of mourning the departed.

Nevertheless, the game was running hopefully. That she did not rebuff him, did not pull her hand away when he squeezed it, seemed to him proof of her weakening. Like a boy, he felt content with small exchanges of affection, and a glance could keep him happy for a night, while, should he touch merely her clothing when she passed, he trembled and felt the skin that had touched it burn as though scorched. His own behaviour surprised him, for it was like that of the heroes in the novels that Lydia often read, and at which he had always jeered. In these tales the hero worshipped the heroine from afar until the final chapter when the covers cut you off from contemplating their ultimate bliss in matrimony. The girls were always beautiful, simple, courageous, timid, moral, and well-conducted: indeed, to his mind, they strongly resembled Mary.

And he, the lion of Piccadilly, the terror of chambermaids and the master of Covent Garden, had become, like the heroes in those books, the tongue-tied adorer of a woman, worshipping her from afar.

By God, said he to himself, it works! And he drank to the novelists.

While Mary appeared gradually to unbend towards him—even her stays, he felt, being not so stiffly boned—Lydia turned further from Bertram: a situation which delighted the Corinthian. Each woman was apparently influencing the other. While Mary drew Lydia towards salvation through prayers and prudery, Lydia was turning the innocent Mary towards daydreams of adventure. It was natural, thought the Corinthian, that a mature woman who had known only one man, and that man Bill Corder, and who was no longer exactly young, must speculate ruefully on what she might have missed, when she had a courtesan like Lydia to boast in detail of past sins under the pretence of regretting them. Greatly did he long to discover a way of boring through their bedroom wall that he might listen to their bedtime conversation. That being impossible, he imagined the kind of things they must do and say; and having the sort of imagination that had made him so popular in Piccadilly and Covent Garden, he quite dazzled himself by his lewd speculations.

Here was being repeated the old tale of the saint and the temptress, and he recalled having read a legend about some old goat who had visited a brothel on the excuse of converting the inmates, only to become an enthusiastic follower of Venus, while the whore he most admired took to his cell in the desert and refused to open her window when he came knocking. He could not conceive Lydia hiring a cell in any desert, but by the way she was behaving, gadding to church three times on Sunday and reading dull books and tracts, he could imagine her retiring into a country cottage and, on the wages of past sin, buying redemption through good works amongst the poor. And Mary? She did not seem quite so enthusiastic about going to church when the four of them sat in the cosy parlour on a cold Sunday morning; and, once or twice, Lydia had to remind her that time was running by and that the church-bells would soon stop ringing.

Determined not to destroy his hopes of conquest by impetuosity, the Corinthian made no attempt to assault more than Mary's fingers, although once, when she dropped her handkerchief, he was careful to kiss it passionately when he knew she was watching; and he was rewarded by one of her rare blushes and a dimpling smile. Otherwise, he remained respectful towards her, her servant, her humble adorer, while she began to coquette awkwardly, fluttering her eyelashes, biting her lips to redden them—she still dared use no paint—and wriggling inside her gown. These gowns remained as unrevealing as before, and so inflexibly boned and metalled underneath that none of her shape might be detected; yet he felt that they had become more feminine, carrying more ribbons and cheap jewellery.

Whatever her changed feelings might have been towards him, she did not falter in her daily visits to the jail, and as the time of the sessions approached, she became quite agitated. The lawyer, Mr. Humphreys, arrived from London and she had many discussions with him about the defence. There was, the Corinthian learned, a difference of opinion here which threatened to upset Corder's case before it was opened, for Mr. Humphreys wanted him to keep his mouth shut.

"If he'll only hold his tongue," he said one evening in the parlour, his eyes, lidded like a lizard's, coldly watching Mary and Lydia, "and leave everything to his advisers, we might bring him off. Otherwise," he shrugged, "I have little hope of an acquittal."

The women conferred together, Mary intent on Lydia's lips, then Lydia lifting her curls that Mary might whisper into her ear.

"Mr. Charnock," said Mary demurely, turning again to the lawyer, "has advised differently. He says that suicide's the only possible defence."

"Mr. Charnock," growled Humphreys, "is possibly a learned man, but I cannot agree with him on this. If you insist on it, I'm afraid I can't continue. In the face of the evidence, I consider such a plea to be a desperate course. If you intend to plead suicide, I'm afraid I can't conduct the case."

"What else can we plead?" cried Lydia, squeezing her hot hands together. "Something must be said. He can't stay silent."

"My dear lady," said Humphreys wearily, "I will accept this case only if I'm allowed to advise on what I consider best. It has become notorious and I have my reputation to consider. Should the verdict run against us, as it most certainly will if you persist in this attitude, I will suffer for it. My client may defend himself on the grounds of provocation. And on no other. I might then possibly induce the jury to reduce the charge to manslaughter, although I can make no promises."

"That would mean jail, transportation! No," cried Mary, "I forbid it. William's innocent and he must stand on his innocence."

"Please, please," sighed Mr. Humphreys, raising a wrinkled hand. "I have had many, many years' experience in these matters, and I assure you I really do know best. Provocation is the only possible defence. Such a plea, dear ladies, will give our client a far better chance of his life than the pretence that the unfortunate girl killed herself. He might say that angry words passed between them, that the deceased struck him, and that she was levelled in her turn by a blow that proved fatal. Let him not say with what instrument he struck that blow. This appears to me to be his sole chance if you persist in obliging him to make any defence."

The women would not agree. They shook their heads, dark head, fair head, ringlets intertwining in their agitation. "Impossible," they cried, "when he's innocent!"

"Then," said Mr. Humphreys, "I regret that I must decline to act further in the matter."

"But," sobbed Mary, "you can't desert us like this!"

"I'll double your fee," cried Lydia.

"It is not a question of money," said Mr. Humphreys, although a dim spark glowed in his eyes at the offer. "And you know, dear ladies, that I have done everything I could for you. I approached Mr. Adolphus, but his fee, as I warned you, was too high. Two hundred guineas, exclusive of expenses, retaining fee, and fee for his clerk. I didn't like to mention it to you at the time, but such a demand was made in the hope of its being refused; as it was. For the sake of his reputation, Mr. Adolphus wanted nothing to do with the case so long as this defence of suicide was persisted in. As you know, I then applied to Mr. Serjeant Andrews and he agreed to accept one hundred guineas. After reading the brief, however, he declined to continue with it."

"They don't know William, that's why!" cried Mary.

"They know the law," said Mr. Humphreys, "and they know

251

judges and juries. I warn you, dear lady, if you persist in pleading suicide, I, too, must, with reluctance, withdraw from the case. Unofficially, I will give you all possible advice; but officially, I decline to act any further."

The women implored him to reconsider his decision, they almost went on their knees to him, they wept and they plied him with sherry and biscuits and tearful glances; but Mr. Humphreys remained adamant. As a man, he said, he was naturally flattered by these attentions from such charming ladies; as a lawyer, however, he had his professional reputation to remember. And taking up his tall-hat, he stalked out of the room, leaving the ladies to weep in each other's embrace.

When he heard, the Corinthian chuckled, thinking that after this even they must realize that Corder was guilty; but they remained as staunchly prejudiced as before. These legal men were cowards, they declared, and didn't know poor William, and a good counsel would yet be discovered. And discovered he was, a Mr. Broderick agreeing to act for one hundred and forty guineas, exclusive of the retaining fee, expenses and so on. This large sum was beyond Mary's means, and although old Mrs. Corder helped with a little, Lydia had to pay most of it.

"And she's never lent me a penny in all her blasted life!" cried the Corinthian ferociously.

As the assizes approached, the women lived in a near-swooning condition. They walked on weakly jointed legs, they drooped, they moaned, they could not eat, they bathed their foreheads with eau-de-Cologne and sniffed sal volatile, and amidst anguished cries they encouraged one another with loud proclamations of their faith in Corder's acquittal. During this period of fever, the Corinthian's wooing of Mary began to languish, as most of the time she seemed unaware of him hovering about her, although once, to his astonished delight, she spasmodically seized his hand and pressed it into her whalebone-protected bosom, swaying and sobbing, her eyes half-shut. Before he could take advantage of this distress and slip his arm about her waist, Lydia entered and Mary collapsed. Just in time he caught her and carried her to the sofa, but he was not allowed to assist in her recovery. Haughtily, Lydia ordered him from the room before she unlaced Mary's stays; and he slunk out, loudly grumbling.

The women's agitation at least saved him from being interrogated about the religious tracts which Mary had forced into his hands. Struggle though he did to read how sinners were saved by the voice of a small child, how God had rescued a woman from the streets by leading her into a church instead of a brothel, how from petty theft ruffians had finished at the gallows, and so on and so on, he always ended by stuffing them into his pocket and hurrying off for a drink. Desire Mary he might, but, even to attain the heaven of her embrace, he could not struggle through the hell of such nonsense; and he was relieved to find that she had apparently forgotten that she had given them to him. Everything, indeed, was forgotten before the impending trial.

When, on the evening of August 2, the judges arrived in Bury dressed in their scarlet, the javelin-men could scarcely force a path through the excited populace; and on the following day, Sunday, St. Mary's Church was so crowded that it was impossible to enter without influence or a heavy bribe. As Mary had mentioned her desire to be present, the Corinthian slipped half a sovereign into the verger's hand so that he and Mary and—damn it—Lydia were given comfortable seats in the most conspicuous part of the church. Wearing her leghorn bonnet with the green ribbons, and the black lace veil to conceal her face, Mary sat one side of him, Lydia, as unbending as a statue, on his other side; and gravely Mary followed the service, although she could have heard very little, while pretending not to notice how everybody stared at her. Even the judges in their scarlet splendour, even the gold-chained mayor with his aldermen, were ignored when the audience could gape at this woman whose face they could not see.

After the prayers and the lesson of the day had been read, Luther's hymn on the Last Judgment was sung; then followed the moment for which all were waiting. Still tingling within after the flourish of the organ and the echoes of the choir's singing, they sat and gazed at the pulpit in which stood the Rev. Mr. Sheen, the high sheriff's chaplain. A little man with the neck of a plucked fowl, he peered malevolently over the heads of the congregation, and in an awesome resonant voice implored the divine blessing on behalf of the corporate body before him, and especially upon the vicegerents of the Sovereign who were come to execute truth and justice and to maintain them in the county of Suffolk. With a certain briskness, he turned from these conventional exordiums to his sermon, the important Assize Sermon, and for the motto of the discourse, he boomed, he had selected the 13th verse of the 2nd chapter of the 1st Epistle of St. Peter: *Subject yourselves to every ordinance of man for the Lord's sake.*

Had he been alone, the Corinthian would have fallen asleep—but then, of course, had he been alone he would not have been in church—and only the feel of Mary at his side kept him wakeful while he squeezed his knee against hers. This was a delusion of his, although a satisfying one, as, under her skirt, Mary wore two heavy petticoats and a thick pair of drawers, yet he fully believed that he could feel her knee and that it answered his pressure. Behind that dark veil it was impossible to detect what she was thinking, and her hands remained resting in her lap, while, had she been even deafer than she was, she could not have avoided hearing the unctuous baying of the Rev. Mr. Sheen.

He ranted about the Almighty and about Moses the Lawgiver, and of those divine laws which all must obey. Otherwise the Almighty would take revenge on the sinner, visiting him with sickness or loss of property, and sometimes with the dreadful punishment of death. He added that there were, of course, differences between the laws of God and man, the Lord promising rewards and the law threatening punishment.

The Corinthian's jaws ached with suppressed yawning and the lids drooped over his eyes. Only the knowledge that his knee and hipbone pressed close to Mary's kept him wakeful. For hours, it seemed to him, the parson orated, and he was both relieved and disappointed that no reference was made to Corder. It was plain by its shufflings, whisperings and snortings that the congregation considered itself cheated by this Christian forbearance which pleased nobody; and when all was over, there was half-suppressed grumbling at the parson for not having known his duties.

"It was a beautiful sermon," said Mary, leaning heavily on the Corinthian's arm as he conducted her across the street. "Very beautiful indeed," she whispered and, as though about to faint, she swayed against him.

The intimacy of that gesture, as if they were avowed lovers for her to want his support, exalted him and he looked down proudly at her hidden face, noting that the black veil was wet where she had sucked the lace between her lips. She was looking up at him, he knew by the tilt of chin and ribboned bonnet, but he could see only the white blur of her nose and the gleam in her eyes.

"I love you," he whispered, "I love you with all my heart."

He felt her shudder against him while her hand gripped his convulsively, almost painfully, only for her suddenly to move away, sighing, towards Lydia who, previously held back by the people pushing out of church, now scampered to stand protectively on her other side. Sharply, suspiciously, she glared at him and seized Mary's gloved hand, while he glanced expressionlessly back into her angry eyes; and thus, the veiled woman between them, these two who had once been lovers walked back to the inn, hot with hatred of each other.

No longer did Mary seem so self-confident in her righteousness, and often she complained of the migraine. After dinner she would sometimes retire to lie down in her darkened bedchamber. Her face, if possible, looked whiter than before, and sudden pains in her side would cause her to sway, the world whirling before her eyes, and to clutch at what was near to keep her on her feet.

"Poor child," clucked Lydia who was not many years the elder, "the strain has been too great. It's this terrible waiting. How cruel it was of the judge not to hold the trial on the first day! The others can be of no comparable importance."

"I'm well enough," sighed Mary with a wintry smile, hand still pressing on her whaleboned side.

"No, you must rest. It is this excess of sensibility," cried Lydia, staring adoringly into her eyes, "that racks a body that is not really strong, poor darling. Rest your little feet." She swung Mary's legs on to the sofa, then drew down the shirt to hide her feet. "Would you like me to read to you?" she asked. "That charming young curate with the prominent teeth, poor man, brought some new tracts this morning."

"No," sighed Mary, lying back and shading her eyes with her hand, "not for the moment."

On tiptoe, Lydia returned to her chair and took up her knitting, and over the clicking needles she watched her friend, delighted that the men were not present so that she could have Mary to herself, while troubled to see how heavily she breathed, troubled to hear her sigh and to see her toss over on her side.

"Have no fears, my love," she said, "God is with us. No harm can come to William."

Mary did not answer. Restlessly, she moved again, hand over her eyes, and Lydia concluded that she had not heard what she had said. This seemed confirmed when, suddenly, she asked:

"Why did you never marry Mr. Barsett?"

Grimly, Lydia laid her knitting in her lap and in the cold voice she always assumed when speaking of the Corinthian, she said: "I suppose because I didn't love him, God be thanked."

"Yet you lived with him for years," said Mary, peeping through her fingers. "I know I'm very ignorant about what people call Life. Mama brought me up strictly and I only learned from books and newspapers the kind of things some people do; and they always leave you guessing. But you must have cared for Mr. Barsett a little?"

"I was a wicked woman," said Lydia harshly. "I was a vicious, heartless beast lost to decency and God. When I look back now I can't believe that it was me who did those terrible things, and I pray I may forget them and start a new life of good works and devotion. If we had real nuns in England, I would take the veil. And you could take it with me, my dear. Then we'd be safe from the infamous designs of dissolute men. . . . Please God you never know such things!"

"What kind of designs? Do tell me, pray, that I'll be warned."

"There's only one design that need trouble you, pretty, and that is a plot against your virtue. I suppose I really ought to warn you. In your innocence, you don't realize the dangerous effect on certain monsters of the pretty little airs you give yourself, the way you look sideways through your curls, and when you toss your head when you're angry and all those little curls start dancing. . . . I don't wish to lecture you, but Mr. Barsett has declared his intention of bringing about your ruin."

"O, no!" she gasped, sitting up, red-cheeked.

"Alas, yes, my precious, so you must be careful and never remain alone with him for a moment. Many a good woman has lost her honour and her reputation through the treachery of a servant, by a false message decoying her from home, or being hustled into a carriage and gagged under her own skirt. I could tell you terrible tales. Whatever you do, never be alone with that man."

"O, I wouldn't, not for anything!" gasped Mary, lowering her hand to gaze with huge blue eyes at Lydia. "I promise you."

"And don't trust strange women either. They might well be bawds he's paid to lure you out of the inn. Trust only me."

"Only you, dear," sighed Mary.

To Lydia's distress, Mary seemed quickly to forget her lesson. That night she chatted with the Corinthian in a corner, and laughed, and gave him sidelong glances through her curls; and later when they had retired to bed, Lydia spoke sternly to her about such thoughtless goings-on. Mary wept and promised that in the future she'd be good. But, she sobbed, she was so worried about poor William that she really didn't know what she was doing half the time, and she liked, when possible, to try to forget that he was lying in that cold jail.

Dimly, Lydia saw her face through the gloom, and heard her sniff and gurgle, and she felt suddenly old and helpless. Until recently, Mary had seemed to her a brave woman serene in her faith in God, fearless of life because she was assured of heaven, but since their arrival at Bury she had gradually altered. They had changed rôles: Mary had become weak while she had grown strong; Mary now was the one always about to weep, with sick headaches and pains in her side and swiftly changing moods; while she had become cold and withdrawn, shrinking with physical disgust from Bertram when he tried to embrace her, and so loathing the Corinthian that she was barely able to look at him and often had to shut her eyes when he spoke, shivering to think that she could ever have believed that she had loved such a man.

Now, in her simplicity, meeting such a handsome gentleman after years of living in drab surroundings with drab companions, Mary was becoming fascinated by him. Horrified, Lydia recognized in her symptoms from her own greensick youth, the swooning, the pains in the side, the giddiness, the sighing without reason. Tight-lacing might have helped to accentuate these ills, as it did with most women, but it was not wholly to blame. The body aching for love, swollen with sighs, rebelled against the pinch of metal and whalebone in its yearning to be free. Fortunately, she tried to reassure herself, Mary was too ignorant to recognize what these symptoms foretold, and there was time yet to save her from herself and the seducer. Had she known what was happening in her heart,

S.O.T.R.B.—R

undoubtedly she would have been appalled that she, a newly married woman with a husband in danger of his life, should have considered any other male even remotely attractive.

Soon, thank God, the trial must come and be over. Then, whether Corder was convicted or acquitted, Mary would be saved from the Corinthian. Taking the sobbing woman into her arms and, as though she were a child, endeavouring to soothe her with kisses and petting, Lydia swore that she would never let that villain know where she was hidden. Peacefully, until death, would they live together, flowers and birds and beasts their only friends, in a house possibly somewhere in Suffolk, in Lavenham perhaps amongst her own people and not too far from Polstead that they might help console Mrs. Corder in the loss of her unfortunate son. For, although she would never confess it to Mary, Lydia no longer doubted that Corder must hang. The evidence was too damning, spun by that witch Mrs. Marten, for him to break through. And no longer did she want him to escape the gallows, for that would mean the loss of Mary. Once she became Corder's wife again there would be no room in the house for a female friend; and had she been able to choose between the two, she would have chosen poor deluded innocent Mary rather than her husband, love him also though she did in her way.

"My child," she whispered, kissing the tear-wet cheeks, the damp lashes and quivering mouth, "I will protect you. I've seen so much of life, such horrid things, things you'd never believe, and I pray God which you'd not understand. Never. Never. Never. I will see to that." Trembling in her agitation, she smoothed Mary's ringlets, whispering endearments which she knew could not be heard, and caressing her throat and cheeks; then vigorously she gripped her in her arms as though to hold her from ravenous men in the dark, and kissed her hard on the mouth. "Trust me," she whispered loudly into her ear, "trust only me."

"Only you," said Mary drowsily, pretending to be half-asleep that she might dream without interruption; besides, she felt uneasy in the grip of this large woman and did not like being touched so intimately.

Lydia, however, would not release her, and although, remembering the lessons she had taught at school of what one must do when pursued by a bear, Mary lay as if dead, the bear still clutched her, whispering of how she would guard her from temptation; and sometimes it kissed her to prove her detestation of men, so that it was many hours before Mary truly slid to sleep and into troubled dreams of hangmen's ropes with the Corinthian tapping at her window-pane.

Chapter Twenty

LOVE MAKES THE DEAF TO HEAR

THE trial of William Corder had been fixed for Thursday, August 7, but very few people believed this. A trial so fascinatingly horrible, one in which, because of Mrs. Marten's alleged dream, all England had become passionately interested, could not, it was felt, be delayed by cases of lesser importance. When the assizes opened on Monday, the roaring, pushing, kicking crowd, struggling to gain admission into the Crown Court, was such that it remained a miracle that nobody was trampled to death. The only people to prosper by the riot were the pickpockets who made a gala-haul. So confused and vast was the concourse that when the sheriff's carriage appeared it could not penetrate the mass, and even the pawing of frightened horses' hoofs forced only a comparatively small space, driving those nearest to them to terrified squeals and shrieks while those in safety further back refused to budge. There were as many, if not more, women than men in the hurly-burly and some of them, the Corinthian noted sardonically, were what might be called ladies. All they received for their passion to quiz a woman-murderer were torn and muddied gowns, pulverized feet and bruised and scratched skin.

Having been reliably informed by Lea that there was no possibility of Corder's case being called before Thursday, he had come purely to watch the crowd, and he returned to the inn to tell the uproarious tale only to find that Mary and Lydia listened with glum faces.

"Disgusting," shuddered Mary, half-closing her eyes. "What savages some people are! What can they expect to see or hear?"

"Smut," said the Corinthian, "blood and smut. That's the way to draw a crowd these days."

"And women there, too!" cried Lydia. "They should be ashamed of themselves, a disgrace to their sex."

This virtuous indignation drove both the Corinthian and

Bertram to the bar; and while they sat there in miserable dudgeon, they saw Lea stride in, his bright little eyes darting glances on every side, his sharp nose seeming to quiver at the point. At sight of the Corinthian, he gave his friendly yet condescending grin, and swaggered over.

"A rum, hot?" asked the Corinthian.

"That's very good of you, sir," said Lea, taking the chair indicated. "I always like a drop of rum to oil the innards. I've seen too much of the effects of Blue Ruin, Old Tom, Jacky, Stark Naked, Fuller's Earth, or any of the thousand names you want to give that poison, gin. And it's not only the poor that drinks it. I've known many a squeamish fair one who takes her daffy regularly on the sly to cure the vapours with, only she always calls it white wine. But it's rot-gut gin all the same. Therefore, gentlemen, I bid you good health, in rum."

They drank and Lea smacked his lips.

"Further business this way, Mr. Lea?" asked the Corinthian. "More women-killers to nab?"

"It's the same one," growled Lea. "I've come up for the trial, got to give evidence. Kind of holiday, but I like my work, and doing nothing makes a fellow rusty. I've been over to the jail to quiz some of my old pals and to mark the dials of some I ain't met before so I'll know 'em next time if they're ever let loose."

"Did you see Corder?" asked the Corinthian.

"Your pal?" Lea laughed at the Corinthian's annoyance and at the way his face reddened. "No offence, sir; no offence," he said with arch joviality. "It's your sister, ain't it, what's so interested? He's taking it very well, you might tell her, considering. . . . Pious, too, reading good books instead of those smutty ones and listening to the parson, though he don't say much. I weren't there, of course, but on Sunday I'm told it was a rare sight in the chapel. Old Stocking—he's the parson—went for him as though he was the devil in boots, preaching on *Thou shalt do no murder*. And he spoke wonderful powerful, too, they say, and everybody weeping and your pal keeping his dial behind his hand most of the time. Now, between ourselves, I think old Stocking went too far. After all, ain't your friend suffering enough without getting insulted? Ain't he going to get himself hanged? And that's no tempting prospect for a brisk young fellow like him."

"Why," asked Bertram, "what exactly did Stocking say?"

"He preached straight at your pal, said he'd never known a murder so diabolical as one of his congregation had recently done: he named no names but he looked at Foxy. They say that when he heard this, your mate struck himself on the forehead as though he wanted to knock himself out. Most of the time he kept his handkerchief over his eyes, so's you couldn't see whether he was weeping, laughing or just trying to hide. The others wept and made noise enough to drown the parson."

"So," said the Corinthian softly, "he was honestly affected? Poor devil! I can't help pitying him."

"Affected?" laughed Lea. "He don't want to die, that's all; and who the hell does want to die except at about two o'clock in the morning? Why, on his way back to the ward, a friend of mine who was there heard him say: 'Ah, that text was a slap at me!' Affected? Don't you believe it, sir. To the very end, they all think they'll wriggle out somehow. Until they meet the hangman in the morning, they're cheerful, waiting for the reprieve that rarely comes. He's not got a hope in hell, yet he still hopes."

"I suppose hope's all he's got left," sighed Bertram. "Another drink, Mr. Lea?"

"Seeing that I'm on holiday," said Lea, "certainly, sir, certainly. . . ."

It was late before the Corinthian lurched to bed, haunted by criminals. After numerous hot rums, Lea had become garrulous, yet even when drunk his eyes had retained that sharp suspicious look which made both the Corinthian and Bertram careful of what they said. Not that they had wanted to say anything, Lea's conversation being too interesting for them to wish to interrupt. He told of crimes and criminals and arrests, and he spoke of his victims with amused tolerance, calling them usually by their first names as though they were not enemies but friends who had merely tried to be too clever. Nobody, it appeared, was too clever for Lea. Wherever he went, men and women flinched before his gaze and confessed to villainies at a quiver of his inquisitive nostrils. There was a joviality in his bullying, an amused comradeship in his voice and manner, that apparently unnerved thieves and even murderers; and the Corinthian could understand how they must feel trapped once he grinned at them and reprovingly waggled his finger, like an omniscient master to a naughty boy. He prayed that he might never fall into his hands.

This renewal of their relationship was to prove valuable, the Corinthian soon discovered. It was Wednesday evening, the night before Corder's trial, and the women were near swooning with fear and excitement when Bertram lounged into the parlour before supper. Tossing his hat on to a chair, he began peeling off his gloves, and in a deliberately casual manner he announced that no females were to be admitted into the court.

"Good heavens," cried Mary, turning pale, "why?"

"Because," said Bertram, "according to the judges' announcement, for the sake of humanity—don't ask me what that means!—and because they wish, they say, to perform the duty imposed upon them by the higher powers."

"Who's going to stop them performing their duty?" shrilled Mary, bouncing on the sofa and glaring at him. "How can a few poor harmless females stop them from doing their duty? Do they expect us to charge the bench and beat them with parasols? I've never heard such nonsense!"

"Don't blame me," shrugged Bertram, "blame the judges; or if you like, blame those lunatics who've been battering at the court-house every day trying to kick their way in. They'll be reading the Riot Act to them soon. We were damned lucky to get here when we did. The cheapest room now to be had in Bury'll cost you a guinea a single bed at the least, and you'll be lucky to get that. They're sleeping on billiard-tables, in sheds and hen-roosts: women, too; and the court-house can't hold a million. You can't blame the judges."

"But why should women be excluded?"

"They've got to exclude somebody and, anyhow, few of the men'll be able to get in. God knows why they want to go. It's a grim case: young girl ripped up and shot and strangled. Not the kind of thing respectable women should want to listen to."

"I'm his wife!" cried Mary, red with rage. "And if a wife can't be present when her husband's on trial for his life, I don't know who can. If I've got to see the Lord Chief Justice himself, I'm not going to be kept out; and Lydia's coming with me."

"O, I suppose they'll have to let you in," yawned Bertram; "but no other woman," he added with a malicious glance at Lydia who had laid her sewing in her lap and watched him with cold eyes.

Trembling, Mary sank back. "O, you men!" she sobbed. "The way you go on you'd think this was all about nothing! But he's my husband, don't you understand? He's my husband who's being tried for his life, and I'm going to be there to watch him and see that he gets justice. He'll need me; he'll see me watching and then he'll know I've still got faith in his innocence. Mr. Barsett, I have trust in you, and I'm sure you'll not fail me. You must arrange that I have a seat tomorrow."

"The time's so short," he muttered. "There's only tonight . . ."

"But you'll do it for me, won't you? I know you will." And before that melancholy smile, the appealing look in her tear-bright eyes, the Corinthian knew that he was helpless.

"I'll do what I can," he groaned.

There was nothing, he found, to be done officially that night. At both jail and court-house he was told that, outraged by the behaviour of the crowd, and the brawling and lechery that went on throughout the nights in streets and fields, the judges refused to countenance such saturnalia when a man was being tried for his life.

On being informed by a constable where he might find Lea, he saw him in a crowded public-house near the river where, with a smile of malicious glee, he was listening to the confidences of a drunken fisherman; but even he could not help to gain admittance for Mary into tomorrow's court. In the chill night-air, walking on the quiet river's bank with boats and barges drawn up on the mud, the Corinthian explained Mrs. Corder's distress and her need to be present at the trial.

"I'm very sorry, sir," said Lea, sucking the knob of his stick, "but you're too late. I don't mind waiting on her tomorrow night and telling her how things went; but she can't get in. No women can get in, 'cept friends of the mayor and judges. Now, if I'd had warning, her being the wife of the accused, I don't doubt something might have been done about it; but not now. On Friday, I should be able to manage it, but not tomorrow. Old Baron Alexander's got 'em all dancing with terror, for, says he, if anybody sneaks into that court—'cept the officers, of course—he'll fine or commit the under-sheriff and jailor for contempt. Those to be allowed in, such as newspaper reporters, are to be given tickets. It's no good pressing any honorarium on me, sir; even I can do nothing about it."

Miserably, the Corinthian pushed through the mob back to the "Angel", going empty-handed to Mary. And he could not blame the baron for his decision to keep the court as clear as possible. The orgies at Polstead during the inquest had been innocent compared with the rioting at Bury. Here there were numerous taverns and lanes and byways in which criminals and whores could lurk, and the streets, day and night, were crowded with a noisy throng out for mischief, or worse. Against so many, the police were almost helpless. A few they might arrest, but hundreds, nay thousands, of other ruffians remained; and all, it seemed, were viciously drunk.

Gentry also had raced to Bury, with respectable citizens and their wives, to enjoy the excitement of a murder trial and the hope of watching a fellow-creature jerk on the end of a string. Few of these ventured out at night. Paying extravagant sums for a couch, they skulked indoors, peering out of windows at the roaring multitude singing obscene ballads and dancing over the cobbles, many of them in rags, and dirty after lying in the fields. Women had brought their children with them, some had babies in arms, and their uncorseted flesh, shapeless after yearly child-bearing, sagged inside torn dresses. St. Giles, thought the Corinthian, and Wapping were Sunday schools compared with Bury, while the consumption of gin was astronomical. Old men and women, lads and lasses, all swilled the daffy which Lea had denounced, and urchins, boys and girls, children and babies, drank the poison while staggering after their parents.

When the moon rose and lighted up these drunkards' faces, it seemed to the Corinthian, who was no fastidious fellow, like a scene out of hell. They squabbled, fought, embraced and laughed, or wept while someone sang of a pure maid, Maria Marten, seduced and carved up by a fiendish Corder; and some, too drunk to care who watched, lay semi-naked, men with women, as though alone in bed together, lust, fired with gin and the thought of a violent death, driving all else from sodden minds. Their friends laughed and stumbled over them, poured gin and ale over them and blasphemously blessed the unborn.

Sickened, he turned away, appalled that humanity could be so base, and aghast at the thought that these depraved females were of the same sex as a delicate creature like Mary. Their lascivious postures, their piercing shrieks and bawdy laughter, their rampant dancings, skirts thrown high with bodices unbuttoned, their guzzling of daffy through the necks of bottles, and the way they clutched at men and dragged them down on the backs of others, with mad laughter and legs kicking, made him long to be alone in green fields, far from humankind. And these were the monsters who had already condemned Corder, who had gathered like wolves for his blood!

Back, sweating, at the "Angel", he drank two large brandies quickly before he dared face Mary. She was not angry with him, as he had feared she might be. The long wait while he had sought for Lea had apparently brought resignation and she had prepared herself for the worst.

"It was my fault," she said. "I should have asked Mr. Orridge long ago; but who would have thought this would happen?"

"Lea has promised to see that you have a seat on Friday," said the Corinthian.

"Thank you," she whispered, and leaned her face on Lydia's shoulder. "Perhaps it is for the best," she said with an assumption of cheerfulness. "I don't know if I'd really be strong enough to listen to those people swearing his life away; and that horrid Mrs. Marten. . . . So they don't expect it to finish tomorrow?" she asked, sighing deeply as she turned to watch the Corinthian's mouth.

"I can only go by what Lea tells me," he explained, "but he's a man of great experience in such matters. Apparently, the bill of indictment's a particularly long one, and he grew quite lyrical when he spoke of it. It should take hours to read, he said. Then the prosecutor has to state his case, which will doubtless take some time. After that, he'll call his witnesses, of whom Mrs. Marten will be the chief one, of course."

"That woman," shuddered Mary, "and her dreams! Did you ever hear such nonsense! She knew where her step-daughter was because she'd buried her there herself."

The Corinthian was startled by her percipience and he glanced at Lydia to see whether the suggestion had come from her; but Lydia lay back with closed eyes and said nothing. . . .

Although sorry to have disappointed her, in the morning, when he strolled towards the court-house, the Corinthian was relieved that he had been unable to smuggle Mary in. The drunken crowd of last night was still there, looking greenish and feeble-legged yet vociferous enough, and it had been joined by hundreds of better-class people, men and women attempting to push through to the doors while being elbowed and kicked back. The shouting and cursing mingled to a deafening clamour, a savage howl in which every now and again could be heard the words: "He's coming! He's coming!"

Wriggling out of the hurly-burly, he sought refuge in a tavern and, for the price of half a guinea, was permitted to walk upstairs to watch from a bedroom window. Others were there before him; a stout farmer, his wife, his son and two daughters, all dressed in their best, were leaning over the window-sill and one another, and at the sound of his entrance they turned to scowl at him.

"Sir," said the farmer, "I paid a guinea for this view."

"Then I've been robbed," said the Corinthian. "There are five of you for one guinea; and I, who am alone, paid ten and sixpence. I think I must have my share of that window, if you don't mind."

His gentlemanly manners, his beautifully cut coat and trousers, disposed the ladies towards him, and the young man was too bashful to argue with such an exquisite. Only the farmer grumbled, but against his womenfolk he was helpless, and the Corinthian was permitted to squeeze amongst them. The women, seated on a small sofa, had the best view, as though in a theatre-box, while over their backs the men leaned and bobbed their heads together. Through that small space there was little to be seen save the walls of the court-house and the multitude of heads below, but the Corinthian feigned great interest that he might not be trapped into conversation with the women who had become very arch and ladylike, fanning themselves and ejaculating many a "La!" and "Mercy me!" while rolling their eyes towards him.

At last the shouting grew, if possible, louder. The cry, "He's coming!" became more confident and shrill. Then into the human mass was edged a cart, the driver beating a way with his whip, while people clambered up the sides and on to the wheels, waving hats and holding up bottles. Corder had arrived. There he sat, pale and smiling, between the governor of the jail and one of his officers; and he did not appear to be afraid. Rather, thought the Corinthian, he seemed to enjoy the situation, smiling tightly and looking around him in an amused, condescending fashion, like a king in his coach. By God, he thought, the man has courage! And, sickened by the spectacle, to the distress of the women, he turned suddenly and, without saying good-bye, hurried from the room. . . .

That night, in the "Angel" bar, Lea recounted the day's proceedings, the Corinthian thinking it might be best for him to hear the tale that he might retell a purged version to the women. Yet the tale proved of surprisingly little interest, the evidence having been similar to that which had been already given at the inquest, only more elaborate because there had been counsel to ask questions. As he had expected, after the prosecutor's opening speech, Mrs. Marten had been the first witness called and she had told what she had told before, except that this time there was no mention of her dream.

"There was talk for and against using it, I'm told," said Lea, "but it was decided not to bring it up. It was thought, and I think rightly, that it would only confuse the case. All right for a country-inquest but not for the assizes. They want Corder hung on facts—facts, gentlemen. And, of course, if—I'm only *saying* if, mind you—he should be found not guilty, there'd be the devil to pay if they'd relied on a supernatural thing like that. It's made this case more famous than any in the *Newgate Calendar*, so let it rest."

"How was Corder?" asked the Corinthian. "How did he behave?"

"Remarkably well," said Lea, passing his glass to have it replenished, "considering his awful situation. Well-dressed he was, too, in a new corbeau surtout with a velvet collar, and a black waistcoat and blue trousers. And he had a white neckerchief round his collar, and silk stockings and pumps. Very handsome, I tell you, quite the swell, 'cept for them eyes; better dressed than when I nabbed him. Wife bought 'em for him, I'm told."

"O?" said the Corinthian, who had heard nothing of this before.

"There's one person he really does abominate," said Lea, watching him sharply, "and that's this Mrs. Marten. Perhaps because of that dream, eh?" He paused as though expecting a reply, glancing from the Corinthian to Bertram, but as neither made any comment, he continued pensively: "Rum things, dreams. Don't believe in 'em myself and I've never come across one quite so convenient before. Makes you think, don't it?"

"It does indeed," said the Corinthian.

Lea grunted. "Anyhow, dream or no dream," he said, "Corder hates her like spiders. The way he looked at her when she stepped into the box made you grateful he didn't have those pistols with him. He put on his spectacles and took out his red morocco pocket-book and began to scribble in it, and while he scribbled, every now and again he'd look up and squint at her. She didn't look at him. She looked at the counsel and never wavered, not for a blink. It was strange to see, I tell you, as though there was some nasty secret atwixt them, or something."

The Corinthian called for further drinks while Lea watched him with an ingratiating grin, awaiting revelations he was not to receive.

"I saw his arrival at the court-house," said the Corinthian, "and the behaviour of the people was disgusting, really disgusting."

"Not only the common people neither," said Lea, gracefully accepting his defeat over Mrs. Marten, "but gentlemen, and ladies, too! Why! ladders were raised and a whole pack of 'em—ladies amongst 'em, I'm telling you, not ashamed to climb up a ladder with that dirty mob yo-hoing below—climbed the tiling of a house, they did. There they could see Corder if they twisted themselves. The court, you know, has got a round hole in the roof to let the air through. Usually it's closed by two flap-doors, but the day being hot, these were open and a whole crowd of 'em got up there. Don't ask me how," he sniggered. "But court officers don't get much in the way of pay. Anyhow, up there they got, lying flat on the joists— ladies amongst 'em, I repeat—and peering over the cornice just to have a squint at that squint-eyed rat in the dock. Mighty queer they looked when you looked up at 'em. Do you know what I felt for a moment? Sounds silly when you think what dirty minds they had, getting up there to quiz a woman-killer, but I thought they was like angels. Just heads and shoulders and a bit of neck to be seen. You could hear the roof crack under their weight and old Orridge made a fine to-do about us all being crushed if they fell. Anyhow, he got 'em down. Even when that thunderstorm burst over us, you couldn't wash 'em away; they were still yelling outside, females louder than the worst of 'em, and it was shocking for the sheriff's lady to hear, not to speak of the chaplain's wife and two female friends of theirs."

"What!" cried the Corinthian. "There were women present!"

"Lord love you, sir," chuckled Lea, "you couldn't lock them out when there's a good murder or a rape case going. Aw, you don't

269

know what they're like when they sniff blood, and the sheriff'd never dare say no to his wife; and as for the chaplain . . . Ho, ho! he's a good preacher 'cause the pulpit's the only place where he knows he can talk without being interrupted. But don't you worry yourself, sir. I've arranged with the sheriff that you and Mrs. Corder can be present tomorrow. I'll call for you in the morning, so wait for me."

"Thank you," said the Corinthian, beckoning the maid for further drinks. "But about the trial: wasn't there anything of interest?"

"Nothing, sir. Just like the inquest it was. The prisoner remained calm, and ate well, and he drank deep—'cause of the heat, they was bringing water in in pails—and it was only towards the end that he seemed to lose some of his confidence. At first, he didn't seem to care a rush. He stood there smiling, 'cept when the surgeon, Mr. Lawton, was telling about the wounds. He didn't like that, I can tell you. Those squint-eyes of his were fixed on Mr. Lawton all the while, and his examination wasn't short. But, Lord love you, it was sport when I went into the box. I treated that man fair, gentlemen: I acted like a friend to him; yet, would you believe it! he looked at me as if he'd cut my throat for twopence. When I was telling about the pistols I'd found in his place, he stamped his foot and set his teeth and I heard him growl that I'd swear to anything. That's the kind of return you've got to expect from scamps like him! I know one should get used to it, but somehow I just can't. One doesn't expect gratitude from villains: no man likes being nabbed for what he's done; but one does expect a little appreciation, a little consideration. I don't care who his mother may be, that man, sir, is no gentleman. I've done less than I done for him and I've been thanked for it from the heart by fellows you'd think hadn't a grain of politeness in 'em. They was nature's gentlemen. But this Corder . . . No, sir: I only hope they hang him."

Being free, the rum was so much to Lea's taste that it was with difficulty that the Corinthian escaped from the bar. But leaving the man in Bertram's charge, he hurried to the parlour that he might tell Mary about the trial before she retired to bed; for it was growing late. Eagerly, she looked up as he entered, and she put down the copy of *The Lady's Magazine* she had been reading.

"Tell me," she cried, "everything that's happened! How is he? Is the evidence as strong as we feared?"

Lydia left her chair and, placing a cushion on the floor, sat at Mary's feet, leaning her dark head against her thigh; and both women watched the Corinthian with a wide cat-like stare.

"There's nothing to tell," he said. "According to Lea—he's still in the bar if you want to question him—it was just a repetition of the inquest, only prolonged because of the cross-examination. Corder, he says, behaved very well, leaning against a pillar to ease his limbs and taking a great interest in the proceedings. But I've not come to tell you things you can read in tomorrow's newspaper. Lea's arranged for you and me to be present."

Mary took a deep breath, her eyes almost closed, and she shivered. "Thank you, good friend," she said. "It will be a melancholy pleasure, but I would be lacking in all marital duties were I to evade going. William will be encouraged by my presence."

"What about me?" asked Lydia.

"I'm sorry," said the Corinthian, "but Lea can only manage two tickets."

"Then I'll go with Mary," she said. "It would look more decent."

"She will need a man's protection. You saw the crowds today. Anyhow," he shrugged, "I'm taking her; I've arranged for the seats and I'm going with her."

Breathing fast and trying not to lose her temper, Lydia glared at him, sitting up while leaning her shoulder against Mary's skirt. Then suddenly she turned and, seizing Mary's hand, held it to her cheek in a passionate gesture of possession.

"Mary," she wheedled, "you must not go out alone with this creature. I've warned you what to expect from a man like him. He has no honour, no respect for women. Most likely, he'll not take you to court tomorrow. He'll have his rascals handy to drive you to some hot-house in the country. I forbid your going."

Timidly, Mary glanced at the Corinthian. "I'm not afraid of Mr. Barsett," she said, wrinkling her nose at him in a conspiratorial smile.

"That is your inexperience talking, and inexperience and trust and curiosity have ruined more women than anything," said Lydia severely, still clutching her hand. "You think you're safe because you've been lucky enough to have had no dealings with certain types of men. O, my dear, the devil doesn't run around like a roaring lion seeking whom he might devour; he comes in well-tailored breeches with a smooth tongue; he wears a mask of sentiment with which to cheat a woman. She believes that she's safe, trusting to his lies; her virtue will protect her, she thinks; but virtue itself can tempt such monsters who lust to corrupt what is pure and good. I, too, suffered from the lying promises of such a man when I was a girl; and look what it has led me to!"

Mary glanced down at her and saw her expensive gown and the jewels around her throat and on her fingers. "What has it led you to?" she asked, smoothing the cheap cloth over her knees.

"To shame!" cried Lydia. "To remorse, to the gnawing of conscience! Until I met you, I had no heart, I scorned men and despised good women. But you changed all that. Seeing you so cheerful, so contented, so calm in your faith and knowing the angry resentments in my own heart, I became ashamed, utterly ashamed of myself."

"Cheerful, contented, calm!" repeated Mary in a bitter voice. "How little you know me!" and with great sad eyes she looked at the Corinthian standing silent before them.

Lydia saw that look and twisted furiously, writhing against Mary's gown. "Of course you're not happy now," she cried, "with your husband in this terrible situation!" She glared into Mary's eyes as though commanding attention and obedience. "Listen to me," she said. "You must not go to court tomorrow. If you asked him, I am certain Mr. Barsett would surrender the tickets to you, then you and I could go together."

"That would not be right," said Mary, "after all the trouble he's taken."

"You'd prefer to go with him than with me!"

"It's not that. It just wouldn't be right. . . ."

"Ingratitude!" cried Lydia, springing to her feet. "After the way I've cared for you in your trouble, tried to protect you, lent you money from my savings, for you now to turn on me like this!"

"I'm not turning on you." With angry dignity, Mary looked up at her. "And I'll pay you back every penny you've lent."

"It's not the money, I don't want the money!" Sobbing, Lydia twisted her hands together, that splendid bosom swelling above her stays, and there were tears in her eyes. "Don't I mean anything to you?" she gasped in a choking voice. "Does all my care, my love, my watching over you mean nothing, nothing whatever to you? Mary darling, I've never asked a thing of you, have I? I've been happy to serve you, but now I do ask, please, please don't let this man take you out alone tomorrow!"

"O, dear," said Mary, hunching her shoulders and half-closing her eyes in her distress, "I don't understand what all this fuss is about. What possible harm can there be in going to court where I'll be surrounded by the police and judges and heaven knows whom? Really, Lydia, this is most unpleasant and very unnecessary."

"You have to choose," cried Lydia: "him or me!"

"I'm not making any choice. Since Mr. Barsett's been so kind as to get these tickets, and it must have caused him a great deal of trouble, the least I can do is to accompany him."

"Then you choose him?" cried Lydia in a voice of tragedy.

"I'm not choosing anybody. . . ."

"But you're letting him take you tomorrow?"

"Of course I am."

"That is sufficient," said Lydia gruffly, drawing up her skirt and striding to the door. "I wish you good night," she said and, in her haste to escape before she burst into tears, she almost caught her skirt in the door when she slammed it behind her.

"O, dear," sobbed Mary, "now I've upset her again, and I do hate scenes. Tonight when we're in bed she'll talk and cry and, O, it's all so silly! Why shouldn't I go with you tomorrow?"

"Because," said the Corinthian with a passionate look, "she knows what you've failed to see. I love you, Mary."

"O, don't talk like that!" she shrilled, hands almost to her deaf ears, "I won't listen to you, I won't. I'm a married woman and it's not right to talk to me like that!"

"I didn't intend to speak of it yet," he said, stepping towards her while she shrank back on the chair. "I meant to wait until . . . I meant to wait and live on hopes. But this scene of Lydia's tonight was too much and I can't keep silent any longer. I love you, Mary, as I've never loved any woman before. What Lydia told you about me is the truth. I have been a villain, a despoiler of innocence, a gambler, a cheat, and many other vile things; but that lies in the past and God has promised pardon to those who repent. You with your goodness and beauty have brought that repentance, Mary, my darling; would you have me lose my soul again? for if I lose you, life will hold no further meaning for me, and I daren't think what I might do."

"Please," she whimpered, "this is unmanly of you. We must think of poor William and . . . and . . . No, I can't, I can't!"

"What is it, my pretty?" He caught her hand and kissed it, squeezing it against his lips and cheeks.

"Don't, please," she moaned. "Why must you ruin our friendship in this way? No, don't touch me : I beg of you, please."

They did not hear the door open. Already in his excitement the Corinthian had an arm about her adamantine waist and was drawing her towards him that he might kiss her mouth, and she was weeping and not struggling hard. Within a moment their lips would have met. . . . Then they started guiltily apart as Lydia jeered :

"Exactly what I expected. I warned you, Mary! No woman's safe near that blackguard. I thought I'd let you learn, and I waited outside and listened. And I was right."

"You were spying!" shouted the Corinthian; and in his rage, his impulse was to kill her. "You bitch!" he cried, clenching his fists.

"There, you see what kind of a man he is," said Lydia. "My child, you had better let me take you up to bed."

Weeping, her hands over her face, Mary did not speak; and she remained silent, as though dumb with shame, when Lydia caught her by the waist and, lifting her to her feet, guided her to the door. Then with a look of triumph mingled with loathing, Lydia turned to glare into the Corinthian's eyes. Words were not needed to give force to that challenge. And furiously, threateningly, the Corinthian glared back at her, as though to tell her that he would fight to the end and would not scruple about what tricks he used that he might win from her this woman whom he loved.

Chapter Twenty-One

THE FIGHT FOR A LIFE

WITH the help of Lea and the court officials he had suborned, the Corinthian and Mary Corder were given seats in the court the following day. They were not placed on the bench, where ladies sat with bouquets to drive off the smell of so many people crowded into one place; they sat amongst the barristers and lawyers and their clerks at the table in front of the dock. Although the besieging populace remained in the same state of almost lunatic excitement, they were being managed more cleverly than on the day before. Special constables had been posted to hold back the invaders that a passage might be formed through which the judge, officials, witnesses and the privileged few might enter without being assaulted. Nor was the ruling against the admittance of women maintained; many ladies, apart from Mary and those on the bench, were allowed seats and, with everybody talking and laughing, the atmosphere was more that of a theatre than of a court of justice.

For the first time alone on an expedition with Mary, the Corinthian felt very gay, even though they were present to witness her husband fighting for his neck; and after last night's emotional scene he had expected that he would have to surrender his ticket to Lydia. Although Mary had not fought him and unquestionably had been prepared to let him salute her lips, he feared lest she might later have grown ashamed of her weakness, particularly after a curtain-lecture from Lydia about male perfidy. But it would seem that Mary and not Lydia had won that bedtime battle. Alone, she had descended to breakfast, excusing Lydia's absence on the plea of a headache, and had made no reference to anything that had happened. Almost gay had she looked, blushing now and then when she found the Corinthian watching her, becoming girlishly, charmingly selfconscious with fluttering eyelashes and downcast eyes and almost clumsy gestures, for all of which he loved her.

Had the show been anything other than the trial of Corder, the Corinthian would have proved himself a captivating companion, but he kept his quips to himself and attempted to look grave; and he could not help becoming excited by the tense atmosphere of the court with the audience whispering and tittering in anticipation of cruel and amorous details from the witness-stand, and the counsels shuffling briefs and glancing through fat books and chatting together. So interested was he in watching them, prosecution and defence friendly together as though they had not met to battle for a man's life, that only by the sudden hush did he realize that the prisoner had arrived, and he squirmed round to see Corder in the dock with officers either side of him.

He blinked at the change in the man. It was not merely that Corder had grown thinner but that there was a hunted look in his shifty eyes, although he managed to force a smile and to assume an air of cheerful indifference. He stared about him, then, taking his spectacles from his pocket, he set them on the bridge of his nose and hooked them behind his ears that he might see his audience more clearly. Leaning against a pillar, he swayed from side to side, arms folded, until suddenly he stiffened. He had noticed Mary.

Behind the glasses, he blinked, and his chest rose in a deep sigh, while Mary waved to him with her lace handkerchief. Not wishing to be noticed, the Corinthian sank into his chair, but within a second Corder had seen him, and his face paled. Fists clenched, he stepped forward, but the officers closed about him and he sank back with folded arms, to lean on the pillar, and somehow he managed both to smile at Mary and to defy the Corinthian.

The entrance of the lord chief baron attended by the high sheriff and the chaplain made everyone rise swiftly to their feet, and the Corinthian was glad of the opportunity to turn away from the prisoner. Despite the presence of Mary, he was not, he feared, going to enjoy the day as he had anticipated. Under the most comfortable circumstances it could prove embarrassing to make love to a wife when her husband was present, but when the husband was fighting to save his neck, it seemed scarcely in the best of taste, and he groaned to think that he would have to guard against any look or gesture which might too openly display his feelings.

While his lordship was speaking to the jury, hoping that they had spent a pleasant night, and making polite bows to the ladies, the Corinthian stared at his shoes. Nor did he look up when the clerk read over the jurymen's names, but from the corners of his eyes he noted that Corder was busily writing, frowning, and tearing up what he wrote.

Determined not to stare at the poor wretch, he shifted his chair to face the bench and tried to interest himself in the proceedings; but he was too conscious of those malignant cross-eyes watching him balefully, and of the presence of Mary so close that he had only to turn to touch her.

A surgeon was the first witness, but he had little to say; and he was followed by John Baalham, Polstead's parish clerk and constable, a man with a twisted face and a projecting jaw, who related how the body had been disinterred for the second time. Then, on the surgeon being recalled, there began a tiresome argument with the defence counsel about when the wounds on the corpse could have been inflicted, the defence striving to show that they might have been caused by old Marten when he first found the body in the barn. To prove various points, Maria's skull was produced out of a bag and a loud humming noise ran through the court, women squeaking and men hissing, and Mary gripped the Corinthian's hand. The polished bone turning in the counsel's hands shone brightly, and it grinned. The lower jaw had been wired in place, and when it fell down it gave an impression of silent laughter, the empty eye-sockets darkly watching the prisoner who wrote furiously and passed his notes to his counsel who tore them into tiny pieces. Then, in his turn, counsel answered on another piece of paper, and this Corder, in his turn, tore into scraps after reading it. Otherwise he gave no sign that he had been affected by the girl's fleshless, hairless head taken from the grave to accuse him of murder.

After this moment of gruesome sensation, the court settled into boredom until another surgeon appeared to contradict what his predecessor had sworn. Whereupon the first surgeon took the skull and, holding it up before the jury, rammed a sword through the base of the skull and out through the right eye. The Corinthian almost expected the skull to squeal, so callous appeared that brisk assault, but it remained grinning with hanging jaw, showing gaps where teeth had been lost, and he found it difficult to believe that, when clothed with flesh and adorned with hair, the owner of that bone had been an attractive female, desirable, the mother of children, a wench whom many men had kissed. Under Mary's bonnet, under those bright curls and that delicate flesh, there was insensate bone like that, expressionless, ridged and bumpy, showing a zigzag crack circling above the ear. He shut his eyes to shut away that thought.

How could Corder, he wondered, remain silent before that accusing bone? And he twisted round to look at him over Mary's bonnet. No blink of horror showed on his face. Through his spectacles he stared anxiously at the jury, troubled, it was plain, only by what the effect might be on those men in their box.

I hope to God, thought the Corinthian, that they hang the dog!

Demurely, Mrs. Marten, eyes downcast, fluttered to the box to identify certain articles of clothing as having belonged to Maria; and Mary looked up to stare at her. Face and lips so pallid she seemed about to die, Mary turned to look with loathing on this little woman primly repeating that this and that had been her step-daughter's property. But soon—whether it was the basilisk glare of Corder or the smell of the rotting garments could not be told—she began to falter; her head drooped and she almost fell.

Officials ran to hold her up, water was brought for her to sip and a bottle of smelling-salts was opened under her nostrils, as she sank down. Murmuring their sympathy, everybody stood up, her husband loudly weeping, while Corder lounged against the post, arms folded, his underlip out-thrust with the satisfied smirk of a good man contemplating God's judgment on a liar.

Soon, however, Mrs. Marten had sufficiently recovered to identify the remainder of the garments, portions of a leghorn hat and rotting stays; then she was helped from court. She kept her head down, but as she passed the Corinthian she turned in the bonnet and her round blue eyes gleamed malignantly while her lips moved as though she cursed him. Mary saw that look and pressed against him, and Mrs. Marten grinned tight-lipped to see that gesture of affection. Then the bonnet concealed her face again and the Corinthian felt certain that he had heard her chuckle, witchlike, as she padded on, raising her head one moment that she might look triumphantly on Corder.

Her step-daughter, Ann, took her place in the box and answered in a timid voice, identifying her sister's garments and the tortoiseshell comb and other articles. She could not recall, however, what kind of garters Maria had worn to hold up her stockings.

Gown rustling, wig tilted over his forehead, the prosecutor rose to speak of the passport which Lea had found in Corder's desk. This, he said, was a passport for France. . . .

"I think," said the lord chief baron, puffing out his rosy cheeks and rolling from lady to lady on the bench, "that it would be safer not to receive evidence of this, especially as, in a case of this grave nature, all doubtful points ought, from the importance of this trial to the prisoner, to be decided in his favour."

As though he were already acquitted, Corder smiled delightedly and thrice bowed to his lordship who, pretending not to notice, sank down amongst the crush of fragrant femininity with which he was surrounded.

Back into court was Mrs. Marten called, to swear that Maria on leaving home had worn white tape garters, similar to those which had been found on the legs of the corpse. Her voice was low and breathless, and, concealed within her bonnet, she did not raise her eyes; nor, when again she passed the Corinthian and Mary, did she look again towards them or Corder. Swiftly she had entered, and as swiftly she departed in her black gown; and it seemed to the Corinthian, easing his neck from the points of his collar, that he could breathe more freely with her departure.

The remaining witnesses were soon examined and dismissed, the defence not troubling to cross-examine them. Baalham reappeared to swear that the parish of Polstead lay within the liberty of Bury St. Edmunds; Maria's earlier lover, Peter Matthews, a burly, elderly man looking most uncomfortable and sweating profusely, deposed that Maria was able to write and that she had written to him frequently. She could write very well, he added. Lastly, Thomas Marten, looking immeasurably aged since last the Corinthian had seen him, agreed that he had been present when the body had been disinterred from the bay of the barn. The soil, he said, was loose loam, stones and gravel, and very dry.

When the prosecutor, switching forward the tail of his gown, sat ponderously on a chair and crossed his legs, the court relaxed. The prologue, it was felt, which had taken altogether almost fourteen hours, was now concluded and the curtain was about to rise on the real drama, the defence. On what possible defence?

Blowing out his cheeks, the lord chief baron leaned back in his chair and frowned at Corder lounging against the post. In a slow, deep, menacing voice which seemed to be drawn upwards through oceans of gravy, he announced: "It now becomes my duty to call upon you for your defence, and to answer the charge upon which you are indicted. You will speak distinctly, and the court and jury will then be able to hear what you have to say."

The Corinthian did not want to look towards the dock; he did not want to embarrass the wretched man, much as he disliked him; but he could not keep his eyes from watching him furtively while he pretended to look at the floor. Unashamedly, everybody else in court who could possibly see Corder stretched their necks and hissed to one another, craning forward, staring as though at a monster at a fair.

Whether it was fright before such an excited audience, or horror at his perilous situation, Corder began to shake. Mary's hand tightened over the Corinthian's until his knuckles were twisted painfully together, as she stared, scarcely seeming to breathe, at her husband who would not look towards her. From his pocket he had drawn a largish blue-covered copy-book, and, after adjusting his spectacles, he bowed respectfully, but rather unsteadily, to the judge and jury; then in a tremulous voice he began to read aloud.

He craved the court's indulgence if, owing to his state of mind, some of his observations might appear obscure or improperly arranged, and he pleaded for it to forget what it had read about him in the press. As he continued, his voice grew stronger, and when he referred to the press, there sounded almost a savage tone; and a note of horror came when he cried that it was believed that he could be the most depraved of human monsters, one who, while professing to become the husband of Maria, had meditated murdering her!

He talked too much and too vaguely, thought the Corinthian; stumbling away from incriminating facts, he burbled about the press and popular prejudice, then pretended horror that the coroner should have been chosen to conduct the prosecution; and with shrill indignation he referred to the handling of the inquest from which he had been excluded. The behaviour of the coroner had apparently infuriated him, and while his audience settled back in disappointment, he rambled on, the minutes ticking away; and it was long before he reached that moment for which all were waiting, the moment when Maria in his dead brother's clothes had met him in the Red Barn. By this time, he had begun to sweat a little.

"Gentlemen," he said in quavering tones, "this was the origin of the fatal occurrence: As we proceeded across the fields to the barn (which I beg you to bear in mind was a place where we were in the constant habit of meeting and passing hours together, and even nights together), I gently reproved her for giving way to tears, and observed to her that that was not the way she should conduct herself towards one who was willing to make every sacrifice to render her happy. By this time we had reached the barn, when, in consequence of this and other observations which passed, and whilst she was changing her dress, she flew into a passion; told me that she did not care anything about me; that I was too proud to take her to my mother's, and when married she did not think she should be happy, as my mother and family, she was sure, would never notice her. She upbraided me with not having so much regard for her as the gentleman before alluded to had shown. Much further conversation arose, the particulars of which it is useless to detail, but I felt myself so insulted, and became so much irritated by her observations, that I told her if she would go on in this way before we were married, what could I expect afterwards; that I had then seen sufficient to convince me we should never live happily together, and I was, therefore, resolved, before it was too late, not to marry her, informing her that I should return home, and that she might act as she thought proper respecting her future conduct.

"In consequence of this determination I turned from her, and had scarcely proceeded to the outer gate of the barnyard when I heard a loud report, like that of a gun or pistol. Alarmed at this noise, I immediately ran back, and to my horror I found the unhappy girl on the ground, apparently dead. Astonished at the suddenness of the occurrence, and overwhelmed by my own feelings at the awful event, I stood for some moments in a state of complete stupefaction.

"When I had in some measure recovered from this stupor, my first thought was to run for assistance, and well had it been for me had I acted on that impulse; but the dreadful situation of Maria deterred me from quitting the spot. I endeavoured to raise her from the ground in the hope of affording her relief, but to my horror I found she was altogether lifeless. I then placed the body on the ground, in doing which, I perceived the fatal weapon, which I took up, when, to add to my terror and the extraordinary singularity of my situation, I discovered it to be one of my own pistols which I had always kept loaded in my bedroom.

"The danger of my situation now flashed upon my mind. There lay the unfortunate girl wounded to death, and by an instrument belonging to me, and I the only human being present who could prove how the circumstance occurred. I will not attempt to describe to you (because it would be impossible) the agitation of my mind at finding myself surrounded by such suspicious and unfortunate circumstances. My faculties for the time seemed suspended. I knew not what to do, and some time elapsed before I sufficiently recovered myself to become thoroughly sensible of the awful and responsible situation in which I stood.

"When once I had paused, my course was fixed; for having delayed to give an alarm the instant the mischief had happened, it seemed to me that it would only have added to the suspicion that would have been directed against me had I an hour or two afterwards reported what had befallen the unfortunate Maria. Concealment, therefore, I confess, appeared to my distracted and agitated mind, the only possible mode of escaping from the consequences of that day's occurrence.

"The evidence you have heard is, therefore, easily explained. Having once resolved to conceal what had occurred, I buried Maria as well as I was able and afterwards accounted for her absence in some such manner as the witnesses have described to you, sometimes saying one thing, sometimes another. It may be asked, if I were innocent, why should I do all this. I answer that observation by stating that a man may, through fear, pursue the same conduct that another man may from guilt; and, situated as I was, I ask whether it might not have occurred to you or any other man to act as I did. It may be said, why don't I prove this statement as to Maria's death, by witnesses? How can I? Are there not many circumstances in this life which happen between two individuals which can only be proved by the individuals themselves? and as Maria is now no more, how can I, by any possibility, prove it other than by a representation of the real circumstances, in the manner I have done? Neither can I offer any direct proof of the manner in which Maria possessed herself of my pistols, which I always kept loaded in my bedroom. I mention pistols, as I afterwards found the other one in her reticule. She obtained them, there can be no doubt, during the time she was in my bedroom, while it was believed by Thomas Marten, her father, that she was gone to Sudbury, as before related; and as I had no occasion to use the pistols, they were not missed by me.

"It has, I believe, been represented by some of the witnesses that the body had the appearance of having been stabbed and contused. All I can say in answer to this is that no stab or wound was ever inflicted by me; and I believe the surgeons would never have thought of stabs or wounds had it not been that a small sword was found in my possession which gave a probability to their testimony . . ."

"It will not do," groaned the Corinthian, "it really will not do!" This defence was hopeless, so blatantly a mess of lies, that he wriggled with embarrassment and tried not to listen. Corder had answered nothing and he had striven to arouse sympathy by arguing that he had not known what was to be the evidence against him: this was untrue: his solicitor had been given a full copy of what had been sworn at the inquest, and from that this trial differed little, save for the details of stabbing and shooting discovered after the body had been for the second time disinterred. Then his attack on the coroner because he acted for the prosecution was irrelevant. Indeed, most of his speech was irrelevant. And there was no twisting from the medical evidence and the fact that he had had a sword ground before the murder, saying that it was to be used at his cousin's wedding.

It was the sudden pressure of Mary's hand on his that roused the Corinthian from his gloomy thoughts, and he looked up to hear that Corder was talking about the passport to France which Lea had found. And he had said, "my wife".

"This," he was saying, "like other circumstances, has been caught up to show that I meant to leave the country. I say it means the reverse, and so I could prove were I allowed to call my wife as a witness. It was at her request that this passport was obtained in order for us to visit a friend of hers in Paris. I declined going on account of the expense. . . ."

"Liar," hissed Mary under her breath so that only the Corinthian could hear, "liar! Why does he tell such lies!"

The Corinthian squeezed her hand to silence her, afraid lest others hear, and behind her veil he saw her eyes gleam. Then she turned her stiff back on her husband and would not look towards him again, and that meant that, being unable to watch his lips, she could understand little of what he said. Not that it was worth understanding. He rambled on, claiming, with a certain justification, that he had made no attempt to hide, and concluding, opening both his arms, by saying:

"It now rests, gentlemen, with your consciences either to award me an acquittal or an ignominious death. To the former, my own conscience tells me I am fairly and honestly entitled—to the latter fearful alternative, I feel assured your justice and humanity will not consign me. Gentlemen, I have nothing more to say. My life is in your hands."

There was sweat on his brow when he stood back against the pillar, and all the court seemed to sigh, a wind of satisfaction, of surprise and even of pity from the bellies of listeners held tense for over half an hour. Back on chair and forms they sat, relaxed, to whisper and giggle into one another's ears, while, with much rustling of papers, counsel rose to open the defence.

His first witness was a William Goodwin of Sudbury who deposed that Corder had taken apartments in his house during the spring of 1826. Later, a young woman, whom he learned was Maria Marten, came and stayed two or three months, during which time she bore a child. The prisoner, declared Mr. Goodwin, had visited her about two or three times a week and they appeared very fond of one another. He remembered her going to a gunsmith's, but was uncertain whether Corder had accompanied her. On April 16 they had left in a chaise, taking the baby with them.

Evidence that meant nothing, as the lord chief baron pointed out with a grunt, only the dead girl's alleged word being given for it.

Mrs. Goodwin followed her husband into the box and confirmed his evidence; and except that she added that Maria had been "frequently in bad spirits during her stay, but not always", she need never have been called.

The same might have been said of the evidence of the next witness. This was a Thomas Hardy, one of old Mrs. Corder's servants, and he remembered cleaning the pistols. He had seen Maria in the prisoner's company, and there were two staircases in the house, he said, so that anyone could have entered the prisoner's room without being seen by his mother.

Another servant, Lucy Baalham, also remembered seeing the pistols and said she considered the prisoner a good-natured young man.

Next a doctor swore that, as he showed symptoms of consumption, he had advised the prisoner to leave Polstead and had suggested he might stay at Hastings.

Then came evidence of character. A Theresa Havers, a John Bugg, John Pryke, a Mary Kersey, a Jeremiah Boreham, and a William Baalham all swore that he was a kind, humane, good-tempered young man.

And what they swore meant absolutely nothing.

Everybody settled comfortably into their seats as, grunting and blowing out his chubby cheeks, his lordship took up his notes and began the summing-up. Only Corder and Mary stayed stiff and tense; and as the judge continued, Corder's face grew whiter and he began to tremble. After concluding his defence, he had appeared exhausted and had sighed loudly and frequently, but while his witnesses had spoken of his good character he had begun to look more confidently about him and had even tried to catch Mary's eye; but she had persistently looked away. As his lordship continued recapitulating the evidence, however, his courage ebbed and he drooped until he looked almost asleep, as though stupefied at not having had his word accepted. Yet now and then he roused himself and a twinkle of hope showed behind the glasses, as when his lordship exhorted the jury to forget whatever rumours they might have heard, and not to be influenced by a sermon which had recently been preached near the semi-demolished barn to five thousand people and in which the prisoner had been spoken of as the murderer. Then, like a toy on wires, Corder bobbed from side to side, bowing his acknowledgements to judge, jury and audience.

This optimism did not last. When his lordship remarked on how Maria had been enticed from her home by a false statement calculated to intimidate her, the prisoner stifled a groan and his face seemed to lengthen. Longer yet it grew when his lordship continued to speak of the witness Phoebe Stow and how she had alleged that when she had asked the prisoner what had happened to Maria's child, he had answered "the child was dead and buried, and Maria would never have any more". On Phoebe persisting and saying one could never be certain about such things, he had answered: "I can, for I'll be damned if ever she will have any more." Corder flinched, blinking about him, while monotonously, cruelly the judge went on, repeating the evidence: "The witness then asked him whether he was married to her and, if he was, why did he not live with her. He replied to this: 'She is where I can go to her at any day or hour I please.' The witness then said: 'Perhaps you are rather jealous and think that when you are away she is with somebody else.' He said, 'When I am away, I am sure nobody else is with her.' . . ."

Corder wiped his forehead and tried hard to grin, but it was plain that he was near swooning. His eyes rolling, he leaned against the pillar and clutched the iron railing that fenced him from the lawful folk arraigned to kill him. Within a few minutes, by a powerful effort, he recovered his self-possession and stood once more erect, but looking on the floor; only now and then he twitched and his fingers tightened on the rail until the knuckles showed white as cream when the lord chief baron said, with grim humour:

"Gentlemen, you have heard it asserted this day that this truly ill-fated girl had committed suicide; but if that be so, it appears exceedingly strange that, immediately on the prisoner quitting the barn and leaving her alone, she should have used such various instruments in order to destroy herself; for it appears that she must have fired a pistol, and, either before or after she had discharged it, must have stabbed herself in various parts of the body with some sharp instrument. . . ."

No jury could ignore that comment. Ruthlessly, it tore aside Corder's feeble pretences and put the rope about his neck. And the poor devil knew it. All attempt at nonchalance was forgotten. He gasped and sweated, clinging to the rail lest he fall, and swayed from side to side with his mouth open. A glass of water was passed to him by the jailor, and, spilling much of it, he drank greedily; yet still he swayed as though in a strong wind. Spirits of hartshorn were waved under his nostrils until he shivered and opened his eyes; but they did not stop the sweat from running down his forehead until his face shone wetly, and they could not stop his swaying.

When he looked at him, the Corinthian shuddered and tried to stifle pity by reminding himself that this anguish resulted, not from remorse at a bloody deed, but from fear of the rope. Yes, it was terror, not remorse, that shook Corder: terror that came like a wind to that airless court to sway him in the dock and to burn within him, until, as on a lighted candle, the grease ran down. Dispassionately, the judge droned on, scarcely troubling to discuss the feeble defence, and damning the accused with every impartial word he uttered; and all the court stayed hushed.

The Corinthian sneaked a glance at Mary, but she remained hidden under the dark veil. Only by her agitated breathing and the way she clutched his hand did he know how profoundly she was affected. After this, surely she could not possibly believe Corder to be innocent?

For nearly two hours his lordship droned on, and even he, inured though he must have been to judging criminals, showed that the strain was affecting him. He spluttered, wiped his brow, and at times, as when speaking of the medical evidence, he faltered as though the words brought too clearly to his mind the body of that murdered girl. The women on either side of him made no attempt to conceal their feelings; they sniffed into lace handkerchiefs and darted furious, disdainful glances at the prisoner swaying in the dock.

Sickened by the stale atmosphere and the odour of many over-clothed bodies seeming to sweat with their hatred and their lust for blood, the Corinthian shivered. Yes, he felt that he could smell as something tangible this massed loathing of that lonely figure, this craving for Corder's death, and little was needed, he feared, to have turned those genteel people into savages—ay, even those dainty ladies on the bench—screaming and tearing at their victim.

"My lord," said the foreman, rising in the jury-box as his lordship purred to silence, "if it please your lordship, we wish to retire, as this important case requires some time to be spent in deliberation upon it."

"Certainly, gentlemen," said his lordship, "by all means; let an officer be sworn."

While an officer of the court swore that he would not allow communication between the jury and any other person, and the jury shuffled out of their box, Corder sank back on to a chair and covered his face with his hands; and excitedly everybody began to talk. The lifting of tension brought a wild gaiety, people laughed and giggled, and the lawyers and barristers of both sides chattered together, some stalking off for a drink, an example set by his lordship who had been the first to roll out of the room.

As though she realized for the first time that she was holding the Corinthian's hand, Mary swiftly released her grip and placed both her hands out of mischief in her lap. Neither she nor the Corinthian spoke, and he wondered whether she might leave him to talk with her husband. Shyness perhaps before these watchful strangers kept her on her chair, for she made no move towards the dock. Still breathing heavily, she sat, concealed under her veil, while the slow minutes ticked by and the hidden jury argued their verdict. That they should have needed to discuss the question surprised the Corinthian, so clearly proved was Corder's guilt; but, he supposed, they wished to exaggerate their own importance by keeping the court in this suspense.

When Mary leaned towards him, he looked up. He saw her eyes behind the veil bright with tears, and the blur of her nose and the smudge of her mouth. She had intended to whisper, but her voice came loudly. "Why," she asked, choking on sobs, "did he have to lie like that?"

"He had no other defence," said the Corinthian gently, "after he refused to listen to Humphreys' advice. To tell the truth would have hanged him."

"I don't mean that," she hissed. "I doubt if he really killed that horrid girl."

"Good God!" gasped the Corinthian.

"Don't blaspheme," she said severely. "You know how I hate it. What I meant was about that passport. I never did ask him to get me one. That was an untrue thing to say."

It took the Corinthian almost a minute to recollect the evidence about the passport, which he had dismissed as being of small importance, merely suggesting Corder's intention to flee the country.

"What about the passport?" he asked.

"Oh," she gasped, "didn't you hear? He said that I'd told him to get one for me, that I wanted him to take me to France to see some friends of mine. That wasn't true."

"I never thought it was," said the Corinthian.

"Then why did he have to say it? I don't like liars. If he can make up a story like that, he might be capable of anything."

"Indeed, he might," said the Corinthian, trying not to smile.

"I'll speak to him seriously about it when I see him again," she muttered, wriggling on her chair. "Once you find somebody out in a lie, it rather undermines one's faith. It's not the importance of the untruth, it's the principle that matters. I really must say I am most surprised and disappointed."

The Corinthian said nothing. He crossed his arms and hung his head.

He was still in the same mournful position, Mary rigid with indignation beside him, when, after over half-an-hour's retirement, the jury returned with their verdict. Summoned from his cold chicken and port, his lordship apologetically pushed his way behind the ladies' chairs until he had settled into his own; then he sat back, belching and blowing out his cheeks, while the clerk read over the jurymen's names to make certain that none of them had escaped.

Then he asked whether they had agreed on their verdict, and the foreman told him that they had agreed on it unanimously.

"How say you, gentlemen," asked the clerk, "is the prisoner at the bar, William Corder, guilty of the indictment of which he stands indicted, or not guilty?"

In faltering tones, looking at the hairy backs of his hands, the foreman whispered: "Guilty."

Beside him, the Corinthian felt Mary stir, her skirts rustling, and heard her whimper, "No, no." Then he turned to look at Corder. The man stood as though dazed, as though he had been hit between the eyes, and he lifted a shaking hand to his forehead, pressed it there a moment, then let it fall while his head lolled down.

"Harken to your verdict, gentlemen," cried the clerk in ringing tones. "You say that William Corder, the prisoner, is Guilty, and so you say all?"

"Yes," mumbled the foreman, "we do."

Before the court could proceed there was a noise of scuffling near the dock and his lordship glared up in search of the culprits. To the Corinthian's astonishment, he saw Lea struggling with another man, both of them red in the face with fury, fighting over a

S.O.T.R.B.—T

pair of pistols. When by the awesome silence they realized that they were watched, they instantly hurried to the back of the court; and peace having returned, the crier cried for silence, silence, and Corder was asked whether he had anything to say why he should not receive judgment to die according to the law.

He did not answer. He merely groaned and shook his lolling head.

"Silence, silence!" roared the crier again, and gradually the humming of many voices faded as the lord chief baron drew the black coif from a pocket of his robe and tossed it carelessly on top of his wig.

"William Corder," he said, noisily clearing his throat, "it now becomes my painful duty to announce to you the near approach of your mortal career. . . ."

Gripping the bars, Corder shuddered as if on fire, his body writhing. He strove to stand upright, the lips twisting from the teeth in a doggish grin; as though, thought the Corinthian, shivering, his head had already become a skull, like Maria's. Remembering that shining bone he could feel no pity for the man, although he thought that the judge should not have chosen this opportunity to preach at the helpless creature who could not answer back. He had suffered enough, one would have thought, without this constant repetition of the wages of sin, this rubbing of salt into his terror.

"My advice to you," growled his lordship, "is not to flatter yourself with the slightest hope of mercy on earth. You sent this unfortunate young woman to her account, with all her imperfections upon her head, without allowing her any time for preparation. She had not time to lift up her eyes to the throne of grace, to implore mercy and forgiveness for her manifold transgressions—she had no time allowed her to repent of her sins—no time granted to throw herself upon her knees to implore pardon at the eternal throne."

Bravely, Corder tried to remain steady on his feet and to look with indifference about him; but the effort did not last. As though suddenly recollecting his doom, knowing that pleadings now were useless, that there could be no possibility of pardon, he staggered and would have fallen had not a jailor caught him in his arms.

"Nothing remains now for me to do," continued the remorseless voice, "but to pass upon you the awful sentence of the law, and that sentence is—that you be taken back to the prison from whence you came, and that you be taken from thence, on Monday next, to a place of execution, and that you there be hanged by the neck until you are dead; and that your body shall afterwards be dissected and anatomized; and may the Lord God Almighty, of His infinite goodness, have mercy on your soul."

Into the arms of the jailor, Corder sank, sobbing, foam on his lips, while the crowd ran to get closer to him, overturning chairs and applauding gleefully. After him they pushed while the officers of the court tried to hold them back; but in their excitement they would not be restrained, struggling forward that they might gloat on him even in his cell. Somebody screamed, a woman, and sank to the floor, and the Corinthian noticed that she was the Theresa Havers who had given evidence about Corder's noble character. But in his worry about Mary and how to carry her through the crowd, he took no heed.

Motionless Mary sat, her hands in her lap.

"Mary," he cried, "please, don't swoon."

She did not answer and plainly had not heard him, while he could hear her muttering to herself. Then with enormous relief, he saw Lea and called to him.

"What a crush!" gasped Lea, swaggering over. "Never seen anything like it even at the Old Bailey. Why! Thurtell and Hunt never had a show like this! And that old bastard Orridge—did you see him?—trying to nab Corder's pistols. They're mine. Corder gave 'em to me himself. And now the bloody high sheriff's nabbed 'em from both of us and has run off with 'em. You can't trust nobody, you can't."

"Is there no private way out of here?" asked the Corinthian, seizing his arm and shaking him to stop the babble about pistols. "Mrs. Corder's unwell and I must get her into the air."

"In a moment, sir," said Lea, "in a moment. I'll take you out by a side door when the judge's gone. Poor lady," he sighed, "taken it hard, ain't she? I'd have thought it was good riddance myself."

As though slowly waking from an evil dream, Mary looked about her and shivered.

"He's gone?" she whispered.

"Don't you fret yourself, ma'am," said Lea jovially. "He's all right. Safe in his cell where no one can get at him."

"He lied," she whispered. "I didn't want a passport."

Lea raised his eyebrows at the Corinthian and the Corinthian sighed and shook his head to show that he was equally as puzzled.

"No," she said, "once a man lies you can never trust him again, and the other things he said mightn't be true. He might even have killed that girl, after all. Why should I want him to get me a passport? This has taught me a lesson I will never forget. . . ."

Chapter Twenty-Two

BEHIND WHICH DOOR?

A S THE Corinthian might have expected, it was Lydia who began the quarrel. They had finished supper and sat dejectedly about the table, the women sipping tea, the men drinking brandy and water, and talking little. After her return to the "Angel", Mary had sat in a state of sullen misery, refusing to eat, and for all Lydia's coaxing she would not discuss the trial. Sighing, with melancholy eyes she occasionally looked at the Corinthian, and now and then with a tiny lace handkerchief she brushed away a tear, or genteelly, almost apologetically, blew her nose. Hungry for a heart-to-heart womanly talk, Lydia undulated on her chair, trying again and again with sympathetic clucking noises and whisperings of "You poor dear" to bring Mary into her sisterly embrace. But Mary took no heed. Bowed under by melancholy, she sat, and after her first furious outcry that she could no longer trust her husband because he had said that she had wanted to go to France when she had had no desire to visit there again, she said little and did not even weep. And this passivity infuriated Lydia who, angry at having been betrayed in the morning—Mary, against all her pleadings and threats, quietly insisting that she intended to go alone with the Corinthian to the trial—ached for an uproar, to release her anger in tears, quarrelling or kisses.

Like Mary, the Corinthian remained quiet, not answering Lydia's jeers, and only Bertram, drinking with a kind of ferocious desperation, was ready to retort, eyeing her balefully and muttering to himself. But Lydia ignored him save now and then to glare at him with loathing and to shrug when she caught his glances.

"Well," she said suddenly, baring her teeth in a fierce smile at the Corinthian, "I hope you're happy! You've worked for this, haven't you, you cunning, cunning beast? . . ."

The Corinthian raised his heavy lids but was too weary to answer, knowing that all she desired was the excuse to scream at him.

"You and your Mrs. Marten," she cried, her voice rising stridently; "a pretty plot you worked together! You were always the one to hide behind a skirt, getting some woman to do your dirty work, as you used me to hook your flats so's they'd not see how you tricked 'em. And, God save me, I'm much to blame for this! I put the vile idea into your head; yes, I did it and never thought . . . Mary, my love," she wailed, swinging round to face Mary that her lips might be read, "Mary! I betrayed you and William. I didn't mean ever to tell you this, I was too ashamed and kept on hoping that if poor William escaped it might be forgotten. . . . But now that I see you're falling for this smooth devil's tongue, I can't stay silent any longer."

"Lydia!" cried the Corinthian, trembling with hatred and fear, for he knew what she was going to say. "Be quiet!"

She laughed. Leaning back in her chair, holding her side, she laughed and sobbed and groaned, her stays creaking, tears running through the powder on her cheeks.

"Listen," she gasped. "Mary, listen to me! Look at him now. He's afraid. He's afraid of the truth."

Bewildered, Mary turned to the Corinthian and saw the fury in his eyes as he stood up and kicked back his chair.

"I'll kill you, you bitch!" he cried. "Shut your bloody mouth!"

"Kill me," she choked, and giggled, "kill me as you helped kill Bill Corder. Yes, you helped to kill him, you and Mrs. Marten killed him."

With open hand he struck her on the cheek, almost sending her backwards; but, just in time, she gripped the table-edge and managed to swing her chair back on to its legs.

"You coward," she whimpered, and felt her cheek. "You'll pay for that," she said.

"O, don't, don't fight!" shrilled Mary. "Don't hit her, Mr. Barsett; it's wicked of you, unmanly."

"If he doesn't hit her," said Bertram slowly, "I'll do it for him."

For a moment there was silence, a danger-seeming menacing silence like the threat of thunder in the air, and no one moved. Bewildered, Mary crouched on her chair, gazing amazed from face to face; Bertram gripped his glass as though about to throw it at Lydia; the Corinthian, breathing thickly, stood above her with clenched fists; and Lydia panted, grinning, and rubbed her cheek.

"All right," she said. "Now I'm going to tell everything. Mary, it was this man here—this creature, I should say—who plotted with Mrs. Marten——"

"A lie," roared the Corinthian, "a bloody lie!"

"——to tell the story of that dream."

"O, no!" wailed Mary.

"Yes," said Lydia, "I know the whole truth of it, for I was to blame at the start. When we went to the Marten cottage, this fool liked the slut, thought she was all heart, and it wasn't until I pointed out that she was mad with spite and jealousy that he decided how to use her. He thought he was being cunning. He crept back to that cottage by himself, not telling me, but he didn't know I had a faithful servant who watched his every trick. Whatever he did, Nelly knew about it; and then, of course, *I* knew about it. He went back to that cottage and plotted with Mrs. Marten to invent that dream that they might hang your husband."

"This is outrageous!" cried the Corinthian. "You have no proof!"

"Look at him," she said, "look at him, Mary, and you'll see the proof."

Shaking, the Corinthian stood, striving to compose his features that he might appear innocent; but he had been taken too suddenly off his guard, and there was no mistaking the shifty guilt in his eyes. With growing horror, Mary stared at him, and trembled; then with a little moaning cry, she hid her face in her hands.

"He did it!" cried Lydia, raising her voice that the near-deaf might hear. "There was a dream-book in the house and that gave him the idea. I saw him look through it carefully. Then for hours he talked alone with Mrs. Marten in the garden, and Nelly watched them all the time. They talked passionately together, excitedly. It was after that that Mrs. Marten began her dreams. Mrs. Marten the murderess! And the Corinthian the murderer who stabs in the dark! O, Bill might have killed that stupid Maria; and who would blame him if he did! But you and that bitch got together and cold-bloodedly, without heat, plotted to hang poor Bill, Mrs. Marten because she was mad with jealousy and you because you wanted him out of the way so that you might seduce his wife."

"No, no, no!" There was agony beyond bearing in Mary's voice as she rocked herself from side to side; then, hands to her ears, she sprang to her feet. Mad she looked, eyes staring, cheeks flushed, and wet mouth open, as she glared about her blindly. When the Corinthian held out his arms, crying that Lydia was lying, she shuddered from him, swayed, and almost fell, still sobbing, "No, no, no!"

Into Lydia's arms she sank and, with a cold malicious smile, Lydia held her on her feet and guided her to the door.

"Good night, gentlemen," she said.

Just in time she closed the door. The glass, flung by Bertram, splintered on the panels.

"There'll be another hanging soon," he said in a sick voice as though he hated himself. "That woman's given me hell all day. Led me on, then laughed in my face and talked of God and saving souls. She lay there on that sofa and let her skirt ride up so that I could see above her ankles—damn fine ankles, too, damn it—and rolled about to show her shoulders off: and all that she might tell me to behave myself after she'd driven me mad. I wish I were a monk, by God." After a pause, the Corinthian making no comment, he added in a shamefaced way: "I asked the bitch to marry me, the bloody fool I was."

Roused out of his melancholy at the horror of Mary's loss, the Corinthian looked at him with weary eyes.

"You what?" he growled.

"Asked Lydia to marry me," mumbled Bertram. "I'm a fool; don't tell me: I know it. But who the hell isn't a fool when he's after a woman? And I meant it, by God!" he cried with sudden rage. "I meant every damned word of it! I'd marry her tomorrow if she'd have me. O, hell, I blubbered like a kid. Drunk, of course; but that don't excuse it. I promised I'd leave London and settle in the country with her. Anything she wanted. A man's a fool with a woman; and the curse is, they know it."

"Fools, indeed," sighed the Corinthian. "She'll never forgive me for what I did. Can't blame her really. I did help to get her husband hanged. But that bitch Lydia . . ."

"She wouldn't say 'Yes' and she wouldn't say 'No'. Had too much pleasure seeing me on her hook." Bertram groaned and ruffled his fingers through his dark curling hair. "And she led me on, pretending she didn't know what I wanted . . . and showing her legs and rolling her eyes and speaking in that soft, husky voice of hers. D'you know,

Tom, if we'd the brains of lice we'd get out of here damned quick."

"I would if I could," said the Corinthian. "But I'm in love; and she'll never forgive me now."

"That's an echo of what I'm thinking," growled Bertram. "Lydia's not the same woman as she used to be. She hates you so that she hates all men. You can shrug because you've had her and I haven't. I've been in love with her for years and didn't really know it. Used to think she was a fine figure of a woman, like to sleep with her if I had the chance, but never thought I'd make a bloody fool of myself like this about her. Queer, Tom: the worse a woman treats you, the more you seem to want her."

Woefully, the Corinthian shook his head. "Mary's always been kind to me," he said, "and the kinder she's been the more I've loved her. There's no rules for love, old man. If there were, you'd be able to get any woman you wanted, wouldn't you, just by playing the same cards? But they're all different, and what goes down with one sticks in the throat of another. There's some like Lydia who want a man to wipe their feet on, and there're sweet characters like Mary who just want someone to love and cherish 'em. But you never know what they want until it's too late."

"She didn't exactly tell me to go to hell," mumbled Bertram. "Not in those words, she didn't, anyhow. She's too kind, or pretended that she was; and she ran her fingers through my hair. D'ye know, old man, I've noticed two things: if a woman runs her fingers through your hair or lets you put your hand on her knee, she's . . . well, things aren't going too bad. That's about all I've ever really learned about 'em."

"Did you put your hand on Lydia's knee?"

"Well . . . yes; but she's got that amount of clothes on these days you might as well hold a stuffed monkey. And all she did was to look pityingly at me as though I was a bloody fool; which I probably am. Well, who the hell isn't when he's nutty over a woman? I used to think novels were all my eye. You know the kind of stuff. 'Unhand me, villain, never even by brute force shall your infamous designs be consummated!' 'Ha,' says the villain, showing his teeth, 'silly little girl; your vaunted opposition is a stimulus to my evil passions. I love you to madness, darling bitch.' 'Ho,' says she, 'rather will I die, rather shall you hold within your arms a bleeding corpse, than know me by your strength dishonoured!' "

"What the devil are you gibbering about?" asked the Corinthian, looking at him owlishly.

"Nothing." Bertram slouched in his chair. "It's only what I read in a book—*Dangers of the Female Life* or something, it's called—which Mrs. Corder got from the library."

"Mrs. Corder reads stuff like that!"

"All women do, you fool, that's why they're often difficult to get: they always expect the worst from a fellow. Anyhow, this book's not rubbish. When I read it this morning I felt I was reading about myself. By a fellow called Huish or something. Why, here it is!" He picked up a worn volume from the floor to where it had fallen, and, flipping through the pages, found the passage he sought. "If this ain't true to life, by God, if this ain't Lydia, you can cut my throat. This bastard, Lord Partington, has got the poor girl, Rosa, all alone where no one can hear her squeak. Quiet, now! 'The moment was come in which the fate of Rosa was to be decided; the ripened fruit hung trembling on the branch, and the rude despoiler thirsted to enjoy it. Despair now seized upon the heart of Rosa; she saw herself on the brink of ruin, lost, dishonoured for ever. In vain, with uplifted hands she implored mercy from her infamous seducer—another moment and one of the sweetest flowers that ever bloomed was defoliaged for ever'———"

"Hey," cried the Corinthian, "do you mean to tell me that Mary reads dirty books like that?"

"It's not dirty," cried Bertram indignantly; "if you'd only let me finish! It's true to life, that's all. O, don't worry! He doesn't rape her. The dirty bastard dies before she's ruined. . . . Look here! D'ye mean to tell me you don't like hearing the truth about yourself?"

"What do you mean—the truth about myself?"

"Well, ain't this like you and Mary, now? Ain't you an old satyr and ain't she like this poor bloody Rosa? Can't you see it? Lydia and me had a long talk about it. Mrs. Corder's not like one of us. She's like this Rosa here. If you want that type, you can have 'em; but she's simple-minded, she doesn't like It. Now, me and Lydia, that bitch, are different. I told her I'd marry her and I mean it. But we know each other from the toenails up. We ain't fools and if we marry we'll know what to expect. But what'd happen if you married Mrs. Corder?"

"We would be extremely happy," said the Corinthian with dignity faintly marred by a hiccup.

"For how long? You'd soon get sick of her ways, having to bellow every time you wanted to whisper to her, and before you knew where you were you'd be sighing for Piccadilly and the Cyprians and the demi-respectables again. Don't fool yourself, Tom."

"You are my friend," said the Corinthian, his eyes bulging with fury, "otherwise I'd break your bloody neck. But you've made a miscalculation, a bad miscalculation. I happen to be in love with the woman."

"Love, love!" mimicked Bertram. "It makes a fool of a man. But women . . . they grow fat on it. Look at those two bitches! Rosy and bouncing with life because they know they've got us on a gridiron. Even your Mrs. Corder's grown to look not half so bad since you went after her . . ."

"She is," said the Corinthian sternly, "the most adorable creature I have ever known!"

"I approve the sentiment," said Bertram, "without agreeing with it. . . . But, old man, we've both reached the end. In a few days Corder'll be hanged. Then what's going to happen? Your Mrs. Corder'll vanish; Lydia'll go, too, for she's told me she'll never live with you again. So what are we going to do? I suggest this: Tomorrow we'll tear off our masks, we'll insist on a direct answer from both of 'em. We'll force 'em to declare their passion for us."

"And if they have no passion for us?"

"Then," said Bertram with a kingly gesture, almost knocking over the bottles, "we must create one in their bosoms. Damn it, after all, they're only women. . . ."

"I drink to that," hiccuped the Corinthian.

"And I drink with you. . . ."

Steadily through the night and into the morning they drank, both cursing and adoring the Sex until self-pity overcame them and they wept at female cruelty towards unhappy admirers whose only crime was the desire to love and cherish them for ever. . . .

It was late afternoon before they awoke and, after shaving clumsily and dressing and groaning, they staggered to the bar in the hope that brandy might revive their interest in life. Miserably, they sat at a table, feeling too sick to talk and wondering whether the drink would remain inside them for long.

After half-a-dozen glasses they felt capable of exchanging a few words, and these words were mainly curses, curses on heartless females, on themselves and on the drink which they continued to swallow.

"It's no good us moaning here," moaned the Corinthian. "We've got to face 'em sometime. If Mary believes what Lydia's told her . . . Well, we'd better see. . . ."

Squaring their shoulders and trying to appear heroic, they trudged back up the stairs to be met on the first landing by a plump chambermaid with a broom in her hand.

"If you're looking for them ladies in Number 9," she said with a malicious grin, "they've gorn."

"What? What? What's that you say?"

"They've gorn," she repeated with relish. "Went early this morning; asked particular not to wake you up."

"But where have they gone?" almost bellowed the Corinthian and Bertram in one voice.

"Just gorn," she said gleefully. "Asked particular to let you sleep. And they left no address neither."

The wench spoke the truth. They offered her money, which she pocketed, but she could not tell them the ladies' new address.

"This," said the Corinthian, "is the blackest treachery. We need another drink."

Downstairs they stumbled to drink and question the servants, but no one knew the ladies' new address. Early that morning they had left, paying what they owed; beyond that, all was silence.

"Lea'll find 'em!" cried the Corinthian. "That's his job."

But on enquiring at the court-house, they discovered that Lea had returned to London, although he was expected back in a day or two.

"Furious he was," chuckled the clerk, "swore he'd have the law on the county about them pistols. Said he'd be back with a warrant to get 'em. That's all I know."

Bury was not a very large town but it was too large for a house-to-house investigation. Besides, if the women intended to remain concealed, they had most likely changed their names.

"Let's have a drink," said Bertram, "and think about it."

Drink did not help. After the previous night's heavy potations, they were already tipsy, and although they ate a large meal to mop up the brandy, it merely made them somnolent and they staggered back to the "Angel" to sleep.

Waking late in the evening, they raced to the bar and began to drink again, bewailing a squandered day. This was Saturday, and Corder was to be hanged on Monday, which left only Sunday for investigations. And Sunday was a useless day. Mrs. Corder would, of course, go to church, but there were many churches in Bury; and it was the only day on which visitors were not permitted in the jail. Therefore the Corinthian's idea of keeping watch on its gates would have proved a waste of time; and it was unlikely that she would be permitted to see her husband on the Monday when he was to die.

"There's nothing we can do," groaned the Corinthian, leaning his head on his hands.

"I'll not give in," growled Bertram. "Tomorrow I'll search this town from top to bottom."

"And I," said the Corinthian, "will go again to the jail. Somebody there might know her new address."

Nobody there knew it, he discovered, after he had enquired of the turnkey in his lodge the following morning. The warders became genial when he distributed a few coins, but they could not help. Mrs. Corder, they told him, had been there the day before and had had a melancholy conversation with her husband.

"She's a good little body," said one of the warders, wiping the mouth of the flask the Corinthian passed him. "Too good for the likes of him. When he first come here all he could talk about was smut and about the silly women what had written to him in answer to some advertisement he'd put in the papers; but he's mighty different now, ain't he, Jerry?"

"Ay," said Jerry lugubriously, taking the flask in his turn. "After he come back from court all he could talk about was his wife, when he could see her again and all that. Troubled he was about her and some cove called the Corinthian he didn't trust. I had to stay with him that night—always two of us in the cell with him to see he don't cheat the law . . . And that reminds me, when his wife was told of that she got highly indignant. 'If it pleased the Almighty,' says she, 'to take him before the time appointed for his execution, I'd feel most happy,' says she; 'but I'd not interfere,' says she, 'between God and him on any consideration. I wish he may meet his fate,' says she, 'with submission rather than afford him any means by which it might be anticipated.' A very godly lady, my lord; and handsome into the bargain in a homely way, you know. What a fool he were to slice the other 'un up when he had a nice little lawful blanket like her to keep him warm at night!''

"He killed Miss Marten before he met her," said the Corinthian.

"Ain't that just like life," sighed Jerry. "If only he'd seen her first he'd have had no need to cut the other 'un's throat. Woman-mad, he is, always talking about the foolish wenches what answered his advertisement. Mr. Stocking—he's our ordinary—got quite angry about it, he did. 'This is the time to be thinking about heaven, my good man,' says he, 'and not of carnal wickedness.' But I'd say he was thinking of the kind of heaven he liked best. Boasted to me, he did, of the handsome females what had been foolish enough to write to him and what he'd have done to 'em if he'd had half a chance. Then in the next breath—blow me down! —if he weren't swearing his wife was an angel and the only one he'd ever loved! I says to him, I says, just to make him feel good, you know, I says: 'You must have had a brave nerve to dig a hole while that there dead woman was lying in your sight,' I says. He looks at me queer as though he thought I was trying to trip him. 'Nobody,' says he, 'knows that the body lay in the barn, and in my sight, while I dug that hole.' Well, if it weren't lying in his sight, he must have been blinder than he is, and her all bleeding and gashly. Then sudden-like he gives a graveyard groan. 'O, Gord,' he says, 'nobody'll dig my grave!' ''

" 'Tis said he's confessed," muttered the turnkey. "But that's said of all of 'em, even if they're dumb. Otherwise parson feels his reputation's suffered. He's got to put such terror of hell into the poor bastards that they don't know what they're blabbing; and I will say he works hard at it."

"You don't think Mrs. Corder'll be here today?" asked the Corinthian, fidgeting under this talk of Mary's husband.

"Well," said Jerry, " 'tain't allowed on Sundays, which is not to say it ain't done on particular occasions. Seeing as how he's to be strung up in the morning, Mr. Orridge might well let her in for a last cuddle."

The Corinthian sprang to his feet. All morning he had been unable to remain still for long. No sooner had he sat down than he had started up again, feeling that he wasted time by remaining in one place, that Mary might be passing elsewhere at that moment. Too late might he hurry around a corner, glimpsing merely the whisk of her skirt as she turned ahead of him; a door's blank panels concealing her when a lock clicked into place; a window-curtain still shaking after she had let it fall. Always too late. Always to find the street empty of all save nonentities, no sign of Mary, concealed perhaps beneath the cloak of vindictive Lydia. At times, some woman in the distance caught his eye: a gesture, the shape of a bonnet, a daintiness in the walk, quick little steps reminding him of her, and, heart beating fast enough to suffocate him, he sped forward to look into an unexciting face and at a gown that had become drab because it concealed limbs that were not Mary's.

Hundreds of times he saw her yet did not see her. Hundreds of times he peered through windows at domestic scenes empty of her, or entered women's shops to seek her amongst the customers; only always to fail. Bury contained many women, and, to watch the hanging tomorrow, numerous strangers had arrived so that the streets were crowded. Men and women together, men and women laughing, chattering, happy together, while he remained alone, staring into bonnets at pretty faces, ugly faces, jolly faces, sour faces, thin faces, fat faces, painted faces, clean faces, wrinkled faces, young faces, but never Mary's face. The lady and the merchant's wife, the country-woman and the shop-girl, the virgin and the harlot, walked these streets to torment him, gazing into shop-windows and thrilled to think that a man must die in the morning for having killed a woman with whom he'd slept. This execution was their sex's vindication. That Maria had been concupiscent, mother of at least three bastards, was forgotten in the tragedy of her death. They were going to build at Polstead a monument to her memory, the girl who had died for a villain's love.

Grimly pushing through the streets, listening, watching, seeking always Mary, Mary, Mary, the Corinthian smiled tightly to hear the chatter. Poor girl, they said, poor hapless creature, victim of a man's lust; and that monster, that villain, seducer, ravisher, murderer, William Corder! . . . They rolled their eyes and shuddered pleasurably at the sound of the ogre's name.

At a street-corner, a ballad-singer stood, a roll of ballads in one hand, and mournfully he intoned:

"Come all you thoughtless young men, a warning take by me,
And think of my unhappy fate, to be hanged upon a tree;
My name is William Corder. To you I do declare,
I courted Maria Marten, most beautiful and fair.
I promised I would marry her upon a certain day,
Instead of which I was resolved to take her life away;
I went into her father's house the 18th day of May,
'O, come, my dear Maria, and let us fix the day.

If you will meet me at the Red Barn, as sure as I have life,
I will take you to Ipswich town, and there make you my wife.'
I straight went home and fetched my gun, my pickaxe and my spade,
I went into the Red Barn and there I dug her grave.
With heart so light she thought no harm, to meet me she did go.
He murdered her all in the barn, and laid her body low;
The horrid deed he had done—she lay bleeding in her gore,
Her bleeding and mangled body he threw on the Red Barn floor."

Many people stood and listened, men and women gravely frowning, some dabbing at their eyes and sighing and groaning; while some gipsy children danced in the roadway, the little girls lifting their frayed skirts to show strong brown legs, and clapping their hands to the ballad-singer's drone. The Corinthian paused to watch them, marvelling at the perfection of these wild girls, children yet nubile, who would too soon grow lean and wrinkled like their mothers. Knowledge beckoned in their tawny eyes, their greasy hair dangling to their waists, while with every gesture, every shrug of shoulders, waggle of hips and wriggle of arms, they impudently coaxed a man to loving.

"Now all things being silent she could take no rest,
She appeared in her mother's house, who suckled her at her breast.
For many a month long or more, her mind being sorely oppressed,
Neither night nor day she could take no rest.
Her mother's night being so disturbed she dreamt three nights o'er,
Her daughter she lay murdered upon the Red Barn floor.
She sent her father to the barn, when in the ground he thrust
And there he found his daughter, mingling with the dust."

Not fame but immortality had become the lot of Bill Corder; yet, wondered the Corinthian, what satisfaction could he have in that when he cringed in his cell under the threatening admonitions of the Rev. Mr. Stocking? He slipped a coin into the singer's hand but would not take a broadsheet. Listening like this was wasted time, for he must find Mary before she left this town.

He hurried on, and the ballad pursued him:

" *'My trial is hard, I could not stand, most woeful was the sight,*
When her jawbone was brought to prove, which pierced me to the heart' ;
His aged mother standing by, likewise his loving wife,
And with her grief her hair she tore, she scarcely could keep life.
'Adieu, adieu, my loving friends, my glass is almost run.
On Monday next will be my last, when I am to be hung.
So you young men that do pass by, with pity look on me,
For murdering Maria Marten, I was hanged upon a tree.' "

He prayed that Mary might not hear that ballad, but she could scarcely have avoided hearing it, or others like it. Boys and girls sang it, danced to it, with relish shrieking of gore and a mangled body; and children in the roadways performed the murder, little girls squealing while small boys spectacularly slew them with chunks of wood to represent pistol or sword. "You're Maria, I'm Corder!" For all her deafness, Mary would not have been able to escape that cruel mockery; often, usually at unwanted moments, the Corinthian had noticed that she could hear perfectly even a whisper. Stone-deaf would she have had to have been to shut out this bawling, this fiends' delight in bloodshed, in a dream sent from heaven and a live man in a noose.

Crowded Bury might be, but to the Corinthian it was empty because he could not find his beloved; and as daylight faded and lamps were lit, he grew frantic, feeling he could never live without her. Not since youth had he felt so desperately in love. Then had he walked night-long, tormented by dreams, sighing in the dark before some girl's window, imagining her in her chaste bed with him shut out in the unfriendly dark. Later, when he had learned to smile unconcernedly into the face of a wench who recently had seemed a miracle of perfection, he had jeered at those pangs, but now they returned to fret his blood, to drive him tirelessly in search of one woman amongst thousands, of one woman who—he did not shy

S.O.T.R.B.—U

from the truth—was little different from many others, who was indeed not even beautiful, who was deaf and even rather stupid, ignorant of life and timid of loving, but who nevertheless was to him a goddess without whose healing embrace he felt he could not live. Mad: yes, he was mad; he knew that he was mad; and he trembled and in agitation had to lean against a wall when he saw a couple kissing in a doorway, and for one wild moment thought that Mary was the woman in that stranger's arms.

Jealous of ghosts; jealous of Lydia, of the mere inanimate things with which Mary was surrounded, of the chair to feel her weight, the cup to taste her lips, the bed to know her body's warmth, the clothes to touch her skin, the shoes to nestle round her feet, the food to be eaten, ay, the very food to be swallowed and the fork that grazed her teeth . . . he was as jealous as a boy in first love, drunk on desires he dared not visualize, and near to tears when he thought he might not see her again. Lydia would be sure to smuggle her out of town, repeating lies about him, insisting that he had been the inspiration of Mrs. Marten's dream, as indeed, he groaned to recall, he had inspired it. Guarded by that she-devil who now inexplicably detested him, she would be walled like a nun, and England was a vast haystack from which to ferret out one woman. But he would do it; ay! he'd employ Lea and other police officers, and they must find her in the end.

But he could not wait. They might take months, years, in their search, and his heed for her was urgent, a constant irritation like a rash in the blood; and it was exasperating to think that he might be within a foot of seeing her if only he knew her address. Why, in this twilight she might be any of these rustling women, their faces shadows in their bonnets; any of these shuffling creatures, shawls about their shoulders and skirts whispering both fear and shy invitation, who hurried to be safely home before dark. Only whores and ragamuffins soon would roam abroad, all honest women locked away from danger; then would his last hope be gone. . . .

Miserably, he slouched back to the "Angel" to find an angry Bertram resting his hot feet on a chair while he lounged back on the couch. At the Corinthian's entrance, he cocked one eyebrow, then slouched down again when he recognized by his despondent air that he also had failed in his search.

"I've looked everywhere," he groaned. "I've even knocked at

doors and asked if they lodged there. They've vanished. They've left Bury for good."

"No," said the Corinthian, buying a brandy and taking it with him when he sat beside his friend, "they'll not leave until after the hanging. Until the last moment, she'll hope for a miracle. And I'm going to find her if it takes a hundred years!"

"What's the use?" Bertram seemed to sink inside his coat. "They don't want us. We're acting like silly boys. She thinks you hanged her husband and I was fool enough to gammon myself that Lydia liked me. She likes only herself. It's no go, Tom: we've failed."

"We have not," said the Corinthian, setting his teeth. "They might be at the hanging. Anyhow, I'm going to see."

"They'd not go there, to see the fellow they love on a string!"

"You never know. Women are queer cattle and they like to weep. What better opportunity could they find to blubber than at a hanging? As it says in the ballad:

"*His aged mother standing by, likewise his loving wife,*
And with her grief her hair she tore, she scarcely could keep life. . . .

Anyhow, I'm going. And that means an early night for a change. Besides, I'm half-dead. I must have walked a hundred miles, and I'm going to sleep . . . I hope."

Chapter Twenty-Three

THE QUICK AND THE DEAD

A S HE had feared, the Corinthian could not sleep that night, save fitfully, and he rose in the morning as tired as when he had lain down. Resolutely, ignoring body's weakness and thought's despair, he roused Bertram, and they shaved and dressed in the early morning, then joined the happy throng hurrying out of town. It was impossible to hire a coach or horse, or even a cart, and they had to walk the long way to the jail on the road to Sudbury. Merrily, jesting uproariously, the crowd trudged into the country, some dancing, all as gay as if off to a wedding; in that multitude, only the Corinthian and Bertram looked glum.

Thousands were tramping to watch Corder die. Around the prison, the press was so great that the two friends, tall though they were, had to stand on their toes to see, above men's hats and women's bonnets, the scaffold raised against the prison door. It was an unusually shaped scaffold and much smaller than the one used at Newgate, while the crossbeam from which Corder was to be strung curved up like a bow. Before it, a space had been railed off and there the newspaper men and various officials lounged with an appearance of professional boredom, talking lazily together.

The day was warm, too beautiful a day for any man to wish to leave this earth, and the green hills bounded by the masses of dark trees gave an air of peaceful unreality to the thought of death. Many an execution had the Corinthian witnessed in London but they had been spectacles that had not moved him save with excitement; even when he had known the condemned, they had been merely Covent Garden acquaintances in whom he had had no real interest. This hanging of Corder, however, seemed in some peculiar way a hanging of part of himself, not of his body, but of some portion of his soul. He thought of Mary, doubtless praying at that moment, and tears came to his eyes. Angrily, he blinked them away and looked about him, hoping, while knowing that the hope was absurd, that he might find her amongst the multitude. Bertram, of course, had been right. So sensitive a lady would have shrunk from the thought of seeing her own husband hanged. Perhaps she was within those thick walls, consoling him with talk of God and making a rendezvous with him in heaven; and the idea made him jealous. Even to bid her husband good-bye, he grudged her seeing another man, so greatly did he crave her for himself. And he might never see her again. . . .

Resolutely, he put that terrifying thought aside and attempted to appear nonchalant. Never had he pretended to love his fellow-creatures, the mass of whom he despised, but his scorn turned to loathing when he looked about him. At other executions he had laughed and jested. Now he found the influence of Mary too strong for him to maintain his usual cynical mask, and he was revolted by what he saw, as though he were a respectable citizen who had never mixed with criminals. What astonished him—he had seen it often enough, but had not troubled to consider such things morally—was how in some perverted fashion death and love became one; these people, drawn like a pack of hounds to the kill, were excited lecherously, men and women taking advantage of the sweaty crush to rub against one another, even women with the appearance of honesty becoming flushed and lewd-eyed while they panted, flashing their eyes and licking their lips, like damned whores, he thought with disgust.

He had expected the riff-raff, the harlots decked for custom, the pickpockets fast at work, but he had not expected to see ordinary folk behaving in this abandoned fashion, and using words which normally they would have been ashamed to utter in mixed company. Shop-girls and servants had come for sweethearts, and soon they found them; and the dirtiest draggletail of a woman did not have long to wait in that itching multitude. At any moment, he felt, this crowd, trembling joyously in expectation of seeing a violent death, might have turned the occasion into a debauch. Those without partners sang bawdy songs or threw dirt and ordure into the air, while bottles were continually raised to twinkle their ends in the sunlight.

Traders pushed through the crowd selling gin, gingerbread or broadsheets detailing Corder's alleged confession or some ballad on the murder, their bawling rising above the laughter and shouts.

Dead cats and dogs were suddenly tossed, to howls of merriment, at somebody's hat; and handfuls of filth were thrown wherever the crowd was thickest. To ruin somebody's best coat, to soil some dainty lady's gown, was the ambition of the rascals' spite, and while, with curses, they surged forward, they kicked with boots and knees, the women as vicious as their men, some with razors slyly slashing expensive dresses at the back. Nor were these noisy rascals always ruffians, many of them were young rips on a spree, drunk and out for mischief, urging on the others to bawdier blasphemies or crueller frolics.

As the slow hours passed, the Corinthian regretted having come, being certain that Mary would never mingle with such creatures, but it was now impossible for him to escape, people on every side pressing against him, whistling, singing, men tickling women and dragging up their skirts from the back. Impossible for the assaulted women to do more than squeal and wriggle. They were trapped, and those nearby jeered at their screams; the Corinthian saw one girl weep, hands over her face, at being thus publicly shamed—perhaps, he thought, because her undergarments were not over-clean. At any rate, it served her right, for having come to such a spectacle. . . .

"It's silly to pity the bitches," he growled to Bertram. "Had they any of the vaunted delicacy of their sex, they'd have stayed at home."

Beside him a woman wriggled, a lean elderly creature whose enamelling was cracking in the heat, and she glared at him haughtily.

"Sir," she cried, "as a woman, I have a right to witness the end of a man who inhumanly butchered one of my sex."

The Corinthian looked her up and down as well as he was able in the pushing crowd.

"Madam," he said, "you need have no fear of such an end. Your virtue is too plain to attract even a Corder."

To stamp on his toes was her only revenge, and his boots were of good leather. Sweetly, he smiled as though she had caressed him; then he turned again to watch the scaffold.

It was nearing noon, the hour of execution, and, amidst whistling and shouted encouragement from his vast audience, the hangman with his assistant began to attach the rope to the curved crossbar. In the railings below, officials and reporters had ceased to chatter and now stood in silence, looking up expectantly; and gradually the crowd became quiet, even lewdery forgotten as all held their breath in voluptuous excitement. Beside him, the Corinthian could feel the little woman with enamelled face begin to tremble, her hip, through the many skirts, knocking against his, only the pressure of others, it seemed, keeping her upright. As though drowning, she gasped and shuddered, rolling up her eyeballs to show the whites.

On to the platform stepped Mr. Orridge, and all were silent now that the moment of death approached. Behind him, with other officials and the ordinary, Mr. Stocking, Corder appeared. Thin he looked and pale-faced, yet, to the Corinthian's surprise and satisfaction, he did not seem afraid. At sight of him, a shrill murmur rose, and soon was hushed. Even this vile crowd had some respect for a man about to die, thought the Corinthian; and hats began to vanish. Hat after hat slid from men's heads in respect, if not for the condemned, for his fate; and hearing an angry growl behind him, the Corinthian quickly doffed his beaver.

With no wink of cowardice, Corder stared at the rope looped for his death, then he turned to Mr. Orridge who spoke quietly to him. What they said, the Corinthian was too far away to hear, although, like the others, he held his breath and strained to listen. Then calmly, Corder stood aside while the executioner drew the cap down over his head. Before the rope could be adjusted, however, Mr. Orridge stepped up and again spoke to Corder, and the cap was lifted from his eyes. And at this second vision of the world he had expected to leave, he trembled, his face as white as flour. Had not one of the officers caught him about the waist, he would have fallen, while he muttered something too low to be heard.

"What's that? What's he saying?" shouted the crowd. "Speak up! . . . Hey, tell us what he said. . . . Come on . . . what was it?"

Holding up his hand as the crowd surged forward, Mr. Orridge stepped to the end of the platform.

"Silence!" he bellowed, and he would say nothing further until the noise sank into an angry hum; then in a loud voice, he announced: "The prisoner acknowledges his sentence to be just and declares that he dies in peace with all mankind."

"Does he?" roared the multitude, some in mockery, some with pity; while others bellowed: "May the Lord have mercy on his soul!"

More mercy, hoped the Corinthian, than these blood-hungry creatures would have given him, for all that they might take off their hats at his appearance. He shut his eyes before the flushed faces, the hungry eyes, the wet lips of men and women, doubtless many good folk amongst them, enjoying this terrible moment.

Again was the cap adjusted over Corder's face; but again, there was further delay, the officials talking together, and from their gestures it appeared that they were dissatisfied about the drop. Furiously, the hangman argued, waving his arms, plainly outraged by this interference in the mysteries of his craft; and at last with a very ill grace, scowling, he submitted to officialdom. Even to the Corinthian, far though he was from the scaffold, it was plain that the man was almost beside himself with vexation while he shortened the rope; and all the while, the pinioned figure of Corder stood, supported on his feet by Mr. Orridge, with a cloth face, seeming inhuman save for the trembling legs.

So enraged was the hangman that he did not even wait for Mr. Stocking to begin his prayers. Suddenly he leaned down and with a knife slashed the rope supporting the platform. Immediately, the lower half of Corder vanished to appear under the platform, legs kicking as though he trod invisible water. To one side jerked his head behind the cloth while he raised his arms as if striving to pull himself up. The hangman seized him about the waist, almost throwing himself down with his victim, and pulled; yet still Corder's arms rose and the legs kicked and kicked and kicked. . . .

"Christ!" groaned the Corinthian, and shut his eyes. "Let's get out of here, for God's sake. . . ."

They had to fight their way out; and when at last they stood, gasping and wiping the sweat from their faces, on the edge of the crowd, the Corinthian started guiltily, as though he were the hangman with Corder's death on his conscience, when he heard somebody call his name.

With relief such as one must feel after being drawn to land from drowning, he turned and saw Lea grinning at him in his confidential manner, dark head cocked to one side.

"Well met, gentlemen," he said. "I always like to see my clients worked off. It puts finis to the case. Though they shouldn't have done that to old Foxy, arguing about the drop—I meant Jemmy Foxen, the hangman, not your pal. Foxen's a bit of a bungler, if you ask me: but he can't be blamed. Weak lungs, you know, horrid cough, and he had a bad time last year with young

Charlie White. Remember the case, don't you? Young White, early twenties he was, thought he'd bilk the insurance companies by burning down his house. It was a gruesome hanging. Young White wouldn't be turned off; and Foxy was set on hanging him, as he had to do, of course, hanging being his trade; and there was Whitey clinging to the rope with the trap open under him. Wouldn't leave go, he wouldn't. You should have seen it! Never seen anything like it in all my life before! His tongue came out like a rotten potato. Poor Foxy had a deal of trouble knocking his hands off the rope, then he had to grab him by the legs and pull and pull like hell. Wonderful it was to see his presence of mind! For with lungs like his, Foxy ain't got an easy temper, I tell you. He was all over sweat and gasping and coughing and cursing like he was going to die when it was over. Orridge ought to have known better than to interfere with a man like him."

With difficulty had the Corinthian remained silent during this account of the shortcomings of Mr. James Foxen, but when Lea paused for breath he said hurriedly before he could begin again:

"You're the very man I wanted to see. Can you tell me where Mrs. Corder's living?"

"Mizzled, has she?" chuckled Lea, digging him in the ribs with a fat forefinger. "Naughty, naughty! Would you have an officer of the law help you in your designs against a poor lone hempen-widow?"

"Do you know where she lives?" cried the Corinthian.

"Of course I know where she lives," growled Lea, as though insulted that anyone should suspect the omnipotence of his knowledge. "What do you think I come back here for? I want those pistols I was telling you of; I could make money with 'em, people'd pay to see 'em, and Corder promised to give 'em to me. That bloody sheriff nailed 'em, and when I went to see him, d'ye know what he says? 'Me part with 'em!' he says, laughing in my dial. 'No,' he says, 'not for one hundred pounds; these are all I'll get out of my shrievalty!' he says. Now what do you think of that, eh? And him calling himself a gentleman! But I'll get 'em out of him, don't you fear."

"Where's Mrs. Corder staying?" almost bellowed the Corinthian, hopping from one foot to the other.

"Well, I had to see her, you know," continued Lea imperturbably, "had to get her permission to keep the pistols. Don't be so impatient, gentlemen! I'll take you there in a moment. She's in College Street, if you want to know, but there's no need to hurry."

"There's every need to hurry," said the Corinthian, striding ahead.

Chuckling, Lea followed at his and Bertram's heels until at the end of College Street they stopped.

"Gentlemen, gentlemen," he wheezed. "It's always been my principle to take things quiet. Let the other fellows run, only winds 'em and makes 'em scared——"

"Where does Mrs. Corder lodge?" roared the Corinthian.

"Now, sir, let's not get excited. I should be at the sheriff's, and here I've been spending my time on your business——"

"I'll not forget it," said the Corinthian, pressing half a sovereign into his open hand. "But where?"

"You see that house with the chaise outside?" said Lea. "The one that fellow's carrying the box out of now . . ."

Bowed under a heavy box and turning with the weight of his burden, a man was staggering out of a door towards a post-chaise, helped by Lydia's maid, Nelly. The Corinthian and Bertram did not pause to thank Lea. They left him grinning on the corner, sucking the knob of his stick, and ran up the stairs of the house; and on the first floor they almost ran into Lydia carrying a parcel. Gasping, she stood back, the paint shining on her cheeks as the skin whitened.

"You!" she gasped. "What are you doing here?"

"I've come to see Mary," said the Corinthian.

"I've come to see you," said Bertram.

"You'll not go in there. You'll have to kill me first!" Eyes glittering, she backed away before them, holding up the parcel like a shield. "I'll not have you ruin her life as you ruined mine!"

The Corinthian laughed. "Ruined your life!" he scoffed. "You who came out of a brothel! You Covent Garden strumpet to try these airs on me! By God, the insolence of some women's beyond bearing! Stand back!"

"Who is it?" asked Mary Corder, opening the door and peering out. Then she saw the Corinthian and the bones seemed to give in her body. Limply she sagged, clinging to the door-knob, and he saw that she had been weeping, her eyes red-rimmed and sunken.

"You!" she whispered.

"Me," said the Corinthian, pushing Lydia aside and going to her. "Did you think you could lose me so easily? My dear, I love you and you'll never be able to hide from me again. Wherever you go, I will go; to the ends of the earth, if necessary. I need you, Mary; and you need me. I love you, dear."

"No," she whimpered, and took a deep breath. Then in a low voice, she said: "Now that you're here, you'd best come in," and she opened wide the door.

"Are you mad?" cried Lydia. "You know what you promised! You mustn't see him, he'll trap you with lies; you know how weak you are!"

"Come in, sir," said Mary quietly. Then she turned to Lydia. "Will you wait for me in the chaise?" she asked. "I must first say good-bye to Mr. Barsett. I'll not keep you long."

"I'll not leave you alone with him!"

"Please," said Mary. "I promise not to be long. Wait for me in the chaise. Mr. Bertram will look after you."

"Ay," said Bertram, seizing Lydia by the arm: "I've much to say to you, my duck."

Furiously, she shook off his hand and turned, too late, on Mary. The door had closed when she reached it, and she heard the key turn in the lock. Panting, she stood, one hand to her breast as though to still her heart's wild beating, and for a moment she could not speak.

"She's locked me out!" she gasped at last. "Mary's locked me out!"

Then she sprang at the door and beat the panels with her fists.

"I'll see you soon, dear," sounded Mary's voice. "Wait for me below."

"Yes, pretty," said Bertram, "let's wait for her below."

"She's such a fool," wailed Lydia, "a man could do what he liked with her. So ignorant and so sure of herself!"

"Come," said Bertram gently, taking her hand, "come with me."

She tried to flout him with a look, lifting her chin to stare down at him and thrusting out her bosom; but her lower lip quivered and she began to sob.

"O, Bert," she said, "I've never been so unhappy! Why did you have to come here, just at the wrong time?"

"Perhaps it was fate," he said, and drew her slowly down the stairs, his arm about her waist. "Have no fears for Mrs. Corder. The Corinthian's too nutty over her to do her any harm. Why," he laughed, "he worships her!"

"I pray you're right," she whispered. "But I'm afraid . . . she's so weak at heart, so easily hurt."

Fearfully, over her shoulder, she looked towards the closed door as, drawn by Bertram, she stumbled down the stairs, her hand reluctantly sliding along the banisters. The silence within that room troubled her, cloaking perhaps things of which she dreaded to think. . . .

It was the silence of compassion and love with which the Corinthian and Mary Corder looked on one another. After the locking of the door, she had sunk into a chair and crouched on it, trembling, gazing up at him with huge appealing eyes in dark hollows.

"Did you think you could escape me?" he asked at last, and stepped towards her.

"Stand back!" she cried, flattening herself against the chair. "It's impossible, a dream," she whimpered when he paused. "We must never meet again," she said, "never! It's no good arguing, my love . . . My love? Did I call you my love? There's proof of what you've brought me to! I never thought to use those words to any other man; and I hate myself for them. When I saw William yesterday——"

"You saw him yesterday? Why didn't I wait there for you!"

"Mr. Orridge took pity on me," she said, tenderly, longingly watching his mouth, "and he relaxed the rules. O, it was pitiful! He had changed so much; and, although he sought to hide it from me, he was afraid. I tried to give him courage and we talked of the future life. I could scarcely speak for weeping." At the recollection, she began to sob, rolling her head against the back of the chair; and the Corinthian saw the jerking of her bosom under the stays. "I could talk to him only about God," she said. "I dared talk of nothing else. I told him I didn't care how great a sinner he'd been so long as he died penitent. O, it was pitiful, Tom, it was pitiful! He's little more than a boy, not twenty-five, and now to die like that! And he did repent. He wept and prayed beside me. And he asked me never to marry again."

"He had no right to ask such a thing!"

"He had a husband's right," she said with sudden dignity. "But he didn't mean it in any selfish way. He saw I was reluctant to agree and he didn't press me. He asked me then to be careful and not to marry a gambler or to marry again as I'd married him—not by answering advertisements, he meant, because often bad men used advertisements that they might ruin silly women. And I promised him."

"Not to marry again!"

"Yes," she said, "I promised him."

"You had no right to promise," he cried, rising on his toes to tower above her. "And he had no right to ask such a promise. You're still young, and you love me: don't pretend you don't."

"I'm not pretending . . ." Then with a strong effort as though the words stuck in her throat, she said: "I love you, Thomas. But, no! don't touch me! Think of what it might lead to. You helped to betray my husband; you plotted with that horrid woman. . . . No matter whether he was guilty! O, I know now that he killed that girl. He told me so. But that's not what really matters. You sent him to the gallows."

"He'd have been caught in the end. Besides, I did nothing. It was Mrs. Marten who wanted revenge."

"You suggested that dream to her."

"That's a lie! I didn't. It was her idea."

"Yet you put the idea into her head. . . . We could never forget that, my love. It would always be standing between us. His ghost, I mean. It'd always be there, always; no matter what we did or where we lived, he'd lie between us, always between us. O, it would be like adultery, only worse. He'd be the third in our loving, never forgotten, a chill on our hearts. Besides . . . No, don't!"

She sprang to her feet as he moved towards her and, holding the back of the chair, she fended him off.

"I've something else to tell you," she panted: "something that's not easy for a woman to say to a man. I've tried to tell you before, but I couldn't; and even now, I blush. . . . There wouldn't only be his ghost between us if we married. He'd be with us in body as well. Yes, even if it should be a girl, it'd still be him, wouldn't it? It'd be his eyes watching us, and his voice. . . . Could you marry me after that?"

"You're carrying his child?" he cried.

Flushing, she nodded and kept her head down that he might not see her face.

"O, hell!" he cried, and laughed. "He has the trick on us to the end! He's got his laugh on me, as he always had. . . . You're certain of this?"

"Quite certain," she whispered.

"O, Christ," he sobbed, and strode the floor. This was so unexpected a revelation that he could not think. Corder's child, Corder's damned baby to be suckled and petted, to be rocked in her arms, a tiny rival he could never hope to defeat. To feel in their embrace the mockery of his enemy growing under her heart; to feel, as the months went by, that monster kick beneath his hand; to know it was feeding in there, living within her, living on her, another Corder . . . No, no! . . .

"God," he cried, "what shall I do?"

"There's nothing we can do," she said, love in her eyes and in her voice, "nothing, my dear, nothing. I am his, sworn his before God, and he claims me still, even though he's dead. Don't lie and pretend that it won't matter. You know it will. You might even grow to hate me; and you would certainly hate his child; and I'd not blame you if you did. And what could I do then? It's mine as much as his. And, O," she sobbed wildly, almost laughing in her despair, "if you only knew how desperately I used to pray to become a mother! Yes, night after night I prayed for God to bless me!"

To look at her and not to take her in his arms was agony; but the Corinthian knew that once he touched her, once he kissed her, he would weaken. And she was right. Never would he be able to like Corder's child. He would detest it, this living memory of the man who had loved her first, robber of her virginity; and, being a woman, and a loving one, she would adore her child, regardless of the father. Better to suffer parting, to exist amongst mournful memories, than to live in jealousy's hell.

"I'm right, aren't I?" she whispered.

Her voice was sad, pleading, and he knew that she wanted him to say that he did not care, that he would marry her and cherish both her and her child; and he could not say it. He turned and went moodily to the window and stared into the street. Leaning on the post-chaise's open door, he saw Bertram talking to Lydia who sat

318

nside. Her face showed dimly, a smudge on the shadows; then her gloved hand reached out and caught Bertram by the sleeve. With a pretence of reluctance, he remained in the street, then the Corinthian saw him shrug, lean forward and step into cosy gloom to sit with Lydia, the door slamming shut behind him.

Now that he had been foiled, robbed by a dead man of his beloved, Lydia could graciously take Bertram to her arms. She would take him as she had taken Mary, for the spiteful satisfaction of robbing him of both friend and mistress; then he would be alone.

"Good-bye," he heard Mary say; and he shivered and dared not turn.

He heard her lagging steps, he heard her rattle the key in the lock and very slowly twist the enamelled knob.

Again she said, "Good-bye," in a low voice, choked with sobs.

"Good bye," he muttered, and would not turn.

Softly the door closed, and he staggered, gripping the curtains, half-blind with tears, longing to race after her. With the closing of that door, all his hopes of happiness went. . . . Yet there was still time . . . Within a minute, if he ran, he could catch her. She was half-expecting him, walking downstairs very slowly, waiting for him to follow. . . .

Into the street he saw her step, her head down in the gay bonnet and her shoulders hunched as though she were crying. The post-chaise door swung open and Lydia leaned out to help her in, while the driver turned to watch.

Time . . . there was time . . . He had only to fling up this window and shout.

Within the ribboned bonnet, he saw her pale face, a waxen blur, look up towards him as she leaned out of the window; and when he made no sign, she sank back, only one hand remaining to grip the ledge.

The driver cracked his whip and the horses woke to life. Over the cobbles the wheels clashed, the chaise jolting on its springs, bouncing from side to side.

He saw it turn the corner; and, hands over his face, he sank down sobbing, tearing at the curtains as he slid to his knees. Even now he did not know whether he had acted selfishly, wickedly, or foolishly. All three, perhaps. He did not know; all he knew was that he envied Corder even in his grave, triumphing over him in death, and felt that, alone, life was no longer worth the effort. With the fading clatter of the post-chaise, his hopes of happiness were gone; yet what choice had been his?

Outside, he heard somebody walk and quickly stood up and sought his hat, rubbing his eyes against his sleeve; and he was glad that the room was darkish when the door opened and an elderly woman peered in.

"The ladies have gone?" she asked.

"Yes," he said: "they've gone"; and pushing past her, he strode from the room, down the stairs and into the street. And there he paused, not knowing where to go. Never again, he realized, would he have anywhere to go; love's jealous Ishmael, he would wander lonely until death . . . and death he longed for, having none to love or to love him.

Sunlit was the street, and people laughed. He saw a man and woman smiling, the man squeezing her elbow against his side; he heard a pedlar crying his wares and a chapman singing nasally of Corder's murder; he saw, in a shop-window, a young girl lean forward, arranging flowers, and she smiled at him, then flushed when he looked stonily back at her; he heard, to his astonishment, birds singing, and there was a man with a woman leaning against a wall and laughing as the man whispered into her bonnet. . . . He saw that the sun was bright, he saw a puddle at his feet that showed the blue of the sky; and he stood, blinking, helpless as a cripple, looking about him and wondering where to go.

THE END